THE BURNING CROWN

THE UNFORGIVEN: BOOK TWO

JAYNE CASTEL

WINTER MIST PRESS

Published by Winter Mist Press

ISBN: 978-1-991280-43-5 (paperback)

Edited by Tim Burton
Cover design by Winter Mist Press
Fantasy map design by Winter Mist Press using Wonderdraft design software.

The proverb, "Every ending holds a new beginning … just as every sunset promises dawn", is a variation of a famous quote by Ralph Waldo Emerson: "Every sunset brings the promise of a new dawn."

Visit Jayne's website: **www.jaynecastel.com**

Will she trust the man who betrayed her … or watch her world fall into darkness?

Enemies-to-lovers. Slow-burn steam and a morally grey hero you'll never forget. Celtic mythology meets Frog Prince vibes. The epic conclusion to a Romantasy duology perfect for fans of LJ Andrews and Rachel Gillig.

A year ago, Lara's husband double-crossed her and stole half her kingdom. Now her former overkings circle like hungry wolves at her borders.

But a far greater threat has awakened.

The Shattered Crown—a broken stone circle in the north—has become a conduit for chaos. The veil between worlds is tearing apart, unleashing vengeful spirits upon the mortal realm. The Slew and other nightmares bent on destruction now hunt her people.

Only an impossible alliance between three sworn enemies can seal the breach and stop the rising tide of evil.

But can a betrayed queen, a treacherous half-blood, and the enigmatic Raven Queen set aside their hatred to save both human and fae … or will Albia burn?

For those who never wanted the crown … but wore it anyway because no one else would.

CONTENT WARNINGS

THE BURNING CROWN is a fantasy romance set in a brutal Pict-inspired world. It's intended for mature (18+) readers and contains the following triggers:

Violence
Graphic sex
Discrimination/racism
Coarse language

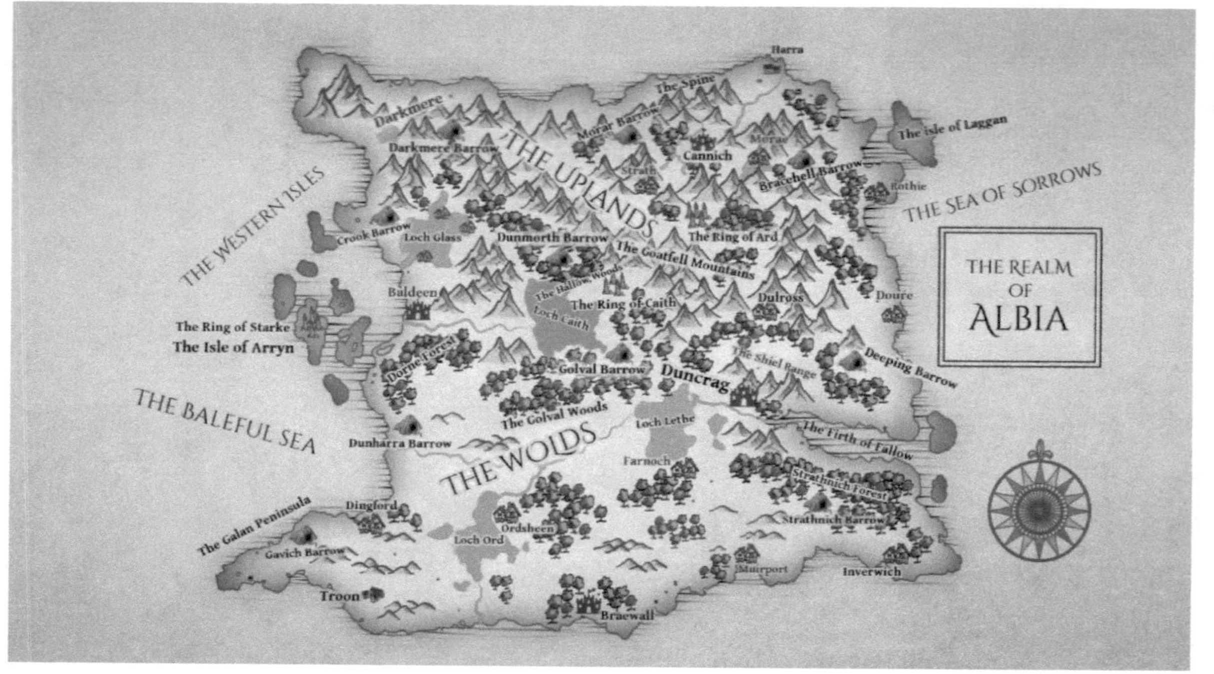

THE REALM OF ALBIA
THE SEA OF SORROWS
THE WESTERN ISLES
THE BALEFUL SEA
THE UPLANDS
THE WOLDS
Harra
The Spine
Darkmere
Morar Barrow
Mora
The Isle of Laggan
Darkmere Barrow
Strath
Cannich
Bracehell Barrow
Rothie
Crook Barrow
Loch Glass
Dunmorth Barrow
The Ring of Ard
Baldeen
The Goatfell Mountains
Dulross
Doure
The Hallow Woods
The Ring of Caith
Loch Caith
The Ring of Starke
The Isle of Arryn
The Shiel Range
Deeping Barrow
Dorne Forest
Golval Barrow
Duncrag
The Golval Woods
Loch Lethe
Dunharra Barrow
The Firth of Fallow
Farnoch
Strathnich Forest
Dingford
Ordsheen
Strathnich Barrow
The Galam Peninsula
Loch Ord
Gavich Barrow
Muirport
Inverwich
Troon
Braewall

MAP

Visit my website to view a larger version of the Realm of Albia map.

1: REVENGE NEVER SLEEPS

The Golval Woods
The Realm of Albia

ROARS OF VICTORY vibrated through the trees. Warriors thrust their swords high, turning their faces to the rain that fell in a gentle mist upon the tangle of oak, beech, and sycamore.

But their queen didn't cheer alongside them.

Instead, Lara guided her mare between the scattered corpses in the clearing, counting. Eighteen Baldeen warriors would never steal another furlong of her land. Satisfying, yet not enough. Not when a village lay in ruin behind her, and her husband still sat smug in Dulross, believing himself untouchable.

She reined in beside one of the fallen—a hatchet-faced warrior with staring blue eyes—and dismounted, her boots squelching in the mud. Around her, standards listed drunkenly. Blood splattered the iron shields of Baldeen. The dead man's sword lay half-buried in the peaty earth—a broadsword, with a double-edged blade. She pulled it free and tested its weight.

"Strip their weapons," she called to the warriors nearby. "Every blade … every pike. The villagers will need them."

Behind her, still seated astride her cob, Bree cleared her throat. "Surely, cottars and woodcutters can't—"

"They can learn." Lara cut her warder a sharp look as she cleaned the sword's edge on the warrior's cloak. "And they will. I won't have Artair's next push catch them helpless."

She looked down at the broadsword once more, her pulse quickening. The iron gleamed dully in the rain. Each weapon here was one more chance for her people to survive what was coming. This win meant nothing if she couldn't protect these lands—and she had bigger prey to hunt than her treacherous overking.

"My Queen!" A big man with wild red hair, riding astride a muscular horse, approached. Splattered with mud and blood, his handsome face gleaming with rain, Roth mac Tav wore a fierce grin. "Well fought! Artair's dogs are fleeing west with their tails tucked between their legs."

"For now." Lara straightened up, frowning. "But they'll be back."

His smile faltered slightly. "Today is still a success, nonetheless." Roth's voice carried a familiar note—one that reminded her of when she'd rejected his advances a year earlier.

His hesitation pleased Lara. Let him mind her.

"Not to the folk of Cobblebrae, it isn't. Tomorrow, we will start building a palisade around the village. I want every able-bodied inhabitant shown how to wield a bow and arrow and a blade."

Handing the sword to one of her Guard, Lara continued picking her way through the corpses. She hunkered down next to another Baldeen warrior, drawing a dagger from the woman's belt and testing its edge against her thumb. A thin line of red welled up. The iron bit deeper than intended, but she didn't flinch. Pain was useful—it sharpened the mind and reminded her of the cost of letting her guard down.

Her husband had taught her that too, and every day that the bastard held onto Dulross was another cut.

"I won't leave those on our borders defenseless," she announced then, rising to her feet. Handing the dagger to another of her warriors, she crossed to Bracken and swung up onto the mare's broad back once more.

Meanwhile, her warriors had already begun stripping weapons from the dead. They obeyed her. Nonetheless, she marked their set expressions and the veiled looks some of them shared. They were suspicious of her these days. On their way west, they'd passed through the village of Croy—where there had been rumors.

The High Queen wielded a forbidden power. Fire magic.

As she'd expected, Alar had revealed her secret to his allies in Dulross, and news was spreading. It wouldn't be long before she'd have to address the whispers. And what then? Would her people rise up against her?

Lara's jaw tightened. She didn't have time for this. They'd had a victory today, but it wasn't enough. Not when the Shee occupied the North, her husband ruled the borderlands, and her overkings had annexed themselves to the south. Enemies surrounded Duncrag now. She had so many battles to fight. Many centuries had passed since Albia had been this fractured.

Her pulse spiked, and her breathing grew shallow. How was one woman supposed to fix such a Gods-damned mess?

"And after we're done at Cobblebrae?" Roth asked, though something in his tone suggested he already knew.

"It's time to look north once more," she replied, fixing him with a penetrating look. "Once we get back to Duncrag, I want our full strength assembled within the moon's turn, ready to march."

Lara strode through the camp, making her way past where warriors erected tents and lit cookfires. Woodsmoke and mist mingled in the damp air. They'd made camp a few furlongs east of the battleground, not far from what was left of Cobblebrae. After Baldeen warriors had sacked the village, the locals had fled into the woods. However, once the battle ended, they'd emerged. Now, many of them were warming themselves by the fires inside her camp. Tomorrow, they'd be able to return home.

The rain still fell gently, soft and silent in the gloaming. Tall trees loomed around the encampment; many had changed color now, from various shades of green to yellow and deep gold. Summer had faded, and autumn was upon them. Over a year had turned since that fateful day when she'd followed corpse candles into the woods and been rescued by the Half-blood.

Tension coiled under Lara's ribs. Was it only a year? It seemed longer. She felt so much older. She hadn't realized it then, but that evening had been the turning point in her life. At the time, she'd been grateful to Alar for saving her from powries.

These days, all she could think about was sinking a blade between his ribs.

Forcing herself to focus, she glanced, not for the first time, up at the western sky. The Slew always flew in from that direction. Her ears strained for the familiar shrieks, but all was quiet—for the moment. Her last encounter with The Unforgiven was two days earlier. She'd driven them off, yet had been wracked with fever and bone-deep exhaustion afterward. The reaction wasn't unusual, although this time, it had lingered. She was primed this evening though, ready to rush to her tent and throw on the voluminous black cloak and leather mask.

Her lips thinned. Many of her followers already suspected that the 'fire wraith' wasn't a helpful spirit but their High Queen in disguise. The next time she went out to face the Slew, she might not be able to slip away afterward.

Next time, the warriors and druids who'd followed her from Duncrag might demand answers.

Ones that wouldn't make her popular.

Reaching the heart of the camp, she ducked into the largest of the tents—the royal pavilion—to find her attendants readying it for her. Florie was lighting a brazier, while Ani and Lilith were shaking out the furs. Nodding to them, Lara shrugged off her filthy cloak and handed it over to Lilith. She then drew the iron-bladed dagger she always carried at her hip, dropped into a fighting stance, and started going through her drills.

Block. Parry. Strike. Her servants continued their chores as she repeated the movements.

They were used to their High Queen doing her daily training while they worked. *Block. Parry. Strike.*

"Good." Her gaze cut right as Bree ducked into the tent. Dressed in mud-caked fighting leathers with a longsword at her hip, she flicked her long oak-colored braid over her shoulder as she straightened up. Fatigue etched her pretty features. "Although I'm surprised you want to spar this evening. Aren't you tired?"

"Aye." Lara flipped the blade, as Bree had shown her, and caught it by the handle. She then flashed her warder a grim smile. "But revenge never sleeps."

Bree huffed a laugh before drawing the knife strapped to her thigh. "Right. Let's work on your counter strikes … you still aren't fast enough."

Lara pulled a face. "I'm getting quicker."

"Aye … but Alar moves like a snake."

At the mention of her husband, Lara's belly clenched. The bastard *was* fast, thanks to the earth magic that flowed through his veins. His wolf's head tattoo had sharpened his reflexes and instincts, making him hard to beat. But she would. When the time came though, the element of surprise could only be used once. She wouldn't waste it.

The two women faced off against each other.

"Remember, the key to making a lethal counter strike is to give yourself enough space to work with," Bree explained, her fingers flexing on her dagger hilt. "Careful though … get too close, and your opponent's blade will find you … stray too far and your strikes won't land."

Lara nodded, impatience bubbling up. "All right. Let's—"

"My Queen!" Cailean shoved his way into the pavilion then.

Lara cast him a sharp look. Her chief-enforcer usually announced himself before entering Lara's private space. However, one glance at his stunned face and her irritation fled. "What is it?"

"The Shee are here," he replied roughly. "And their queen is with them."

2: A LOST LEGACY

"ARE YOU SURE there are just ten of them with the queen?"
Lara peered into the darkness that fringed the bright ring of
torches ahead. "There aren't more lurking amongst the trees …
ready to attack the moment I show my face?"

"We checked." The chief-enforcer's tone was gruff. "Only
Mor's Ravens accompany her. I wouldn't let you anywhere near
them otherwise."

Lara frowned. Cailean and Bree flanked her, while Skaal—
his fae hound—stalked behind them. She trusted her chief-

enforcer's judgment, yet it still felt as if she was walking into a trap. Her last encounter with Mor's Ravens—her personal Guard—had left a bitter taste in her mouth.

"Do you want *me* to meet with Mor?" Bree asked. "It would be safer."

"No," Lara replied firmly, even as heat ignited under her ribs. "A High Queen doesn't cower."

"No … she doesn't." Censure edged Bree's voice now. "But you shouldn't put yourself at unnecessary risk either. And since I have … history … with Mor, she might treat with me instead."

"Or she might kill you," Cailean pointed out.

The warrior druid had a point. Since Bree had once been Mor's assassin—before fleeing Sheehallion and shifting sides— the Raven Queen was likely still looking for retribution.

Lara quickened her stride, one hand drifting to the cairn stone safely tucked away at her belt. She carried her dagger as well, but if things turned nasty, fire would be her greatest ally. She didn't want to wield it openly, for it would expose her secret to all, but if Mor tried anything, she'd have to.

"I'm not facing Mor without you *both* at my side," she reassured her chief-enforcer and warder. "Keep that torch with you, Cailean."

Her pulse leaped into a canter. *This could be your chance to kill Mor. Cut off the head of the serpent.*

Aye, she could—and she longed to—but she'd hear Mor out. Initially, at least. The Raven Queen had threatened to push south within the year, to make The Wolds hers, yet she still hadn't. Maybe Alar's presence in the borderlands prevented her, or perhaps there was another reason. Lara was curious to learn more about her enemy.

She wouldn't trust a word the Shee queen spoke though.

She'd learned the hard way that trust was as dangerous as an aughisky. If you were foolish enough to reach out a hand, it would drag you down to the bottom of a deep, dark loch and feast on your entrails.

A terrible wail rent the night then, a woman's cry full of sorrow. Behind Lara, one of the warriors muttered an oath. Despite that she'd heard it often since departing from Duncrag, the keening made Lara's chest constrict. The Weeper, foretelling grief and loss, dogged their steps these days. It was hard not to let that anguished cry get to her. Worse still, every time the Weeper held vigil near their camp, she watched those around her struggle to hold back the tide of despair. The spirit's mournful cry had a way of sucking hope out of you.

The last of the tents fell away, ghostly shapes in the mist. A line of enforcers and warriors waited there, weapons drawn, faces grim in the light of the torches many held. Roth stood amongst them, his cool blue eyes shadowed as his gaze slid over the trio. "Shall I join you, My Queen?"

Lara nodded. "Bring a few of your warriors and follow Skaal."

Without another word, Roth gestured to the helmeted figures next to him, and they fell in behind the massive dog with a shaggy green coat, plumed tail, and glowing amber eyes.

Something chattered and hissed in the undergrowth then, the sound cutting through the Weeper's wail. The fingers of Lara's right hand brushed her cairn stone's pouch once more. As always, these days, the night was alive. It wasn't just faerie creatures that stalked the darkness, Mor's spies, but spirits too—angry, vengeful ones. Over the past year in Duncrag, they'd terrorized the fort, forcing their way into dwellings through smoke vents and the cracks under doors. And when Lara had set off west to deal with King Artair, the news in the villages they passed wasn't good either. The botach had stolen away bairns, while boggarts—broonies turned bad—had smothered two newborns. And then, there was the Slew.

Lara's skin prickled. The situation was worsening, yet there was nothing she could do about it.

The rain had ceased now, although fog rolled through the woodland in a dense blanket. Wet ground squelched underfoot, and the rich scent of rotting leaves tickled her nostrils.

Up ahead, the glow of more torches beckoned. And as they approached, the outlines of tall, cloaked figures appeared. The Shee waited with a stillness that no Marav could have obtained.

Lara's pulse kicked up another notch.

She couldn't believe it. Finally, the two queens would meet face-to-face.

She drew nearer, stopping when she was around half a dozen yards away from the party of Shee. As Cailean had assured her, they were a small group; lithe and lean, their gazes shadowed by deep hoods. However, they were all heavily armed. Sheehallion steel glinted in the light of the blazing torches. They must have slipped out of Golval Barrow, which lay just a league to the north of here. Unlike the Marav, the Shee could use the ancient burial mounds to travel between Sheehallion and Albia. It had allowed them to approach unseen.

Lara's gaze slid over the Shee. However, she paid scant attention to the black-cloaked Ravens. Instead, she focused on the figure standing in the middle of the group; the one who'd just pushed back her hood.

A large raven perched upon her shoulder—Eagal, Mor's messenger.

Tall and willowy, the Raven Queen was a striking sight.

The torchlight accentuated her sharp high cheekbones, and in this light, her eyes were the color of ink. She wore a long high-necked gown that shimmered like liquid silver, a sword belt buckled around her narrow hips. A necklace of gleaming white stones encircled her throat, their paleness contrasting with her smooth umber skin.

Lara observed her adversary, taking in every detail. In truth, after what Bree had told her about the queen, she'd expected her to be more intimidating. Instead, her expression was solemn, her gaze veiled. "Good evening, Lara mac Talorc." Her voice was low and melodious.

"You're trespassing on my lands," Lara replied coldly.

"We are … but with good reason."

"State your purpose."

Something flickered across the Raven Queen's face—an emotion Lara couldn't quite place. "The spirit world grows unruly." She paused then as the Weeper gave another heart-rending wail. "Something must be done."

Silence followed this response, and when Lara replied, anger edged her voice. "Things only turned bad when you took the North. You threw our world out of balance. If you want to put things right, leave Albia."

Mor frowned. "We aren't to blame for this. Wraiths and wights were causing problems *long* before your father stepped up his campaign against us."

Fire started to pulse in Lara's gut. Easy words, but where was the proof?

Mor's gaze slid from Lara's face down her body, fixing upon her right hand—on where the amber stone of the iron ring she wore gleamed in the torchlight. "So … Fern was right," she said softly. "Albia's rulers still wear the ring."

Lara's heart kicked. Fern? Mor was referring to Alar's half-sister. The Shee warrior who'd tried to assassinate Lara a year earlier before being taken prisoner. She'd escaped Duncrag when the Slew attacked the previous Gateway. It was no surprise that she'd gone straight to her queen. Yet mention of the ring Lara had inherited from her father confused her. "It's the *Ord-ree seal*. What of it?"

"You know its history?"

Lara lifted her hand, studying the ring as if expecting to find the answer to Mor's question in the depths of the amber. She didn't. "No."

"It was made for fire-wielders."

Lara froze, while gasps and mutters rippled through the amassed crowd behind her.

"And that is what you are, isn't it?" Mor continued, her gaze lifting to meet Lara's. "The first in many generations of your family."

Queasiness washed over Lara. *Fuck*. Mor had just ripped off her mask. She wasn't ready for this. "I don't believe it," she whispered finally, her mind wheeling.

"You didn't know about the family connection?"

Lara shook her head.

"The *Ord-ree seal* … passed down from ruler to ruler over hundreds of years. Common-born fire-wielders didn't possess such a ring though … it belonged only to Albia's royal line."

Aware of the gazes now boring into her back, Lara curled the fingers of her right hand into a fist. "How do you know this?"

"The archives of Caisteal Gealaich hold many secrets … if you dig deep enough."

Moments passed, and as they did, the riddle Lara had been trying to solve for a while now untangled itself. Whenever she displayed a strong emotion—anger usually—flames flared in the depths of the amber. And they did whenever she wielded fire as well. There were also times, as she clenched the cairn stone tightly in her right hand, when the ring pulsed hot against her skin.

Over the past turns of the moon, she'd guessed it was connected in some way to her ability. But she hadn't made the link to her family.

"What does the ring have to do with the spirit world?" Cailean spoke up then, his voice sharp.

Mor's gaze never left Lara's face as she replied, "Nearly two and a half thousand years ago, fire-wielders were common in Albia. There was even a class of druid called pyromancers … trained fire-wielders who expanded their abilities through study and discipline."

Cailean stiffened. Clearly, pyromancers weren't part of current druidic lore. The news surprised Lara as well. She hadn't realized some fire-wielders had become druids.

"One of these pyromancers—the High King's brother— rose to become arch-druid," Mor continued. "He encouraged the king to push the boundaries of his power … to take control over life and death itself."

The fine hair on the back of Lara's neck stood to attention. That was quite an ability—one she wouldn't want. To wield it was to make yourself a god. It was risky. Arrogant.

"The arch-druid chose The Shattered Crown for his ritual … a broken stone circle in the far north, on the shores of the Darkmere," Mor said. "The veil was thin there. Like the other standing stones of Albia, it was made long ago by the Ancients … long before my time. However, The Shattered Crown has always been different from its cousins … it holds no earth magic and has never provided a portal between Albia and Sheehallion. No one is sure why the Ancients built it so, or of its original use … but your ancestors decided it was perfect."

"What did they do?" Lara asked, though dread was already pooling in her gut.

"They created a breach in the veil between this world and The Threshold." Mor's expression remained impassive. "The arch-druid had an iron ring forged with a piece of amber set into it … amber he fed with his own blood over many moons of ritual, binding it to his fire magic. He and a group of pyromancers then traveled to The Shattered Crown and, together, they burned a narrow tear in the veil. The arch-druid then used that ring—the *Ord-ree seal*—to stabilize the tear and keep it open."

Lara frowned. The Threshold was the liminal space between worlds, where spirits of the dead lingered for a short while before passing to the Otherworld or Underworld. However, some malevolent spirits, like the Slew, remained there. "I can't believe my ancestors would mess with something so dangerous."

"They had to … if they wished to bring back the recently departed," Mor replied. "Those of their choosing, of course. Shortly after the breach was created, the High King lost his beloved daughter to illness. He wanted her resurrected." She paused. "And through sacrifice at the stone circle, they brought her back from the dead."

Lara's throat suddenly felt dry and tight. *Gods.* They'd actually done it.

"The ring was designed to be worn by fire-wielders," Mor went on. "It needs to be actively maintained … fed power through the bloodline connection. As long as a fire-wielder wears it, the tear will remain stable and controlled. Small enough for their purposes, yet preventing anything *undesirable* from escaping."

"What went wrong?" Cailean asked.

"The fire-wielders were slaughtered." Mor's voice flattened. "*All* of them. Ill-feeling had festered for decades. There were tales of villages burned and power abused … of pyromancers going mad and incinerating everything within reach. When Albia outlawed fire magic, the Marav made it a death sentence … and they hunted the fire-wielders down. They dragged them from their homes and put them to the sword. And when the last one died, knowledge about the tear in the veil and the ring went with them."

"So, what do you know about the ring?" Lara's voice came out hoarse.

"For centuries, the rulers of your line have worn the *Ord-ree seal* as a family heirloom, not realizing magic lay dormant in their veins or what the ring truly was." Mor's gaze fixed on Lara's hand. "Without a fire-wielder to maintain it for so long, it's likely the ring has been slowly failing. Like a fire starved of fuel. The 'controlled tear' has been gradually widening."

Lara's chest tightened. "But I'm wearing it now. Shouldn't that help?"

"You've awakened it," Mor said, her tone softening slightly. "But I fear the damage has already been done. Indeed, given recent events, you may have made the situation worse."

Lara stared at the ring on her finger with new horror. *"I'm the reason the spirits are flooding through?"*

"The *ring* is the reason," Mor corrected her. "Your family created this crisis over two thousand years ago. You simply … woke it up."

A brittle silence fell.

"What if I took it off?" Lara's pulse quickened, panic fluttering up. "Would that help?"

Mor huffed a sigh. "I doubt it … the rift isn't likely to shrink." She paused then. "After consulting with my archivists, I sent warriors to The Shattered Crown a few days ago. It was a risky mission, but they managed to climb up to the stone circle. They returned with ill news. The tear is wide now … wider than it's ever been. Wraiths are flowing through in numbers we've never seen before. And the more of them there are, the bolder they become."

"That's why the Slew are so restless these days?" Lara breathed.

"Aye … they grow in number and in strength. Unchecked, they will likely challenge Shee and Marav alike for the rule of Albia."

Cailean made a noise in the back of his throat. "You believe the Unforgiven are capable of marshaling themselves into an army … of taking us on?"

"They already are."

The chief-enforcer's jaw flexed. No doubt he was remembering what had happened at Duncrag the previous Gateway. Lara didn't argue with Mor on that point either.

Despite the chill night, she started to sweat. There was no denying that the spirit world had grown problematic. There was no denying they were in trouble. She cleared her throat. "Can the gap be sealed?"

"Perhaps."

"That's why you're here, right?"

"Aye." The Raven Queen stepped forward then. Next to Lara, both Cailean and Bree stirred. Skaal began to growl, low in her throat. It took all Lara's self-control not to reach for her cairn stone.

But Mor ignored everyone except her. "I can't make you any promises," she said firmly. "But if we want to have any chance of fixing this, *we* will need to work together."

3: NOT HIM

LARA DIDN'T ANSWER. The moon would rise at midday, and the sea would boil, before she'd ever join forces with the Raven Queen.

Mor cleared her throat then. "Actually … my plan requires the cooperation of *three* of us."

Goosebumps rose on Lara's skin. She didn't like the direction Mor was taking.

"Three is a magic number." Mor's gaze flicked briefly to Cailean. "All druids know this, don't they?"

"Aye." The chief-enforcer was scowling now. "Three points of a triangle have the power to bind ... to create a sacred circle."

Mor nodded before her attention settled upon Lara once more. "I may have discovered how to send the spirits back into The Threshold and seal the veil. We need an 'anchor'—a fire-wielder who bears the *Ord-ree seal*. You." She paused. "A 'weaver'—one of the Shee royal line with the ability to manipulate moonlight with song. Me." Another pause. "And a 'bridge'—someone who possesses both Shee and Marav blood to complete the binding."

Nausea rolled over Lara. "No," she whispered. "Not *him*."

"I'm afraid so," Mor replied. "Half-bloods are rare. We don't have time to go hunting for another. I'm not asking you to forgive him ... after this is done, you can take a blade to his throat. You'd be doing us both a favor."

"He's pissed you off too?" Cailean asked, not without a note of irony in his voice.

Mor pulled a face. "He and his wulvers ... and their Circines friends ... are harrying our borders. The villages around the Ring of Ard have fallen to them."

Lara barely heard these words; all she could focus on was Mor's plan. An anchor, a weaver, a bridge—and an alliance she didn't want. Bile stung the back of her throat.

"This binding sounds"—she paused, searching for the right word— "complicated."

"It is."

"You don't know if it will work."

"The old records suggest it will," Mor replied. "After spending the past year working with my archivists and advisors, I'm confident this is our best chance." She paused, her expression growing more intent. "Though I'll be honest with you ... this has never been done before. Your ancestors used the rift to create an exchange ... the living for the dead, through sacrifice at the stone circle. To my knowledge, they never attempted to close the tear. We'll be the first."

Lara's stomach tightened. "And if it fails?"

"Then we're no worse off than we are now." Mor's eyebrows drew together. "But I believe it *will* work."

"Explain it to me then," Lara demanded. "What exactly happens at The Shattered Crown?"

Mor inclined her head. "We'll need to reach the stone circle by Gateway, when the moon is full. Moonlight is essential for the weaving. Spirits will be gathered there ... and they'll try to stop us." She held up a hand, ticking off each point. "You'll stand on the southwestern edge of the circle as the anchor. The Half-blood will kneel at the center stone ... he must be close to the earth to form the bridge between us. I'll take position on the southeastern side."

"And then?"

"I'll sing, weaving moonlight into a net ... a wind that will push the wraiths in the vicinity of The Shattered Crown back into The Threshold." Mor's gaze remained steady.

"What about me?" Lara asked.

"You hold your position. The *Ord-ree seal* will flare to life as it connects with the tear. It will grow hot ... it may even burn. The sensations will likely be intense, but you must endure them. You're the anchor, keeping us grounded while I work." Mor paused. "Once the spirits have been shoved through the gap, you cast the ring into it. The *Ord-ree seal* is what has been keeping the tear stable and open for so long. When you throw it through, you sever that connection. The ring created by fire-wielder blood must be returned by fire-wielder blood. Only your bloodline can release its hold on the veil."

Lara's mind raced, trying to envision it all. "I won't have to wield fire?"

"No," Mor said. "Your presence and your blood are what matter … the connection to those who made the ring. Not the fire itself."

"And Alar?" Lara forced the name out. "What does he actually do?"

"His presence, as someone who bears both Shee and Marav blood, completes the binding. The third point of the triangle. He simply needs to be there, kneeling on the center stone."

Lara's gaze narrowed as she scrutinized Mor's face. "You said the ritual of old required sacrifice … why doesn't this one? Surely, Alar must bleed?"

Mor gave a soft snort. "No. We're not asking a favor from The Threshold or summoning anything. We're putting things back the way they should be … restoring balance. Closing what should never have been opened. There's no debt to pay for that."

Mor's explanation sounded reasonable. Logical, even. Lara wanted to catch her out, but it tracked with what she knew of druidic magic.

It was a pity Alar wouldn't need to suffer though.

"How long will this take?" she asked.

"I cannot say for certain."

"And what if someone interferes? What if the spirits attack us during the ritual?"

"They will try … but no one else can enter the circle during the binding," Mor answered, her gaze unwavering. "It will break the ritual if they do. Our companions will need to hold the perimeter … keep the wraiths at bay outside the stones." She paused. "Once I've started the weaving, everyone must take cover. The wind will be violent. It will push every spirit nearby into the rift … you don't want to end up going with them."

Beside Lara, Bree made a noise in the back of her throat. Mor's gaze sliced sideways, focusing on her for the first time. Moments passed as the two of them stared at each other. And then the Raven Queen's face froze.

Lara's breathing quickened. She'd recognized her.

Marshaling herself, Mor shifted her attention back to Lara. "This won't be easy. The first obstacle will be getting the Half-blood to join us, obviously. After that, we'll need to survive the journey north. The spirit world knows where its weakness lies, and it guards The Shattered Crown heavily these days. When they realize we're making for Darkmere, they'll try to stop us." She halted, swallowing. "But together, the three of us could put things right."

Lara took a step back, her pulse racing now. "No."

Mor frowned. "Your ancestors caused this mess, Lara. You shoulder some responsibility."

Lara's temper splintered. "Don't you dare lay the blame at my feet. I had nothing to do with any of it," she snarled. "This plan suits you, doesn't it? It's the perfect way for you to rid yourself of two enemies with one swipe of the blade. I'm not falling for it."

Mor's lips pursed. "It's not trickery. Believe me, there are easier ways to rid myself of rivals."

Lara gave her a long, hard look.

The Raven Queen folded her arms across her chest. "You will believe me soon enough. When the Slew hunt every night, and the sky swarms with them. When wraiths outnumber the living. Aye, you fight some of them off with your fire … but you can't protect everyone, everywhere." Mor broke off there, her gaze sharpening. "When you're forced to hide away in your broch, even during the day, while spirits stalk the wynds of Duncrag bringing death and destruction, you'll wish you'd listened to me … and agreed to help. But then, it'll be too late."

"My Queen?"

Lara blinked, rousing herself. She'd been leagues away just then, instead of listening to her council. "What's that, Ruari?"

"You did well to refuse Mor." Ruari was watching her strangely, as were the others gathered in the meeting tent. Straight after her encounter with the Shee, Lara had stalked back to camp and summoned the rest of her advisors. "She cannot be trusted."

Warmth rose to Lara's cheeks. *Shades.* Exhaustion must be catching up with her. She didn't usually go blank like that, in the midst of a conversation.

"You should have done more than that." Hands braced on the table they stood around, the chief-sacrificer's dark eyes glittered in the lamplight. "Why didn't you kill the bitch when you had the chance? You could have—"

"Enough, Gregor." Lara cut him off.

"But you can't believe a word that slips from a Shee's lips." He looked almost desperate now, and it hit Lara how deeply hatred of the Shee ran amongst her people. "They're all manipulators."

"*Mor* is a manipulator," she corrected him, her own anger rising now. "Your prejudice isn't helping matters. Rein it in."

The chief-sacrificer growled another curse. Beside him, Cailean shifted, casting the big man with sharp cheekbones and a shaven head a warning look. They'd never been friends, but had rubbed along well enough of late. However, Gregor was close to crossing a line this evening.

On the way to the meeting pavilion, Lara had weathered stares and whispers. Mor's confirmation had caused a storm within the camp. News that their High Queen was a fire-wielder rippled through the ranks. Everyone who followed her would know by dawn. However, all those in this pavilion already knew her secret, for they'd been present when she wielded fire to save them at the previous Gateway.

No, Gregor wasn't in a foul temper about Lara being a fire-wielder, but about what he perceived to be her inaction. He wanted Mor disposed of, and The Uplands back in Marav hands.

Lara wanted that too, but she wasn't a butcher. As angry as she was, she wouldn't attack Mor and her Ravens unprovoked.

Annis cleared her throat, even as she cast Gregor a censorious look. "The Gods won't approve of violence … not when the Shee approached us in peace."

"Will they return?" Ren, the chief-bard asked. Her sharp-featured face was pinched.

"Aye," Lara replied, her voice roughening. "Our conversation ended badly. But before she melted into the mist, Mor made it clear, she'd seek me out again … in a couple of days … to see if I've changed my mind."

"And this time, you'll torch her," Gregor growled, unable to hold his tongue.

"I think you should heed Mor," Bree said then, as if Gregor hadn't spoken.

Silence fell like a cleaver in the tent. The five senior druids Lara took everywhere with her, as well as her captain, all fell silent. They all stared at Bree.

Lara folded her arms across her chest. "Really?" Heat pulsed under her ribs. She didn't want to heed Mor. She wanted to gather her army, march north, and make all her enemies pay.

Bree raised her chin. "She's telling the truth."

The chief-sacrificer made a disgusted sound. "Of course, you'd say that … you're one of *them*."

"Gregor," Cailean rumbled. "Watch yourself."

The chief-sacrificer's heavy jaw bunched, high spots of color flushing across his angular cheeks. "You're a weak-minded fool, mac Brochan. Your wife has you in the palm of her hand, doesn't she?"

Cailean's gaze narrowed. "Just keep talking."

Trying to ignore the ratcheting tension between the two men, Lara met Bree's eye. "But haven't you always warned me never to trust her?"

"And I stand by that. However, she's never reached out a hand to a Marav ruler like this … or made herself so vulnerable before. Things clearly haven't been going her way of late. She's worried. Humbled."

"The threat she speaks of is real," Cailean agreed reluctantly. "We all know it."

"But can't we find a way to solve it ourselves?" Lara cut her attention to her chief-counselor. "Surely, the druids have enough knowledge?"

Annis's lips pursed. "I'm flattered by your faith in us, My Queen … but earth magic can't mend what fire magic broke." She grimaced then. "Only *your* power can do that?"

Lara's stomach clenched. "So, you believe Mor's story too?"

Annis nodded.

"If that's the case, why does she need the *three* of you?" Gregor interrupted once more. A vein pulsed on his temple now. "And what's this crap about needing that half-breed bastard as a 'bridge' and her weaving moonlight? It all reeks like shit to me."

Lara's gut clenched. Did it? Flustered, she swept her gaze back to Cailean. "Tell me more about your last visit to The Shattered Crown."

"It was five years ago," Cailean replied, still eyeing the chief-sacrificer. "A group of us were in Darkmere hunting Shee who were fleeing toward their barrow." Bree shifted uncomfortably beside him as he continued, "They were too quick for us, and reached safety … but that night we camped on the shore of the Darkmere, under the shadow of the stone circle. None of us got any sleep. Boggarts crawled into our tents and tried to smother us. I woke up to find four of them on me." He paused, his lip curling. "When I fought them off, they turned the air blue with their insults. Nothing has a fouler mouth than a boggart."

"Had you offended broonies?" Annis asked.

Cailean shrugged. "Not to my knowledge … but boggarts weren't our only problem. When I left my tent, a cluster of Loch-Bhàn were drifting across the loch toward our camp, their hair flowing like water."

Lara tensed. 'Lake women' were rarely sighted in The Wolds. The wraiths were said only to appear upon a full moon. Their song was haunting, and if one touched you, you'd lose your memory.

"We didn't linger near the loch after that," Cailean concluded.

"So, spirits were guarding The Shattered Crown ... even five years ago?" Roth asked, alarm flaring in his eyes.

"Aye."

"That would indicate that this has been building for a while." The captain scowled. "Which means Mor was telling the truth ... about that, at least."

"It would seem so."

"You don't want to work with the Half-blood ... I understand that," Bree spoke up once more, meeting Lara's eye squarely. "I too want to see him dead ... but don't let your emotions blinker you. If you must form a temporary alliance with him, do it."

Lara's belly cramped. Bree might want to drive a blade into Alar's throat, but her hate for him was a pale shadow in comparison to what Lara felt. All she thought about these days was killing him. It was the first thought that appeared in her mind upon waking, and the fantasy she played in her head each night as she struggled to get off to sleep.

She couldn't work with him.

"Mor should never be trusted," Bree went on. "But right now, she's not the greatest threat to Albia."

"In your eyes, maybe." Gregor erupted once more. Disgust twisted his face. He'd clearly had enough. Over the past years, he'd suffered Bree's presence at Lara's side, but this evening, his anger at the High Queen for letting Mor live unleashed his deep-seated resentment. "You were Mor's spy once ... what's to say you haven't turned again? Let's face it … you're nothing but a Shee bitch wearing Marav skin."

A blur of movement followed the chief-sacrificer's insult.

Cailean's fist smashed into Gregor's face with a sickening crunch. The chief-sacrificer staggered back. Blood gushed from his nose, but Cailean wasn't yet done. Another punch followed, and this one felled the big man like a tree.

4: NOTHING IS CERTAIN

THE WEEPER'S WAIL echoed through the gloaming. The drawn-out cry made Lara's chest ache. Taking a step forward, she stumbled, her feet suddenly clumsy.

"Lara?" Bree was at her elbow, supporting her, but she gently shook her off.

"It's all right," she muttered.

Bree's brow furrowed. "Are you sure?"

Lara nodded, yanking her cloak close. "It's that howling … it gets to you after a while."

"Aye," Bree agreed roughly. "It gets to us all."

Indeed, lines of strain bracketed her warder's mouth this evening. Her posture, usually as straight as a spear, was slumped, her shoulders rounded.

The Weeper's lament was eroding their defenses, letting despair and hopelessness creep in. Even Bree, the strongest person Lara had ever met, couldn't hold it back.

For herself, Lara could feel the weight of it, pressing down upon her shoulders like two heavy hands. Her limbs tingled with fatigue, and her temples pounded. Jaw clenching, she looked around her. They stood near the northern edge of the perimeter her army had just built around Cobblebrae. Two days had passed since her victory over Baldeen and her meeting with Mor. And ever since, Lara had deliberately kept herself busy.

She didn't want to think about the things the Raven Queen had told her, or what might happen if nothing was done. And she wished to forget about the alliance Mor had proposed between her, Lara, and Alar.

Around her, warriors were hammering in the last stakes to secure the high wooden palisade that now surrounded the clusters of sod-roofed roundhouses. The thud of iron colliding with wood echoed through the grey dusk like a listless heartbeat. One look at the faces of the men and women working—their slack expressions, wet eyes, and shallow breathing—and she knew the Weeper's song was affecting them badly.

One of the men, a young warrior, threw down his mallet and sank to the muddy ground, burying his head in his hands. Two other men cast aside their tools and knelt next to him.

"It's all right, Brodie," one rumbled, slapping the warrior on the shoulder to rouse him. "Pay no heed to that wailing bitch."

A few yards away, two women were bringing in washing from a line outside a roundhouse. They stared at their High Queen as if she'd just sprouted horns and fangs. Wide-eyed and nervous, they whispered together before one clutched at the iron protection amulet around her neck.

Lara murmured an oath, even as the ache under her breastbone deepened. Of course, her army's morale and the mood in Cobblebrae weren't helped by the fact that everyone knew she was a fire-wielder now. "We'll need Ren to sing to us. tonight," she announced then, looking away from the women. "Something cheerful to keep the despair at bay."

"Good idea," Bree replied. "The villagers won't be able to defend Cobblebrae if they can't rise from their furs in the mornings."

Most of the residents had returned to the village now. They'd welcomed the weapons eagerly, and the training that came with them. A few yards away, warriors guided a line of men and women through basic drills—parry, strike, defend—but the Weeper's distant wail kept shattering their focus. Cobblebrae had been fortified, yet fear still lingered in the faces around her.

"No," Lara agreed, her pulse quickening. "Hopefully, when we move on … the Weeper will follow us and leave these people be."

The two women continued their circuit then, around the palisade. Lara had wanted to see it before nightfall, although it was difficult to concentrate. Tomorrow, they'd pack up and begin the journey back to Duncrag.

Maybe I should just give up. Just leave the North to Mor, and the borderlands to Alar. None of it matters. Not anymore.

She caught herself then. *Shades.* The Weeper was altering her thoughts now.

Jaw clenching, she quickened her stride. No, she wasn't giving up. It would take more than a wailing spirit to best her.

"My Queen." She glanced over her shoulder to see Roth approaching in long strides. The captain's auburn brows were knitted together over the blade of his nose. His lips compressed; he struggled like the rest of them. "The Shee are back."

Lara halted and turned to him. "Mor asks for another audience?"

He nodded.

Lara breathed a curse.

"You knew this was coming," Bree reminded her gently.

The last of the light was fading when Lara emerged from the village. As before, Bree and Cailean strode at her side, with Skaal padding silently behind them, while Roth and a group of warriors brought up the rear.

And like two evenings earlier, Mor and her Ravens waited for them—tall, cloaked figures surrounded by flickering torches.

"Have you changed your mind?" The Raven Queen greeted her without preamble. Eagal perched on her shoulder, beady eyes fixed upon Lara.

"No," Lara replied, folding her arms across her chest as she halted.

Mor sighed. "We're wasting time here. The full moon has just passed … we need to get to The Shattered Crown before the next one."

"Off you go then."

Mor's black eyes narrowed. "Not without you."

"Why does this matter to you so much?" Lara demanded. Bree had counseled her to work with Mor, but over the past two, largely sleepless, nights, she'd relived their conversation multiple times. Something didn't make sense. "Surely, the spirits are more of a problem for my people than yours?"

Bree had told her that the Shee couldn't control the spirit world, yet Lara couldn't imagine they were bothered by most of them. Mor had gone to a lot of trouble to search for a way to mend the veil, and Lara wanted to know why.

A nerve flickered in the queen's smooth cheek. "The wights that dwell in our barrows grow … unruly."

Lara stilled. Of course, wights were spirits too, malicious ghosts. The barrows that the Shee used to travel between Sheehallion and Albia were the tombs of ancient kings, and their spirits still lingered.

"Of late, crossing between realms has been … difficult," Mor admitted after a lengthy pause. "If things continue, we won't be able to travel back to Sheehallion."

Or it might drive you back to your realm for good.

Lara's pulse quickened. Perhaps she'd just found a way to rid herself of the Shee.

She caught herself then. Was that really her priority right now? The likes of the Slew were a far greater risk to Albia at present than the Shee. She had to focus on them.

Mor had finally given her a solid motivation, one she could actually believe. Yet, at the same time, there were so many things that were wrong about all of this. Her enemy was proposing that they work together. Every instinct rebelled against it.

And then there was Alar.

Just thinking about him made her stomach burn.

Ironically, she had some things to thank the prick for. Their marriage had helped forge her. It had toughened her up. Even though his support had all been mummery, she'd believed in it at the time. It had allowed her to step into her own power. By the time his betrayal happened, she'd been stronger. Surer of herself. Despite hardships and obstacles, leadership had been much easier ever since.

But now, thanks to Mor, the earth shifted beneath her feet.

After besting the Baldeen army, she'd been unwavering in her resolve. She'd had a plan. She understood what she needed to do and had been ready to do it. But this new development changed everything.

"The idea of allying myself with you and the Half-blood doesn't overjoy me either," Mor said then, irritation lacing her voice now. "If there were another way, I'd have taken it."

Lara pulled a face. "Can you assure me it'll work … this binding between the three of us?"

Mor shook her head. "Nothing is certain. However, with you as our anchor bearing the ring, we have a strong chance." She paused then, impatience flickering across her features. "We shall be traveling fast and light. We must, if we wish to reach The Shattered Crown by Gateway. I have only my most loyal Ravens with me … I suggest you choose just a handful of warriors and druids to accompany you. Send everyone else home."

Lara tensed. Mor was talking as if she'd already agreed, and she hadn't. The Shee queen was making sense—nonetheless, she'd never traveled without an army before. It would make her vulnerable.

When she didn't reply, Mor huffed another sigh. "If this is going to work, you'll have to trust me a little."

Lara's pulse quickened.

Trust is a blade offered hilt-first—dangerous to give, deadly to refuse. Her chief-seer had told her that, and she'd replied that trust was just betrayal waiting for the right moment.

A year on, and she still stood by her response.

Where had trusting someone ever gotten her? Hurt by her father. Abused by her first husband and betrayed by her second. Abandoned by her overkings. But the need to trust was forever raising its head. And now, she was supposed to put her faith in her enemy so they could work toward a common goal.

Suddenly, she was standing on the edge of a cliff with nothing but darkness beneath her. The future was yet untold, but she wasn't powerless. She had a chance to make a difference.

Long moments passed, the weight of gazes pressing down upon her. Everyone, her own people and the Ravens standing behind Mor, was awaiting her answer.

Lara glanced at Bree, their eyes locking for a few moments. "Very well," she said finally, even as her heartbeat thumped in her ears. "I'll do it."

"Your warriors aren't happy, My Queen." Roth's announcement made Lara's fingers tighten around her wooden cup. She stood before a roaring fire in Cobblebrae. Her army had put up tents inside the new palisade overnight, but she and her advisors had gathered around a hearth outdoors. Her council members all nursed cups of warmed wine, their expressions drawn in the flickering firelight.

"That's because you're making a mistake," Gregor ground out. The chief-sacrificer's battered face was set in severe lines this evening. He spoke with a slight lisp through swollen lips. "One we *all* will regret."

A gust of wind shoved at her back, making the flames gutter. The Sweeper had pushed the rain clouds and mist away, yet days of rain had left the air heavy. And all the while, the Weeper continued her lament. But this time, the strains of another voice, female and melodious, joined it. Ren had climbed up onto the watchtower on the palisade and now sang a soothing sain.

I already do. Pain thumped through Lara's temples at the thought of the first stop they'd be making, and the man who waited for her there. The next time she saw the Half-blood was supposed to be on a battlefield. Gods, how this would choke her.

Pushing aside her churning thoughts, she took a sip from her cup. She usually enjoyed plum wine, yet tonight, it tasted sour. "It wasn't an easy decision, Gregor."

"They're calling you a traitor." He stared her down across the fire. "They're saying your father would never have had dealings with the Raven Queen."

"They're wrong on both counts," she shot back, anger rising in a red tide. "I'm doing this for them. And we're in this mess because of my father's choices. Don't compare me to him and expect me to hang my head. I won't."

Silence followed. Gregor looked as if he'd just swallowed a mouthful of nails.

Lara glared at him. *Gods.* Belligerent prick. She wished she didn't need the chief-sacrificer on this journey—that she could send him back to Duncrag with the rest of her army the following morning. As Mor had suggested, she was bringing a small group with her: Bree, Cailean, Roth, Annis, Ruari, Ren … and Gregor. No one else.

A savage howl cut through the village then.

Across the fire, Annis started, wine sloshing from her cup. "The Hag's scythe," the chief-counselor gasped. "What was—"

"It came from the direction of the Shee camp," Lara replied.

Another howl followed, this one filled with rage.

"The Slew?" Ruari asked, his face paling.

"No … it sounds like … wild cats fighting," Roth muttered.

Lara tossed aside her cup of wine and moved away from the fire, gesturing to the others to follow. "Let's see for ourselves."

They did, forming a tight circle around her as she made her way toward the perimeter. The guards there drew the gate open, allowing them through. Beyond, they walked through a line of ward stones that Cailean and his enforcers had dropped earlier. Earth magic prickled Lara's skin.

Ahead, the line of torches around the tiny Shee camp—a roaring fire pit and a hide awning—beckoned.

In front of them, Mor crouched on the dew-laden grass, hands spread wide. Eagal had flown off, yet she hadn't drawn the longsword at her hip. Instead, she sang. Breathless, lilting words in the Shee tongue echoed through the trees, mingling with feral snarls.

Meanwhile, her Ravens appeared to be trying to fasten a steel collar around a beast's neck.

Lara halted abruptly. *Shades!* Although she'd heard about the deep grooves this creature scored in trees, scars that never healed, she'd never actually seen a clag-doo. Big, lean, and feline, it was easily the same size as Skaal.

Hissing, the predator slashed at the nearest Shee warrior. Its spine arched as it pivoted on powerful haunches. Long claws resembling meat hooks whistled through the air, carving black arcs.

The clag-doo's amber eyes burned as it dropped low, belly nearly touching the earth, tail thrashing in violent spirals behind its coiled form. Muscles rippled beneath its black pelt. It sprang sideways, avoiding the glinting steel collar that snapped shut on empty air. A guttural noise rumbled from deep in its chest while it backed up.

The Shee circled closer, but the clag-doo's ears flattened against its skull, and it pounced, front paws extended. Its jaws parted to reveal gleaming fangs as it landed atop one attacker, pinning the struggling male beneath it. The beast's head snapped left and right, gaze tracking each enemy while its body remained perfectly balanced, ready to explode into motion again.

And all the while, Mor sang, her hands spread as if in supplication.

"What is she doing?" Lara hissed to Bree.

"A gentling sain," her warder whispered back. "She's trying to make it kneel to her."

Cailean snorted. "Good luck with that."

One of the Ravens moved then, a blur in the torchlight. Leaping high, the male flung himself on the clag-doo's arched back. Lara caught a glimpse of long black hair and a handsome face.

Her heart kicked. Did she know him?

There was no time to study the warrior further, for he shouted, "Now!"

An enraged howl followed, as did the flash of silver, and the 'snap' of the steel collar fastening—this time around the clag-doo's neck.

The beast thrashed, tossing the male to the ground. However, the warrior rolled nimbly to his feet, unhurt. He then pulled the warrior who'd been pinned underneath the clag-doo to safety.

Heavy chains pulled the beast's head down, bringing it to heel.

Despite her fascination with these events, Lara couldn't concentrate on the enraged feline. Instead, she stared at the Shee who'd just fastened the collar.

The similarity was uncanny. Lean, aquiline features. Black hair that spilled like ink over his shoulders. There was no mistaking he was related to Alar. This had to be his father, Wynn Sablebane.

Feeling the weight of her stare, the warrior glanced in her direction. Swallowing, Lara dragged her gaze away from him, focusing on the Raven Queen once more.

Mor moved forward then, her song growing more strident. The clag-doo tracked the Raven Queen's steps, its lips pulling back into a snarl.

"I wouldn't go any closer, cousin." One of Mor's Ravens approached her in long strides. "Your song isn't gentling it. You'll need time if you want to tame one of these."

Lara stiffened. *Cousin?* Indeed, there was a cast to his proud features that reminded her of the queen; he had the same arrogant tilt of the chin and sweep of the eyebrows. A silver half-moon glinted upon one ear. Short black hair curled close to his scalp. His onyx gaze was riveted upon Mor.

Cutting the male an irritated look, the Shee queen ceased her sain.

His lips curved. "It's a female too … they're more dangerous than the males."

"All females are, Vyr," Mor replied with a soft snort. "Something worth remembering."

Her cousin smirked.

"Why capture a clag-doo?" Lara spoke up, interrupting them.

Mor glanced her way, gaze widening. She hadn't realized she'd drawn a crowd. "An age ago, when faerie creatures still inhabited Sheehallion, my predecessors didn't ride upon an elk or stag … but on a 'black claw'," she replied, her tone growing wistful. "Long have I wished to have one as my own."

The clag-doo made an angry spitting noise, the hackles on its back rising. It was eying the Raven Queen as if it wanted to rip her apart.

"You're a beauty, aren't you?" Mor murmured.

A growl rumbled in the clag-doo's throat in reply.

"I shall name you Dorka … 'Dark One'."

It was a fitting name, considering the clag-doo's plush obsidian coat. However, Dorka didn't look impressed. The huge feline continued to watch Mor with burning eyes.

"You intend to travel north on *this*?" Lara was incredulous. Surely, they had more important things to worry about.

A smile tugged at Mor's lips, excitement kindling in her gaze. "Aye."

5: ASHES

THE NOISE INSIDE the hall was deafening: a roar of Marav and wulver voices. They rose and ebbed like waves upon a shingle shore. Usually, Alar found the sound of conversation at mealtimes soothing, but today, it got on his nerves.

Tonight, he was in the mood for silence.

Leaning back in the carven chair one of his brothers had made him in the days following their victory, he picked up his pewter goblet of apple wine. Taking a sip, he surveyed the faces of those seated around him. Many of the Circines warriors' cheeks were flushed with drink.

There was no high seat in this hall. He and Beathan had decided that from the first. Instead of a long table upon a raised dais at the far end of the hall, where the chieftain of Dulross had once sat, the tables had been arranged into a large square in the center. Here, Alar and Beathan faced each other—as equals.

A fire pit smoldered between them, lumps of burning peat sending oily dark smoke wreathing up toward the smoke-blackened beams that crisscrossed overhead. Smoke vents lined the surrounding walls, but it wasn't enough to clear the fug from the air. Around the two rulers of Dulross sat wulvers and hill-tribe warriors.

"By the Warrior balls." A drunken man shouted above the din. "Not fried fish again!"

Jeers followed these words, and Alar tensed, casting a glance right at where Lyall and Dolph sat. Neither of them appeared offended by the jibe. Instead, Lyall, who had one arm around Dolph's broad shoulders, merely lifted his cup of wine in a mocking toast to the warrior who'd spoken.

Slaves had just carried in platters of fried eel and pike. Wulvers loved fish; they preferred it to all other foods. And since his brothers and sisters had taken over the cooking, they decided on the meals. The Circines were happy to have someone else cook for them; however, that didn't stop them from complaining about the fare. They were mountain people. Hunters of deer, boar, birds, and hares. A rich venison stew was what they really wanted.

Usually, their comments washed over Alar, but this evening, they vexed him.

Upon taking Dulross, Beathan had promised that wulvers and Circines would have the same rank here. Nearly the turn of a year had passed since then, and Alar had noticed a gradual shift. The Circines were becoming dominant, while his brothers and sisters bowed to them. He didn't like it.

"We're doing you all a favor," Lyall called out then, his low, gravelly voice cutting through the heckling. "Fish keeps you lean and quick … meat makes you sluggish."

Snorts followed these words.

Meanwhile, across the table, Beathan mac Glen raised his cup high. "A toast!" he boomed. "To our wulver brothers and sisters … and to victories … past and future." His blue eyes, bloodshot from drink, were still as sharp as ever. A comely lass with thick flaxen hair perched on his knee. Duana, the daughter of the hapless chieftain—Og mac Alpin—who'd ruled here before they arrived, was now Beathan's bed-slave.

The young woman's face was impassive this evening, despite the livid bruise upon her cheek. Duana gave little away. She was strong, which was just as well, for Beathan was reputed to have quite an appetite. The Circines chieftain had given her younger sister to one of his captains. A sneering warrior named Lorc. The man's rough hands were squeezing Eithne's breasts now, as she struggled on his lap. Unlike her more stoic elder sister, Eithne's face was stricken.

Alar's jaw tightened. After seizing Dulross, the surviving residents of this broch were now slaves—including the chieftain's daughters. He'd thought about challenging Beathan over taking mac Alpin's daughters as his prize when they'd seized Dulross, but it was hill-tribe tradition to do so. As such, he'd let it lie. The sight of Duana and Eithne each mealtime though, their bronze bed-slave collars gleaming at their throats, never failed to unsettle him.

He'd crossed so many lines over the past couple of years, another one shouldn't matter. And yet it did.

"And to our ever-widening territory!" Beathan added. His gaze glinted as it met Alar's. "Long may this alliance between Circines and wulver continue!"

Alar raised his goblet of wine. "Aye … here's to that."

There had been plenty to celebrate of late. Ever since taking Dulross, they'd gone from strength to strength. The Ring of Ard now belonged to them, as did the villages around it.

They'd pushed the Shee back.

"I want us to go further," Beathan said then, raising his voice to be heard over the cheering that reverberated around the hall. "Now that we've started, we should take *all* of The Uplands for ourselves."

Alar stilled, his fingers tightening around the stem of his goblet.

He'd been waiting for this.

Power was seductive. First, you wanted just a taste, but as it settled upon your tongue, you grew hungry for more. And over time, the hunger grew to greed.

Together, Circines and wulver ruled a wide belt of territory: Doure on the east coast, all the Goatfell Mountains in the central Uplands, and now the Ring of Ard as well. But it wasn't enough for Beathan. He was drunk on more than potent apple wine tonight. He was drunk on victory.

"We don't stand alone," the chieftain went on. "The other tribes will unite with us."

The rumble of voices around the table died at these words. A bold statement. The three hill-tribes within The Uplands rarely joined forces. The Circines, Druthen, and Lothin had a long history of blood feuds.

"What if they don't?" Alar asked, swirling his wine. "What if the Raven Queen has bought them … as she once did you?"

Beathan's dark eyebrows drew together. "People change sides."

Alar inclined his head. He hadn't been able to stop himself from making the dig. The Circines had initially fought for the Shee. Mor had promised them revenge against the High King of Albia … and then, when she pushed south, she'd promised Beathan could have Duncrag. But the Raven Queen's plans had moved too slowly for the Circines chieftain.

And Alar had exploited his frustration.

After they'd taken back Doure a year earlier, he'd told Lara he needed time to spread word amongst his brethren of their victory and to rally his warriors. And he had. But the *real* reason he'd waited a moon's turn before traveling south and marrying the High Queen was to visit The Goatfells. There, he'd met with Beathan and made his own proposal.

"There are other things to consider," he said after a pause. "What about the Slew … and their *friends?*"

Beathan's brow furrowed. He didn't like to discuss the problems they'd been having of late—problems that were growing—but ignoring them wasn't going to work either. Taking back The Ring of Ard and the lands surrounding it had brought them face-to-face with the fact that various spirits now swarmed in the darkness each night. Some of the wraiths were curious or restless, others mischievous. But many wished to cause harm. And they did.

The Slew had swarmed in on the night they'd taken back the stone circle. Beathan and Alar had camped inside the towering stones and surrounded their warband with huge bonfires. Even then, some of the wraiths had gotten through. They'd taken warriors, and the fight had drawn out as exhaustion hammered at them. They'd been on the verge of collapse when the Slew finally drew back.

"I'm not going to let those fuckers ruin this," Beathan bellowed. The Circines chieftain's expression turned fierce as he raised his cup high once more. "They might stalk the night … but we rule the day."

Alar didn't reply. He admired Beathan's stubbornness in the face of adversity. However, even within the sheltering walls of this fort, their problems with spirits were growing. The Slew hunted with chilling regularity now, and just two days earlier, a grimloch had killed an entire family in the lower fort. It had squeezed through the smoke vent and snuffed out the peat fire, suffocating a carpenter, his wife, and their two bairns while they slept.

No, they couldn't sweep it all away—although the Circines chieftain was making a valiant attempt.

"Just imagine it, Alar." Beathan sat back in his chair, his hand playing with Duana's soft hair. The lass sat, as if carved from stone. Her blue eyes were distant. "The whole of The Uplands … *ours*. From Darkmere in the northeast, to The Spine and Harra in the far north, and the Isle of Laggan in the east. The High Queen can keep The Wolds … but the mountains, glens, and valleys of the North belong to us."

Something in the chieftain's voice called to Alar then.

It was tempting.

Of late, he'd gotten bored. It surprised him how quickly he'd fallen into a routine in Dulross, how quickly he'd forgotten how hard he'd fought to be here.

It was easy to think the solution was to gain more territory, but was it?

Would it ever fill the aching pit in his chest?

Lyall and Dolph exchanged glances then, their gazes glinting.

"The Shee are at their weakest when the weather turns bitter," The chieftain went on, oblivious to the wulvers' reactions. "I suggest we wait until mid-winter and then hit Cannich first … rather than taking smaller villages and forts. Strike fast and hard."

Excited murmuring erupted at this suggestion, and a grin stretched Beathan's face. His attention then shifted to Alar. "You're quiet."

"I'm thinking."

Beathan cocked a dark eyebrow. "And your conclusion?"

"I wouldn't rule such a strike out." Alar raised his goblet to his lips and drained the rest of his wine. It burned a trail down his throat and warmed his belly. "But that doesn't solve our problems with the spirits. And remember too that the Shee will be watching us."

Beathan's lip curled, while around him, some of his warriors snorted derisively. "*Watching* is all those goat-eyed fuckers do," he slurred, holding his cup up for a slave to refill. "The Raven Queen got what she wanted … Cannich and the far north … but she doesn't have the guts to take anything else." He paused then, his dark-blue eyes glassy with drink. "If we push hard enough, she'll yield."

Misty rain coated Alar's face as he stepped outdoors. Summer lay behind them now, and the weather had turned cold and wet. Damp air caressed his bare arms as he walked across the yard, his boots squelching in the mud, nodding to the wulvers who stood guard at the gates. He then climbed the stone steps up to the walls.

None of the Four Winds were blowing tonight, which made a welcome change, and the braziers that burned up here lit up the darkness with their ruddy glow. The broch's perimeter walls, high above the rest of the fort, were his favorite place to come when he needed to be alone. The broch was too noisy—and as airless as a barrow. Out here, he breathed easier.

Not many ventured out after dark these days—only those charged with protecting the fort. And when the Slew hunted, they too retreated to safety.

But although Alar was wary of the wraiths that stalked the darkness, he wasn't afraid of them. The night had always been his time. His routine was different these days though, now he'd fallen into the Marav way of living.

Alar walked along the wall, moving past hill-tribe warriors. Like him, they wore sleeveless leather vests and fitted breeches, although woad tattoos covered their brawny arms. They nodded to him as he passed, and he responded in kind. However, he didn't exchange words with any of them.

He'd come up here looking for solitude.

Finding a quiet spot on the eastern wall, far from others, he halted. He then looked down at where sod-roofed houses tumbled down the hillside. Fires burned on the walls at each of Dulross's three levels, making the fort glow gently in the darkness.

Alar's gaze slid over the rooftops and probed beyond. Longing rose within him then, for the dark forests that had been his home for so long. He had an untamed heart and was his happiest stalking through the pines and sleeping rough on the mossy banks of a burn.

A smile tugged at his lips as he remembered how simple life had once been. He'd chafed at it in the past, believing he and his brothers and sisters deserved better. But these days, he wasn't so sure. Maybe when all this was done, when he tired of sitting on his carven chair next to the Circines chieftain, he'd disappear into the wilds again. He'd leave Beathan mac Glen, Lyall, and Dolph, and the chieftains of the other hill-tribes to rule.

Moving forward, he leaned against the stacked-stone wall that ran around the broch.

His wulvers would be disappointed if they knew he entertained such thoughts, but he did.

Taking Doure and Dulross had been all about justice for him. The wulvers had rescued him, had given him back his dignity and self-worth. He owed them everything, and so he'd dedicated his life to giving them freedom, to showing the other inhabitants of Albia that they underestimated them at their peril.

The Marav—Lowlanders and Uplanders alike—now minded them.

That satisfied Alar, for the Shee had never persecuted his brothers and sisters. However, Lyall and Dolph appeared to want more these days. Previously, they'd owned nothing, yet like Beathan, they were enjoying having their own territory. But were Dulross, Doure, and the borderlands enough?

Alar's mood darkened again, his stomach tightening. Once, he and his brothers hungered for the same things. These days, there was a widening chasm between them.

But there was another reason—one they never spoke about. It was a subject he refused to discuss.

Lara.

Alar rationed thoughts of her, like a pauper doling out crumbs of bread to last the week. It wasn't wise to let his estranged wife intrude. Not after what he'd done to her. He'd told himself that as he'd walked away from Lara before the gates of Dulross nearly a year earlier.

He shouldn't have gone down to speak to her, but he had.

He'd regretted doing so the moment they'd begun talking. She'd shown remarkable self-control, facing the man she'd given so much to before he betrayed her. Her dignity and strength made everything he'd worked for seem petty in comparison.

And that had angered him.

He'd clung to that anger, cloaked himself in it, as he'd returned to the fort.

But the woman was a splinter that had worked its way deep under his skin. No amount of probing or cutting could release him from her.

Reaching out, Alar placed his hands on the rough, wet surface of the ramparts, gripping tight.

A noise roused him then. Something scraping against stone.

Jerking from his thoughts, he turned, drawing his twin blades from where they were always sheathed on his back.

And in the flickering light of the nearby brazier, he saw it.

A hunched form crouched on the top of the encircling wall. Watching him.

Alar's gaze narrowed as he stared back. It had been a long while since he'd come face-to-face with a boggart.

It was small and wiry, like a broonie—its helpful cousin— but the similarity ended there. Everything about the boggart was wrong. Soured. In the flickering firelight, its skin had a jaundiced cast, as did its bloodshot eyes. Coarse, matted hair hung in greasy strands around a pinched face. It wore the stained, tattered remnants of what might once have been humble working clothes—a broonie's traditional garb. Large hands with unnaturally long fingers—perfect for smothering bairns, unraveling carefully woven cloth, and spoiling fresh bread—flexed against wet stone.

Alar's lip curled. "Off with you."

The boggart didn't move, and so he sheathed one of his blades and reached for the large pouch at his waist instead.

Salt.

Everyone in Dulross made sure they carried it with them these days.

Iron worked well against spirits—but salt was even more effective. Especially with the likes of boggarts.

Opening his pouch, Alar took a handful.

The boggart shuffled sideways on the wall. It then sneered, revealing yellowed teeth that were slightly too large for its mouth. "Don't be hasty, half-breed bastard."

Alar stiffened. The insult didn't bother him. He'd heard worse over the years. However, the boggart spoke in an unsettling, high-pitched, sing-song voice, and it seemed to recognize him.

"Do you know me?" He tightened his grip on the salt.

"*Know me. Know me,*" the boggart mimicked, grinning now. "Son of a whore. You think you're king here … but you're *nothing*. Nothing! But I see who you are … I see the real man behind the mask."

Alar stilled. The boggart was treading dangerous ground now. His inane babble, mixed with riddles and insults, was designed to unbalance the listener.

"You sold yourself for a victory that is ashes in your mouth!" it crowed. "Ashes. Ashes!" The boggart gave a shrill laugh that cut through the damp air like a blade. Nearby, one of the guards cursed.

"Stay at your posts," Alar called out. "I'll deal with this."

"*I'll deal with this*," it mocked. "Betrayer. Liar. Exile. Outsider. You will never belong. Never! You found something more precious than gold, but you threw it away … and you will regret it for the rest of your miserable life. Every. Single. Day."

Alar's blood started to roar in his ears. This time, the boggart had gotten to him.

Snarling a curse, he stepped forward and hurled the salt in the boggart's eyes. With a shriek that echoed through the darkness, it tumbled off the wall.

6: UNEASY ALLIES

THE SWEEPER TUGGED at Lara's cloak and whipped hair into her eyes as she rode Bracken through the gateway of Cobblebrae's new perimeter. Her pulse quickened. *This is it.* The first day of the journey that would take her to Dulross.

To Alar.

A familiar heat ignited deep in her chest then, as vindictive thoughts wreathed up. She'd fantasized about meeting him again, about dealing out justice. It choked her that revenge would have to wait.

They needed his help, and if they didn't get it, this mission would end in the borderlands.

A few yards distant, to the west, Mor and her companions waited upon elks and stags. The queen sat astride a magnificent white elk with massive spreading antlers. In one hand, she held a steel chain, and at the end of it, crouched Dorka. The feline's plush black coat contrasted against the bright collar around her neck. Golden eyes gleamed in the dawn light, and a long tail swished furiously. The Shee had buckled restraints above each of her four paws, allowing the predator to walk but do little else.

Steeling herself, Lara glanced east.

The last of her army—which included servants and a supply train—was moving out, taking the road that would lead them back to Duncrag. They'd bring word from Lara about the task she'd been set. And, of course, they'd also let everyone in the capital know that the High Queen was a fire-wielder.

A hollow sensation settled in the pit of her gut then.

If she survived this and returned home, would she find the gates of Duncrag barred?

Don't be a fool. She pulled herself up short. *Mirren and Torran will ensure that never happens.*

With her steward and protector overseeing Duncrag, the fort and the throne would remain hers. Both her former handmaid and Cailean's second-in-command were loyal to her—and to each other. She'd left them in charge the year before, and after Alar's betrayal, had traveled back to Duncrag to discover there had been changes in her short absence. When she'd departed just a few days earlier, their relationship had been awkward and strained, but she returned to find them in love. During the summer that followed, the pair had wed, and Lara was the one to conduct the handfasting ceremony.

Her gaze lingered on the departing warriors and wagons. Spears pierced the drifting mist.

A strange detachment filtered over her then, as if she was dreaming, or watching her life unfold from a distance. It was a sensation that had started visiting her with increasing frequency of late, one that troubled her. Was the stress of everything finally causing cracks to appear?

"You're making a mistake." A rough voice intruded, and she turned to find Gregor next to her upon his stocky grey gelding. The bruises on his face were mottled and colorful this morning, and a scab had formed on his lower lip. However, when their gazes met, his brown eyes blazed with frustration. "But it's not too late to change course. Break with the Raven Queen and join your own people. You can't go through with this."

Anger spiked through Lara. "The Warrior's balls," she muttered. "You're like a baying hound."

The chief-sacrificer flinched as if she'd just struck him. Yet, vexed now, she pushed on, enunciating each word sharply. "Our path lies north now, Gregor. Don't bring this up again."

With that, she urged her mare forward, leading the way toward the waiting band of Shee.

It felt strange to travel with such a small escort. Unnerving and yet liberating.

All her life, Lara had been sheltered. Every time she stepped outside the protective walls of her broch, she was never alone. She couldn't even venture into Duncrag's market without guards, and had only ever left the fort with at least two hundred warriors with her. And she'd always had servants to tend to her needs. On this journey though, she'd sleep under the stars, with no attendants to wait on her.

But Mor was right: they traveled much swifter this way.

There were no lumbering supply wagons. No warriors keeping up on foot.

The Shee led the way along the road, their leggy elks and stags easily outpacing the horses that followed. Mor kept Dorka on a long chain, allowing her to settle into her own ungainly stride, hampered by shackles.

The Sweeper blew leaves in their path, a carpet of red, gold, and pale yellow surrounding them. The air was sharp, laced with the faint perfume of woodsmoke. Albia was beautiful this time of year, although Lara found it difficult to focus on such details.

As often, her thoughts turned inward.

Now that they were traveling to Dulross, Alar kept intruding. Try as she might, she couldn't keep him out. Memories tortured her—of how she'd slowly let her shields down around him, how she'd learned from him, believed in him. Given herself to him.

Gods, the humiliation of it.

When he'd turned on her, the world had spun for a few instants. And after the dizziness had settled, everything had looked different. *She* was different.

"You're thinking about him, aren't you?" Lara jerked out of her reverie, her gaze cutting right to Bree. The two women traveled side-by-side, with Cailean and Roth in front of them and Annis and Ren behind. Gregor and Ruari brought up the rear of their party.

Lara grimaced. "How could you tell?"

"You get that look."

"A look?"

"Aye … hard … hungry … like you were imagining twisting a knife in that fucker's gut as he pleaded for mercy."

She snorted. "That's because I was."

Bree studied her then, her brow furrowing. "And yet, you've agreed to work with him."

"For the moment."

"You're ready to face the Half-blood again then?"

"No." Lara cut her gaze away. "I'll never be ready."

Warming her hands over the fire, Lara looked west. "No sign of the Slew," she murmured.

"And the Weeper hasn't joined us yet, thank The Mother," Ren replied.

Lara glanced over at where the bard tossed a gnarled branch of old pine into the flames. Sparks gushed skyward, illuminating the young woman's tired face. Ren had held vigil the eve before and was clearly hoping to get some rest tonight.

Lara nodded. "Maybe we'll have some respite."

"Aye." Ren's voice dropped to a whisper. "Although I don't think I'll sleep easily … not with *them* so close."

Lara tensed, her gaze flicking to where the Shee warriors had taken their places on the opposite side of the fire. Mor took her place amongst them, folding her long legs into a cross-legged position. Her lips pursed slightly as she tried to get comfortable on the stony ground, and Lara empathized. As queens, neither of them was used to 'roughing it'.

Once they were all seated, the Shee began their supper of crispy bread, cheese, and fruit. They were also roasting chestnuts they'd collected during the day on the glowing embers at the fringes of the fire. The sweet, nutty aroma blended with the tang of woodsmoke.

Mor sat flanked by her cousin Vyr and Wynn Sablebane.

There were no separate camps, no tents, for there were no wagons to carry rolls of hide and poles. Instead, they'd dug a large fire pit, which they'd sleep around. There would be little privacy and no soft furs on this journey. Behind them, Lara and her escort had tethered their horses, while the Shee had let their elks and deer roam free overnight. Their mounts would rejoin them in the morning. Mor's Ravens had staked Dorka's chain to the ground a few yards back from the fire—far from the horses that had eyed the clag-doo nervously all day. Around them burned a perimeter of flaming torches. The Sweeper had died with the dusk. The evening was still and watchful.

"You'll need to get used to it, Ren," Lara replied, keeping her voice low. "Shee and Marav are uneasy allies … for the moment, at least."

The bard's mouth pursed, while next to her, Gregor stabbed at the fire with a stick. The sacrificer held his tongue though. Lara was grateful for that.

Cailean appeared then. "I've laid the ward stones," he informed them.

"Good," Gregor grunted, rising to his feet. "I'll go and sacrifice some pigeons." The druid had brought two cages of the birds, strapped behind his saddle, north with him. "We need to keep the Gods happy."

Lara was about to remind him they shouldn't use up their resources before they reached The Uplands. However, Gregor had already stalked off, disappearing behind the row of hobbled horses.

Meanwhile, his and Cailean's comments had drawn the Shee's attention. Across the fire pit, gazes narrowed, and unease rippled over their beautiful faces.

"We'd rather you didn't ward this camp ... or let your sacrificer or bard weave charms," Mor said, frowning. "Earth magic weakens us ... as you know."

"As does iron," Cailean replied. "But we aren't going north without our weapons either, so you'll just have to get used to them."

His tone was blunt, harsh even, and a stony silence settled over the fireside, broken only by the crackling of the flames and popping of chestnuts.

Mor's onyx gaze narrowed. Meanwhile, Eagal hunched slightly upon her shoulder, as if reacting to her anger. Iron. The Shee couldn't stand it. Just the merest touch left a terrible burn upon their skin, and prolonged exposure killed them.

Lara cleared her throat. She agreed with Cailean, yet didn't want to lock horns with Mor so soon. "We agreed to be your allies ... and won't use earth magic or iron against you. Nonetheless, we can't travel without protection. Especially not now." She paused then. "Iron and earth magic will help keep *all* of us safe from the dangers that stalk the night."

Mor pulled a face, and Vyr raised his eyebrows, while another of the Ravens murmured something rude under her breath.

A young female, slender as a blade, with long dark hair.

Lara stilled. Fern Sablebane. Father and daughter served in Mor's bodyguard.

Alar will choke on this.

She hoped he would.

"No offense, but we don't need your protection," Vyr replied. An amused smile played on his lips now. "We have our own methods for warding our camps." Around him, some of the other Ravens smirked.

"Well, you use yours … and we shall keep ours," Lara shot back, her temper rising. "I'm sure we'll need them *both* in the days to come."

Another silence fell then, one neither party sought to intrude upon. Instead, Shee and Marav alike ate their suppers. Lara and her companions had also brought their own supplies in saddlebags. Oatcakes, dried sausage, hard cheese, and apples. The food would last them until Dulross. Hopefully, they could replenish their supplies there; otherwise, they'd be hunting and fishing for each meal for the rest of the journey.

The chestnuts were roasted, their skins dark and blistered. The Shee then handed them out to everyone.

Taking one and trying to peel it without scorching her fingers, Lara wondered if it was a peace offering of sorts. As she nibbled listlessly on the sweet chestnut—her appetite was poor these days—she noted that Mor kept stealing glances at her. The queen's expression was speculative. Was she trying to get her rival's measure?

Lara met her eye boldly. *Underestimate me at your peril.*

To her surprise, Mor smiled back.

"Where's Gregor gotten to?" Annis drew her attention then. The counselor was brushing crumbs off her white robes. "He's missing supper."

"He's likely sulking," Ruari replied with a wince. He then rose to his feet. "I'll go fetch him."

The seer departed, while Lara shared a look with Bree.

"You need to watch him," her warder murmured before lifting a skin of ale to her lips and taking a gulp.

Lara frowned. "Aye."

"He's always been an aggressive prick," Cailean muttered.

Meanwhile, the Shee were observing their exchange keenly.

"It's more than that these days," Bree answered, frowning. "He's a pot of milk about to boil over. I wouldn't—"

"My Queen!" Ruari rushed toward the fire pit, green robes billowing. "Gregor's gone!"

Her heart kicked. "Gone?"

"There's no need to panic," Roth replied, raising an eyebrow at the younger man. "Maybe he's in the trees taking a piss."

The seer shook his head, his angular face taut. "Then why is his horse also missing?"

7: TOGETHER, YET APART

"PERFECT WEATHER FOR the Fuath."

Pushing a lock of wet hair out of her eyes, Lara cast Bree a quelling look. "Gods, don't summon them."

Her warder snorted. She rode, one hand gripping the reins, the other casually resting upon the pommel of her sword. Bree appeared relaxed, but she wasn't.

She always had her eye out for trouble.

Lara had intended to do the same, but the day had passed in a strange blur. Just before Bree had spoken, she'd glanced up at the sky, alarm flickering through her when she realized the afternoon was waning. It seemed only moments ago that they'd remounted after a brief noon meal and pushed on.

Where had the time gone?

Curse it. She needed to focus. After all, they'd recently formed an alliance with the Shee. Mor and her Ravens, and the restless spirit world, weren't the only things worrying her though. Alar was. They'd entered the borderlands. He was two days' ride away now—and then he'd decide whether they mended the rift in the veil. She hated giving him any leverage, but they needed him. How he'd enjoy that. Imagining the smirk on his face made her belly hurt.

How would she suffer his company? She dreaded journeying north with him; just the thought made her break out into a cold sweat.

And then there was Gregor's desertion. Lara and her escort had searched the nearby pinewood for the chief-sacrificer that night. Mor and her Ravens had even joined them. But Gregor had fled into the darkness on his horse. They didn't have the time to hunt him; they had to keep pushing forward.

Four days on, her mouth still soured whenever she thought about the sacrificer. Only the evening before, she'd found herself studying Annis, Ren, and Ruari's faces by the fireside, and wondering if any of them were considering abandoning her.

"Luckily for us, there are no rivers or marshes close by, or I wouldn't be so confident," Bree went on, oblivious to her line of thought. "Even flooded fields would make me nervous these days."

Lara glanced up at the sky. Purple clouds were boiling in from the north, promising worse weather to come. She too grew nervous when traveling in heavy rain these days. Last year's encounter with the bog wights farther up this road still haunted her sometimes. She remembered the way the water in the marshes had started to bubble, steam lifting from its surface. Moments later, the bog wights themselves had crawled up onto the road. Even now, her pulse quickened at the memory of how close she'd come to being taken by one.

Uneasiness skated down Lara's spine. She'd been on edge all day, but now each sense sharpened. Even the rush of the wind made her jumpy.

"At least the Slew haven't bothered us in a while," Bree said then, as if deliberately changing the subject.

"Aye … but that worries me too," Lara admitted with a frown. "They never usually wait this long between attacks. What if they're watching us … waiting for something?"

Looking ahead, her gaze rested on the backs of the Ravens who traveled in pairs behind their queen. She wished to discuss this with Mor, yet the Raven Queen had been aloof of late. Over the past days, the Shee had led the way while Lara and her escort followed. They traveled together, yet apart. Of course, the iron they carried unsettled the Shee. But there was more to it than that. Lara understood that the elks and stags were faster than horses. Nonetheless, she didn't like that Mor had made herself the unofficial leader of this band.

She wasn't. They were equals.

One of the riders ahead turned then. As they looked on, a Shee warrior upon a pale brown stag approached.

Wynn Sablebane's hood had blown back, his long black hair wet and tangled in the rain.

The sight of him made Lara's heart kick hard. Sablebane appeared no older than a Marav of forty winters, which meant he was old by Shee standards. And today, he reminded her more than ever of his son. But there was one marked difference. Alar was good at veiling his thoughts, yet his face told a story all the same, whereas his father was impossible to read. Alar's smile flashed through her mind then—the way his eyes crinkled at the corners and his cheek dimpled, while his gaze softened.

Her breathing hitched. Hag's teeth. She couldn't let herself go to that place. Ever. Again.

"The queen suggests we halt soon, camp on the hillside, and in the morning take a different road to Dulross," he said, his voice low and flat, with a slight husk to it that reminded Lara once more of Alar. "It's faster … and we'll avoid the marshes."

Lara frowned, even as her pulse quickened. "A different road? Won't that mean doubling back?" Indeed, they'd passed a crossroads a while ago, and there wasn't another until much closer to Dulross.

"There's another path."

"I've traveled this road often and know of no other route nearby," Cailean muttered.

Sablebane gave him a dismissive look. "That's because no Marav has ever traveled the Slighe Fraoch."

A beat of silence followed before Bree spoke. "Mor wants us to take the 'Heather Path'?"

"Aye. It's safer."

Bree scowled. "For Shee maybe … but not Marav."

Sablebane eyed Bree, his lip curling. "No harm will come to any of you. Just don't stray from the path … or touch anything … and you'll all be fine." He paused and studied Bree's face intently, as if trying to catch a glimpse of the Shee female she'd once been. "Regretting our choices, are we?"

Bree scowled at him. "No." Her tone was cutting. She gave Lara a sharp look then. "The Slighe Fraoch can only be used by

Marav by invitation … and even then, Shee magic makes it risky for us. He's failed to mention that the path is a cruel, twisted mirror … it shows you the things you don't want to see." Discomfort flickered across Bree's face. "The Shee don't make a habit of traveling their greenways with Marav … but on the rare occasions they have, some Marav have lost their minds."

"Only the weak succumb," Sablebane replied, his tone dismissive. "Surely, you aren't afraid to face yourself, *Fellshadow?*"

Bree stared back at him, her eyes hardening. "No."

"Good." He shifted his attention to Lara. "This way, we'll avoid any bog wights. It'll rain for a while longer … and if we take the low road, we're likely to draw the Fuath to us." Lara and Bree shared a look at this. "Also, time moves against us, and your husband may be difficult to convince. This route will take a day … no longer … *and* we'll approach Dulross unseen." He paused then, his grey eyes glinting. "The Half-blood won't know we're coming."

The small band made camp a few furlongs above the road, on a rocky hillside strewn with purple heather. They stood under the shadow of the Goatfells now, serrated peaks that pierced the low cloud. The rain fell steadily as they set about getting a fire lit— not an easy task with The Sweeper slamming into them. Both Roth and Cailean had brought rolls of hide with them, and so they managed to put up a windbreak and erect an awning of sorts over the fire pit.

But despite working at close quarters, the Shee and Marav didn't mingle. Even when they sat around the fire at night, the two races kept to their own sides. Lara had marked the wary looks the Ravens gave her escort—and in turn, the suspicious way the likes of Cailean and Roth, especially, watched their Shee companions.

"Cnoc-banes dwell in this area, My Queen," Roth warned as he staked down the hide, even as the wind tried to tear it from his hands. "It wouldn't be my choice for a campsite … especially with the spirit world as churned up as it is."

Lara frowned. She then glanced over at where, a few yards away, the Raven Queen looked on while Sablebane drove the chain that secured Dorka into the ground. "Surely, Mor knows that?"

"Maybe she has a way of repelling them."

"Not likely," Bree answered. "The Shee avoid cnoc-banes as much as we do."

Meanwhile, Mor crouched before the snarling feline, the melodious strains of her voice rising and falling with the wind. She was trying to gentle Dorka, as she did every evening while they made camp. As yet, she didn't appear to be making any headway.

Irritation spiked through Lara as she looked on. Instead of messing about with that oversized cat, she should have been focusing on ensuring this was a safe campsite. Over the past days, Lara had noticed that the Mor left such things to her Ravens while she tried to coax the clag-doo into tolerating her.

Dorka hissed then, a large paw raking the air. Mor leaped back just in time to avoid being clawed.

It wasn't working.

Lara huffed a deep breath. They also needed to discuss how to approach their looming meeting with Alar. Anxiety tightened her belly. She didn't want to lead the meeting. Mor would have to. The less she spoke to her husband, the better.

Her chief-enforcer approached then, after tethering the horses, Skaal padding along behind him. Lara turned to him. "Cailean … you'll know. What's the best way to repel a cnoc-bane?"

Cailean pulled a face. "I'd suggest a ritual where you ask permission to dwell on their hill. Unfortunately, it's one sacrificers usually perform."

Lara breathed a curse. The Reaper take Gregor. His absence left them vulnerable to many dangers. Also, without a sacrificer, Cailean wouldn't be able to replenish his earth magic when the need arose—and it surely would.

"Ren." She turned to the blue-robed woman digging through a saddlebag behind her. "Can you sing something that will appease them?"

The bard's brow furrowed. "I will try … in the meantime, I suggest we place some offerings on the highest point of this hill. It should help."

"A wise idea," Lara replied with a nod. Their food supplies were dwindling, but they'd have to part with some of it. They still had a couple of Gregor's pigeons. The birds would have to be offered up. "Ruari and Annis … can you see it done?"

Both druids nodded and started digging into their saddlebags.

Meanwhile, Roth and Cailean wore frowns. Lara shared their worry. What was the point of avoiding the Fuath on the low road if they awoke to a devastating landslide on this hill? She'd heard cnoc-banes—'hill-destroyers'—were highly territorial.

They were ancient spirits that viewed settlements on their hill, even temporary ones, as a scar on their domain.

None of them wanted to be covered in rubble during the night or sucked into a sinkhole.

Bree threw herself backward, boots skidding on the wet grass. Lara's blade whispered past her throat—close enough that her warder's eyes snapped wide.

"Impressive." Bree straightened, breathing hard. Rain plastered her oak-colored hair to her skull. "If a little *too* aggressive."

Lara's chest heaved. Sweat mixed with rain, running down her spine. She raised her knife then, fingers flexing on the grip. Aye, she'd almost taken their sparring too far. It was Alar's fault. He'd preyed on her mind far too often over the past few days. "Once more."

They circled. Their fire pit, protected by a hide awning, flickered behind them—torches guttering in the downpour, figures huddled under cloaks. The ground trembled. Just a shiver, as if the earth were shifting in its sleep. The cnoc-banes were making their presence known.

Lara lunged. Bree sidestepped, grabbed her wrist, twisted—

"Slower than I remember, Bree."

A voice intruded, and the pair froze, their gazes cutting left to where Mor stood at the edge of their circle, water streaming off her black fur cloak. Eagal hunched on her shoulder, feathers slicked flat.

Bree went still. Her fingers tightened around Lara's wrist, as if she was warning her not to say anything. She wouldn't. In truth, she'd expected Mor to confront Bree sooner.

"You used to move like smoke." Mor tilted her head as she studied her former assassin. "But now you move clumsily … like one of them."

Lara bristled. *Clumsily?* She didn't appreciate the slight.

The ground shuddered again. Longer this time. Lara felt it in her knees.

Bree released her wrist and turned to face Mor fully. They stood around five feet apart, rain falling between them in grey sheets.

"I chose this," Bree said, her tone clipped. "And I have no regrets."

Mor's eyes widened slightly, disbelief flickering over her features. "So, Cailean mac Brochan was worth giving everything up for, was he?"

Bree's lips lifted at the corners. "Aye."

Rain pattered upon the hide while the fire smoked. Shee and Marav alike huddled around its scant heat—on opposite sides, as usual. Even with the shelter they'd erected over the fire pit, the flames guttered. Across the hearth, Mor's shoulders were rounded. She'd pulled her black fur mantle close, although discomfort etched her face. Likewise, the other Shee looked similarly affected.

Of course, they all hailed from Sheehallion, the land of eternal spring.

Dwelling in Albia came at a price, for this realm weathered bitter winters as well as harsh winds and biting rain at any time of year.

All the same, despite that she was Marav born and bred, Lara had to admit the night was a foul one. The damp made her joints ache, and after a day in the rain, her clothes clung clammily to her skin. How she wished she had a warm, dry tent and a pile of soft furs to crawl into.

Sleep didn't come easily these days, but it would be even harder to rest in this weather.

A rogue gust whipped through the camp then, causing smoke to billow up from the fire pit.

Coughing followed.

"Grimlochs?" Roth wheezed. Those around the hearth tensed, their gazes narrowing as they tried to catch a glimpse of the mischief-making smoke spirits.

"No," Mor replied between chattering teeth. "Just foul weather." She caught Lara's eye then through the haze of smoke. "You're a fire-wielder. Can't you do something?"

Lara frowned. She could. However, she'd gotten used to hiding her ability, not flaunting it. She needed to get over that. Her fire-wielding would be both a tool and a weapon on the journey ahead. She'd have to get comfortable using it without hiding behind a cloak and mask.

"Very well." Shivering, she reached for the cairn stone she carried at her waist. She then wrapped her fingers around the lump of smoky quartz, its familiar rough edges digging into her skin. As Ruari had taught her, she found the calm, still place within. Fire magic was volatile. She needed to be in control of her emotions before wielding it—even for this simple task.

Then, she extended her left hand, fingers fluttering as she sought a connection with the smoking embers. "Come on," she murmured. "Dance for me."

Tender golden flames rose from the fire pit, swelling as she extended her fingers fully.

Fire roared to life before them.

Mor watched her work, her face rapt. Then, smiling, she extended her fingers over the flames, while on her shoulder, Eagal ruffled his feathers and preened. Relief flickered across the faces of the Shee, except for Sablebane, who looked as aloof as ever. Even Fern's features relaxed a little, while Vyr smiled. "A useful skill."

"That's but a shadow of what she can do," Bree answered, her tone cool. "You'll see."

Mor leaned forward then, her eyes bright. "How does your magic manifest?" she asked. "Can you *speak* to the flames?"

Lara shook her head. "It's subtler than that. When I focus on them, I feel a connection form … a partnership. It started a few years ago, when I'd ask fire to dance for me."

"Does it respond to emotion?"

"Aye … negatively," Lara replied, aware of Mor's fascination—an interest that immediately raised her hackles. "Ruari and I have worked together so that I only wield fire when I'm in a calm state. It's dangerous otherwise." She paused then. "Didn't the records you found speak of this?"

Mor leaned back, shaking her head. "It was all about history … not the specifics of the magic."

"Really?" A groove had etched itself between Bree's eyebrows. "That seems odd."

Mor flashed her an irritated look.

A deep rumble rolled over them then, and the ground they sat upon shuddered.

Lara's breathing caught. The cnoc-banes were indeed restless. In response to her reaction, the flames guttered. But she flexed her fingers again, and the fire flared bright once more.

"We too left some food as offerings upon the summit of the hill," Mor assured her then, even as her spine stiffened. "Hopefully, it's enough to keep the 'hill-breakers' happy."

8: TAKING THE HEATHER PATH

LARA WATCHED THE Shee lead the way onto the Slighe Fraoch. Mor went first upon her elk, dragging the shackled Dorka behind her.

A grey dawn greeted them, the sun a pale glow in the eastern sky. A collective sigh of relief had rippled through their small camp with the rising of the sun though—for their precautions had worked. Apart from the odd rumble during the night—

warning tremors that shook the hillside—the cnoc-banes had left them alone.

Lara peered through the murk toward where the Shee headed north, disappearing into the mist. The rain had lessened to a drizzle for the moment, but the iron-colored clouds to the north warned that more bad weather would soon roll in.

Soon you'll face him again.

Aye, there was no getting around this. She was going to have to work with the Half-blood.

Jaw set, Lara straightened her spine and urged Bracken on. Cailean and Roth led the way, with Bree and Lara following. Annis, Ren, and Ruari brought up the rear.

Lara didn't look back at the three druids. She hoped they were all ready for the Heather Path. She'd heard of roads like this one, invisible to Marav but used by the Shee to travel unseen throughout Albia. Bree had told her there weren't many of these ways, but that if a mortal trod the path, they had to keep their wits about them.

Indeed, Mor had given them a few 'rules' the night before.

Don't leave the path.

Don't touch anything.

Prepare to face yourself.

The mist swallowed them, as dense as porridge. Rain continued to fall in a soft veil for a short while longer, the caw of ravens echoing across the hillside, and then the air changed.

It grew lighter, scented with thyme, and the rain stopped.

The mist drew back then, revealing a swathe of blue sky arching overhead. And a path stretched before them. It was a greenway, a road of short grass fringed on either side by banks of heather.

Lara stared, entranced, while behind her, some of her companions murmured oaths under their breath. She'd never seen heather in so many colors. In Albia this time of year, the heather had faded, but here, it grew as it did in high summer, in profusions of creamy white, dusky-rose, custard-yellow, and even robin's egg blue as well.

Bracken whickered as they started upon the path, her heavy hooves sinking into the soft carpet of grass. The mare's head lowered slightly, her large muscular body relaxing. Of course, animals responded well to the Shee and their magic. Her horse felt at home here. Likewise, Skaal loped alongside Cailean's stallion, her ears pricked. The fae hound didn't have a problem with this place either.

Lara did though. Aye, the Slighe Fraoch was beautiful. However, from just a few yards in, her mood shifted. Heaviness descended upon her, as well as a nagging sense that something was wrong.

"Breathe slowly," Bree said then, raising her voice to ensure everyone heard her. "And keep reminding yourself … no matter what you're faced with on this path … you're strong enough to stare it down. You are more than the darkest parts of yourself."

Cailean twisted in the saddle, his gaze settling upon Bree's face. Husband and wife shared a long, intense look. Of course, both her chief-enforcer and warder had bloody pasts. They'd both done terrible things, followed orders without questioning them. These days, they made different choices, but this place wouldn't let them forget.

"The Heather Path will try to shame … and break you. It's a distorted mirror of sorts that exposes and twists the things about us we'd rather not face … and if you let it, it'll make you despise yourself." Bree continued, her gaze never leaving her husband's. "Don't let it."

"Any suggestions on how to protect ourselves?" Ren asked then, her tone subdued.

"It helps if you can imagine something guarding you," Bree replied, glancing over at the bard. "A wall. A cocoon. Whatever works. Keep your shields up … it'll help muffle the sensations."

They rode on, traveling at a brisk canter along the path. The Shee drew slightly ahead, their cloaks fluttering. None of them looked back to see how their Marav companions were faring. Lara wondered if it was deliberate.

Meanwhile, the Slighe Fraoch stretched out before them, undulating over heather-clad hills, while a cloudless blue sky swept over them. The sun bathed their faces, a balm after so much rain and smothering cloud.

The loveliness of this place should have lightened Lara's heart, but it didn't. She found herself slumping in the saddle, clinging to the reins as if they were her anchor. The warmth of Bracken's body against her legs was reassuring too, but the sense of 'wrongness' intensified with every furlong.

At first, she took Bree's advice, imagining a shimmering veil protecting her. It helped, for a while. But eventually, the thoughts broke through.

The first blow struck without warning—a sudden certainty that clawed its way up from her gut.

Her father's rage lived in her bones. The same fists that had beaten men bloody, the same voice that held no mercy, the same savage pleasure in watching enemies suffer—in torture. She could feel it coiling in her chest, hot and familiar.

Her fingers tightened around the reins until her knuckles went white. Bracken's mane blurred before her eyes.

Then came the names. One by one, they marched through her mind. Alar and his wulvers. The Circines. The overkings. The Raven Queen. Each name carried weight—stone after stone piling onto her chest until she could barely breathe. The path knew. It showed her what she'd become: a woman who kept lists, who nursed grudges like bruises, who would spend a lifetime feeding her anger until nothing else remained.

And when it was done—when the last name was crossed off, the last throat slit, the last score settled—what then? The path pressed the knowledge into her: nothing. No peace. No satisfaction. Just the hollow echo of her own heartbeat in an empty alcove.

Sweat broke out along her spine despite the mild air. Was she already too far gone? Sometimes, in the quiet times before dawn, she'd wondered if betrayal upon betrayal had left her beyond repair. Not broken cleanly but shattered into so many pieces that no amount of vengeance would make her whole again.

The pressure built behind her eyes. Her throat tightened. Bracken's steady gait became the only real thing in a world that was trying to unmake her.

Around her, the others had gone silent, presumably as they waged their own battles.

They stopped briefly at noon to rest their horses and eat the last of their bread and cheese. The Shee had halted around a dozen yards farther up the path, still keeping their distance.

Lara hardly paid them any attention though. She could barely force down a mouthful of food. Instead, she looked around at her escort.

They were indeed struggling too.

Roth stood by his horse, head bowed, one hand braced against the stallion's flank as if the animal were the only thing holding him upright. Cailean had moved apart from everyone, even his wife and fae hound, and now gazed sightlessly into the distance, his jaw working. Bree had walked away from the others as well. Her shoulders were rigid, her hands clenched at her sides. Meanwhile, Ruari's eyes were wet and bloodshot, his breathing coming in shallow gasps. Ren and Annis clung together for support, their faces the color of milk.

"I'm a coward!" Ruari cried out then, his voice cracking. "I'll only let you down, My Queen!"

To Lara's horror, he now lurched toward the edge of the path, staggering as if drunk.

"Gods!" she cried out. "Stop him, Roth!"

Mor had made it clear what would happen if any of them strayed from the Slighe Fraoch. The beauty surrounding them was just an illusion. Once you stepped off the road, you entered a liminal space that burned you to ash within moments.

Her captain moved fast, grabbing Ruari by the arm and dragging the seer back to his horse.

Lara approached him. The young man trembled. Sweat beaded upon his brow, and his eyes darted back and forth as though tracking things she couldn't see. "Hold fast, Ruari." She reached out then and placed a hand on his thin shoulder. "The arch-druid sent you to me for a reason … you're the youngest to serve as chief-seer in a long while." She squeezed tightly then. "When I look into your eyes, I see strength, not cowardice. Don't you dare stray from the path."

The young man stared back at her, a nerve flickering under one eye.

Lara held his gaze, and as she did, something inside her hardened. Earlier, as she'd dismounted Bracken, she too wondered how she was going to make it through the day. But the things she'd just said to Ruari helped her as well. This road was cruel, and Gods knew it found the soft places in her armor with unerring accuracy, but it wouldn't break her. It couldn't. She wouldn't let it.

Nonetheless, when they resumed their journey, the assault began anew.

The weight of ancestral guilt pressed down on her, as though generations of the dead now rode upon her shoulders. She was the inheritor of their mistakes. The rift in the veil—the spirits that clawed their way through to torment the living—all of it traced back to blood she carried. Her ancestors had opened the door, and she was expected to close it, but the path whispered a darker truth: what if she only made things worse? What if her meddling tore the veil wider still?

Her chest constricted. She could feel her heartbeat in her throat, rapid and unsteady.

Then came the fire. Not the physical flames she could summon, but the hunger for them. The path showed her what she tried to hide even from herself—that every time she called upon her fire magic, it answered more eagerly. That the rush of power through her veins was becoming sweeter, more necessary. What if, one day, she reached for it, only to find she couldn't let go? The magic would consume her from the inside out, burning away everything until only the fire remained, wild and mindless. Ravenous.

Her breathing grew shallow, then shallower still. Black spots danced at the edges of her vision.

No.

The word came from somewhere deep, somewhere the path hadn't reached yet. She dragged in a breath, then another, forcing air past the tightness in her throat. "Your words are venom," she whispered aloud, her voice hoarse. "They have no sway over me."

The path didn't relent. But this time, Lara didn't try to argue or deny its cruelty. Instead, she reached for Bree's words like a lifeline thrown across dark water. "I'm strong enough to stare you down." Her lips barely moved. "I'm more than the darkest parts of myself."

The whispers continued, but she met them with the same words. Again. And again. A sain. A shield. A defiant snarl in the face of everything that wanted to drag her under.

And slowly—so slowly she almost didn't notice at first—the crushing weight eased. Not gone, but bearable. There was space now between her and the poison the path poured into her mind. A sliver of distance that let her breathe.

She wouldn't let self-loathing take her. Not today. Not on this cursed road.

The afternoon dragged on. The sun moved across that impossibly blue sky while Lara fought a war inside her own skull. Her jaw ached from clenching. Her shoulders burned with tension. Bracken's steady rhythm beneath her became a prayer: *One step. Another step. Keep moving. Don't stop.*

They made their way down a steep hill now, strewn with gold and pink heather, where bees buzzed and butterflies fluttered. A soft, scented breeze tickled Lara's cheeks, yet she barely noticed. Every sense was turned inward, focused on the battle for her own mind.

She'd never thought beauty could be such a trial. She just wanted to be free of this place.

And then, moments later, she was.

As they neared the bottom of the hill, the sunshine faded, the breeze grew cool and damp, and mist rolled in. The multi-colored swathes of heather drew back, and familiar clumps of faded dark purple dotted the roadside. The soft grass beneath their horses' hooves turned to rough pebbles.

The crushing pressure on Lara's breastbone eased all at once, like shackles falling away. The vicious whispers cut off mid-word, leaving a ringing silence in their wake.

Her spine straightened. She threw her head back and sucked in a lungful of air—real air, clean and cold and blessedly free of magic. Tears stung her eyes. Relief. Bone-deep, overwhelming relief.

"Thank The Mother," Ruari rasped from behind her.

Aye. They were through. The Slighe Fraoch hadn't beaten them.

Ahead, the mist parted, and they rode into a stand of pines. The sharp scent of resin, reminiscent of earth magic, filled the air. Lara's hands still clenched the reins, but the worst had passed. They were home.

She glanced over at Bree then, and they shared a long look. No words needed. Just the understanding of two people who'd walked through fire and emerged on the other side.

Twisting in the saddle, her gaze slid over the three druids riding behind them.

Annis, Ren, and Ruari were all pale and drained, their eyes hollow and haunted. But like her, they'd survived.

The Shee waited for them up ahead. Mor watched Lara intently as she approached. "All is well?"

Lara lifted her chin, eyeballing the Raven Queen. "We're still here, aren't we?" If she'd known just how hard this 'shortcut' would be, she'd have willingly faced the Fuath instead. Perhaps the Raven Queen had known that.

"You are," Mor murmured.

The two of them locked gazes then, and Lara had the impression she'd just passed a test.

"Come on." Mor jerked her chin east. "Our destination is close."

The tall trees encircled them, their tips brushing the pale sky. The ground squelched underfoot, but the rain had ceased.

A short while later, the pines drew back, and they rode into a wide glen. The Goatfells rose directly overhead now. Huge jagged peaks of coarse dark rock with sheer sides. And ahead, in their shadow, perched upon a high hill, was a fort—three tiers of wooden and stone palisades rising to a broch at its crown.

Lara's heart kicked hard. The Brooch of Albia.

9: SAFE CONDUCT

"WHAT'S THIS THEN?"

"A messenger."

"I can see that." Irritation laced Beathan's voice. "What the fuck does he want?"

Standing at Beathan's shoulder, Alar gazed down at the lone rider waiting before the fort gates, on the other side of the spike-filled ditch. A big man with a shock of red hair. Even at this distance, he recognized him. Roth mac Tav. "To find that out, we'll need to speak to him."

The chieftain muttered another curse under his breath. "This reeks."

"There are barely twenty of them in the pinewood," Lyall rumbled. The big grey wulver had followed Beathan and Alar up onto the walls at the base of the fort. "Two queens and their escort hardly make an army on our doorstep. They'd be wise to move on."

Beathan cut Lyall a sharp look. "How is it that your wulvers have only just noticed them?"

"They appeared from nowhere through the pines," Lyall replied gruffly. "We've got sentries on the highway … but they didn't arrive that way."

Beathan snorted. "So, how did they get here? On the backs of ravens?"

Alar didn't care how they'd managed to get by their sentries. What mattered was that Lara and Mor had turned up *together*. His breathing grew shallow then. His wife was here. She—

He caught himself then, cutting himself off, mid-thought. Enough. He couldn't let himself think of her as his 'wife'. They were enemies now.

Alar glanced at Lyall. His captain was staring down at Roth, his golden eyes narrowed. Like Beathan, he was suspicious. Alar was too, but his curiosity was stronger—and they wouldn't get any answers standing up here.

He stepped back from the edge of the wall. "Come on … let's see what he has to say."

The wind whipped Roth mac Tav's red hair around him as he waited astride a large bay stallion. The beast pawed the ground, nostrils flaring. They'd just lowered the drawbridge, and Alar, Beathan, and Lyall walked out to meet the captain.

Roth watched them approach, lantern jaw set, cool blue eyes slitted.

And when his gaze settled upon Alar, something ugly rippled across his face.

Hatred.

Aye, Alar hadn't just betrayed Lara the year before; he'd stabbed them all in the back. He'd find few friends amongst the High Queen's escort.

"Good evening, Roth," he greeted the captain with an offhand tone that made red flush across the man's cheeks. "To what do we owe this visit?"

"The High Queen seeks an audience," he replied, biting out each word as if it cost him.

Warmth kindled in Alar's gut, but he swiftly shut his response down.

"Tell her and that Shee bitch she travels with to fuck off," Beathan growled, charming as usual. "They'll get no meeting with us."

"They don't want to talk to *you*, mac Glen," Roth answered coldly. His gaze flicked back to Alar then. "It's the Half-blood who has been summoned. No one else."

Alar walked across the meadow toward the dark wall of pines that rose up to the west. The wind had gotten up. The Whistle whined in his ears and slapped his cheeks. He welcomed the sensation though. It kept his senses sharp. He'd need his wits about him for the meeting to come.

As asked, he was alone. Only Roth rode beside him. He'd left his weapons behind too, divesting himself of the twin daggers he always wore upon his back. He felt naked without them. Vulnerable.

Beathan and Lyall hadn't wanted him to go.

"It's a trap," Lyall had muttered, placing a heavy hand on his shoulder. "Don't walk into it."

"Both queens promise 'safe conduct'," Roth had replied tersely. "The Half-blood shall not be harmed."

Silence had followed these words. 'Safe conduct' was a bond, a formal promise of immunity. One that wasn't taken lightly by anyone in Albia.

Eventually, Beathan spat on the ground at this. "Stick your safe conduct up your arse."

It had gone on like that for a short while longer before Alar had finally spoken up, cutting Beathan off mid-insult. "Very well."

Beathan and Lyall had still tried to put him off as he removed his weapons and handed them to his captain.

"There's no such thing as safe conduct in Albia," Lyall had warned him. "Not anymore."

"Maybe … but it's a rare thing for Marav and Shee rulers to unite on anything," he'd replied. "I'm curious to see what they have to say." It was strange indeed for the two queens to be traveling together. The two races were like frost and fire—they rarely shared the same space. The fact that they did now suggested that they had a problem, and he needed to know what it was. It could be something that affected them all.

"Your curiosity will end when your wife stabs you in the balls," Beathan had muttered, but Alar had merely shrugged. They were wasting time bickering.

And so, here he was, making toward their camp.

"How is Lara these days?" Alar asked Roth then.

The captain cut him a glare. "You will refer to her as the High Queen."

Alar caught something in Roth's voice then—jealousy perhaps. Aye, he'd marked the way the captain looked at Lara sometimes a year earlier. They were stolen glances, but Alar was adept at reading people. He'd seen the longing in the man's eyes.

He wondered then if Lara had turned to Roth for solace in the past turns of the moon. If they now shared the furs.

His gut twisted. Painfully.

Stop it.

"And why is she here with Mor?" he asked, changing tack.

"You'll find out soon enough." A muscle flexed in Roth's jaw, his fingers tightening around the reins. "Make no mistake. If it were up to me, I'd cut you down where you stand, you treacherous piece of shit."

Alar smirked. Roth's threats didn't scare him. Like a loyal dog, the man would follow orders.

They approached the pines then, and Alar spied the glow of torches amongst the trees. The daylight was fading. The days had grown short. Summer was now a memory that would have to sustain them until the following spring.

The sharp scent of pine filled his nostrils as he followed Roth into the trees. Up ahead, the outlines of cloaked figures became visible.

Lara was waiting.

His heart started to kick against his ribs then. *Ashes.* He needed to leash himself. Lara had gotten to him all those turns ago. She'd cut through the tough cloak he wrapped himself in. On their last night together, he'd been on the brink of giving it all up for her.

All his plans. His reckoning. The justice for his people he'd fought so long and hard for.

He'd been ready to turn his back on it. For his wife.

But sanity had prevailed. And despite that the victory he'd sought had ultimately felt hollow, he needed to find that place again. He had to go before Lara with a cool head.

The Shee and Marav stood in a semi-circle waiting for him.

It was an incongruous sight, seeing both races together like this, and his step slowed.

Two regal figures stood at the center of the horseshoe. One was Shee: tall, slender, and dark, with a raven hunched on her shoulder. The other was Marav: small and pale, wearing a jade-green fur-edged cloak.

Alar focused first upon the Raven Queen. Mor was exactly as he'd imagined. Regal. Intimidating. He noted then the black cloaked Shee warriors standing to her left, as well as Bree, Cailean, and the robed druids waiting to Lara's right. Bree's glare could have cut through granite, while Cailean, Annis, Ruari, and Ren—there was no sign of Gregor—stared him down. He couldn't blame them. Once, he'd sat with these people in Duncrag's hall. Once, they'd worked together, planning their campaign north. But all the while, he'd been playing a double game. One they'd lost.

But then he shifted his gaze to the High Queen, and everything else faded.

Suddenly, he couldn't hear anything except the thunder of blood in his ears.

She was as lovely as he remembered. Her auburn hair coiled in a braid around the crown of her head. Strands had come free and curled softly around her heart-shaped face. She looked tired; her features were strained, her eyes hollowed, yet the torchlight highlighted the creaminess of her skin, the scattering of freckles across her nose. Her cloak hung open, revealing a thick woolen tunic beneath that clung to her soft curves. Curves he'd once worshipped. Skin he'd once tasted. He remembered *everything*, including the feeling of being wrapped around her. Like he'd come home.

Lara stared at him as if a bog wight had just crawled into the pinewood. Her face drained of color, and for an instant or two, she swayed on her feet.

But then, their gazes met. Cold washed over him, slicing through memories that made his gut ache.

There was no warmth in her pine-green eyes. No softness.

Just bitterness and loathing.

10: INDULGE HIM

BILE STUNG THE back of Lara's throat.

She'd readied herself for this moment and employed the same toughness that had gotten her through the Slighe Fraoch. But all of it fled when Alar emerged through the trees.

The air rushed out of her lungs. Dizziness barreled into her.

For a few instants, the world tilted before she yanked herself back.

Shades. She couldn't faint.

The humiliation of crumpling onto the carpet of pine needles with Mor watching, and with the Half-blood standing a few feet in front of her, wouldn't be borne.

She clenched her hands at her sides, her nails biting into her palms.

That was better. She was back in control now.

All the same, the sight of him—tall, lithe and leather-clad, his dark hair spilling over his shoulders, his iron-grey gaze upon her—made her pulse betray her.

Her heart was pounding now.

"Finally," Mor spoke up then. "We meet … Alar … *King* of the Wulvers."

Did Lara imagine it, or was there a sneer in her voice?

Alar, who'd been staring at Lara, his face taut, cut his attention to the Raven Queen. And as he did so, his expression veiled. "Mor."

Their gazes met and held for a few moments before Mor inclined her head. "We have much to discuss … but first, there's someone here I'd like you to meet."

Lara turned to see Mor gesturing to her left. She should have known. Mor wanted to kick things off by delivering a shock. It was clever and would put the Half-blood on the back foot.

"You've met Fern before." The young Shee warrior stood, arms folded across her chest. She watched Alar with a look of thinly veiled distaste. "But I believe you've yet to be acquainted with your father … step forward, Wynn."

Sablebane did as ordered. In the torchlight, his handsome face was remote, his grey eyes—the same shade as his son's, although with slitted pupils—emotionless. He regarded his son as he might a spider crawling up the wall.

Meanwhile, Alar had gone still.

He stared back at his father, his expression stony now. Neither spoke, and a strained silence followed.

Lara's attention flicked between them. When she'd first seen Sablebane, she'd found his resemblance to Alar uncanny. They were both lean, both dark-haired, with the same arrogance and leashed power. But seeing them together, she realized they were as different as iron and Sheehallion steel.

Everything about Sablebane spoke of control. Detachment. She found it strange that he'd ever done something so reckless as tumble a Marav lass and get her with bairn. In contrast, his son burned with restless energy. Thanks to his tattoo, covered now by his vest, earth magic coursed through his veins, anchoring him to Albia, with all its roughness and beauty. It struck her then that despite his bitterness toward her people, Alar was far more Marav than Shee.

"Don't you have anything to say to each other?" Mor asked finally.

Sablebane's chiseled features tightened, while Alar folded his arms across his chest. He shifted focus to Mor then, meeting her gaze.

"My thanks for the family reunion," he said, iron edging his voice. "I'm touched. However, why don't you just tell me what you want?"

Alar didn't speak as Mor explained about The Shattered Crown, about 'the anchor, the bridge, and the weaver', and how the three of them were needed to mend the tear in the veil.

His expression never changed. Only the slight narrowing or widening of his eyes betrayed his surprise at certain points in her story. Lara also sensed his growing wariness and suspicion.

As she had, he was examining every word, waiting to expose a lie.

But Mor told the tale plainly. Honestly. The starkness of it reminded Lara of everything that hung in the balance. At a certain point, Alar's gaze flicked momentarily to her. She glimpsed the questions in his eyes, ones she wouldn't be answering.

"Will you join us?" Mor asked once she'd finished.

"It's convenient that I'm required at all," he replied, brows drawing together. "What exactly does 'the bridge' do, beyond kneeling on a stone?"

"You form a conduit between Lara and me," Mor said evenly. "We are three points of a triangle."

Alar's frown deepened. He glanced over at where Annis stood, watching the exchange. The counselor's white robes gleamed in the torchlight. "Correct me if I'm wrong, but don't rituals like these require a sacrifice of some kind? Blood-letting?"

His question echoed Lara's own from days earlier. She imagined he'd have directed his question to Gregor, but since the sacrificer was absent, Annis would suffice.

The druid grimaced. "They did in ancient times," she replied. "When seeking favor or summoning—"

"But we're not *summoning* anything," Mor interceded, her tone surprisingly patient. "We're sending wraiths back into The Threshold and closing the rift."

Alar studied her. A weighty silence followed. Lara watched his face, saw him turning Mor's words over in his mind.

"Your presence is all that's needed, Alar," Mor said eventually. "Your mixed heritage ... the bridge between our peoples ... completes the binding. That's all."

Alar's scowl remained, but something in his posture shifted slightly. His shoulders lowered. What Mor said made sense—restoration didn't require the same price as intervention. Balance could be achieved without sacrifice.

"We're all risking our lives by making this journey," Mor added. "The spirits will try to stop us. You're in no more danger than the rest of us."

He snorted softly, though his suspicion had eased somewhat. "That's not particularly reassuring."

Mor's lips tugged up at the corners. "No … but I think you'd prefer the truth." She paused then. "If you have any more questions, now would be the time to ask them."

Another silence settled, and everyone waited.

Right now, the Half-blood had them all in his hand—and he knew it.

Lara clenched her back teeth together. How he'd be gloating. Gods, to ask anything of him was humiliating.

"I do have questions … but not for you," Alar replied. His gaze snapped to Lara then. "I want to speak to my wife first … before I give an answer."

Heat rolled over her. *My wife.*

How dare he speak about her as if she belonged to him? As if they were together.

"I have nothing to say to you," she replied.

He looked her way then, his gaze pinning her to the spot. "If you refuse … I'll walk away."

Her pulse went wild. The selfish prick meant it too.

"Indulge him, Lara," Mor said, shattering the weighty silence that followed. "Just this once."

She cut the Shee queen a sharp look—a warning to stay out of this—even as panic clawed its way up.

Fuck.

She still bore the scars from their last conversation, still recalled his callous words. His betrayal remained etched on her skin; a tattoo she'd wear for the rest of her days. She demanded the truth, and he'd given it to her.

And she'd been plotting his downfall ever since.

She drove her fingernails harder still into her palms and sought that calm, still place. She had to find that quiet loch before wielding fire, but if she was to face the Half-blood in private, she needed the same self-control.

And so, she slowed and deepened her breathing, letting her churning emotions settle before she finally answered, "Very well."

"Speaking to me alone isn't necessary."

"Actually, it is."

They stood together in the pinewood, around ten yards from where the others waited. The faint glow of torchlight filtered through the tight press of trees. However, Lara carried her own torch.

Glaring at him, she drove the torch into the soft damp ground before folding her arms across her chest. "Spit it out then."

She'd agreed to this under sufferance; he should tread carefully.

Aye, he should—and yet a sudden recklessness burned in his veins. He hated her coldness, especially when he recalled the heat that burned just beneath the surface.

This wasn't the woman he remembered.

You did this.

He took a step forward, and she retreated. "Keep your distance."

Alar heeded her. He was on borrowed time here; he had to make the most of it. "Do you believe Mor's tale?"

"Aye."

"Why?"

"Cailean visited The Shattered Crown around five years ago … even then, he marked something strange about the place."

Alar inclined his head. "And that's all it took for you to agree to this?"

Heat flickered in her eyes, and upon her right hand the *Ordree seal*—the amber stone set upon an iron ring—flared gold. That ring. It was far more than royal jewelry, but something that had the ability to regulate a gap in the veil between the living and the dead. Powerful indeed. And dangerous.

"I didn't want to believe Mor," she replied, her tone brisk now. "But her story rings true." Her hand lifted then, and she stared down at the gently glowing ring. "I guess I've always known … but never wanted to admit it."

Alar considered this. He wanted to disagree, to call her a fool for being taken in, for forming an alliance with the Raven Queen. But something stopped him. He'd heard many stories about Mor, and none of them engendered trust. And yet, she'd never have approached Albia's High Queen. Not unless she was worried. Desperate.

"It must hurt," he said after a long pause. "Asking me for help."

Her gaze hardened. "How I feel about this is none of your business."

No, it wasn't. He'd turned his back on her and her people. He had no right to answers. And yet, he couldn't help but push.

"And what if the rift can't be shored up? What if what's broken can never be mended?"

She stilled. He'd just reminded her of the things he'd said before they left Duncrag all those turns of the moon ago—of how there was no returning to how things were. Her father's kingdom was fractured, and even Lara's iron will, her fierce determination, couldn't put it back together.

He'd just reminded himself too of how deep his betrayal of her had gone. There was no going back.

"Bastard."

"Aye."

"You enjoy breaking things, don't you?"

"Sometimes."

Loathing burned in her eyes now. "Do you want Albia to collapse?"

"Maybe it should. Maybe none of us deserve it."

"I'll not stand by and let the darkness swallow us," she shot back. "Unlike you, I *care* about this world."

"Do you?" He couldn't help but take the bait. "Or are you just wanting to put the Marav back in control again?" He flashed her a goading smile, even as a voice in the back of his head warned him against taunting her. "Face it, Lara, you play the role of the protective High Queen ... but in reality, you're just as self-serving as the rest of us."

She snarled something then. His words had hit a raw nerve.

And then, a heartbeat later, the dam burst.

Dull iron flashed, and an instant later, she'd closed the gap between them. One hand fisted the collar of his leather vest.

The other held a cold thin blade to his throat.

11: I DESERVE WORSE

"I'VE IMAGINED THIS moment so many times." Lara marveled at how steady her voice was. Her temper had boiled over, heat pulsing under her ribs. Fury yanked like a beast on a leash, and yet she was in control. "You taught me much during our marriage … especially how to turn resentment into a weapon. Ever since you betrayed me, I've hardly slept. Instead, I lie awake thinking about killing you."

Alar stared down at her, his eyes wide. They were standing so close, she could see the flecks of charcoal in amongst the iron-grey of his irises. He hadn't realized it, but his words had yanked her right back to The Heather Path, to the things it had shown her. And this time, she'd reacted.

"You're a lot faster than I remember," he murmured. He didn't move though. Not with her blade pressing against his windpipe.

"I've been practicing." The urge to press the knife in hammered into her. "And during every session, I imagine I'm cutting up your smug, sneering face."

He didn't reply. Indeed, her own venom surprised her. *Gods.* She didn't sound like herself at all. And yet, the rage was liberating. Anger and bitterness had built a prison around her over the past year, but she'd just broken free. She'd walked that cursed greenway and been faced with the twisted truth. Now, she'd own her darkness.

"Food has lost its taste. I no longer enjoy warm sun on my face or appreciate a cup of sweet plum wine," she went on, the words tumbling out of her now. She hadn't realized her hatred went so deep, yet it did. "My need for reckoning is all that matters. And I don't care if I die getting it. You will pay, Half-blood."

He swallowed, carefully. There was no taunting light in his eyes now.

Her venom shocked him.

"Do it," he replied, his voice roughening. "You'll never get a better chance. Take your revenge now."

White-hot rage consumed her then, blotting out all reason. All sense. She pressed the blade harder against his throat. Blood welled against iron. And as she watched, crimson trickled down his pale skin.

Surprisingly, he didn't flinch. Instead, his stillness unnerved her. "Again," he said quietly. "If it helps."

"Don't tempt me," she ground out, even as she leaned into the dagger. Blood welled again, more of it now, running over the iron blade. And still, he didn't move.

"I deserve worse."

Lara stiffened, even as her fingers flexed around the dagger's bone hilt. Finally. There was complete honesty in his voice. He'd dropped the arrogance, the taunting. There was no barrier between them now. "You do."

But even as she whispered the words, something inside her shifted.

The bastard wasn't supposed to submit to her like this. She wanted him to fight, to sneer, so she could enjoy watching him bleed out over the pine needles. His submission disturbed her. Revenge didn't feel like victory when he offered himself up for it.

Neither of them moved. Instead, they stared at each other. It was a moment of raw honesty, and she didn't want it. She didn't want any closeness between them. Hatred was easier.

"Lucky for you, we need the three of us to perform the binding at The Shattered Crown," she said finally. "My reckoning will have to wait."

"You're wasting an opportunity," he replied softly. "It won't be so easy to catch me unawares next time, Lara."

"No, but we both have an important job to do."

She stepped back then, releasing her grip on his vest and removing the blade from his throat. Blood slicked his neck, running down into the hollow between his collarbones. His chest rose and fell sharply then, as if in the grip of a strong emotion.

Indeed, he wore a strained expression, his skin pulled tight over his high flat cheekbones.

"Will you come north with us or not?" she asked, shoving the observation aside. Of course, he was flustered. An inch more and blood would be pumping out of his neck. "Will you form the third point of the triangle, so we can push the wraiths back into The Threshold … and close the door behind them?"

He swallowed, blood glistening in the lamplight. And when he answered, his voice held a husky edge. "I'll think about it."

Alar walked back to the fort alone.

Night had fallen, and a waxing crescent moon was rising. Away from the glow of torches, the darkness was alive. Whispers followed him, and icy fingers brushed his cheeks.

He hadn't let on, but Mor's story had shocked him. Even so, there was no denying reality.

The spirit world was growing increasingly troublesome.

He didn't quicken his pace though. Instead, his hand rested on the pouch of salt at his waist—just in case something went for him. He didn't want to hurry his path to the gates.

He needed this time to think, to untangle everything he'd been told and make sense of it all.

He'd agreed to consider traveling north with Mor and Lara at dawn. They'd told him he could bring a small group of wulvers with him, if he wished—generous of them—but he wouldn't.

Lyall and Dolph would be incensed.

No, if he agreed to this, it was a journey he needed to make alone.

One he wouldn't return from.

He'd had one shock after another this evening. He'd hidden his reaction well, but seeing his half-sister and his father standing with Mor had been a punch to the gut. He'd still been reeling when Mor began her tale. At first, he'd barely listened, but as she talked about The Shattered Crown and the wraiths that poured out nightly through the gaps, he'd focused. He'd only half-believed the Raven Queen though, which was one reason why he'd insisted on speaking with Lara alone.

His free hand lifted, tracing the cut on his neck. He then grimaced. It stung.

There had been a moment back there, as he'd stared into Lara's furious green eyes, when he'd thought she'd throw caution aside and kill him anyway.

But he'd counted on her to do the right thing and stop herself.

She needed him alive.

Even so, as blood had warmed his neck and the cold iron blade burned against his skin, he'd wondered if he was breathing his last.

Lara had withdrawn in the end though, and despite the relief that had weakened his legs, he'd mourned the loss of contact. When she'd been standing close, the familiar scent of her had crowded his senses.

It had brought every memory back into sharp focus. If he was going to die this evening, he wanted to do so in her arms.

Shaking himself free of unsettling thoughts, he drew in a deep, steadying breath. *What's wrong with you?*

He was losing himself these days. The old fire that had burned in his belly had gone out.

"Have you lost your Gods-damned mind?"

Beathan mac Glen slammed his cup of ale down on the low table beside the hearth, making Duana startle. The young woman sat on his lap, her face set in a rigid expression.

He'd been casually fondling her, one hand up her skirts, when Alar, Lyall, and Dolph had entered his alcove.

Alar had called his brothers to him, but wouldn't reveal what had transpired in the camp until they met Beathan too. He didn't want to repeat this tale.

Standing in the middle of the large alcove, warmed by a roaring hearth, Alar had recounted what Mor had told him.

All of it.

There wasn't any point in leaving things out. Everyone needed to know about the danger that threatened to engulf them all. He'd responded flippantly to Lara when they'd been alone, goading her into anger.

He hadn't given her a firm answer either, yet he knew how serious it was.

If wraiths continued to pour into Albia, everything he'd worked so hard for would be lost.

His brothers and sisters would be forced to flee Doure and Duncrag, to return to the dark forests and cower in the shadows. But, even there, they wouldn't be safe.

He couldn't let that happen.

Aye, victory had left a bitter taste in his mouth, but the reason he'd done all this remained. It didn't matter if the wulvers didn't look at him as they once had.

Their leader. Their savior. He still owed them more than he could ever repay.

If traveling to The Shattered Crown and taking part in this binding ritual would save them, he'd do it. And if he didn't return from the North, so be it. Fatalism had descended upon him during his walk back to the fort, and he hadn't fought it.

And so, he told his companions that he'd leave with the party waiting in the pines that following dawn.

Lyall and Dolph had gone still, their amber eyes narrowing, as the tale had progressed. Beathan had stopped groping Duana, while across the chamber, Duana's sister, Eithne, who'd poured everyone fresh cups of ale, had gone still.

Beathan hadn't reacted though, until Alar announced that he intended to travel to Darkmere with Mor and Lara, and see this through. "This must be done," he concluded, swirling the ale in his cup before draining it in a long draft. "The binding needs the three of us."

"It sounds like horse shit to me."

"I agree," Lyall growled.

"You aren't usually so easily convinced, brother," Dolph added.

"No, but I can tell you why," Beathan shot back. "The stupid prick is in love with his wife."

"Watch yourself, Beathan," Alar said softly.

The chieftain sneered, dragging his gaze over Alar. "That cut on your neck ... did she do it?"

Alar's pulse quickened. Beathan was far too sharp. "It doesn't matter."

"Don't take us for fools." Beathan's dark-blue eyes bore into him. "You've been pining for the bitch ever since we took Dulross. You're a fucking fool. Women need to know their place. You *never* let one weaken you." To make his point, Beathan grabbed a handful of Duana's hair and yanked hard, pulling her back against him. "They're for humping, bearing bairns, and serving their men." He then twisted her breast with his free hand, and she cried out. "Nothing else."

Angry now, he shoved the lass roughly off his lap. "Get out … the pair of you!"

She didn't need to be told twice. Picking up her skirts with one hand, Duana swept from the alcove, pulling her younger sister after her.

Silence settled after their departure. Eventually, Beathan broke it. "That's how you treat women. Instead, you walk out there, and hand your balls over to that Shee bitch and your wife, like some fucking *eunuch*."

"So, you don't believe the threat is real?" Alar asked, not rising to the bait. The chieftain's insults washed over him.

Beathan made a disgusted sound in the back of his throat. "This is just a power play."

"And what if it's not?"

Beathan snorted. "Then we just drink, fight, and fuck until the end."

"Let them leave tomorrow, Alar," Lyall said roughly. "Let the two queens play their game … without you being part of it."

Beathan screwed his face up. "No … let's *deal* to them instead." His blue eyes speared Alar then. "They're a small band. We wait until just before dawn, and then we kill them."

Silence followed these words.

The two wulvers exchanged veiled looks, while Alar's heartbeat started to pulse in his throat.

This wasn't going as he'd hoped.

Eventually, Dolph cleared his throat. "You shouldn't even be considering helping them. You're needed here."

Am I?

He wasn't sure his brother believed that. Both Lyall and Dolph were happier at Dulross than he was. Beathan encouraged them to expand their territory further—pushed them to want more than Doure and Dulross. But Alar was tired of it all.

He'd recently begun to realize that it would never be enough. He wanted no part of it.

He didn't say as much to his companions though, for he didn't like the way all three of them were eying him now: like *he* was a problem. One they weren't sure how to solve.

As a rule, Beathan got on better with Alar than he did with Lyall and Dolph. Like many Marav, he'd once scorned wulvers. Although he'd swallowed his prejudices to side with them, he still wasn't that comfortable with Alar's captains. Things were better here between the two races than they'd ever been in Duncrag, yet over the past turn of the moon, Alar noticed cracks appearing.

Beathan's jibes about the stink of frying and smoking fish had started to wear thin. The chieftain often disregarded Lyall's opinions at meetings, always asking Alar for his thoughts instead. This evening was the first time in a while he'd actively sided with either of them.

If anything, Alar's absence would likely unite them.

They were all wary of what he might do next. He needed to tread carefully.

"I shall sleep on it then," he said, moving over to the table where Eithne had been standing earlier, and replacing his empty cup.

"There's nothing to sleep on," Beathan growled out. "Ready yourself, Half-blood ... and be at the gates with your wulvers before dawn.

12: CHOOSING A SIDE

ALAR LEFT THE alcove, his pulse thumping in his ears.

No one told him what to do—least of all the Circines chieftain. They were equals here.

However, he let the dog's pizzle have the last word, let the three of them think they'd won. Lyall and Dolph made no move to leave with him. Instead, they stayed with Beathan. It was a silent yet powerful gesture.

They'd chosen a side. But he'd chosen his.

He wasn't killing Lara, or Mor.

He was going. Tonight.

Out on the landing, he nearly collided with Duana and Eithne. The two women had been waiting there, listening in on their argument through the curtain. The lasses reeled back at his sudden appearance, panic flaring in their eyes.

Acting on instinct, Alar raised a finger to his lips, warning them to be silent. He then jerked his chin toward the stairwell, indicating for them to follow him into it.

Faces taut, the sisters obeyed, even as fear vibrated off them.

They still expected him to turn on them.

Unlike Beathan, he hadn't touched either lass in his year at Dulross, nor had he mistreated them. It didn't matter though; they likely hated him as much as they did the chieftain. He'd led the force that had taken this fort, and his wulvers had killed their parents. He'd also let the chieftain and his captain claim them, and he'd been present while they groped the women, humiliated them.

He hadn't stopped the abuse *then*—for doing so would have broken things between him and Beathan—but he would now.

"We're leaving Dulross," he whispered as they made their way down the winding stairwell, within the cavity between two thick stacked-stone walls, which circled down from the top floor of the broch to the entrance hall. Cressets guttered as Alar quickened his pace.

There wasn't a moment to lose.

"What?" Duana hissed back. "Now?"

"Aye."

"They'll stop us."

"Only if they know you're going."

Both lasses slowed their pace, and when Alar looked back, he saw them exchanging worried looks.

Halting, Alar turned to them. "I've given you little reason to trust me," he said, keeping his voice low. "But you must now." He paused then. "Ask yourselves. Whom do you fear more … me or Beathan?"

That decided it. Duana's lips pursed, while Eithne swallowed audibly. Without another word, they followed him down to the entrance hall.

The hearths burning on the other side glowed through the thick curtain that shielded this narrow area from the main hall. The rough voices of men and higher-pitched responses of women, accompanied by the lower, growling tones of wulvers, drifted out.

Alar stilled a moment. They were arguing.

He tensed, wondering if he should move closer and discover what the problem was. He stopped himself though. There was no time to linger. The affairs of Dulross were no longer his concern. He'd given his brothers and sisters their freedom, but they had to find their own way now, without him.

His gaze swept the shadowy entrance hall.

Fortunately, there were no guards in here, although there would be a couple just outside these thick oak and iron doors. Duana and Eithne needed disguises.

Plucking two cloaks down from pegs on the wall—mantles that belonged to warriors arguing just a few yards away—Alar handed them to the sisters. He then took one for himself.

Their blue eyes were huge on pale faces. They were both looking at him as if he were mad.

It probably seemed that way.

"Pull your hoods up over your faces," he ordered, keeping his voice low. "Don't talk to anyone. And if I say 'run' … do it."

"Where are we going?" Duana asked.

"I'm taking you to the High Queen." He paused then, urgency tightening his gut. They had to move. "Come on, it's time."

He waited until both women had donned the voluminous cloaks and yanked the cowls up to hide their faces.

Only then did he pull open the doors.

Outside, two hulking Circines warriors flanked the entrance. Torchlight played across the woad tattoos that curled down their bare arms.

"Alar," one greeted him gruffly.

"Evening," he replied.

"Off somewhere?"

"I have a meeting in the lower town."

"And these two?"

"My slaves."

The big man's heavy brow furrowed. As far as any of them knew, the Half-blood didn't keep any slaves. However, things could have changed.

"It's after curfew," the other warrior said then.

"Aye … we'll be careful."

Neither of the men answered, and Alar walked on. He made his way across the dirt-packed yard in front of the broch toward the closed gates. The scuff of the women's soft-soled boots behind him reassured him that Duana and Eithne were following. He deliberately didn't hurry his pace; if anything, he walked a little slower than usual.

The guards behind him were watching.

Fortunately, he found four of his wulver brothers guarding the gates.

All he had to do was nod, and they opened for him. Moments later, he led the way out onto the road beyond. However, instead of taking the long, winding way that would eventually take him down to the lower gates, he cut right and slipped into one of the narrow vennels that dropped down into the residential area of Dulross's highest level.

The sisters followed him, hurrying now to keep up with his long stride. Out of sight of the guards, he moved faster, taking the stone steps in twos.

Along the way, they passed the headman's roundhouse—each level of the fort had one. These men had once kept order, although those who hadn't lost their lives a year earlier were now powerless. They did Alar and Beathan's bidding or risked hanging by their neck from the walls. The dwelling was bigger and better constructed than most. Light glowed around the door of the roundhouse as Alar and the women slipped by, the rich aroma of blood sausage drifting out into the darkness.

They continued down a network of narrow vennels, heading toward the archway that would take them to the lower levels, passing well-kept roundhouses with turf roofs. This was the wealthiest area of the fort, where most of Dulross's 'elders' lived, venerated men and women whom locals came to for advice. Before the Circines and wulvers' arrival, they'd settled disputes and warned the headmen or the fort chieftain if there was any trouble brewing among the residents. Now, they kept their own counsel.

Since it was after dark, Dulross's residents had locked themselves away behind sturdy oak doors. If Alar had any sense, he'd be inside too. The Slew hadn't attacked in a few days now, but that didn't stop other wraiths from stalking the wynds and vennels of Dulross, looking for a way inside homes or an idiot who didn't respect the curfew.

"Things are moving in the shadows," Eithne whispered, her voice catching.

"Aye … there will be," Alar replied. He thought then of the boggart who'd visited him days earlier. "Don't look at them … and keep moving."

They reached the archway that led out of the top level then and slipped through, moving past two brightly burning braziers. Dulross glowed like a beacon each night—something Lara could have used against them if she'd wished. Perhaps she planned to, once her mission in the North was complete. Nonetheless, fire was necessary. Spirits didn't like it. They were born from the shadows and preferred to linger there.

As such, Alar avoided some of the darkest, dankest back streets now, sticking to the better-lit paths.

On the way down to the gates, they passed no one. At one stage, a large brown rat scuttled across their path, and then farther down, a rail-thin cat hissed at them.

Finally, they crossed the market ground, a wide dirt area before the gates.

Both wulver and Circines warriors flanked the way out.

"A bit late for a walk, isn't it?" One of the Circines greeted him. Alar recognized the man. His name was Ewart. Tall and blunt-featured with long curly straw-colored hair, he was one of Beathan's trusted senior warriors.

"I'm off on an errand," Alar replied, flashing the man a cool half-smile. "Beathan and I have met. I have a proposal for the queens."

Ewart raised ruddy brows. "He's sending you out *now?*"

Alar shrugged. "We prefer not to wait. None of us wants the Raven Queen or that *fire-wielder* to linger at Dulross."

Ewart nodded, although his gaze was still wary. He glanced then at the two hooded figures who stood behind Alar, heads bowed. "I've never known you to take an escort anywhere?"

"These two are slaves … offerings. They carry gifts."

The warrior frowned. "You're trying to buy the queens off?"

"It's part of our plan, aye." Alar was starting to sweat now. If these questions continued, he'd have to draw his blades and kill Ewart—and anyone else who tried to stop him. "Do you want me to send up a runner to the broch, haul Beathan out of the furs, and get him to explain this to you?" He paused then. "When I left him, he was about to give his bed-slave a tumble … shall we disturb him?"

Behind him, one of the sisters—Alar wasn't sure which—squeaked.

Shit.

A moment passed, and Ewart's lips pursed.

Everyone knew Beathan was as randy as a ram in rutting season. After supper each eve, he retired early to give Duana a seeing to—and he didn't like being interrupted.

"He should keep me better informed," the warrior grumbled then, stepping back and gesturing to the men standing by the large iron bolts that kept the gates locked.

Alar didn't answer.

A rumble followed as the drawbridge on the other side lowered over the spike-filled ditch. Moments later, the warriors and wulvers pushed the gates open, just wide enough for Alar and his companions to slip through.

"How long will you be?" Ewart asked as Alar moved forward.

"If I don't return from the pines by the witching hour, I'm likely dead."

Alar departed then, with the sisters right behind him. The moment they walked out onto the drawbridge, their boots thudding on wood, the gates started to close. But as they did, the faint echo of shouts reached Alar's ears.

His heart kicked. Someone had raised the alarm.

Fuck.

Halting, he whipped around, grabbed Duana and Eithne by the arms, and pushed them ahead of him. "Run."

Neither lass reacted as he hoped. Instead, they stumbled and smacked into each other, fear turning them both clumsy.

"Run!"

Choking out a curse, Duana took her sister's hand. Together, they fled like hunted hinds across the drawbridge and into the meadow beyond.

Alar was right behind them.

Fortunately, all three of them were wearing black cloaks, which helped them blend in with the shadows. Unfortunately, though, the waxing crescent moon was high and bright, and the sky was clear. A faint veil of silvery light bathed the grass.

Alar's gut clenched. Suddenly, the stretch between the walls of Dulross and the pinewood to the west seemed endless.

They'd hardly gone more than a dozen yards when arrows flew from the walls above them, peppering the ground like deadly hailstones.

"Don't run in a straight line," Alar called, even as heat rippled out from his chest. His tattoo was awakening, earth magic channeling through his veins. Good. His instincts would be sharper now. He'd run faster. "Cut left and right."

He wasn't sure the women had heard him, but he could hear their ragged breathing and panicked gasps.

Something whistled past his right ear then, so close the feather fletching brushed his skin.

Teeth clenched, he bowed his head and sprinted on, dreading the impact of something slamming in between his shoulder blades. They just had to hang on for a few more yards. Soon they'd be out of range of the archers on the walls.

A woman's cry split the night.

One of the cloaked figures that fled before him was down.

An instant later, both Alar and Duana were at Eithne's side. "Where did it get you?" Duana asked, her voice high and panicked. All the while, arrows flew around them.

"It didn't," Eithni ground out. "I twisted my ankle."

Relief barreled into Alar. Grabbing Eithne under the arms, he hauled the lass to her feet. She shrieked as he threw her over his shoulder. "Run!" he barked at Duana. "And no matter what happens to us, don't stop."

13: THE LURE OF THE LIGHT

"HE WON'T JOIN us."

"It's too early to make that claim ... he has until morning."

Cailean snorted. "The Half-blood's loyalty is to his wulvers ... no one else."

Leaning forward, Lara poked the embers of the fire with a stick. The flames had a hypnotic effect. It was hard to concentrate. "He'll know this affects them as well." Her belly tightened then. She was keeping up a stoic front, but the truth was that ever since Alar had stalked off into the darkness, she'd worried he wouldn't return.

She'd nearly cut his throat, after all. The Reaper take her, she'd been close to losing it. What if he refused to help them?

She'd admitted none of her worries to her companions. Nonetheless, some of them must have marked the blood running down Alar's neck as he'd walked by.

Shades. They didn't have time for this. The days were racing by. They had to reach The Shattered Crown by Gateway.

"Sitting out here like a fat grouse on a moor is making me nervous," Roth grumbled then. The warrior kept glancing east, to where the home fires of Dulross glowed faintly through the trees. "They'll know we're vulnerable."

"I don't like it either," Mor replied with a grimace. "But we need the Half-blood. We have to risk it."

A tense silence settled around the gently crackling fire then. Of course, they'd already taken precautions; it would be foolish not to. Their mounts waited a short distance behind them. The horses were saddled and ready to go—although the elks and stags didn't wear saddles and bridles.

Mor had chained Dorka to a tree a few yards away so that she could scratch. The clag-doo's claws grew constantly, and she needed to blunt them often. Now fresh scratches marred the pine's trunk, oozing sap. Dorka watched them. Her eyes glowed in the firelight, and her tail twitched. After Alar's departure, the Raven Queen had spent time, as usual, trying to gentle her *pet.* However, Dorka had merely spat and hissed at her.

"Are you well, Lara?" Bree whispered then, leaning close.

Lara stiffened. "Aye. Why?"

"When we were talking earlier, you just sat there, staring into the fire. It was as if you'd left us."

Lara blinked. She didn't remember blanking, although this wasn't the first time one of her companions had made such an observation. Her pulse quickened then, a sickly sensation stirring in her gut. This was happening too frequently now to ignore it. Something *was* wrong with her.

"We must be patient." Mor's voice intruded then. Reaching up, she stroked Eagal's soft feathers. The raven roosted on her shoulder, eyes closed. "He needs time to think it over."

Next to her, Vyr huffed. "He doesn't *have* time. We can't linger here. After things soured with the Circines, their chieftain might decide to have his reckoning with you … or he might just take the opportunity to bring down two queens with one stone."

Mor pulled a face before casting her cousin an irritated look.

"What happened with the Circines?" Lara asked.

"I made a deal with them … and they broke it," Mor replied.

"They didn't want to wait five years to get the territory they'd been promised," Vyr added. Firelight played over his handsome face, the silver half-moon on one earlobe glinting. "You Marav are impatient."

"Can you blame us? We don't have centuries to play with like you do," Roth replied.

Vyr shrugged, giving him that.

Lara dug her stick into the embers once more, sending up a spray of sparks. She too was nervous waiting here. If the Circines and wulvers attacked, they didn't have the resources to face them. They'd have to flee into the night instead, leaving Alar behind. And since they couldn't perform the binding without him, they wouldn't be traveling to The Shattered Crown. Instead, she'd have to return to Duncrag, knowing that she'd failed her people.

The spirits plaguing them would grow in number, and the world would grow dark indeed.

Her pulse quickened.

Gods. She hoped she hadn't ruined everything.

Her gaze traveled around the fireside then, taking in the faces of their small band. The Shee all looked tense, their gazes wary, whereas Cailean and Roth wore deep frowns. However, when her attention shifted to Annis, Lara stilled.

The counselor's face had gone slack. Her dark eyes were glassy as she stared off at a point behind Lara's shoulder. Lara observed her for a moment, wondering if that was what *she* looked like when she drifted away.

The hair on the back of her neck prickled then. She hadn't been herself of late, but Annis was usually as sharp as a boning knife. Something was wrong.

Tensing, she twisted.

A light in the darkness winked back at her.

Lara's breathing caught.

The golden light flickered. A heartbeat later, another appeared a few feet away from the first. Flames dancing.

Corpse candles.

And as she had a year earlier, she felt their pull. *Follow me.*

But this time, the urge didn't overwhelm her. Warmth suffused her chest. It was like seeing old friends.

"Annis?" Ren's voice drew her attention back to the fire. "Where are you going?"

Indeed, the older woman had just lurched to her feet and was stumbling away.

Lara motioned to Roth. "Stop her!"

Standing up, he caught Annis by the arm. She barely noticed him though, as she stared into the trees. And when the warrior followed her gaze, his expression changed. Wonder filtered over his rugged features.

"Shit," Lara muttered as she got up. "It's the corpse candles. Lower your gaze to the fire … and *don't* look behind me."

Cailean growled an oath. Gaze averted, he rose to his feet and moved toward Annis and Roth. Then, keeping his back to the dancing flames, he faced the captain and counselor. "Shake it off, you two."

Neither answered. Instead, Roth tried to push past the chief-enforcer. His lips were parted, his eyes shining. The faerie lights had him.

The 'crack' of Cailean's palm colliding with his cheek echoed around the glade.

Roth stumbled back, while Cailean caught Annis by the shoulders, shaking her. "Annis!"

She blinked, surprise rippling across her face. "What—"

"Corpse candles," he cut her off, turning her sharply around.

Rubbing his stinging cheek, Roth also turned his back on the flames.

Lara glanced over at the Shee then. They watched the unfolding scene with interest; of course, corpse candles didn't affect them. They could stare at the lights with impunity.

Mor raised an eyebrow. "You resisted them … how?"

"I don't know," she answered honestly. "A year ago, powries used corpse candles to lure me into a trap." Anger flickered to life under her ribs then. Of course, the powries were Mor's servants these days. Had the Raven Queen ordered that attack? "But tonight, it's different."

"How?"

Lara shook her head, confused. "I don't know … I still feel their lure … but it just … *washes* through me."

Her companions all looked puzzled by this.

"Maybe it's the fire magic?" Ren suggested hesitantly, even as she took care not to glance up from the fire lest the faerie lights ensnare her. "It might be protecting you."

"Or perhaps it calls to them," Annis added. Her round face was pale, her expression shaken.

Lara didn't answer. Instead, uneasiness twisted in her belly. *Or could it be another sign that something is wrong with me?* The lapses. The blanks. And now her surprising reaction to the corpse candles. It could all be connected.

"How many of them are there?" Cailean asked, his voice sharp. He'd placed a hand over his eyes.

Lara glanced over her shoulder. More lights winked into existence then. Moments later, they illuminated the surrounding pinewood. "A great number now," she replied. "Keep your gazes averted or—"

The snap of twigs and the tattoo of running feet intruded then. Like skittish fawns, the corpse candles scattered.

In a burst of movement, Mor and her Ravens all sprang to their feet, blades sliding from scabbards. Likewise, Lara and her escort all drew their weapons, swiveling toward the noise.

And then Alar appeared.

Face glistening with sweat, he carried a young woman over one shoulder, while another lass followed close behind. Both women had long flaxen hair and wore voluminous black cloaks. Their hoods had fallen back, and bronze glinted at their throat in the firelight. Bed-slave collars.

"What's this?" Mor greeted him.

"I'm coming with you," he gasped, lowering the trembling lass to her feet.

"Who are these two?" Lara demanded.

Alar glanced her way, straightening up and pushing hair from his face. "Duana and Eithne. They're mac Og's daughters. Beathan and his second took them as bed-slaves. I didn't want to leave them there."

His explanation made something jolt deep in Lara's chest. An instant later, heat washed over her. Surely, she wasn't relieved that these women weren't his?

Mor made an irritated sound in the back of her throat. "You were supposed to bring a small escort of *warriors* with you."

"That wasn't possible," he shot back. "And while we stand here blethering, trouble is coming. We need to go."

The thunder of approaching hoofbeats shook the ground then, torchlight flickering through the trees.

No one argued with Alar after that. Leaving their fire pit burning, for there was no time to kick dirt over it, Shee and Marav alike rushed to their mounts. Mor untied Dorka, dragged her away from the tree, and vaulted upon her white elk's back.

Lara mounted Bracken, noting that Roth had yanked one of the lasses up onto his stallion's back. Meanwhile, Cailean had hauled the other one up behind him. However, Alar was still on foot. Her heart kicked against her ribs. Curse it. He was fast, but even with his earth magic, he'd never keep up with them.

He was going to have to ride with someone.

Just not her.

Skaal stalked up to Alar then, pushing hard against his shoulder. He flashed the fae hound a wary look. "What is it?"

She made a growling noise in the back of her throat and lowered herself down next to him.

Surprise flickered over his face. "Really?"

Her tail swished.

"Get on her back, Half-blood," Cailean grunted.

Alar obeyed, climbing astride and grabbing hold of her thick ruff. An instant later, they were off, bounding through the trees.

Lara dug her heels into Bracken's flanks and followed.

They fled north, through the dense pinewood, weaving between tall, bristling pines. Branches thwacked her in the face, nearly unseating her. And all the while, the thunder of their pursuers drew closer. Angry shouts echoed through the woods now.

And when she emerged into a clearing, where a burn glittered in the moonlight, she found Mor and her Ravens waiting, as was Alar upon Skaal. Dorka crouched behind Mor, her hackles raised.

"Why have you stopped?" Lara pulled up between Cailean and Bree. The others were right behind her.

"They've got us surrounded," Sablebane replied.

No sooner had he spoken than the glow of torches flooded the clearing, chasing away the moonlight. Tattooed warriors astride stocky horses emerged. Firelight glinted dully off iron.

"Fuck," Cailean growled. An instant later, his own tattoos started to glow silver as he readied himself to fight.

"We're badly outnumbered," Roth grunted.

"Aye … but that doesn't mean we'll go down easily." Vyr's black eyes glinted as he raised his sword, while his elk tensed under him.

Lara's fingers flexed around the hilt of her dagger. By the Gods, everything was unraveling.

"No sign of Beathan," Alar observed.

Mor muttered something under her breath in reply.

An instant later, warriors attacked with a roar. Circines. There were no wulvers amongst them. The clang of iron meeting iron and steel splintered the air. Lara found herself hemmed in by the others as they fought back.

Sheathing her dagger, she knotted the reins. She then retrieved her cairn stone from its pouch, clenching it in her right hand as she extended her left, reaching for the flames. It was hard to catch hold of them though, for many of the Circines carrying torches tossed them to the ground so they could fight.

Lara struggled to find that peaceful place within that enabled her to wield fire safely.

Sweat beaded on her forehead as she reached again for the flames.

And this time, she connected with one of the torches. A tongue of fire roared upward, curling like a vine around the torso of a hill-tribe warrior. His screams knifed through the clearing as he toppled off his horse.

But he was just one amongst many.

A host of Circines had poured out of Dulross. They pressed in on all sides now, so close that Lara could see the whites of their eyes.

Eagal had wisely flown from Mor's shoulder. The Raven Queen's sword slashed silver, biting deep as her elk lowered its antlers and plowed into the Circines. No one could get near her. Not yet, anyway.

But even Mor would tire eventually. She'd dragged Dorka into the melee, yet the clag-doo held her ground, clawing at any Circines warrior foolish enough to stumble close.

Alar had leaped from Skaal's back and fought with his twin daggers. The fae hound remained at his side. A wet, ripping sound filled the glade as her teeth tore into flesh. Of course, the fairy dog's howl would have been enough to send the Circines fleeing in terror—and three howls in a row would stop their hearts. The problem, though, was that Skaal would kill *all* the Marav present, not just their attackers. Luckily for them, the Shee were immune.

Among Lara's own escort, only Cailean, Roth, and Bree were fierce fighters. Ren, Annis, and Ruari had been trained to wield weapons, but they were no match for the Circines. As such, they pressed close to Lara, doing their best to protect their High Queen as the enemy closed in. Eithne clung to Cailean as he fought, while Duana, still seated behind Roth, now wielded a dagger and slashed at their attackers.

And then, beyond the crush of Circines, Lara spied familiar flickering flames amongst the trees.

The corpse candles had returned.

After witnessing their fellow warrior set alight, those still wielding torches had tossed them aside as well. With the wall of bodies around her, Lara couldn't reach the flames now.

Yet, she did have a direct line of sight with the corpse candles.

Acting on instinct, she raised her left hand high and focused on the flickering lights. Yearning filled her. She flexed her fingers around the cairn stone, even as the *Ord-ree seal* started to gently pulse. Her breathing deepened, and then calmness descended.

Aye, that was better; she'd connected with them now. Whispers and soft laughter filled her head.

"Help us," she whispered, clenching her left hand and then extending her fingers. "Lure them away."

The flickering flames danced through the trees. They were skittish. Approaching and then halting, but she persisted. Beckoning them with gentle words. As they drew nearer, she made out the shapes inside the golden flames. They were faeries, winged with slender limbs and long flowing hair.

And all the while, around her, the fighting grew more frenzied. Mor and her Ravens had formed a ring with Alar, Cailean, Bree, and Roth, but the Circines had pushed them back. The clang of metal and the grunts of fighting echoed through the night.

One of the corpse candles sailed overhead. And then, to Lara's surprise, it landed on her shoulder, spinning and dancing there.

Next to Lara, Ruari breathed an oath.

And despite their dire situation, Lara was entranced. Wonder filled her.

How could she ever fear these lights? Right from the first moment they'd caught her attention on that night outside Doure, she'd longed to get closer to them, to dance with them in the woods. Their presence now filled her with quiet strength.

We're running out of time.

A soft chattering noise filled the woods as corpse candles crowded around the fringes of the clearing. As yet, the hill-tribe warriors hadn't seen them. They were too busy driving against the ring of Shee and Marav in the heart of the glade.

Lara clenched both fists then—her father's ring on her right hand pulsed now, in time with her heartbeat—before she slowly extended the fingers of her left hand. Over the past year, she'd learned to be gentle with fire. It didn't like to be forced to bend to her will. Instead, it preferred to be coaxed. It was a partnership.

Stillness settled deep in her chest as a second corpse candle landed lightly upon her other shoulder. It sat down, its tiny heart-shaped face turned up as it gazed at her.

Lara's breathing caught. Quite simply, it was beautiful. She couldn't believe it was responding to her like this, but she couldn't just admire the corpse candles. She needed their help.

"We will die in these woods," she whispered. "Unless you help us."

She paused then, while lights swirled and danced around the clearing in a ring. She waited, knowing how fickle the faerie and spirit world could be. No good ever came from ordering them about. They helped you if it suited them, and if she gave offense, these corpse candles would flee, leaving them to die upon Circines blades.

One of the Shee fell then. A slender male with flowing silver hair crumpled to his knees only to be beset upon by warriors. Iron daggers rose and fell, the wet sound of sharp blades puncturing flesh echoing through the glade.

Sablebane cut his way into their midst, but it was too late.

Sweat bathed Lara's skin. *Now. Please.*

The circling lights moved quicker now, and then a bright golden flare exploded from the fringes of the clearing.

"Close your eyes!" Lara gasped, hoping all her Marav companions had heard her.

This time, the Circines noticed that something had changed. Those farther back in the crowd, hemming them in, turned.

When they did, the corpse candles ensnared them.

They stood there a few moments, oblivious to the fighting that raged around them. And then, one by one, the men and women stumbled from the clearing, following the lights. Those left behind continued to slash and stab, not realizing they were being deserted.

When only a handful of Circines remained, Mor, her Ravens, and Alar fell upon them.

Lara watched the slaughter, unflinching, but her escort didn't. Instead, they surrounded her, all facing in, gazes lowered to avoid the lure of the lights.

Fighting alongside the Shee, Alar didn't appear to be affected by the corpse candles either. That surprised her. Did his fae blood protect him? She remembered then that he'd been in the woods that fateful eve a year earlier when the lights had lured her into that trap; the corpse candles hadn't bothered him then.

Eventually, the last of their attackers fell. Tattooed bodies sprawled to the ground, blood seeping into the mattress of pine needles and moss beneath them.

However, there was no time for celebration. Instead, breathing hard, faces gleaming with sweat, the party of Shee and Marav turned their mounts north once more and fled into the darkness.

14: A BLOOD DAWN

A ROSY DAWN filtered across the eastern sky, chasing away the shadows.

Watching it, Lara blinked. Where had the night gone?

Shit. It had happened again. She'd lost time. Her mind churned then, as she tried to recall their path north. However, she could remember nothing but their initial journey through the pines.

Dread settled on her chest then, a weighty sensation as if the margins of her world had suddenly shrunk. She'd never suffered from ill health before, apart from colds and fevers over the years. Never had she felt so … fragile. It frightened her.

Pulse fluttering in her throat, she leaned forward and stroked Bracken's sweaty neck. Although she couldn't remember the last while, the horse had taken care of her. Bracken had held fast during the Circines attack and then carried her north.

Glancing right then at where Bree rode next to her, Lara met her friend's eye. "Well, we all lived to see the dawn … that's something at least."

Bree flashed her a weary smile. "Thanks to you."

Cailean, who traveled to Lara's left, made a sound in the back of his throat. "Aye … but it was a close thing though. Too close." Behind him, Eithne's face was pale and strained. Lara wondered if the sisters now regretted fleeing from Dulross.

Lara's stomach tightened then. She understood why Alar had brought the women with him, yet Duana and Eithne shouldn't be here. They were in the wilds now, but if they passed a village en route, they'd need to leave the lasses there—for their own good.

The Goatfells towered above them, casting long shadows across the hill they now climbed. The pinewood and the Circines lay far behind, yet they didn't slow their pace. From this point on, any delay would cost them.

The Shee rode ahead of Lara and her escort, just as they had on the Slighe Fraoch. They'd fought side by side earlier, yet now a distance yawned between the two groups once more. The lack of trust between Shee and Marav wasn't something that could be easily overcome. They were still aloof with each other, still sizing each other up.

She glanced over her shoulder then, half-expecting to see horses boil over the top of the hill behind them, tattooed warriors bent low over their necks. Beathan mac Glen would be incensed when he discovered what had happened to his band.

Instead, all she saw beyond where the rest of her escort traveled was a lean figure, jogging alongside a huge wolf. Now that they were out of imminent danger, Alar no longer rode upon Skaal's back.

"I can't believe she offered to carry him," Bree said quietly. "Fae hounds don't suffer such things."

"No." Lara cast her gaze over Skaal. She moved in long lithe strides, her thick pelt stirring in the light breeze. "But she and Alar share a bond." She paused then, hesitating. She shouldn't be worried about sharing Alar's secrets, for he hadn't guarded hers—and yet, she did. "He bears a tattoo on his chest … infused with earth magic. It draws wolf-kind to him."

"That's forbidden." She looked at Cailean to find his woad-blue eyes burning with anger. "Only druids are permitted to bear such tattoos."

"It was a former sacrificer, I believe … who inked him," Lara replied, wishing she'd kept her mouth shut. There was enough tension within their group as it was without her making things worse.

The chief-enforcer's eyes narrowed. He then cut a glare at Alar. "That explains much," he growled.

Lara could almost taste his resentment. Cailean's bond with Skaal was a special one. Although now he knew why the fae hound was smitten with Alar.

Her attention traveled once more to her husband. Sweat gleamed on his cheekbones, and strands of dark hair stuck to his face. If he'd run since leaving the pinewood, he'd demonstrated considerable endurance. No doubt the earth magic helped with that, as did his Shee blood.

"The Shee are stopping," Bree announced then. Lara turned forward once more to see that, indeed, the knot of elks and stags had slowed at the crown of the hill, their proud silhouettes outlined against the dusky morning sky.

"A Blood Dawn bodes ill," Mor greeted Lara as she approached. Despite that she'd battled Circines before riding all night, the Raven Queen looked irritatingly fresh. Eagal had returned to her shoulder, and her curly black hair hung in glistening curls down her back. Her plush black fur cloak wasn't dirty or blood-splattered either. Likewise, her Ravens—one fewer now—didn't look sweaty and disheveled like Lara and her party did.

"Bad weather doesn't bother us," Cailean answered.

Mor cut him an irritated glance. "I wasn't talking about the weather." She paused then, her gaze lifting to the sky. "I was hoping we'd get a day or two of travel under our belts before the spirit world closed in … but I sense that won't be the case."

Misgiving fluttered through Lara, although she covered it up with a frown. "Well, we've survived our first trial."

Next to Mor, Sablebane gave a derisive snort. "Flesh and blood is much easier to fight than shadows."

Silence fell then, and Mor met Lara's eye. However, there was wariness in her gaze, almost as if she wasn't sure what to make of her. "You did well back there," she murmured. "I never thought to see the day when a Marav could command corpse candles."

"I didn't command them," Lara corrected her, even as her pulse skittered. Mor's comment reminded her of the dread that now sat like a brick upon her breastbone, of the fear that everything was about to unravel. "I *asked* them for help … and they gave it."

The sun warmed Alar's face as he walked at the rear of the party.

He was the only one on foot, and so he lagged behind. Not that any of them, Shee or Marav alike, waited for him to catch up, or offered for him to ride with them.

Alar didn't care. Mor and Lara thought they were putting him in his place by ignoring him, but he was happy enough here, journeying on foot as he'd done for years with the wulvers.

Something tugged deep in his chest then.

The wulvers.

He'd just walked out on them.

There hadn't been any of his brothers and sisters amongst the band that attacked them the night before. Nonetheless, Lyall and Dolph would be incensed. Wounded.

He'd disappointed them. Again.

Before he'd made that alliance with Lara, he'd had to push his brothers into striving for more. But once he had, Lyall and Dolph's attitudes had changed. Lyall especially had wanted Duncrag. He'd hoped Alar would turn on his wife shortly after their handfasting and stage a rebellion. He didn't know their commander had made Lara a promise.

It was a cruel irony. He'd betrayed her, stolen one of her most valuable forts, but it mattered to him that certain lines had never been crossed.

Lara. She couldn't bear to even look at him now, but he hungered for the barest glimpse of her. It was foolish—and dangerous. The truth was that her proximity unsettled him, as had their argument. The cut on his neck was starting to scab, but it was a reminder of the hate she bore him.

She'd asked him to join them out of necessity and believed he'd agreed for the same reason.

But he hadn't. He'd done it for her.

They traveled through a narrow glen now, sheer scree-covered sides of mountains, streaked in green, ochre, and grey, rearing up on either side. The Goatfells were magnificent, dwarfing the small band that traveled beneath it.

Alar's skin prickled as he lifted his gaze to them.

This mountain range reminded him of how insignificant they all were. Kingdoms would rise, shatter, and fall, and power would shift like sand on a beach. But these mountains would stand until the breaking of the world.

The reminder should have unsettled Alar, yet it didn't.

If anything, it unshackled him. He'd been so driven, for so long, caught up in things that could never last. He'd realized that these past moons in Dulross. He'd thought taking the borderlands for the wulvers would be the end, but it wasn't. It was merely the beginning of a new story.

One he wouldn't be part of.

He'd walked free, and although it pained him to cut ties with his wulver kin, he understood this was his path.

And yet, he wasn't himself today. Whenever he thought about the journey ahead, misgiving pitched in his gut.

Sounds like horse shit to me. Beathan's coarse voice taunted him then. The Circines chieftain had brutally dismissed Mor's tale about The Shattered Crown and what was needed to restore balance. Alar now worried that he'd swallowed the Raven Queen's explanation too readily.

Maybe Beathan was right. Maybe Lara distracted him.

Maybe he was walking into a trap.

They traveled all morning, while hunting goshawks dove overhead, their cries echoing through the vastness. Despite that the air held a bite, sweat dampened Alar's back and forehead. The band he'd joined traveled fast, urgency in every stride. It was a relief when they stopped at noon.

One of the Ravens approached him, a grim-faced male who shoved some bread and cheese into his hands. Alar took it with a nod, but the warrior had already turned and stalked off. Settling down onto a lichen-encrusted rock, he ate his meal in silence.

Meanwhile, Skaal, who'd remained with him all morning, wandered over to Cailean. The chief-enforcer murmured something to her, and she pushed against him, her plumelike tail swishing from side to side.

As he ate, Alar observed his companions. Not the Marav, but the Shee.

For years, he'd wondered about his father's people. His feelings toward them were complicated. They were part of him, and despite the persecution he'd suffered because of it over the years, he'd secretly been proud that powerful fae blood flowed in his veins. But he had a reason to loathe them too.

His gaze lingered on Wynn Sablebane.

The warrior stood apart from the others. He'd finished his light meal and was now looking north. Ashes, he was an ice-cold bastard. How had his mother fallen for him?

Memories of Struana mac Aedan fluttered up. Small and dark-haired with bright blue eyes. A dimple puckered her cheek whenever she smiled, although his mother hadn't smiled often. Indeed, with the years, her lovely face had grown stern, her gaze increasingly shadowed. She'd done her best to protect him, but he hadn't been able to protect her.

And neither had this Shee bastard.

He'd planted a seed in her womb and then disappeared, never to be seen again.

Hate now pounded in Alar's chest. Finishing his scant meal, he rose to his feet and made his way over to Sablebane.

Along the way, he skirted around the clag-doo Mor held on a chain. The predator crouched on the ground, a growl rumbling low in its throat as it eyed the Raven Queen. Long and sleek, the feline looked to be female.

Mor crouched just out of reach, eyes bright as she whispered what sounded like a gentling sain.

Incredulity wreathed up within Alar. When he'd met with Mor and Lara in that pinewood, he hadn't seen the beast chained up nearby; its black pelt made it blend in with the shadows. Clag-doos were dangerous, yet pity stirred within him to see it leashed and shackled. Just like fae hounds, they were wild creatures. He didn't know why Mor wished to gentle it, but they weren't meant to be pets.

Sablebane turned then, watching him approach. A few yards away, Fern also tracked Alar. He noted the way her hand strayed to the pommel of her sword. She was readying herself for trouble.

Meanwhile, their father's mouth puckered. His iron-grey eyes with their goatlike pupils narrowed.

His reaction made something ugly flare inside Alar. "I bet you regret that tumble," he greeted him. He hadn't intended to open with something so aggressive, yet he couldn't help it. He was aware then of gazes upon him. Mor and her Ravens were observing him, as were Lara and her party. All of them had been waiting for this moment, wondering how it would play out. Did they want him to put on a show for them?

A heartbeat passed, and then Sablebane's lip curled.

Alar's blood started to roar in his ears. How he wanted to reach for his blades and deal to this whoreson. If he dared insult his mother, he would, and fuck the consequences.

"You're here because of it, aren't you?" Sablebane's voice was low and eerily like Alar's own.

Alar's hands flexed at his sides. "Is that all you have to say?"

"What do you want to hear?"

"The truth."

Their gazes locked for a long moment before the Shee warrior's expression hardened. "No, you don't."

"Tell me."

Something glinted in those iron eyes. "The truth is I made a mistake," he replied softly. "And *you* were the consequence."

15: A FOUL WIND

AS THE SHADOWS grew long, a strange wind kicked up.

Lara tried to place it, but it wasn't any of the Four Winds she recognized. It wasn't shrill like The Whistle, or aggressive like The Sweeper. Nor did it peck at them like The Sharp Billed Wind or blister the land like The Gales of Complaint.

No, this warm, dry wind gusted in from the west, feathering across Lara's skin as if she were pushing through old cobwebs. Usually, the winds brought the smell of the mountains or sea with them, yet this one had an unsettling odor. Musk and mildew. Uneasiness tightened deep in Lara's chest as she raised her gaze to the sky, cloudless and pale pink.

But when voices reached her, tangling and overlapping as if each strove to talk over the last, her pulse lurched into a canter.

She cut her gaze right to where Bree rode. Her friend frowned as she looked up at the sky.

"It's The Gaulas, isn't it?" Lara asked.

Bree's lips compressed. "Aye."

"It sometimes blows in the far north," Cailean added then, "especially around Gateway."

"But we aren't yet *in* the far north," Lara reminded him.

She'd grown up listening to chilling tales of The Gaulas. It sprang from The Threshold and carried the voices of those banished there. The damned souls of the Slew—traitors, kin slayers, oath breakers—didn't merely whisper. They infected. Their words burrowed under your skin like splinters.

The first gust hit her in the center of the chest, and then the voices began.

This mission is doomed. None of you are prepared for what waits for you at The Shattered Crown … not even Mor.

Her lungs seized. The air turned thick. It wasn't like on the Slighe Fraoch. The Gaulas didn't risk crippling her. Instead, it undermined her confidence. It made her doubt her choices. It knew exactly how to strike the soft places where doubt already lived.

You can't trust any of them. Not Mor. And certainly not that traitorous bastard you married.

Sooner or later, they'll both turn on you.

You'll fail your people.

Albia will slip into darkness, and history will blame you.

Lara's belly started to ache. *The Gods spare me.* With spirits like these on the wind, who needed enemies? The Gaulas was exhausting. Relentless.

The wind shrieked past her ears, but beneath it—woven through it—she could feel *them*. Not voices exactly, but presences. Thousands of them, pressing close, their hatred and despair lashing her.

Lara started to sweat. It didn't help that she was exhausted. All of them were after a sleepless night. However, in the wake of wielding her fire magic to gain the assistance of the corpse candles, her limbs were leaden and weak.

And underneath it all, a dull dread gnawed at her.

What if something was terribly wrong with her?

What if she failed those she'd sworn to protect?

Her gaze slid ahead to where Mor rode upon her elk. Dorka was giving her trouble this afternoon. She twisted against her chain, snarling and spitting. Mor's long curly black hair flew around her as she fought to control the clag-doo. Her face was set in grim, tight lines.

Aye, The Gaulas had dug its hooks into her too.

"I shall sing something to take the edge off once we make camp." Lara dragged her attention from Mor to see Ren urge her sturdy garron alongside Bracken. The bard's eyes were hollowed.

Lara nodded, relieved. Ren's songs had helped against the likes of the Weeper. Hopefully, she'd provide a barrier against this foul wind too. "Aye … do that."

Sinking down before the crackling hearth, Lara heaved a deep sigh. "Thank The Mother."

They'd traveled for as long as they dared before stopping for the day on the eastern side of a steep hill that provided some shelter from the wind. It wasn't yet dusk, but since everyone was tired and hungry, they'd ended their day early. Two of the Shee had gone hunting, and as Roth dragged branches of dusty whin onto the fire, they returned with five large hares and two fat red grouse.

They'd eaten all the food they'd brought with them, and resupplying at Dulross had turned out to be impossible. From this point onward, unless they stopped at a village, they'd be hunting and foraging for each meal. Thirst wasn't an issue though. They filled their waterskins from burns on the way; the Shee knew which ones were safe to drink from, as did Cailean, Bree, and Alar, who'd all traveled The Uplands extensively.

Looking on as the Shee gutted and skinned the hares and plucked the grouse, their long slender fingers moving with deft precision, Lara reflected on just how vulnerable she was out here in the wilds. Aye, she'd shown her mettle over the past years, but the truth was that she'd never had to hunt for her own food. She'd never gutted a hare, let alone spit-roasted one. She'd grown up in an environment where others rushed to do her bidding.

They'll all abandon you. The Gaulas's cruel refrain was back. *They'll leave you to fend for yourself. Turn back now!*

Lara clenched her jaw, forcing the words away. She reminded herself then that she wasn't helpless. She'd learned how to wield a dagger and defend herself, hadn't she? She'd learn survival skills too. And no matter what happened on the road ahead, she'd hold fast. Even so, the spirit wind's cruelty got to her. She felt bruised this evening. Tender.

Digging into a pouch she carried at her waist, she pulled out one of the rosewood figurines her brother had carved for her. The Hag. A bent crone, leaning upon a stick. Her thumb smoothed the artfully carved lines as she murmured a prayer to the Goddess of the Dark. The Hag presided over sleep, dreams, death, winter, and the earth. They were entering her time of year, and Lara needed her grace.

The rich smells of gamey meat drifted over their camp, making Lara's empty belly rumble.

"Settle, my lovely." Mor's voice drew Lara's attention then. "I mean you no harm."

She had to hand it to the Shee queen. Mor was diligent. Every evening, she attempted to gentle Dorka. Longing gleamed in her eyes now as she whispered to the feline. But she wouldn't be tamed.

Ears back, hackles raised, Dorka hissed viciously. And then, as Mor edged closer, the clag-doo swiped at her. She was pushing things. Her voice was more strident than usual, even as The Gaulas continued to wrap itself around them.

Heaviness pressed down upon them—a thousand frantic voices crying in the wind.

The sky had gone the color of deep rose now. It was no longer as cold as it had been before this eerie wind began, although Lara found herself wishing for the bite of The Sharp Billed Wind or the bracing slap of The Sweeper.

Dorka yowled, lashing out once more. A ripping sound followed as its claws caught Mor's sleeve. She reeled back, and with an outraged caw, Eagal took wing. Mor's song cut off before she snarled something in her own tongue—Lara didn't need any translation to understand she'd just cursed.

"You're wasting your time. Clag-doos won't respond to Shee songs." Alar appeared by the fireside. Like everyone else, his face bore lines of fatigue this evening. His shoulders bowed slightly under the weight of The Gaulas. He'd been out collecting wood and just dumped an armful on the pile already gathered. They were traveling through largely open country now, although whin, broom, and other shrubby bushes were still plentiful.

Mor cast him a glare. However, embarrassment edged her irritation. "Know better, do you?"

His lips quirked into a wry smile. "I've spent most of my life sleeping rough in the forests of the North," he replied. "The wulvers have had a few brushes with clag-doo over the years. They have ways of dealing with them."

Mor sighed, her chin dipping. Steeling herself against The Gaulas while trying to tame Dorka was taking its toll. She then glanced over at where the clag-doo now strained at her chain, teeth bared. "Go on."

"The clag-doo once resided in Sheehallion but were cast out. They no longer respond to Shee magic. If anything, your song is incensing her further."

Mor's features tightened, and she cast Dorka an almost apologetic look. "What do they respond to then?"

"I've never been foolish enough to try and tame one … but if I were, I'd try earth magic."

Mor's face screwed up. "*Earth* magic?"

"Aye … it's rawer. Primal. You'd likely have more luck."

Silence fell as The Gaulas continued to batter them, the fire crackled and guttered, and the skin of the roasting hares and grouse blistered.

Mor then turned, her gaze spearing the young woman clad in flowing blue robes who knelt by the fire. "Maybe a bard's song will help."

Ren frowned. "It might … but I'm busy." Indeed, the bard was readying herself for an exhausting long night. Once supper was over, she'd hold vigil over their camp.

"Not right now, you aren't." Mor beckoned to Ren. "Come here."

It wasn't a request but a command. The bard scowled. Lara didn't blame her. Ren wasn't a dog to be ordered around. The Gaulas rose to a howl then, as if tasting the tension around the fireside. Mor's Ravens had all stilled, anticipating trouble, as had Cailean, Bree, and Roth.

"You're used to others doing your bidding, but Ren doesn't answer to you," Lara said finally. Shades, she didn't have the patience for this. Not tonight. The chatter of the spirit wind made her head ache, and she was so tired, her skull felt as if it were stuffed with wool.

A muscle flexed in Mor's jaw. Lara was aware then that Alar was watching her, his gaze penetrating. She ignored him.

Moments passed before Mor huffed an irritated sigh. Her gaze then sought Ren's once more. "The Gaulas will plague us for a while yet, I fear," she said eventually. "You can't shield us from it every night. You're just one woman. It'll break you in the end. Let me deal with the wind tonight, and in return, you help me tame Dorka."

Ren frowned. "How will you *deal* with The Gaulas?"

Mor's lips tugged up at the corners, and she cast her cousin a knowing look. Vyr grimaced. "The ruling bloodline of my people is gifted in magical song too. But our power is different from yours. It's why I'll be able to weave moonlight when we reach The Shattered Crown. Together, Vyrnek and I can take turns in coaxing starlight into a net of sorts, one that will keep the worst of the wind at bay."

Ren didn't look convinced. However, the dark smudges under her eyes revealed just how tired she was. She'd held vigil often over the past nights and would be desperate for a night of unbroken sleep. Rising to her feet, she dusted off her robes. "All right then," she muttered. "I have no idea if I can help … but I will try."

Mor inclined her head in thanks and stepped aside to allow the bard to approach the clag-doo.

Dorka crouched on all fours now. Her golden eyes fixed upon Ren. Unblinking. Hungry. Earlier, one of the Ravens had thrown her a hare carcass, but ever since Mor had taken her captive, she hadn't been able to hunt.

Ren studied Dorka for a while. The wind tugged at her robes and pulled tendrils of red-gold hair free of the tight braid she wore. Extending both hands, she then closed her eyes, and as everyone looked on, the tattoos on her exposed forearms and neck started to glow.

Mor's nostrils flared, and she moved back farther.

The scent of pine and ash swirled through the air.

And then, Ren started to sing. It was a soft, haunting melody—one that Lara had never heard before. It made her breathing quicken and caused something to twist deep in her chest. Without meaning to, she glanced over at Alar. He too was watching Ren, a groove etched between his dark eyebrows. But, somehow, he marked her gaze, and his attention flicked back to Lara.

They stared at each other for a heartbeat, as Ren's song swelled.

An ache rose under Lara's breastbone. Longing.

Heart pounding now, she tore her gaze away. *Gods.* It was the song. It was worse than The Gaulas, for it was tearing down her defenses. Confusing her. Weakening her.

Meanwhile, Dorka continued to watch Ren. Her tail had been beating against the ground, yet it stilled now—and as the song continued, the hackles on her neck, shoulders, and spine smoothed.

Eventually, Ren's voice died away, and when it did, another sound vibrated through the air.

A deep, rumbling purr.

It was coming from the clag-doo.

To Lara's shock, Ren then moved toward Dorka before reaching out a hand and stroking her sleek forehead. She bowed her head and pushed against Ren's hand, her purr loudening.

Mor whispered something before stepping up next to the bard. "What manner of song was that?"

"An old one," Ren murmured, her voice soft now. "A lullaby of sorts my mother used to sing to me when I was afraid of the dark … when no amount of reassurance would quieten my fears. It's a surrendering sain." The bard glanced Mor's way then. "Dorka was afraid. She has now lowered her guard."

16: SHAME

LARA WALKED THROUGH the woods. Weaving in and out of the trees, she was alone, barefoot, and wearing nothing but a thin linen tunic that brushed her ankles as she moved. Cold air kissed her naked arms, causing goosebumps to rise, and she quickened her step.

She wasn't sure where she was going, and yet urgency beat in her breast.

The ground was damp underfoot, wet leaves sticking to her feet. Rustling in the undergrowth warned her that others were watching, but strangely, she wasn't afraid.

Lights flickered in the distance, and her breathing caught.

Corpse candles.

Lara hurried on. She didn't fear them now. These flickering flames were her allies.

The lights led her deep into the woods, darting out of reach every time she neared them. And when she finally caught them up, the corpse candles hovered in a ring around a large dark tree.

The ancient yew stood like a sentinel in the heart of the misted wood, its massive trunk twisted and gnarled. The bark was a patchwork of deep russet and silver-grey, peeling away in long strips. Its base spread wide, buttressed roots disappearing into the soft loam where fungi grew in ghostly pale clusters.

Above, the canopy formed a living vault. And upon one of the ancient limbs, Lara spied the shapes of perching birds.

Crows, large and black with glossy feathers and sharp eyes.

Seven of them—all watching her.

She froze, her pulse now thudding in her ears. And as the moments slid by, the smell of burning caught the back of her throat.

Smoke, drifting like mist through the air, started to curl around the heavy trunk. Crackling split the deep silence of the woodland. Flames erupted then, devouring the yew tree. The crows started to shriek, and she stumbled back, shielding her face.

Lara's eyes snapped open.

Breathing hard, her heart pounding, she stared up at the night sky. Patches of drifting clouds and a waxing moon. Swathes of twinkling stars. She wasn't in a woodland. She was on a hillside, lying beside a smoldering fire pit. The outlines of her companions, Shee and Marav alike, surrounded her. Gentle snores rumbled through the air. The Gaulas's cruel chatter was muffled now, as a male voice, soft and sure, carried through the night.

Vyr was taking his turn.

Lara sat up, clutching her thick fur-lined cloak about her.

Not that dream again.

Over the years, it was always the same one. Others blessed with seer abilities received visions that varied. But with her, it was always the same.

Seven crows in a Gods-damned yew tree.

Someone near to me guards a dangerous secret.

She dragged a hand down her face. *Shit. Shit. Shit.* More betrayal. Just what she needed.

Her dream years earlier had warned of Bree's treachery, and then a year before, of Alar's. Both those individuals were with her now, yet she didn't doubt Bree these days.

Alar had double-crossed her once. He'd do so again without hesitation.

Teeth clenched, she rolled to her feet. Her gaze then searched those slumbering by the fireside. As always, the Shee and the Marav slept apart from each other on opposite sides. Mor slept at the heart of the group, surrounded by her bodyguards.

Alar wasn't sleeping near the Shee though.

Lara's gaze skirted her side of the fire.

He wasn't there either.

Duana and Eithne were curled up together like kittens, while Roth slept next to them; a protective gesture that was endearing. Stepping carefully around where Cailean and Bree slept, wrapped together in the chief-enforcer's cloak, Lara slipped away from the fire.

"Alar."

A woman's voice made Alar turn swiftly, his hand rising instinctively for one of his daggers.

However, it stilled when his gaze settled upon a small figure wrapped in a jade-green fur-lined cloak.

"Lara," he murmured, dropping his hand. "Why aren't you sleeping?"

In truth, he was surprised to see her. Ever since their 'conversation' back in that pinewood, which had ended with her knife at his throat, she'd barely spoken to him.

But here she was.

One look at her, and he could see she was exhausted. Her heart-shaped face was pale and strained, her eyes hollowed. She'd lost weight over the past year, and despite her iron will, there was a fragility about her that hadn't been there earlier.

His chest tightened.

He was the reason, the cause of her suffering.

He frowned. "Something wrong?"

She lifted her chin, her green eyes narrowing. "I had that dream again" —her voice was sharp with accusation— "the one about the seven crows in a yew tree."

Alar went still. He knew where this was going. Meanwhile, Vyr's haunting song rose and fell, muffling the cry of The Gaulas. Mor's cousin was holding vigil on the western edge of their small camp, while Alar took his turn at watch on the eastern perimeter. "You think I'm keeping secrets again?"

"Aye … you lied to me once, twice should be even easier."

Alar's heart kicked. She was wrong there.

"I never lied, Lara," he said after a pause. Like her, he spoke quietly. They were far enough from the fire pit not to be overheard, and Vyr's singing and the whispering wind masked their voices. Nonetheless, this wasn't an argument either of them wanted overheard. "I just didn't tell you what I was planning. There's a difference."

"Treachery is treachery." She moved toward him then, halting when they stood around a yard apart. "What are you hiding from me this time?"

The rage glinting in her eyes made a warning ripple through him. Torches burned brightly around them. All Lara had to do was summon those dancing flames, and she could incinerate him. He should tread carefully, and yet when it came to Lara, he was foolishly reckless.

"Nothing. I came alone … without my wulvers. Without allies. There's no trick. No plan."

Her lips pursed. "I don't believe you."

Alar raked a hand through his hair, even as something twisted under his breastbone. "Asking you to trust me is too much," he said roughly. "I know that. I burned that bridge behind me. But I need you to believe me. The person hiding a dangerous secret from you isn't me this time."

She folded her arms across her chest, a nerve flickering in her cheek.

"I swear … upon my mother's memory … that I'm not plotting against you."

Her lip curled. "You'd even drag your *mother* into this?"

Heat flared in his gut. *Enough.* "My mother's memory is precious to me," he growled. "If I make an oath in her name, I mean it."

She snorted.

"I mean it," he replied, his voice lowering once more. "Because I *killed* her."

Lara jolted as if he'd just slapped her.

His pulse quickened. This wasn't a story he wanted to tell. To do so would slice him open. It would reveal the core of who he was, and what had driven him all these years. His hunger for justice. His restlessness. The uneasiness that gave him no peace. The fact that wherever he went and whatever he did, nothing truly satisfied him. All of it was down to this.

Lara remained silent. She was waiting for him to explain himself.

He hesitated. They'd all taken a battering from The Gaulas today, him included. They had a temporary reprieve at present, and it made him want to shore up his defenses, not spill his guts. But he had to.

"When I was around ten, I started following my mother when she left our cottage," he began, each word halting. "She'd become distant … secretive … and took to disappearing at odd times. I tracked her to a glade deep in the woods, a sheltered spot surrounded by dark-green sycamores. I then watched as she circled the clearing, whispering charms and prayers. She even sprinkled rose petals. She called *his* name as she walked … *where are you, Wynn Sablebane … come to me, Wynn. My brave Shee warrior. My love* … but he never appeared." His throat grew tight then. "Finally, she sank to her knees and began to weep."

Lara's brow furrowed.

"He abandoned her, but she still pined for him." He looked away then, unable to hold her eye now. "I was angry. Jealous. My mother wept over a *Shee* … a lover who'd used her and then abandoned her … while she only gave half of herself to me. In the evenings, she'd stare into the flames of our cookfire, barely listening as I prattled on. She was still sweet, still tucked me up in the furs each night, kissed me on the brow, and told me she loved me." His gut clenched. "But it wasn't enough. I wanted all her love and affection. I didn't want to share."

He halted then, sucking in a deep breath. "So, I came up with a plan. I thought that if she stopped going to that clearing, she'd forget about him … that she'd focus on me again."

Lara made a sound in the back of her throat, and he met her eye once more. "A group of lads from the village liked to go hunting for frogs in a nearby burn. Sometimes, when they allowed it, I joined them. One day, I told them that my mother often went to the glade where she'd once met my father … a *Shee*, obviously … hoping to see him again." He halted then, his throat aching now. "I knew they'd tell their parents. My plan was that they'd shame her into letting go of my father's memory. It didn't work out that way." His pulse started to thunder in his ears. "Instead, a group of women—the mothers of the lads I'd told—followed her into the woods two days later … and when she reached the clearing, they stoned her to death."

He stopped talking then.

Bile stung the back of his throat. *Ashes.* That had been even harder than he'd thought.

Lara still didn't speak. He didn't blame her.

"So, there you have it," he said finally, aware that cold sweat now trickled down his back. "I betrayed the person I loved most. And nothing has ever mattered so much since."

Lara swallowed, her lips parting as if she might answer. However, he spoke first. "There are few things I hold sacred in this world, Lara. But my mother's memory is one of them." His gaze ensnared hers then. "So, heed me when I swear by it."

Silence swelled behind them as Vyr's voice rose and fell.

Eventually, Lara cleared her throat. "All right … so if you're telling the truth, someone else is hiding something from me."

He moved closer to her, even as his pulse still raced. After cutting himself open like that, he wanted to reach for her, to find comfort in her embrace. But since she'd likely whip out her dagger and stab him if he touched her, he restrained himself. "This dream ... where does it take place?"

She swallowed. "In the middle of dark woods. I'm walking through it ... and there's an ancient yew tree with seven crows perched upon its branches. There's—" She halted then, her eyes snapping wide.

He stiffened. "What?"

She breathed a curse. "This dream was different from the others. I can't believe I forgot that."

"How?"

"The tree caught fire."

Alar frowned. "The prophecy isn't the same then."

"It isn't?"

He shook his head. "I suggest you have a word with Ruari tomorrow. Fire cleanses and transforms ... but it also destroys. This time, your dream is sending you a *different* warning."

17: A BREAK IN HOSTILITIES

LARA EYED THE man who stood before her.

That had been quite a story earlier. There had been moments throughout when she'd doubted him. But then his words at the end had moved her.

I betrayed the person I loved most. And nothing has ever mattered so much since.

His single-minded hunger for justice. His blinkered loyalty to the wulvers. The layers of secrecy that surrounded him. His walled-off heart. Suddenly, all the missing pieces clicked together.

Aye, she was a soft-hearted fool, yet she believed him.

And now they stood awkwardly together, neither knowing what to say. In the flickering torchlight, Alar was paler than usual, his twin scars starkly silver against his skin.

"I will speak to Ruari," she assured him, stepping back then.

She felt oddly deflated. When she'd awoken, heart pounding, all she'd been able to think about was the seven crows sitting in the yew tree. The fact that it had started smoking before catching fire had gone straight over her head. Alar was right. This change might mean something significant.

"We must work together over the coming days, Lara," Alar said then, his voice husky. "And it'll be easier for us both if you put your knives away."

She harrumphed.

"Can we be allies again?"

Her pulse accelerated. She wasn't sure about this.

His lips quirked. "Or at least until our task is done."

"Maybe," she said, eyeing him.

"I'll take that." To her consternation, he moved forward and held out his hand. "Let us shake on it."

Lara's pulse fluttered. She didn't want to touch him.

She considered shaking her head and taking another step back, but something about his expression stopped her.

There was no guile in his eyes.

Steeling herself, she reached out and clasped his hand.

The shock of their skin meeting dragged her right back to the past. The familiar strength and warmth of his grip. His scent enveloped her then: leather, oak, with a faint note of mint. She resisted dragging it into her lungs.

For an instant, their gazes met and held. Alar then gave her hand a gentle squeeze. "Allies," he whispered.

Lara swallowed hard before she gave a jerky nod, ripped her hand from his, and turned on her heel. Face flaming, she strode away.

The Reaper strike her down, she was an idiot for approaching him. Alar had disarmed her with his sincerity and vulnerability, yet she couldn't help but feel manipulated. Ducking around where Bracken dozed, head hung low, weight resting on one hind leg, she headed back toward the fire.

But as she walked behind the tethered horses, her gaze alighted on a tall cloaked figure standing on the northern edge of their camp. Her pulse skittered. She hadn't realized someone else was taking their turn at the watch. They hadn't been there earlier.

As she walked by, the individual turned. Torchlight gilded a pale face with chiseled features. A sharp gaze glanced off her. Wynn Sablebane.

His expression was impassive, yet her cheeks burned even hotter. The things she and Alar had just said to each other were private. They'd kept their voices low, yet there had been moments when they'd both forgotten themselves.

Had Sablebane heard Alar's story too?

Alar surveyed the magnificent red stag. It stood with regal stillness. The first glimmers of dawn highlighted a coat of deep russet red dappled with patches of burnished gold and cream—a masterwork of autumn hues. His massive antlers crowned him, twelve points of polished bone spreading wide enough to frame his noble head.

Tearing his gaze from the stag, Alar glanced over at where the Raven Queen looked on from astride her white elk. Dorka sat next to her, oddly placid this morning. "You're giving him to me?"

"For the time being," Mor answered.

"He wasn't with you yesterday … where did he come from?"

"I hailed him."

"We thought you might like to ride a stag," Vyr added. "You are half Shee, after all."

Surprised, Alar shifted his attention to Mor's cousin. Unlike Sablebane and Fern, who both watched him with shuttered expressions from atop their own stags, Vyr was smiling. His face was slightly drawn this morning though—no doubt since he'd ended up warding the perimeter for most of the night. Mor had risen from the fire pit near dawn and taken her turn, yet her cousin had done most of the work.

Alar tensed, searching the male's face for mockery or scorn. He found none. Vyr was in earnest, it seemed. His sincerity made Alar wary.

"Go on, mount," Vyr urged, leaping up onto his elk's back.

Alar hesitated. The stag was eyeing him with its head lowered, as if considering whether to charge him. These beasts likely only permitted Shee to ride them. Was this a test he was about to fail? He was also aware that the rest of their company— Lara and her escort—had already mounted and were watching him. Was he about to be humiliated?

"There's no saddle or bridle," he replied.

"You won't need them," Vyr assured him.

"You do realize I can't touch minds with animals?"

"You won't need to," Mor said, amusement flickering across her face. Upon her shoulder, Eagal gave a short, barking caw.

"Reedav will follow the rest of us … and if you speak to him, he will understand."

"Aye … although he may not choose to obey," Fern quipped, her tone cutting.

Alar glanced back at the waiting beast. *Stag king*—the name was a noble one. His dark liquid eyes, full of sharp intelligence, held a challenge.

Bracing himself, he moved forward and swung up onto the stag's back—not easy, for Reedav stood taller than most horses. However, Alar was nimble.

The stag didn't move, and as Alar settled himself onto the beast's back, the warmth of its body burned like a furnace through his leather breeches and into his skin. Wonder filtered up, and his breathing grew shallow. It was an honor to travel upon such an animal.

Alar looked around then, his gaze sliding over the surrounding Shee to where Lara and her escort waited. Eithne and Duana observed him with frank fascination, while curiosity gleamed in the gazes of the others, Lara included. Bree even looked a little envious. Of course. He'd heard that she'd once ridden a white stag, one that had run as swiftly as the Four Winds. He wondered if Reedav was just as fast.

He glanced back at Mor then, to find her watching him intently. "Thank you," he said softly, oddly humbled.

They set off, and like the day before, the Shee quickly outpaced the Marav on their faster steeds. They rode deep into The Goatfells this morning. The huge peaks loomed overhead, blocking out a pale-pink sky. Unfortunately, The Gaulas whirled around them. The air was oddly mild, yet it smelled musky.

Rank. The protective net Vyr and Mor had woven overnight had fallen away, and the wind found them immediately.

The first assault came swift and precise, a blade between his ribs.

They only gave you the stag out of pity.

The gift—something that had pleased him—now curdled in Alar's gut. How easy to please he was. All the Shee had to do was throw the mongrel a bone and watch how he wagged his tail.

He locked his jaw tight enough to ache then, resisting the heckling.

Lara will use the things you told her against you. The voices slammed into him again. *She will exploit your weaknesses.*

His stomach twisted. The hollowed-out feeling that had settled in his chest after their talk deepened, spreading through his ribs. The truce they'd forged felt gossamer-thin now. He could sense its fragility. One wrong word, one misstep, and it would tear. Part of him had dared to hope—fool that he was—that honesty might build something between them. But the wind stripped that delusion away.

The truth was that Lara tolerated his presence out of necessity, nothing more. The moment their task was complete, the moment she no longer needed him—

The certainty hit him like a physical blow: he was a dead man. She'd see him on his knees, and her hand wouldn't tremble when she struck.

And beneath it all, woven through every other sensation, came the wind's gleeful agreement. *Aye! On your knees. Begging. Bleeding. She will have her revenge.*

Alar's gut clenched so hard he nearly doubled over. The stag beneath him seemed to sense his distress, its gait faltering slightly.

Ashes. He'd rather face a horde of iron-wielding Circines than this vicious wind.

He focused on Reedav then, in an attempt to distract himself. The stag's stride was different from a horse's, longer and more fluid. Powerful muscles moved beneath him. Surprisingly, it was easier than he'd thought to keep his seat. Reaching forward, Alar ran his hand down Reedav's sleek neck. Envy stabbed at him then. How lucky the Shee were that they could touch minds with animals, and that creatures such as these willingly served them.

All his life, he'd denied the Shee part of himself.

As a bairn, he'd noted that animals were drawn to him. It was different from Skaal's devotion to him—for the wolf in his blood called to her. Nonetheless, even skittish sheep approached him, his mother's cat curled up with him every night in the furs, and stray dogs followed him when he ventured out to explore the surrounding woods

But his closeness with animal kind had embarrassed him. It made him different from the other lads. He'd turned his back on them, shunning contact so others wouldn't notice. He needn't have bothered though, for the locals had turned on him anyway. And along the way, he'd lost something precious.

It was one of the many things he now regretted.

Lara watched Ruari intently, wishing she could read thoughts.

She'd told the seer about her dream, and the changes to it, but he hadn't yet answered her. Instead, he appeared deep in thought. Not long after they'd begun the day's journey, she'd left Bree's side and reined Bracken alongside Ruari. All the while, The Gaulas heckled her, yet she did her best to ignore it. They were lucky that it wasn't as oppressive as the Heather Path, or none of them would have lasted this far.

"Well?" she pressed, finally losing patience.

Ruari pulled a face. "Fire in dreams can signify many things … but in your case, My Queen, it's … complicated."

Her breathing grew shallow. "Aye?"

"Well, apart from the fact you're a fire-wielder, fire in dreams represents intense emotions … like rage … but also desire and love. Usually, it signifies that these feelings have been repressed."

Heat washed over Lara. Unfortunately, unlike the night before, she couldn't hide her embarrassment under the cloak of darkness. She cleared her throat. "Anything else?"

"Fire turns a vision inward. In the past, your dreams indicated that someone close to you held a dangerous secret." Ruari met her gaze squarely then. "But this time … *you're* the one with the secret."

Lara stilled. She was aware then that around her, the others of her party were all listening in on their conversation.

"I'm not," she assured them, her voice catching. The Shee and Alar were riding around a furlong ahead. Fortunately, they wouldn't overhear them, especially with the voices on the wind.

"Are you worried about something, My Queen?" Annis asked gently.

Lara cast the counselor a rueful look. "Besides our current situation?"

Annis held her gaze, steady and unflinching. "Perhaps you're embarrassed to share your concerns."

Lara shook her head, even as her belly clenched.

"Ruari could be right … you might be repressing it."

Irritation spiked through Lara's chest like a hot needle. But beneath it—worse than it—panic unfurled its wings. She *was* hiding something. From them. From herself. The heat that had pooled low in her belly when she'd shaken Alar's hand. The way her pulse had quickened despite her anger. Her body's traitorous response to a man who'd destroyed everything. She could feel it now—that shameful wanting coiled in her gut like a serpent. Still hungry. Still aching. After everything he'd done.

Her fingernails dug crescents into her palms. What kind of woman burned for the man who'd betrayed her? What kind of fool let desire override reason, let her body sabotage every vow of vengeance she'd made?

Lara squeezed her eyes shut, as if darkness could keep the knowledge from taking root. But it was too late.

Curse Alar. And curse her too for seeking him out. She'd avoided him ever since, though she'd been unable to stop herself from watching when Mor gifted him that magnificent stag. The confusion on his face first. The wariness. Then—the Gods help her—the wonder that had rippled across his features. Something in her chest had warmed at the sight, an ember she'd thought long dead suddenly glowing.

He'd spent his life as an outcast, accepted by neither Shee nor Marav. The Raven Queen had made a generous gesture, one that would mean everything to a man who'd never belonged anywhere.

But the wind twisted even that moment of sympathy into something darker. *Too generous.* The warmth in her chest turned to ice. The certainty crept up her spine like frost: Mor had plans for him. Plans that might unite them against her. She could see it now—how easily the Shee might turn on her once she'd served her purpose. How Alar might choose his people over her. Again.

Her breath came shorter, shallower. The boundaries between The Gaulas's poison and her own thoughts blurred.

"Lara?" Bree's voice cut through the spiral, and she opened her eyes to find her warder had reined in her cob alongside. Concern etched lines around Bree's eyes. "Are you all right?"

"Not really," she ground out, the words scraping her throat raw. Her jaw ached from clenching. "Those voices never let up, do they?"

Bree's gaze shadowed. "No … but you just withdrew from us again."

"Aye, and you sometimes stop talking in the midst of sentences," Cailean added gruffly. As always, Eithne perched behind him, and she watched the High Queen with wide, curious eyes.

A sickly sensation washed over Lara. Of course, her complicated feelings for Alar weren't her only secret. There was another, one that soured her belly and made her pulse falter. Her fear that she was in the grip of a strange illness.

"Do I?"

Her gaze swept around her companions. One by one, they nodded.

"At least four times since we departed from the Golval Woods," Roth confirmed, brow furrowed. Duana still rode with him. Like her sister, she watched Lara, although with a sharp, speculative gaze.

Lara's heart started to pound in her ears. There wasn't any point in denying this. It was time to tell them the rest. "I've also been losing time." Confusion flickered over their faces, and so she elaborated. "Half a day will go by, but I have no recollection of it."

Her gut churned once more, especially when alarm flared in their gazes.

"When did this start?" Annis asked, her tone gentle, like a healer dealing with a skittish patient—one who was in denial about a grave sickness. No one liked to admit The Reaper was standing over them.

"It's happened occasionally over the past turn of the moon … although more frequently since we began our journey north."

"That's worrying, indeed," Ruari murmured.

"It's not a secret though, is it?" Roth pointed out, frowning.

"Perhaps not." Lara looked away, dread dragging at her lungs. "But it indicates there's something seriously amiss with me, doesn't it?"

18: THE WRITHING SKY

FINISHING HER LAST mouthful of roast grouse, Lara threw the bone into the fire. The hungry flames devoured it within moments. Her appetite had been poor of late, yet now that food was scarce, it had returned with a vengeance. She could have eaten twice what she had.

The Gaulas whispered and eddied around them. Later, Ren would take her turn at warding their camp, but for now, they'd clustered close around the hearth tonight, for although The Gaulas wasn't cold, its horrid lament had gotten to them all. Around the fire, everyone's faces were strained.

She was vaguely aware then that the others were talking. Catching herself, Lara blinked. There it was again. She'd just drifted away. Her pulse fluttered, and she clenched her hands into fists, digging her nails into her palms. *Focus!*

"We'll travel the mountain path tomorrow," Alar announced then, taking a deep draft from a waterskin. "The Hog's Back is the fastest route to Darkmere. The rough terrain of The Uplands will slow us down as we head north. We likely won't make it in time for the full moon, if we don't take this path." Lowering the skin, Alar met Cailean's eye across the fire. To Lara's surprise, the two men shared a long look.

Her pulse quickened. What was that about? Turning her attention to Mor, she found the Shee queen observing Alar, her gaze narrowed. "Have you traveled The Hog's Back before?" Lara asked her, disconcerted by the glint in the Shee queen's eyes.

Mor shook her head, cutting her attention to Lara. "We usually move about Albia using barrows."

"Aye, well … prepare yourself," Cailean replied, picking up a stick and poking at the fire. "The road across The Goatfells isn't for the faint-hearted."

Vyr snorted. "Just as well none of us are cowards then."

"Are you worried the Lothin will cause us problems?" Roth asked.

"They could," Alar answered warily. "But they aren't the only thing to watch out for."

"If you're worried about The Hog's Back, we could take another route?" Lara suggested. His behavior, and Cailean's too, was starting to unnerve her.

Alar shook his head. "There isn't any other … not one that will get us to The Shattered Crown before Gateway."

"The Hog's Back it is then," Vyr said, with a hearty tone that didn't quite match his expression.

Uneasiness rippled through the air.

At that moment, Lara noticed something had changed. "The Gaulas has stopped," she murmured. Around her, the others glanced up at the star-sprinkled heavens.

"Thank the Gods," Ruari huffed. "Some reprieve. I was beginning to—"

The seer never finished his sentence, for a piercing shriek cut him off.

Lara froze. *The Slew.*

Next to her, Bree spat out a curse.

"They're late." Alar rolled to his feet. "Dusk fell a while ago."

Heart hammering, Lara struggled up and fumbled for her cairn stone. As she did so, she twisted west. Winged dark shapes moved fast over the face of the waxing moon.

Mor craned her neck, staring up at the sky. "So many."

"Aye." Alar's voice cut through the darkness somewhere to her left. "Dozens. Maybe a hundred."

Silver light erupted around the fireside, Cailean and Ren calling their magic. The sudden brightness seared Lara's vision, turning the Shee into shadows. Her companions stumbled backward, weapons scraping from sheaths.

Ren's voice ripped through the night, raw and primal; a song that raised every hair on Lara's arms. The tethered clag-doo answered with a terrified howl.

"We need to light more torches!" Sablebane shouted.

"It won't be enough!" Cailean snarled back. "Ready yourselves!"

Lara's gaze snapped upward.

The Slew were diving now, arms outstretched. Long hair and tattered cloaks swirled around them.

Her pulse hammered against her ribs. The cairn stone in her right hand had gone slick with sweat. She raised her left hand, fingers snapping straight.

Fire shot skyward.

Screams answered: thin and terrible, like iron scraping bone.

Heat slammed into Lara's body, a wave that stole the breath from her lungs. It blistered across her skin, scorched through her veins until it felt as if her blood were boiling. The fire wanted more. Finding that quiet, still place inside herself—the place where she could wield flame without fear or fury—was impossible when the air itself was screaming.

She sucked in a breath that tasted of ash and forced her fist closed—and then opened it again.

Flame erupted from every torch, a wall of light and heat that painted the night in shades of gold and crimson. The cairn stone pulsed against her palm, burning now, and the *Ord-ree seal* on that same hand blazed like a fresh brand.

She sent tongues of fire skyward. Again and again. But the Slew kept coming, wave after wave of them pushing against her barrier. For every wraith that wheeled away, screaming, two more dove through the gaps.

Her breath came in ragged pants now. The pressure of holding the flames steady was an iron band crushing her chest. Her raised arm screamed, muscles locked in place, trembling with the strain. Her legs shook so badly she wasn't sure how much longer they'd hold her.

Movement flickered at the edges of her vision. Their small band had fractured: Shee fought on one side, and Marav on the other. Even now, even with death diving from the sky, they couldn't unite. Bree's blade flashed as she cut at grasping hands. Roth bellowed something Lara couldn't hear over the roar of flames and screaming. Cailean moved in a silver blur of speed. Skaal's teeth snapped at shadows. Behind them, smaller figures—Annis, Ruari, Eithne, Duana—huddled, iron daggers clutched in white-knuckled grips.

Alar fought alone, no one at his back.

The Shee formed a protective circle around Mor, their blades singing.

A cry—different from the others, higher, tinged with real terror—cut through the chaos. A Raven lifted off the ground, a Slew gripping each shoulder, her legs kicking uselessly at empty air. Two figures leaped, grabbed her ankles, and yanked her back to earth.

Lara forced her focus back to the fire. She couldn't help them, couldn't afford to let her concentration slip even for a heartbeat. They'd have to save themselves.

The flames surged higher, so bright they turned night to noon. Light gilded the surrounding hills, painted the scree-covered slopes of the Goatfells in shades of copper and gold. She'd never burned this fiercely before. Never pushed this hard. The fire sang in her blood, wild and exultant, and hungry for more.

But it still wasn't enough.

Dark shapes burst through her wall of flame. Some burned, collapsing into columns of black smoke. Others made it through, wings spread wide, mouths open.

Fighting erupted around her—shouts, grunts, and shrieks. She didn't dare look. Didn't dare break the thread connecting her to the flames.

Wings filled her vision, leathery and tattered like storm-shredded sails. The wraith dove straight for her.

Suddenly, Alar was there, blades flashing. The Slew recoiled, its face twisting with rage. Then Cailean appeared on her other side. Then Bree. The three of them moved as one, driving the wraith back until it fled, wailing, into the smoke-choked sky.

Relief crashed through Lara's chest, so intense it nearly broke her concentration. Together. They could do this together. They could—

Something massive dropped from the sky like a stone, landing a few feet away with an impact that made the ground jolt.

Then it rose. Unfolding. Growing. Taller than any man. Broader.

Fear hit her like a fist to the gut.

The flames around her guttered. Died.

Slew poured through the gap above her head, but Lara barely marked them. Her gaze had locked onto the thing standing before her, and she couldn't look away.

Hair like knotted kelp. A melted face that might have been Marav once. Empty eyes. That gaping maw full of splintered teeth. Smoke coiling around black-clad limbs.

She knew this one.

It had come for her at Gateway in Duncrag, had nearly killed Alar to reach her. The other Slew had been smoke and fury, but this one had been solid. Her fire had barely driven it back.

And now, it had found her again.

Mor tore free from her warriors, blade singing through smoke-thick air.

The steel bit deep into the massive Slew's shoulder. The wraith snarled, the sound bestial, and one sinewy arm whipped out. Long fingers fastened around Mor's throat.

The Raven Queen's mouth gaped. Her free hand clawed at the fierce grip crushing her windpipe while she drove her blade in again, deeper, the steel disappearing into shadow-flesh.

Alar flew at the Slew, twin blades flashing. Its head snapped toward him—that was all it took, that shift of attention—and it flung Mor aside like a discarded poppet. Shadow coiled around Alar and the wraith as they clashed, dark tendrils writhing.

Lara locked her knees, even as her legs threatened to buckle. Sweat soaked through her tunic, cold against her skin despite the heat still radiating from her raised hand. Her vision blurred at the edges. The exhaustion wasn't just tiredness, but a weight dragging her down toward the ground.

But she couldn't fall. Not now. The others couldn't fend off the restless dead. Without her fire, they had no chance. Especially not against *this* Slew.

She had to regain control.

Her gaze dropped to the fire pit still burning a few feet away. Usually, she coaxed the flames, whispered to them, let them flow through her like water finding its course. A partnership. A dance. Everything Ruari had taught her about stillness and control and the quiet place inside where fear and fury couldn't reach.

Gone. All of it. Unraveled.

Desperation hammered against her ribs. Her usual way wasn't working. The fire was slipping from her grasp. That Slew was going to kill Alar, and then it would come for her.

She had no choice.

Her left hand clenched tighter, nails biting crescents into her palm. She stared at the flames in the pit, not asking but demanding. *Now!* The word tore through her mind like a blade. *Incinerate them all!*

The fire bucked against her will like a wild pony. She slammed back, threw the full weight of her desperation and rage against it, forced it to bend. Her fingers snapped straight.

Fire exploded from her fingertips.

A roar filled the glen—not from her throat but from the flames themselves. Triumph and hunger. Golden light seared away every shadow.

Screams answered. Not just the Slew's thin shrieks but voices—Shee and Marav both crying out in terror. "Get down!" The words ripped from her throat. "I can't control it!"

She couldn't. The fire had stopped listening. It poured through her, consuming her, burning her from the inside out. Heat blistered her skin. Her blood turned molten in her veins. Copper and ash stung her tongue.

She wasn't wielding the fire anymore. She was just the doorway it rushed through, the conduit, and it didn't care what it burned.

The flames slammed into the Slew. They recoiled, arms wheeling, mouths gaping.

Alar wrenched himself free of the massive wraith and rolled, his body a dark blur. He flattened himself as the wall of flame roared overhead and crashed into his opponent.

The huge Slew twisted and writhed, trapped now, its milky eyes fixing on Lara. Those clawed hands reached for her, grasping at air, but the fire held it pinned.

Lara staggered forward, her legs moving of their own volition. Heat pulsed through her with every heartbeat—and with it came something else. Something like joy. Like power. Like invincibility.

She was unstoppable. She was a Goddess of Fire who'd set the world alight, and everything would burn if she willed it. Everything would bow or break.

"Burn!" The scream tore from her throat, raw and wild. She unleashed another torrent of flame, this one so bright it hurt to look at, so hot the stones at her feet began to crack.

The fire drove into the Slew like a spear. Even the massive one couldn't withstand this.

They broke. All of them. Screeching, the Unforgiven scattered into the darkness, their cries fading into the night until only silence remained.

And the fire burned on.

19: FLAME AND FURY

"LARA!" A HAND fastened around her right arm. *Bree.* "Stop!"

"I can't!"

Swaying on her feet, Lara looked up at the sky. The Slew had departed, yet fire still flowed from her outstretched hand. She couldn't sever the connection. The elation drained from her then, cold fear replacing it.

The fire held her in its thrall.

"Let it go." Alar's voice reached her then.

A sob ripped from her throat, even as sweat trickled down her face. Her skin felt as if it were smoking.

Alar moved close. Fingers fastened around her extended wrist, holding it firmly, while his other hand slid over the back of her hand. Panic thudded against her breastbone as his fingers started to press hers into a fist. What was he doing? He risked incinerating himself. "No!" she gasped. "Don't."

"Fight it, Lara," he commanded. "You're stronger than the flames."

"Go inward. Find the stillness." Ruari was there too, his voice raspy yet strong. Soothing. "You know the place. The peaceful loch where nothing can touch you."

Lara swallowed, her throat painfully tight. And all the while, Alar's fingers continued to push against hers. But still, she resisted him.

Squeezing her eyes shut, she struggled against the roaring in her ears, pressing through it to find her quiet center of power.

"Are you there?" Ruari asked.

"Aye."

"Walk into it … let the cold water put out the fire."

Lara obeyed, even as the fire magic rebelled with every step. Her skin hissed as water lapped around her ankles. She waded in, up to her knees now. The water began to steam.

Throwing her head back, she screamed. And then, she dove under. The chill hit her like a fist, and the fire's roar nearly deafened her. An instant later, it went out.

Alar's fingers closed over hers, successfully bringing her left hand back into a fist.

A deep silence settled.

Lara opened her eyes.

The fire pit smoldered nearby. The sky was clear. Around her, strained faces smeared with ash and soot stared back at her. Disappointment soured Lara's mouth. The Slew had nearly bested them, and not just because her fire magic had almost failed her.

"You didn't work together," she rasped, her throat raw. Even now, the Shee and Marav stood apart as if an invisible fence divided them. "At this rate, we'll never *reach* The Shattered Crown … let alone carry out our task."

Discomfort rippled across their faces. Aye, they knew.

Something sharp and cold settled in the pit of her belly then. She'd never lost control like that before. When she'd tried to find that calm, still loch, her mind had refused to cooperate. She wasn't just losing time or blanking during conversations. No, it was worse than that. She was slowly unraveling and powerless to stop it.

Lara's gaze met Alar's. The ends of his hair smoked, and an angry burn marked his left shoulder, but he paid none of that any mind. Instead, he gently released her hand. A half-smile tugged at his lips, and when he spoke, his voice was rough with relief. "You did it."

"I did," she whispered.

The world started to spin then. Suddenly, she couldn't hear or see. Darkness rushed in, her knees gave way, and she toppled forward into the abyss.

Stepping forward, Alar caught Lara in his arms. Her head fell back, her lips parting. Alarm punched into him, and he ground out a curse. Twisting, he carried her to the fireside and laid her down. Reaching out, he felt for her pulse upon her neck. Sweat slicked her hot skin.

Her heartbeat fluttered against his fingers then, and he let out a shuddering sigh before sitting back on his heels.

The others had gathered close. They were all watching him. "She's alive," he assured them.

"She needs water." Bree retrieved a waterskin and moved close, kneeling next to them. Lifting Lara's head, she carefully let water trickle into her mouth. The High Queen swallowed before a moan escaped her.

Alar studied her flushed cheeks and flickering eyelids. That had been too close. The fire had almost consumed her. He'd sensed its power as he held onto her wrist and hand. Her skin had scalded his, yet he hadn't let go. His palms were blistered in the aftermath. The skin now stung and throbbed.

He lifted his gaze then, taking in his companions' faces. "She's right," he said curtly. He wasn't blind; he'd marked how neither Shee nor Marav had moved to help each other. Or him. "We should have united tonight ... but we didn't."

They'd fought together against the Circines, forming a circle in that glade. But that fight had been different. They'd clashed with men and women. Flesh and blood. "That's the second time Lara has saved all our sorry hides," he added.

No one answered, and the anger smoldering under his breastbone flared hot. "Do you disgust each other so much?"

Faces grew taut at this challenge. Cailean and Roth exchanged looks. The druids averted their gazes, while Eithne and Duana clung together, faces ashen. Only Bree met Alar's gaze. She alone knew what it was to be torn between two worlds, and yet she hadn't cooperated with their allies either. Meanwhile, the Shee bristled.

"It wasn't deliberate," Vyr said stiffly. "It's just ... instinctual ... to protect our own."

Tension rippled around the fireside. Meanwhile, Lara groaned.

"If I had my way, Shee and Marav alike would burn," Alar said finally, even as ire pulsed in his chest. "You're not worth saving." *Ashes.* He missed the wulvers. Right now, he wanted to turn his back on these people. When the darkness came, let it take them.

"I share your anger, Alar." His gaze cut to Mor, surprise rippling through him. Even sweaty, singed, and coated in ash and soot, she stood proud. Her face was all sharp angles, and her black eyes burned. She hadn't yet sheathed her sword. Firelight glinted off its thin folded steel blade. "That was a near disaster," she said as she surveyed her Ravens. They bowed their heads under her wrath. "If we don't start working together, we'll not last the distance."

When Lara's eyes flickered open, the first thing she saw was Alar.

Groaning, she shut her eyes once more.

"Lara?"

She made a sound in the back of her throat.

"Are you thirsty?"

She swallowed. Her throat was parched. Her mouth was sticky with a bitter taste. "Aye," she whispered.

"Here."

She opened her eyes to see him unstopper a waterskin. He then lifted her head, cradling the back of it with one hand, while he raised the skin to her lips. It was an intimate gesture, and had she not felt as weak as a newborn foal, she'd have pushed him away. However, she had more important things to focus on right now.

Lara gulped thirstily; the stale water tasted like summer ale.

"How are you feeling?" Bree's face appeared then. Her friend's brow was deeply furrowed.

"Weak," she replied. "What happened?"

"You fainted after you severed the connection with fire," Alar said, drawing her attention once more.

Lara wet her parched lips with her tongue. She was warm. That was to be expected though. She always came down with a fever and chills after wielding fire against the Slew. It took a lot out of her.

Her pulse stuttered then. *Too much.*

Fear slithered through her gut—a familiar sensation these days. She was tough, had proved her mettle over the past years, but she couldn't fight whatever it was that now ailed her. She hated feeling so vulnerable. It was the last thing she needed, especially when the days ahead required her strength. She couldn't let everyone down.

"Do you remember the attack?" Cailean asked. He too had knelt, next to Bree. They both had burns on their faces, minor compared to the one on Alar's shoulder. Her gut clenched. That was her doing. She'd nearly immolated them all.

Lara nodded, even as her pulse started to thud in her ears. "I lost control … I'm sorry."

Cailean huffed. "Don't apologize. We're all here because of you."

"We are." Mor's voice intruded then, and Lara glanced right to find the Raven Queen seated, cross-legged, a few feet away. Eagal had returned to her shoulder. "Thank you."

Lara held her gaze for a moment. "Did we lose anyone?"

"Not this time," Mor replied, reminding her that one of her Ravens had fallen during the Circines attack. "Although some of us got scorched worse than others." She glanced over at Alar. "That shoulder needs seeing to."

"I can help." Ruari approached then, mixing something with a small wooden pestle and mortar. "Our healer, Eldra, gave me this and some of her herbs for the journey. Boar weed soothes scalds and burns."

The seer knelt next to Alar then before gently smearing the green paste over the blistered burn on his shoulder. He then turned his hands over and dressed his raw palms too.

Alar's jaw flexed, and he hissed through his teeth. Ruari cast him a rueful look as he continued to work. "You can thank me later."

20: NO SAFE PLACE

LEANING FORWARD, LARA let Bracken pick her way up the slope. Mercifully, The Gaulas didn't plague them this morning. Just as well, for her defenses were low; she'd barely had the strength to mount her horse earlier. She now slumped in the saddle, sweating despite the cool breeze that feathered her face. The fever still hadn't lifted. Every bone and muscle in her body ached.

But the physical discomfort wasn't the worst of it. At the back of her mind, dread lurked. Sometimes it would prod at her, causing her skin to pebble. No, she wasn't frightened about what lay ahead—but the beast within. There were few things more terrifying than feeling as if your mind were betraying you. Her thoughts were woolly, scattered. Every time she failed to concentrate, panic grasped at her throat.

At this rate, she'd be demented by the time they reached The Shattered Crown.

They had just left the highway that wound its way north to Cannich. That wouldn't be their road. Instead, they were taking The Hog's Back—a narrow mountain path that led over the Goatfells. Cailean had told her it would take them three days to cross it. The road then dropped down to the west, on the edge of the Hallow Woods. From there, it would be another three-day journey to Crask, the largest of the crannogs that lined the eastern edge of Loch Glass.

They were in the heart of The Uplands now, yet still far from their destination.

Lara was painfully aware of time passing. When they'd set off from The Wolds, it had seemed they had many days ahead of them. But every night when she glanced up and saw the moon steadily growing fuller, impatience swelled inside her.

We have to keep moving.

Her fingers tightened around the reins. If she had to weather another night like that one, she wouldn't make it to their destination. The Slew had been vicious, and that wraith—bigger and more substantial than the others—had come for her again.

The spirits were actively trying to stop them now. Did they sense that she bore the *Ord-ree seal,* and that she was carrying it back to The Shattered Crown? Were they afraid of what she might do?

The ring had been used to keep the breach open, and now it would close it. Forever.

The path was too narrow to ride two-abreast, and so Lara followed Cailean with Bree behind her as they made their way up the mountain. Eithne clung to the chief-enforcer's back, her flaxen hair snagging in the breeze.

Misgiving plucked at Lara.

The sisters had shown surprising mettle the night before. However, she didn't want to drag Eithne and Duana into this. She couldn't abandon them either. They couldn't go back to Dulross, and the road ahead led into Shee territory. She'd hoped they'd pass a village where she could leave them, yet there hadn't been any. There was no safe place for them now. *There isn't for any of us.*

Despite that all their party survived the night, the mood had been subdued when they packed up at dawn. The Slew attack had rattled them, even Mor. The Raven Queen went first up the mountain, leading Dorka. She loped alongside Mor's white elk now, far more placid. Alar was among the leaders of the group, astride that magnificent red stag.

Lara had to admit that he looked right on its back.

She checked herself then.

Alar. Wherever she turned these days, there he was.

He'd helped her fight back against the fire that threatened to consume her—had risked himself to do so. He'd been standing nearby when she collapsed. It was likely he'd been the one to carry her over to the fire. Heat rolled over her then, a warmth that had nothing to do with her fever.

His face had been the first she'd seen after waking. He'd been watching over her.

She'd been aloof with him ever since. She wasn't ungrateful. She just didn't want to rely on him. Ever again.

It galled her that she'd feared for his life as she'd watched him fight that terrifying Slew, that his burns had concerned her, and that some traitorous part, deep inside, had melted at his protectiveness.

No, none of that mattered. *He* didn't matter. All that did was reaching their destination with her sanity intact.

"Gut it like this." Eithne dug her knife into the hare's belly. "You then get rid of everything inside." Reaching into the body cavity, she pulled out its guts in deft, practiced movements. The rank odor of offal made Lara's nose wrinkle. Nonetheless, it was a useful lesson.

Following the lass's lead, she sliced open the hare she'd just skinned and plunged her hand inside its still-warm body, fighting squeamishness. She was still sweating from her fever, chills crawling over her skin, and her body trembled from exhaustion, but this task was a welcome distraction.

They'd made camp against a steep scree slope, just off the narrow path. Beyond, there was a dizzying drop that plunged down to a deep corrie. The setting sun gilded the sea of craggy peaks, bringing out the streaks of gold, ochre, grey, and black rock. The wind was sharp up here. The Whistle echoed off stone. Nonetheless, Lara was so relieved to be free of The Gaulas, she didn't care.

"Fucking grimlochs."

Lara glanced up. A few yards away, Roth was bent over smoking tinder, clutching his flint. As Lara and the sisters looked on, he struck it once more. Flames flared, and then something doused it, like a puff of wind.

Lara frowned. Dark shapes writhed around the fire pit, eyes glowing in the gloaming.

Aye, the smoke spirits were making trouble.

Still, Roth persisted, his curses growing ever more colorful as his efforts were blocked.

A few feet away, Fern muttered something in her own tongue. She eyed the warrior as if he was inept. She and her father were gutting and skinning a wild pig they'd taken down earlier in the day.

"Shall I help?" Lara called out.

Roth looked up, his brow furrowing. "Is it safe?"

She nodded. In truth, she was wary about wielding fire again, but surely, she could manage something simple. She wouldn't even need her cairn stone.

Pulling out the last of the hare's entrails, she passed Duana the carcass. She then wiped off her hands, rose to her feet, and crossed to the fire pit.

"Try again," she instructed.

Casting her a wary look, he did as bid. The flint sparked, and flame spurted upward.

Lara wiggled her fingers, and a line of fire shot across the laid hearth, igniting the dry grass and twigs he'd arranged. "Off you go," she murmured to the swirling smoky shapes. "Bother someone else's hearth tonight."

The shadows grew frenzied, and then, buzzing like an angry swarm of wasps, they departed.

Lara sat back on her heels, meeting Roth's eye. His lips quirked. "You've pissed them off."

She huffed. "No doubt, they'll be back."

Singing intruded then—the same haunting melody from a couple of nights earlier. Lara glanced over at the path, where Ren stood at Mor's side, hands outstretched, tattoos glowing. Dorka crouched before them, ears back. Mor was tense, her lips tight. Being so close to earth magic pained her, yet she needed the bard's help with this. Eagal had flown from Mor's shoulder and now looked on from a scraggly hawthorn a few yards distant.

Meanwhile, Eithne and Duana had busied themselves pushing the hare carcasses onto spits. Likewise, Fern and Sablebane readied the boar for roasting. It would be a hearty supper tonight, and anticipation of it had lightened the mood slightly.

Mor and Dorka also provided a welcome distraction.

"She's going to get on its back," Alar murmured, dumping his whin bush near the fire. "Look."

Indeed, Mor moved forward, one hand sliding along Dorka's neck to her shoulder.

The feline had relaxed now though. Her tail no longer swished, and the rigidity of her spine had softened.

"I don't understand why this matters to her so much," Roth muttered.

"For a Shee ruler to ride a clag-doo carries much prestige," Fern replied, favoring him with an arch look. "If Mor can gentle Dorka, she will earn herself great respect among our people."

Roth raised an auburn brow. "Doesn't she have their respect already?"

Fern sneered at him. "Of course."

Lara glanced back at where Mor now ran her hand gently along Dorka's spine. Realization dawned then. This wasn't about prestige or respect for the Raven Queen, but about something far more primal. As a ruler herself, Lara understood. To rule was to be alone. A queen always had to be on her guard. But if this clag-doo would submit to Mor, would agree to carry her on its back, she'd have a special relationship with it. Intimacy. Something of her own.

Ren sang on, her soft song drifting through the gathering dusk.

Mor took her time. Continuing to stroke Dorka's plush black coat until she purred. And then, gathering her skirts, she climbed onto her back.

The feline stiffened, her long tail starting to whip from side to side.

"Stop singing," Mor called to Ren. "I need to touch minds with her."

The bard ceased, dropping her hands to her sides.

As Lara looked on, Mor reached forward, stroking Dorka's neck. "That's it, my lovely," she murmured. "Listen to me … trust me. We shall be friends, you and I."

A shiver rippled through Dorka's sinewy body. And then, she made an odd chirping sound. "Pass me the chain," Mor said then, glancing Ren's way once more.

The bard hesitated, clearly wary of coming any closer to those deadly jaws and claws.

However, Mor nodded to her, and she did as asked, retrieving the end of the chain and handing it to her. She then backed away, joining Lara and the others by the fireside.

Dorka threw back her head then and gave a loud howl.

The surrounding Shee muttered oaths. Some of them even reached for their weapons. But an instant later, Dorka leaped forward. The Ravens rushed toward the clag-doo. It was too late, for she bounded up the mountain path, disappearing within moments with Mor clinging to her back.

"Well, that's it," Roth murmured, watching clag-doo and rider go. "We won't see either of them again."

But the Raven Queen wasn't so easily rid of.

They were sitting by the fire pit, while the carcasses of the hares and the boar sizzled, when she appeared once more—still astride Dorka's back.

Mor's Ravens rose smoothly to their feet, their gazes riveted upon their queen.

Mor flashed them a grin.

"Well played, cousin," Vyr greeted her, approval shining in his dark eyes.

Nodding to him, Mor slid to the ground and led Dorka over to where a dead hare had been left for her. She then looped the chain around the hawthorn. Eagal still perched upon a branch, glaring down at the clag-doo. After that, she joined everyone at the fireside, dropping down into a cross-legged position with loose-limbed ease next to Alar.

He glanced at her, surprised. As was Lara. Mor usually took her place amongst her Ravens in the evenings. However, when Lara's gaze slid around the fire pit, she realized they were no longer segregated. Sablebane and Fern sat with Ruari and Annis, and Vyr had taken his place to Lara's left, while Bree and Cailean sat to her right.

Had last night's near disaster shaken them? Maybe. The atmosphere had definitely shifted. For the first time since setting out together, they seemed like one group rather than two.

Eagal swooped down then, landing upon Mor's shoulder. She reached up a hand, stroking his back in greeting. "I timed my return well, I see," she said, glancing over at where Eithne and Duana were gingerly removing the hare carcasses from the spits. Her gaze then flicked to Ren. "My thanks to you, bard."

The young woman's spine stiffened. "My name's Ren."

Mor flashed her a warm smile. "Your skill with song is quite something, *Ren*."

The bard's cheeks flushed, and she dropped her gaze.

"Will you be riding Dorka from now on then?" Vyr asked.

"Aye … I've let my elk know it can return to Sheehallion."

Fern grinned, nudging her father in the ribs with an elbow. In response, Sablebane's lips actually tugged up at the corners in a ghost of a smile. Mor's elation, her success, had buoyed their moods. The other Ravens were all smiling. Likewise, even Lara's escort wore softer expressions this evening.

Eithne and Duana pulled the carcasses apart and handed them around the fire. The bed-slave collars around their necks caught the ruddy light as they worked. The boar would take longer, for it was a much bigger beast, although the rich scent of it made Lara's mouth fill with saliva. Her fever was drawing back now, and her aches and pains subsided with it. She was still tired and looked forward to wrapping herself in her fur-lined cloak and stretching out on the ground, but the numbing fatigue was lifting too—and with it the gnawing dread.

At moments like this, she could almost forget there was something wrong with her.

Even so, as conversation rose and fell around the fire pit, she found her mind kept wandering. It was difficult to concentrate. Bree nudged her with an elbow then, passing her a hunk of roast boar.

Lara blinked. Didn't the boar have a while to cook yet? Her gaze flicked to where Sablebane carved the roasted carcass.

Where did the time go?

She stilled then, cold creeping over her. *Shades.* It had happened again. She'd had another lapse.

Her chest constricted, her dread sliding into panic. *No. I can't go to pieces ... not yet.*

She had to hang on—had to keep her wits together long enough to reach The Shattered Crown. Otherwise, she'd let everyone down. Otherwise, the shadows would win.

Feeling queasy, she looked across the fire, her gaze meeting Alar's for the first time all day. He was watching her. His expression was serious, his eyes slightly narrowed.

Her skin prickled. Curse him, he'd noticed. The Half-blood always saw too much.

21: FOOTSTEPS IN THE FOG

"I HEAR YOU wield earth magic."

Alar glanced left to find Vyr riding beside him. The path had widened for a spell, drawing back a little from the precipitous edge of the mountain. They'd set off at dawn, with Mor leading the way upon Dorka. A knot of Ravens upon stags and elks followed the queen, with Alar and Vyr behind them. The morning was dull; a helmet of cloud had descended, bringing the sky oppressively close.

As always, Lara and her escort lagged a little farther back.

Alar eyed Mor's cousin. Clad in black, the silver half-moon stud in his ear glinting despite the lack of sun, he was an enigma of sorts. Alar had heard about Mor's acrimonious relationships with kin. Frankly, it was surprising that Vyrnek still breathed. In truth, he was the only one among their Shee companions that Alar had warmed to. "I have few secrets, it seems," he replied.

Vyr inclined his head. "I've watched you fight." He grimaced then. "And I smelled pine and ash on you … so I asked the chief-enforcer."

Alar snorted. He wasn't surprised Lara had told others his secret. After all, he'd revealed hers to his wulvers and the Circines. He imagined Cailean wouldn't have received the news well; druids didn't like common folk messing with earth magic. "My tattoo allows me to channel earth magic, to make me faster and stronger."

"But Shee blood runs through your veins. Earth magic should harm you, not help you."

"I have Marav blood as well," Alar replied with a shrug. "It balances things."

An emotion Alar couldn't quite place flickered over Vyr's face. Like his cousin, he had proud aquiline features. "The very smell of earth magic turns my stomach," he admitted. "And even now, I can feel the bite of iron on my skin from those daggers on your back." He pulled another face. "Those things have always been our weakness … but if we are here to stay in Albia, that must change."

Alar observed Mor's cousin for a few moments. Vyr intrigued him. He wondered then at the cousins' relationship. They seemed to get on well. However, appearances could deceive. Did Vyr secretly covet the throne? If he did, he wouldn't be the first of Mor's kin to consider overthrowing her. Lara had told him about the Raven Queen, and how she'd hunted her brother after he tried to usurp her. The Shee were as ruthless as they were beautiful. To rule them was a double-edged blade. You gained power, but you could never let your guard down.

"Why are you here, Vyr?" Alar had conversed little with his companions since fleeing Dulross. Everyone had kept their distance from him, yet he sensed Vyr was ready to talk a little. And, in truth, he was curious to learn about the dynamics between Mor and her cousin. "I don't imagine Mor suffers rivals."

The Shee warrior's lips curved. "She doesn't … but she chose her escort carefully for this journey. We all have skills she values. Like her, I can wield moonlight and starlight with song." He winked at Alar then. "Or in other words … I'm useful."

Alar regarded him speculatively. Aye, he wasn't sure what to make of Vyr. He appeared easy-going, charming even, yet that wasn't the whole story. Alar knew what it was to wear a mask—often your survival depended on it.

And yet it was exhausting.

"Are you close to Mor?" he asked then.

Vyr huffed a laugh, eyeing him. "*No one* is close to Mor … and that's the way she likes it." He paused then. "Back in Sheehallion, my territory is in the far north. In truth, I've had little to do with her over the centuries."

Lara dragged a hand across her forehead. It came away slick. The air bit like winter this high on the mountain pass, yet heat rolled off her skin in waves. Worse was the coppery taste coating her tongue. Her throat was tight. And beneath it all, something gnawed at her insides, a wrongness.

"Your cheeks are flushed," Bree said. They rode two abreast now, forced to crawl through the thick fog. A few yards to their right, the world simply ended—a sheer drop into nothing.

"Aye." The word scraped out. "The fever's back." Lara met her friend's eye. "What time is it?"

Bree's mouth tightened. "Hard to tell in this soup … but our break at noon was a while ago. Cailean said we're almost at the summit. Didn't you hear him?"

Ice slid down Lara's spine despite the heat pulsing under her skin. She had no memory of Cailean speaking. None at all. "I've lost time again."

Alarm flashed across Bree's face. "It's the fire magic … it's doing something to you."

Ahead, Cailean twisted in his saddle. Behind him, Eithne did the same, her young face pinched with worry.

"I feared this," Cailean said quietly.

Lara's fingers tightened on the reins. "Feared what?"

"Our *gifts* demand payment. When I became an enforcer, earth magic bound itself to me. I use it, and I must refill the well after. Without the blood-letting, I weaken. Eventually, I die."

The words reminded her of the cost of Gregor's desertion. They'd need to find Cailean a new sacrificer after this. But at least he understood the power burning in his veins.

She didn't.

"So, is my price fire-madness?" The question stung the back of her throat like bile. "But that would mean all the fire-wielders of old would eventually have succumbed to it."

Neither Bree nor Cailean answered, yet their expressions were grave.

"Gil found almost nothing in those scrolls." She looked down at her right hand, at the *Ord-ree seal* gleaming against her skin. Her chest began to tingle. Cold washed over her fevered flesh as fear sank its claws in. "Nothing about what happens when you wield fire regularly."

"Mor said the Marav destroyed most records about fire magic," Bree replied. Her gaze traveled forward to where the Shee had vanished into grey nothing. Her expression tightened then, and Lara was about to question her when Eithne interrupted them.

"Can you hear that?" The lass's fingers dug into Cailean's waist hard enough to make him grunt.

"What?"

"Footsteps."

Lara frowned. She'd been listening to the roar of blood in her own ears, the wheeze of her breathing. But now—

"Halt!" Cailean's shout cut through the fog.

The group stuttered to a stop. Lara glanced back. Ruari, Ren, and Annis had frozen in place. Meanwhile, Vyr and Alar had pulled up in front of her.

Then she heard it.

The crunch and drag of heavy footsteps.

Something climbing the mountainside behind them.

The sound of it—rhythmic, patient, inevitable—made her still. Her pulse thudded slow and thick in her ears. Despite the fever burning through her, her fingers went numb with cold. "By The Five," she whispered. "What is that?"

"I'd hoped to avoid this." Cailean's voice had gone flat.

Lara swallowed. "Avoid what?"

"The Grey Ghost." He looked at each of them in turn. "Can you feel it?"

"You mean the certainty I'm already dead?" Roth's face had pinched. Behind him, Duana paled.

"That's it," Cailean ground out. "The wraith is following us."

"Why have we stopped?" Mor materialized through the fog astride Dorka, Sablebane and Fern emerging like shadows behind her.

"Do you hear footsteps?" Vyr called out to his cousin.

"No, I—" Mor's words died. Her expression went rigid. Her dark eyes swept over the group clustered on the narrow path.

The footsteps were louder now. Heavier. Closer.

Lara's grip on the reins tightened. Beneath her, Bracken shifted and trembled. She glanced back over her shoulder, peering into the wall of grey.

A shape loomed there. Massive. Taller than any man or Shee she'd ever seen. Not quite solid. Not quite smoke. Something in between.

"Gods!" Annis's choked voice tore through the mist. "It's coming!"

Aye. No doubt. No question. The knowledge settled in Lara's bones with absolute certainty. She whispered a prayer, the words tumbling over each other. Beside her, Duana and Eithne clutched the iron charms at their throats.

Lara's breath came fast and shallow. She looked back again.

The shadow had vanished.

Bree cursed, her blade scraping from its sheath. "It's above us now. Look!"

Lara's gaze jerked upward. Tors rose through the fog toward the hidden summit. And there—moving through the drifting grey—the tall silhouette approached.

How had it moved so fast?

Crunch. Drag. Crunch. Drag.

The sound came from everywhere now.

Ruari choked on a prayer. Ren opened her mouth to sing, but the note came out strangled and died to a whimper. Fear had wrapped itself around the bard's throat and squeezed.

"Don't let it take you." Alar's words cut through the fog. "We need to keep moving."

An anguished cry echoed across the mountainside.

"Eithne!" Duana gasped.

Her sister had launched herself from behind Cailean, skirts bunched in her fists, and now bolted back down the way they'd come. Her hair streamed behind her like a battle standard.

Ren tore past on her pony, sobbing, her small body hunched low. Ruari galloped after her.

"Fuck!" Cailean wrenched his horse around. "You're all going the wrong way!"

They didn't hear. Couldn't hear. Terror had them now.

Annis sat frozen in her saddle, eyes locked on the shadowy figure. The mist rolled in, swallowing them. Lara felt the pull then—the urge to run, to flee, to do anything but stay here with that presence bearing down on them. Sweat poured off her despite the mountain cold. Her body trembled.

"We have to get them back!" The words burst from her. "Cailean. Roth. Go—"

"You won't find them in this fog." Mor's voice sliced through Lara's panic. "But we can. Wynn. Vyr. With me."

The Raven Queen leaned forward and pressed her palm flat against Dorka's neck. The clag-doo's tail lashed, fighting the connection. A yowl ripped from her throat as she submitted and lunged forward, vanishing into the mist with Mor. Vyr and Sablebane plunged after her.

"Lara." Alar appeared at her side.

His hand clamped around her arm, and the contact jolted through her. The crushing dread pulled back. Just slightly. Just enough to breathe. His eyes burned into hers. "Ride!"

"The others—"

"Mor will find them. We cross the summit now, or the fear takes us all."

He released her arm, grabbed her reins, and urged his stag forward. They surged up the path. Shapes blurred past—Shee on their elks and stags, phantoms in the fog.

Lara's heart hammered against her ribs, as if it were trying to break free.

Shouts echoed through the grey. Weeping. Cursing. Prayers.

She twisted in the saddle. Bree rode right behind her, face set and pale. Cailean had caught Annis's reins and was dragging her forward. The counselor clung to her horse's mane, tears streaming down her cheeks. Behind them, Roth wrestled with Duana. She snarled and clawed at him, desperate to chase after her sister, but he was bigger, stronger, and he held on.

Terror tightened like cruel fingers around Lara's throat.

Even through the thunder of hooves, she could hear the heavy footsteps.

Patient. Relentless. Inevitable.

Cold air rushed past her burning face. A sob tore itself from her chest.

Panic took her then. *There is no escape.* They could run until their horses collapsed, until their hearts burst, and that thing would still be there. Their journey ended here on this fog-shrouded mountain. None of them would see the other side.

They galloped blind into the mist. Madness—for the drop was right there, just yards away, waiting to swallow them. But staying would have been worse. Staying meant the fear would

burrow so deep they'd throw themselves off the mountainside
just to make it stop.

22: HIS GAME

NO ONE HAD much to say when they finally made camp for the night, yet the relief was palpable. They'd left the terror behind on the mountain's summit, where it belonged.

Roth went to light a fire, his face pale and strained. He bore livid scratch marks upon his left cheek, where Duana had raked him in her panic to get to her sister. Like the night before, grimlochs gave him trouble, and Lara eventually knelt by the smoking hearth to help. A short while later, a fire crackled merrily.

They'd stopped halfway down the other side of the mountain, far from the summit. The gloaming had grown deep by the time they halted upon a ledge that looked west. Below them stretched the dark carpet of the Hallow Woods. Tendrils of milky mist drifted above the treetops.

Mor, Vyr, and Sablebane had caught them up not long before they made camp. Eithne perched in front of Vyr, eyes red-rimmed and tearstains upon her cheeks, while Mor and Sablebane towed two ponies with the druids behind them.

There had been no time to hunt, although there were slabs of boar meat left over from the previous night's supper. They sat around the fire pit, chewing in silence. Lara surveyed her companions' faces, marking their haunted gazes and tense faces. Even the Shee looked shaken by their encounter with The Grey Ghost.

"Mark me," she said to Cailean then, breaking the heavy silence. "If we survive this, I'm *not* taking this road home."

"Thank the Gods," he replied with a rueful shake of his head.

Lara's gaze flicked between the chief-enforcer and Alar. She recalled the look they'd shared that evening—just before the Slew attacked. They'd both known what awaited them up here.

"Have either of you seen that wraith before?"

Alar grimaced. "Almost," he admitted. "I didn't actually *see* it, but I was near the summit of the pass when I heard dragging footsteps crunching on gravel behind me. I kept turning, but there was nothing but swirling mist." His mouth twisted then. "I'll admit, I broke into a run ... and didn't slow my pace until I'd passed the summit and was far down the other side."

"I saw it," Cailean answered quietly. "A tall dark shape advancing through the mist." He paused then, discomfort flickering over his face. "I'm not easily scared ... but there's something about its presence that strips the flesh off your bones."

A brittle silence fell after this admission.

Aye, they'd all felt it. Thank the Five, The Grey Ghost was behind them now. The Hog's Back wasn't an easy road, but if they survived it, they'd cut precious days off their journey. Gateway inched ever closer. Lara was aware of time slipping through her fingers now, like dry sand.

"Just one more night up here," Alar said as he reached for a skin of water. He then took a measured sip. Their supplies were running low. There were few burns or rivers on this path. "We should reach the end of The Hog's Back by dusk tomorrow."

Sighs of relief rippled around the fireside. Ren sat, shoulders rounded, head low, while a nerve twitched in Ruari's cheek. Duana glanced over at Roth then, her features tightening. "Sorry about your face."

He snorted.

Meanwhile, Ruari roused himself, reached for a saddlebag, and started digging around. "Those scratches need tending. I'll fetch you something."

Lara listened to the murmurs of their voices as Ruari located the dried woundwort and mashed up a paste with a little water in his pestle and mortar. However, she was listening to them as if from afar. Her fever had broken again, yet she found herself strangely lightheaded. Distracted.

"Lara." Alar gently nudged her with his elbow. "Mor just asked you something."

She blinked and forced herself to focus. "Sorry," she muttered. She then met Mor's gaze across the fire. "What did you say?"

A groove etched between the queen's brows as she watched Lara. The intensity of her stare made Lara's skin prickle.

"You're often leagues away when the rest of us are talking," Mor said. "Is something worrying you?"

Lara sighed, rubbing her eyes, gritty and sore from fatigue, with the back of her hands. "I'm fine."

"No, you aren't. I've noticed how distracted you are … but it's getting worse."

Lara's pulse quickened as everyone around the fire now watched her.

Curse it. Of course, she'd already spoken to some of her escort about this—but discussing it so openly made her uneasy. Vulnerable. However, judging by the stubborn set of Mor's jaw, she wasn't going to let this go.

"Aye … I'm not myself at the moment," she admitted after a long pause. "My mind is muddled. I'm often exhausted. Feverish. Every day, there are now periods I can't remember."

Mor's frown deepened. "Fire-madness."

Lara leaned forward. "I know little about the power that burns in my veins. But you discovered scrolls about fire magic in your vaults. What did you learn?"

Mor regarded her for a moment. Eagal sat on her shoulder, roosting. "I read some of the history regarding your bloodline," she replied finally. "But I don't recall a remedy for fire-madness. I'm sorry."

Lara's breathing grew shallow. "So, it's incurable?"

"I don't know."

"And what happens," she asked, "As it progresses?"

No one answered. They didn't need to. Lara was already imagining her descent into madness. Distraction would slide into paranoia, and then into rage. Eventually, she'd see enemies everywhere. Eventually, she'd turn on those she cared for.

"Your dream," Ruari spoke up then. "The dangerous secret it warned of …"

Lara glanced over at him, aware that the Shee had all tensed. Irritation spiked through her. She'd asked Ruari not to say anything to Mor or her Ravens about her premonition, yet he'd just blurted it out. "Aye," she snapped. "The one that referred to me?"

"It seems clear now that it *was* referring to fire-madness," the seer replied, meeting her eye, even as his cheeks flushed. "It's slowly taking you."

A fragile silence settled around the hearth.

"Maybe it's time to stop wielding fire, Lara," Alar said then, an edge to his voice. "Your symptoms might subside if you do."

"After our task is complete, I don't intend to use magic again," she answered, surprised by the vehemence in her voice. This wasn't something she'd articulated before, even to herself. It didn't ease the knots in her belly though, or the tightness in her chest—the fear of what would happen if the fire-madness took hold.

Mor's gaze met hers across the firepit. "Fire magic is a part of you. Could you resist its lure?"

Lara nodded. If the alternative was madness, she would.

A sickly sensation flooded through her then. *What if it's too late?*

Lara's mind whirled as she retreated into silence. *Gods.* She didn't want to think about that. What if she ended up a danger to those she'd sworn to defend? What if her own people—her friends—would be forced to turn on her in the end?

Around her, murmured conversation rose and fell around the firepit. The atmosphere among their band had definitely shifted tonight. Despite her worries, Lara had marked it. Shee and Marav were still wary of each other—that would likely never change—but today, they'd worked together.

"It grows late," Alar said finally. "We should all get some sleep."

Many of their group nodded, stifling yawns. It had been a harrowing day; everyone needed to rest. Moments later, they stretched out by the fire, trying to get comfortable on the hard stony ground.

Lara was exhausted too. Despite that the fever had receded for a spell, her limbs felt weak, and her temples ached dully.

Alar rose to his feet then, catching her eye as he did so. He'd sat next to her all evening, and she'd been too distracted, too drained to demand he move elsewhere. It would have seemed petty. However, his proximity now put her on edge.

"You'll weather this, Lara," he said, his voice low and firm. "You're strong … and after we've sealed the veil, you won't have to use your fire magic again. You *will* recover."

Her breathing grew shallow at these words, and for a few moments, she let warmth suffuse her. However, she then pulled herself up short. After their handfasting, her husband had believed in her, supported her, encouraged her. Thanks to him, she'd grown in confidence. Blossomed. It had made his betrayal all the harder to take.

His reassurance now was a slap across the face. She'd agreed to be his ally, but he'd just overstepped.

"And you'll be there to hold my hand, will you?"

His gaze shadowed. "I—"

"Save it." Turning her back on him, she rose to her feet and went looking for somewhere else to sleep.

Lying on her back, Lara stared up at the night sky. Around her, everyone else was sleeping—everyone except Alar and Fern, who'd taken the first watch—yet she silently fumed.

The gall of him.

She knew his game. It was the same one he'd played the year before. Her husband couldn't open his mouth without manipulating others. It came as naturally to him as breathing. And worse still, for a heartbeat, she'd been drawn to his words.

Above, the mist had cleared, and this high up, the belt of twinkling stars looked close enough to touch. The moon was well over half full now, a reminder that Gateway was breathing down their necks.

Nearby, the fire crackled, while a low rumble reverberated across the mountainside. A growled curse followed, and then the noise abruptly halted. Despite her black mood, Lara's lips curved. Skaal snored like a hibernating trow. Over the past days, Cailean had often been forced to nudge the fae hound with his foot.

Her smile faded then, her temper smoldering once more. Not at Alar this time, but herself.

Don't let the bastard get to you.

Every time she snarled at him, she played into his hands. She had to master herself. She had to crush that ember of longing that burned deep in her breast.

The rumbling started up again, and Lara stifled a groan. Skaal would keep them all awake tonight.

However, the noise grew louder, rolling in waves over the mountainside. Moments later, the ground started to tremble. Nearby, the horses squealed and pulled at their tethers, while Dorka yowled.

Something pinged off Lara's cheek then. A sharp sting followed.

Cursing, she rolled onto her side as a rock the size of her fist punched into the ground where her head had just been.

Her heart lurched, and she rolled to her feet. Around her, some of the others sat up, dazed.

"Rockslide!" Alar shouted as he and Fern rushed to the fireside. "Run!"

There was no time to grab their bags. They scrambled away from the fire to free the horses. Mor dashed across to Dorka. Luckily, the elks and stags all roamed free overnight.

The rumbling grew louder, deeper.

Lara rushed to Bracken, untying her and hauling the mare after her. As she went, she looked over her shoulder and froze.

Moonlight frosted the mountainside, illuminating the craggy slope above their campsite as it gave way. Rocks, debris, and dirt rolled toward them in a great wave.

Her breathing hitched. It was the end of the world.

Alar materialized beside her, blood trickling down his forehead. Wordlessly, he vaulted onto Bracken's bare back and grabbed Lara's hand, hauling her up in front of him in one wrenching motion.

Screams cut through the night. Then the mountain swallowed them—a roar like a thousand fists pounding stone, drowning out everything human.

The Shee warriors sprinted past, cloaks billowing behind them. Cailean heaved Eithne onto his stallion's withers, while Roth hauled Duana up, both girls dangling half-on, half-off. Bree dragged Annis by the arm, their horses plunging and rearing. Vyr threw himself onto Ruari's pony, the seer clutching his waist. Sablebane did the same with Ren.

"Move! Move!" Someone shouted—maybe Cailean, maybe Roth—the words shredded by the thunder of the landslide.

A rock the size of a skull slammed into the ground three feet away. Then another. And another. The air turned to grit, dirt boiling up in choking waves that scraped Lara's throat raw.

Black fur streaked past—Mor and Dorka, the clag-doo's muscles bunching and releasing. Green followed—Skaal, low to the ground, ears flat.

Lara wrapped her fists in Bracken's mane. The mare's body heaved beneath her, foam already flecking her neck. Behind her, Alar's arm locked around her waist like an iron bar.

"Go!" he urged the mare forward.

The path unwound before them—too narrow, too dark, each turn coming too fast. Bracken's hooves skidded on loose stone. A drop yawned just beyond the path's edge, a void waiting to swallow them.

The mountain bucked. Shuddered. Tried to throw them off its back.

Lara's lips moved—a prayer to the Gods, though she couldn't hear her own voice over the deafening roar behind them. Every instinct screamed at her to look back, to see how close death was riding.

But she didn't.

23: NO SOFT WORDS

"REMIND ME TO never piss off a cnoc-bane."

Cailean's gravelly voice shattered the eerie stillness that had followed the rockfall.

Vyr muttered something under his breath in response. "We should have offered them something before retiring … even a song or two might have helped."

Ren, who now rode with Vyr, grimaced. "Aye … but we were all exhausted," she murmured. "We forgot about them."

They'd just pulled up their horses, farther down the mountain. Fern and those who'd fled on foot were bent over, panting from their sprint.

Fortunately, the Shee were fast. None of the Marav could have outrun that deadly wave.

The rockslide had ended, and a deep hollow silence had settled. In the moonlight, Lara could see that many of her companions—Shee and Marav alike—bore cuts from the rocks and stones that had rained down on them before the mountainside gave way. Skaal was limping.

"We should keep going," Alar said roughly. "There isn't enough space here for us to camp."

"Aye … there's a ledge farther down," Cailean agreed. "Let's go."

They urged their mounts on.

"Where's your stag?" Lara asked, suddenly aware of how close she and Alar were sitting. The heat of his body was a furnace against her back. Now that they were no longer fleeing for their lives, embarrassment flushed over her. The front of his thighs pressed against the back of hers. It was too intimate.

"Reedav and the others traveled farther down the mountain when we made camp," he replied. "They'll rejoin us at dawn."

Bracken stumbled then, and Lara lurched forward. Alar's arm looped around her waist, catching her. She fell back against him. For an instant, the hardness of his lithe body pressed indecently against hers.

And then, mercifully, he released her.

Lara pulled herself forward onto Bracken's withers. It was uncomfortable to perch there, but preferable to the distracting strength and heat of his body.

"Your cheek was bleeding earlier." Alar's voice was subdued, with a wary edge to it now. "Did you get hit anywhere else?"

"No." *Gods.* Why did her voice sound so breathless? "And you?"

"Just a knock to the forehead." He paused then. "We were lucky."

"Thanks to you." She forced the words out. They needed to be said. If Alar hadn't reacted so swiftly, they'd have been swallowed by the rockslide. "You acted fast."

The clip-clop of their horses' hooves on the rocky path echoed through the night. They rode in single file now, keeping close to the scree-covered slope to the south, and away from the edge.

"About earlier," Alar said finally. His voice had lowered now, so that only Lara could hear him. "I meant what I said … I wasn't trying to manipulate you."

She stiffened. "Can we *not* talk about this?"

"Aye, we must." An edge crept into his tone. "If you continue to misunderstand me."

Heat washed over her. "What's to misunderstand?"

"That I'm trying to crawl back into your good favor. I'm not." Her heart started to punch against her ribs, but he wasn't yet finished. "We agreed to be allies, remember? That means you need to stop snarling at me."

Her cheeks started to burn, and she was glad he couldn't see her face.

Was her estranged husband—the man who'd dealt her a savage blow—telling her off?

Angry words surged up her throat, but she choked them down. No. She wouldn't engage.

Even so, her temper simmered, looking for an outlet.

But there was another problem. Their proximity. With each stride, she slid farther off Bracken's withers and straight back against Alar's crotch. Her cheeks started to burn. The fever hadn't returned though. Instead, embarrassment pulsed like an ember in her breast. It was ridiculous, really. They'd lain together. He'd parted her thighs and feasted on her sex. He'd sunk his teeth into her shoulder as he spilled deep inside her. She'd nearly passed out as ecstasy pulsed through her womb.

Lara squeezed her eyes shut. *Gods.* She couldn't go there. Why was she thinking about those lewd things when she was so angry with him? She had to stop. But curse her, the memories kept intruding. Her breathing grew shallow, warmth kindling in her lower belly.

She was aroused now, painfully aware of him. Her fury melted away like spring snow; she couldn't hold onto it.

The musky scent of his skin, the smoky smell of leather, and that hint of wild mint that was uniquely him made her pulse quicken. His nearness overwhelmed her senses.

She tried to slow her breathing, tried to think of something else, yet when Bracken stumbled again on the rough road, he caught her once more to stop her from toppling over the mare's neck. She slid back against him, their bodies flush.

Alar made a strangled noise and grabbed her hips, pushing her away from him. But it was too late. She'd felt it.

Something thick and hard was pressing against her backside.

Lara bit down on her lower lip. Even as desire jolted through her. *Fuck.*

The journey down to the ledge Cailean had mentioned was the longest ride of Alar's life.

Every jolting stride brought Lara's delicious arse up against his groin. The chafing was unbearable. His prick had turned to wood, straining against the tight leather of his breeches. Much more of this, and he'd humiliate himself.

The feel of her soft body against his, the tickle of her hair against his face, was driving him mad. Like him, she hadn't bathed in a few days, yet he could still smell a hint of lavender on her.

Lara perched rigidly in front of him, no doubt horrified by his erection.

He hadn't wanted her to know. She already thought he was an animal—and now she'd think him a degenerate beast.

And he was.

His body cried out for her. He longed to halt their horse, let the others go ahead, while he pulled Lara to the ground, spread her out under him, and sank into her heat. He'd make her his again.

You wouldn't get that far. She'd knee you in the balls.

The reminder punctured his heated thoughts like an iron spike through a bladder.

All the same, he'd had to make things clear earlier. He wasn't Lara's adversary. He never had been, not really. Her hostility had gotten under his skin. What was he supposed to do? Prostrate himself before her. Tell her he was a maggot that deserved to be ground into the dirt?

No. He'd made mistakes—ones there was no coming back from—but he had his pride. They were equals on this journey.

And yet, she now knew he wanted her. Badly. It was humiliating. Her nearness was a cruel punishment, a reminder of everything he'd cast aside. Everything he'd lost.

Closing his eyes, he prayed to the Hearthkeeper for this ride to be over.

Sliding from Reedav's back, Alar's gaze swept over the line of trees stretching west. The carpet of sycamore, oak, and birch was changing hue now, bright-yellow and deep-gold leaves amongst the darker greens of evergreens like yew and pine.

The Hallow Woods.

After three days of travel, they'd made it over The Hog's Back. The woodland stretched right up to the edge of the foothills. The mountains reared above them, slicing into an overcast sky. It had been a dull and windless day, eerily so. The Gaulas hadn't returned—not yet anyway—yet the stillness made everyone quiet, watchful.

Around them, the shadows were lengthening. They still had some distance to travel today, for they planned to reach a cave farther north, in the foothills of the Goatfells, before nightfall. However, since a burn bubbled across pale stones nearby, this was a good spot to water their animals and take a short breather.

The sight of the woodland brought gusty sighs of relief from everyone.

Finally, The Hog's Back was behind them. Of course, Alar had been the one to suggest taking this route. He didn't regret it, yet the journey had been even harder than he'd expected.

Aye, it felt good to be standing on the other side of The Goatfells. Even so, he noted that none of the Marav appeared comfortable here, especially Cailean. The chief-enforcer wore a grim expression as he led his stallion over the burn. Of course, Alar had heard of the massacre that had taken place here a few years earlier. The news had traveled far and wide over Albia. Several enforcers had fallen that night.

For his part, Alar had crossed the Hallow Woods a few times over the years, yet he always avoided the ancient burial site on its southern edge. The Slew dwelled amongst these trees, and it was best not to disturb them.

The Shee didn't gaze upon the woods warily though. Mor and her Ravens looked west, their eyes soft with longing. Dunmorth Barrow lay at the heart of the forest—a sacred place for Shee. Only fae-kind traveled easily in this place. It was safe enough in daylight, if you kept to the paths and didn't stray into its dark corners—thankfully, they wouldn't be going in that direction.

Skaal stared into the shadowy trees, golden eyes sharp. The blood on her left shoulder had dried now, and her limping had eased as they made their way down the mountainside. Dorka yowled before scraping her claws feverishly upon the ground. After three days without trees to blunt her claws, she was desperate.

"Come now, sweet one." Mor swung down from the clag-doo's back. "Let's help you out." She led Dorka over to the tree line, looking on then as the feline clawed at a sycamore trunk in a frenzy. Alar noted the soft expression on Mor's face, the affection in her eyes.

Meanwhile, Reedav walked over to the bubbling burn and started to drink. Alar knelt next to him, scooping up water in his hands and slaking his own thirst. They had fewer waterskins with them now, although they'd fill what they had before moving on.

Shifting back from the water's edge, Alar stroked Reedav's ruddy coat, warmth kindling in his chest. He'd been relieved to see the stag at dawn.

He glanced then over at where Lara was watering her mare. Like the others, she now rode bareback, as their saddlery and saddlebags lay under a pile of rocks on the western slope of The

Hog's Back. Head bent close to her horse, she stroked its neck and murmured soft words.

The warmth faded. His breathing quickened, and his gut hardened. She had no soft words for him.

Ashes. Was he jealous of a horse?

He cut his attention away—to find his father watching him.

Wynn Sablebane stood barely more than two yards away, next to his own stag.

Father and son hadn't spoken since their tense exchange the day after leaving Dulross. But the Slew attack and their journey across The Goatfells had taken their toll.

Their gazes locked, and then, to Alar's surprise, Sablebane favored him with a faint smile. "Reedav has taken to you," he said gruffly. "An honor indeed."

Unnerved, Alar stared back at him. An awkward pause ensued before he found his tongue. "It would seem so," he replied before turning away.

Uneasiness churned in the pit of Lara's belly as she led Bracken toward the cave's shadowy entrance. Her mouth was dry, her skin clammy.

A fever had plagued her for most of the day. But that wasn't the worst of it. Her mind had wandered constantly, and she'd lost time twice.

She was getting sicker.

Pausing before the cave mouth, she glanced up at the sky, shivering. The sun had now dipped behind the edge of the woods. Mist had snaked in as they rode, drifting from the trees, blocking out the bulk of the mountains rearing above them. It felt like days since she'd last seen the sun, and she wondered if the spirits that plagued the night now influenced the day too. Heaviness lay in the air, and although she didn't wish for the return of The Gaulas, she found herself missing the Four Winds. The shriek of The Whistle would come as a relief, would shatter the oppressive stillness.

Inside the cave, her companions were already busy with their evening routine. Four of the Shee had gone hunting as they'd traveled north, catching up with the rest of their party later, each with a brace of fat red grouse. A fine supper awaited.

Duana and Eithne sat with the Shee as they plucked and gutted the birds. Next to them, Roth lit a hearth—without Lara's assistance this time—while others went out to collect firewood.

Lara led Bracken to the back of the cave, where Annis, Ruari, and Ren were seeing to the other horses, rubbing them down and checking their feet and legs for injuries. Forcing herself to ignore the dread that clenched under her ribs like a fist, she tied up her mare.

"You've done me proud, lass," she murmured to Bracken, stroking her neck. The contact soothed her. "You have nerves of iron."

The horse snorted, tossing her head.

Lara huffed a sigh. "I know … you're hungry. Let me get you some supper."

Slapping Bracken on the rump, she went outside to pick grass with Ren. They had no grain to feed the horses with, and there had been little time to allow them to graze.

Outdoors, the light was fading fast.

The two women set about their task. It relaxed Lara to focus on something practical. Riding gave her too much time to think.

And when she did, her mind drifted. Concentrating became difficult, like trying to catch hold of water.

But this repetitive job steadied her.

Some of the grass was dry and stalky; it was late autumn now, and the greenery was dying off. However, their mounts would no doubt eat it. As they worked, Lara and Ren filled the skirts of their over-tunics, and when they were full, carried the grass back into the cave. The horses snatched at the grass immediately. They were hungry. This task would take several trips.

Annis joined them when they went back outside.

Tearing off clumps of grass, Ren cast a nervous glance over at the dark line of trees. The back of her neck prickled. "It feels as if something is watching us," she muttered.

Annis harrumphed. "There will be … more than the Slew live in those woods."

"We'd better make sure a line of torches burns outside the cave entrance then," Lara replied, deciding it was best to be practical rather than let the shadowy forest unnerve them. "Best we take all the precautions we can."

"Cailean lost his ward stones in the rockslide," Ren said then. "But I will hold vigil after supper."

Lara glanced the bard's way. Even in the dimming light, the lines of fatigue on the young woman's face were clear. Her eyes were bloodshot and hollowed. "You need to rest."

Ren pulled a face. "We *all* do, My Queen."

24: SHARING SECRETS

LARA ENTERED THE cave carrying the last armload of grass, stems poking through her fingers. Behind her, Sablebane shoved torches into the ground—a ring of fire between them and whatever hunted in the dark.

She walked past the hearth, where grouse carcasses dripped fat into the flames. Her companions sat in a rough circle, their voices a low murmur that didn't quite reach her.

She stopped and stood there, watching.

Fern's slender hands moved through the air as she explained something to Duana and Eithne. The sisters leaned in, faces intent, while two Ravens edged closer to listen. A few feet away,

Vyr and Ruari debated something—she caught the word 'Gateway' before their voices dropped again. Closer, Alar sat beside Mor, their heads bent together.

Shee and Marav. Sitting together. Talking like *allies*. Like people who might actually trust each other.

Something twisted in Lara's chest. Not quite hope—it was too fragile for that—but something akin to it.

This wouldn't last. She knew that. Once they reached The Shattered Crown, once they sealed the rift, everything would fracture again. Old hatreds ran too deep. She'd go back to Duncrag, and Mor would return to Cannich or Sheehallion, and the brief warmth of this strange fellowship would freeze over.

Her stomach clenched. Gods, she was so tired of fighting. Tired of keeping lists of enemies, of nursing grudges. She'd seen what waited at the end of that road: a woman alone, consumed by her own rage, becoming the very thing she'd denied being.

Her father's daughter.

If the fire-madness didn't take her, bloodlust would.

Her boot caught on something—a stone, jutting up from the cave floor. She stumbled, grass spilling from her arms.

Hands grabbed her, steadied her, and pulled her upright.

Alar.

Of course, it was Alar.

Their faces hung inches apart. She could see the flecks of black in his grey eyes. The smell of leather filled her nostrils. Heat radiated off him. Her pulse kicked hard against her ribs. Why? Why was it always him? Why did he appear every time she faltered, and why—Gods help her—why did his nearness scramble every coherent thought in her head?

"Are you all right?" Concern roughened his voice.

"Aye." The word came out too husky, too raw. "Fine. Thank you."

Releasing her arm, he stepped back, putting distance between them.

Lara walked on, legs unsteady. She made her way to the back of the cave, where Ren and Annis had dumped their grass before joining the others. Alone now with just the horses for company, she added her grass to the pile. She then brushed stalks off her tunic with hands that trembled slightly.

She didn't go to the fire. She couldn't. Not yet.

Instead, she moved to Bracken's side and pressed her cheek against the mare's warm neck. The horse's solidity anchored her. Everything was piling up—the fever, the lost time, the fear of what the fire was doing to her. And underneath it all, threading through every other worry: him. Always him.

"Enough," she whispered into Bracken's mane. "No more doubts. I must stop worrying about things I can't control." Her fingers curled into fists against the mare's shoulder. "Just let me get through the next few days. I'll face the future then. I'll face *him* then."

She lifted her head. Straightened her spine. Pushed her shoulders back.

Something fluttered in her chest—not nerves, but determination clawing its way back to the surface. She'd survived the Heather Path. Survived the Slew, The Grey Ghost, and a deadly rockfall. Survived seeing herself clearly for the first time and not breaking under the weight of it.

She could survive this too. They were making good time. If they kept pushing on, they'd reach The Shattered Crown for Gateway. They wouldn't be able to slow their pace though.

Tonight's waxing gibbous moon was a reminder that time was running out.

The task ahead was too important. The rift wouldn't seal itself. The dead wouldn't stop pouring through. And if she failed—if she let herself get distracted by old wounds and inconvenient feelings—everyone she'd ever loved would pay the price.

She couldn't let anything distract her.

She couldn't fail.

Even if it meant ignoring the part of her that still ached when Alar looked at her. Even if it meant burying the treacherous warmth that bloomed in her chest every time he steadied her fall.

Especially then.

Seated by the fire, Alar watched Lara take her place.

On the far side. As distant as possible from him. He marked it, yet he didn't blame her. It didn't help that he kept staring at her like a lackwit. Kept helping her. Kept stepping in where he wasn't wanted.

Irritation twisted in his chest. He needed to pull back, to give the woman room to breathe. But the truth of it was that she consumed his thoughts—she had for a while. He'd made a choice a year earlier and had been on the wrong path ever since.

His gut clenched.

He might as well admit it to himself. It was time to stare the truth in the eye. Justice for his wulver brothers and sisters had meant everything to him, but his decision had been about more than that. He'd wanted revenge against the people who'd spurned him, hunted him, and turned him into an outcast. He'd been as bitter as wormwood, unable to see past it.

But he did now—only now it was too late.

Mor handed him some grouse then. Nodding, he took it, even though his current thoughts had just killed his appetite.

Across the fire, Cailean was ribbing Roth about something. Both men's faces were drawn with fatigue, yet Roth's gaze gleamed with amusement as he replied.

Alar envied them both.

Neither of them had grown up knowing they were a mistake. They were proud Marav men. He would never be accepted by them. Once, he hadn't cared. He'd have spat at their feet rather than try to befriend any of them. However, tonight, tiredness had lowered his defenses.

A hollowness filled him.

Worse still, those two men had Lara's respect. Her trust. Yet, he'd cast it aside like it hadn't mattered.

"Aren't you hungry?"

Alar dragged his attention from Cailean and Roth and glanced at where Mor sat, cross-legged, Eagal perched upon her shoulder.

"Not overly," he admitted, looking down at the greasy hunk of grouse he held. His stomach had firmly closed.

"Well, I'll have that if you don't want it."

Gratefully, he passed it over, watching as she tucked into it. She appeared to be enjoying her food. Eating in a dingy cave like this would be new for her, but she seemed at ease all the same.

"You're subdued this eve," Mor noted after swallowing a mouthful.

"I'm tired," he answered, guarded now.

She studied him for a few moments. "Those scars are impressive," she said softly. "How did you get them?"

Alar tensed, aware that others nearby were now watching them—Fern and Sablebane included. Lara was the only person he'd told about his scars. He didn't like having an audience and thought about refusing to answer. However, a challenge glinted in Mor's eyes now.

His pulse quickened. She was testing him.

"Both are testament to how much the Marav despise your kind," he replied.

That got everyone's attention at the fireside. Lara glanced up from where she'd been staring absently at the flames, while beside her, Cailean frowned. Focusing on Mor once more, Alar lifted his hand, tracing the scar that slashed down his cheek. "This was from when a villager tried to kill me as a child." His hand lowered to the second scar around his throat. "And this is from when the local overking's brother attempted to string me up a few years after … as you can see … they both failed."

He wasn't sure why he did it, but he glanced over at his half-sister and father then.

And what he glimpsed there surprised him. Fern's expression was almost … anguished, while Sablebane's face was all taut angles, his eyes shadowed.

Alar stared his father down, issuing a challenge of his own.

Did you think I had an easy time of it, you rutting bastard?

"A half-blood must weather much," Mor murmured, drawing his attention once more. "You are a reminder of a truth that neither of our races wishes to accept."

Sourness flooded Alar's mouth. He wasn't enjoying this conversation. "And what's that?"

Mor's lips curved into a rueful smile. "That there are more things that unite us than separate us."

"Maybe things need to change then," Lara spoke up, her voice carrying across the hearth. "After we're done at The Shattered Crown, you and I need to talk, Mor."

The two queens locked gazes then, Alar forgotten.

The silence drew out before Mor slowly nodded.

After supper, Alar gratefully took his turn at watch. Standing at the entrance to the cave, listening to the murmur of voices behind him as his companions tried to get comfortable on the hard ground, he stared moodily through the line of torches.

A long, harrowing wail split the night.

Alar stiffened, murmuring an oath under his breath. The Weeper had found them.

They'd had regular visits from her at Dulross, but had been spared of late. He grimaced then. Not that they didn't have other, far more dangerous, spirits to contend with.

Even so, the keening cry made his temples ache. Numbness settled over him. Hopelessness dug its claws deep.

The scuff of heavy boots on hard-packed earth made him turn. Cailean stepped up at his side. A moment later, Skaal pushed in between them, tail wagging. She nudged at Alar, demanding affection.

Trying to ignore the despair that rolled over him in dizzying waves, Alar reached out and stroked her neck. He glanced up then, marking the severe cast of the chief-enforcer's face. "You know it's my tattoo, don't you?" he said, lifting his other hand to his chest as Skaal nuzzled into him. "It gives me a bond with wolf-kind."

Cailean snorted. "I don't give a fuck about that."

Alar lifted an eyebrow. *Liar.*

Cailean met his eye then, his gaze narrowing. "But what I *do* care about is my High Queen's well-being." His voice was low and gruff, almost a growl.

Silence fell while Cailean's words hung in the air. Alar stiffened. He wanted to tell him that he too cared about Lara, yet he wisely refrained. Such a response would likely earn him a fist in the mouth.

"You want to see her broken." The accusation fell like an axe.

"No." Heat rolled over Alar. "You're wrong. I don't." He'd never wanted that.

"But you *could* break her." Cailean's lips twisted. "She's strong … but she has a weakness. *You.*"

Alar stared back at him. His heart started to kick against his ribs. He was still reeling when Cailean leaned in, as if about to share a secret.

However, something else rolled off his tongue. A threat. "Hurt her again, and I'll kill you."

25: A BRAVE FLAME

"WELCOME TO CRASK, My Queen!"

The slender man with a thick mane of flaxen hair swept into a bow. "You must take my roundhouse while you're here."

Lara studied Connor mac Garth's face—young and open, despite the shadows under his eyes. "That's kind, but we're a small party. Another dwelling will do."

He smiled, although the expression was strained. "Of course. And you'll be wanting supper?"

"Aye," Roth cut in. "Blood sausage. Bread. Cheese. Ale. Lots of it."

Connor's blue eyes widened slightly.

Lara shot Roth a sharp look. "Forgive my captain. We've had a few lean days."

Lean barely covered it. They'd hunted what they could since the cave, but game had been scarce—unnaturally so. The land felt wrong, like something had curdled in the soil itself. Their last two suppers had left everyone hollow-bellied and irritable.

And all the while, as they'd pushed hard toward Crask, they'd been aware that the full moon loomed like a specter. As hungry and tired as they all were, their stop here would have to be a brief one.

Seeing Loch Glass's dark surface through the fog had been a relief. Crask rose from the water on its man-made island, the largest crannog on these shores. Roundhouses clustered at the center—wood and wattle walls, turf roofs sagging with damp. More dwellings perched on wooden walkways that radiated outward like wheel spokes, their pilings sunk deep into the loch bed.

Woodsmoke curled through the air. The aroma of baking bread threaded through the resinous scent, making Lara's mouth flood with saliva. But other smells also intruded: fish left too long in nets, the sour tang of spoiled grain, and underneath it all, something she couldn't name. Something dank and disturbing. The spirit world was closing in, tainting their own.

Her stomach growled despite the unease prickling her skin. Like her companions, she was starving.

Her nose wrinkled. She also stank—they all did. First thing: a bath.

"We'll need supplies for our journey," Mor said, her voice cutting through Lara's thoughts.

Connor's gaze snapped to the Raven Queen.

His expression shifted, going from welcoming to cold in an instant. His shoulders went rigid.

Lara tensed as well. Mor had suggested the Shee 'guise' themselves as Marav warriors. Their magic allowed them to wear the skin of others for a short while. It would make things easier, less tense, but Lara had refused. If their races were ever going to move past centuries of hatred, they needed to start appearing together. United.

Even if it made moments like this excruciating.

"Connor," Lara said quietly, drawing his attention back. She kept her voice low, conversational. "Could we speak? Just for a moment?"

Something flickered in his eyes—relief, maybe, at being pulled away from Mor's unsettling presence. He nodded and stepped aside with her, far enough that their words wouldn't carry.

Lara glanced back at the crannog—at the roundhouses with their sagging roofs and the walkways where fog clung like cobwebs. On the approach, she'd seen the fields on the shore, where late-season crops should have been standing tall. Instead, brown stalks listed sideways, leaves curled and blackened. Dying.

"I saw your fields," she said softly.

Connor's throat worked. He looked away, toward the grey water. "Aye."

"And the spirits? They've been worse?"

"Much worse." The words came out rough. "The Loch-Bhàn took two fishermen last week. The aughisky drowned a child. And the Slew" —he swallowed hard— "they hunt regularly now." He cut himself off, as if worried he'd said too much.

Lara stepped closer, lowering her voice further. "Connor, look at me."

He did. Reluctantly.

"We're going to Darkmere," she said. "To The Shattered Crown. There's something there … something the Raven Queen and I believe can help fix this." She gestured vaguely toward the dying world around them. "All of this."

His eyes searched her face. Looking for certainty. "What kind of something?"

"I can't say more. Not yet." She held his gaze. "But I need you to trust me. Can you do that?"

A long pause. Around them, the fog pressed closer, muffling any sounds. The water lapped against the pilings with a soft rhythmic slap.

"The Shee," he said finally. His voice had dropped to barely a whisper. "You're traveling with them? Working with them?"

"I am."

"My Queen." Censure hardened his voice.

"I know what I'm asking." Lara glanced back at where Mor stood with her Ravens, a dark cluster of cloaks and gleaming eyes. She understood the wrongness they represented to people like Connor. To them, the fae were dangerous. Cruel and capricious. "I know what they are to you. But Connor" —she turned back to him— "If we don't do this, if we don't work together, there won't be anything left to protect. The veil between the dead and the living is failing. You've seen how the world has changed. You *know*."

His throat worked. A nerve jumped in his cheek. He looked quietly terrified—not of her, but of everything her words implied. Of the choice she was forcing him to make.

Behind him, his wife, Orla, stood watching, their wee daughter swaddled against her chest. The bairn was too quiet, Lara realized. Babies should fuss, should cry. This one didn't.

Seeing the direction of her gaze, Connor glanced over his shoulder. And when he turned back, the shadow in his eyes told her that he understood there was something wrong with the bairn as well.

"Six days," Lara said softly. "We need supplies to get us there and back. Food, water, whatever you can spare. That's all I'm asking."

Connor looked at her for a long moment. Then at Mor. Then back at the crannog—his home, his people, all of it slowly dying under a grey sky.

"Aye," he said finally. The word sounded like it cost him. "Aye, My Queen. For *you*."

"Thank you." She touched his arm briefly. "I won't forget this."

He nodded, but his eyes remained shadowed. He gestured to Orla, who stepped forward with the too-quiet bairn. "My wife will show you to your lodgings."

A short while later, as they followed Orla deeper into the crannog, Lara couldn't shake the feeling settling in her bones like winter cold. The dying crops. The silent baby. The fog that wouldn't lift. The chill that had nothing to do with the season.

The spirits were taking over.

And she was running out of time to stop them.

Inhaling the scent of lavender, Lara then sighed. *Gods. What a relief.* Washing away days of dirt and grime was beyond satisfying. She leaned over the earthen washbowl in her alcove and soaped up her hair. Then, picking up a ewer of cold water, she rinsed it clean.

Back in Duncrag, she enjoyed long soaks in an iron tub. She'd lean back against the rolled rim, eyes closed as the hot water soaked into her limbs. Standing at a washbowl wasn't the same, but she didn't care.

Being clean against was what mattered. For a few moments, she could put all her worries behind her.

Her extra clothes had been in the saddlebags the rockslide had taken. As such, Orla had given her one of her tunics to wear. Likewise, all the members of their party would leave their old clothes here to be laundered and picked up when they returned from The Shattered Crown.

Lara's pulse quickened. *Just three days.*

When they'd set off on this journey, the destination had seemed distant. No longer though. Now, it breathed down their necks.

Reaching for a drying sheet, Lara toweled off her wet hair. As she did so, she cast an eye around her alcove. It was simple. A sleeping nook with a nest of furs. A ledge where she'd placed her rosewood figures of The Five. A clay pot for her to relieve herself in during the night, if necessary. A soft sheepskin beneath her feet.

Longing wreathed up. How she'd love to stay here for a few days. The alcove was much more rustic than she was used to, yet she liked that.

But no, time raced against them now.

If they departed tomorrow, they'd arrive at The Shattered Crown just in time for Gateway.

This alcove will be waiting on the way back, she reminded herself. *You can rest then.*

Orla had also left her a wooden comb. Picking it up, she gently teased out her tangled hair. She was still bone-weary, but being clean again made all the difference.

A short while later, she pushed aside the heavy curtain and emerged from the alcove, stepping out onto the rush-strewn floor. Her gaze swept over the shadowy interior. Carven oak pillars held up a vast conical roof. A hearth burned brightly in the center of the space while half a dozen curtained alcoves lined it—spaces many of their party would sleep in. The rest would find a spot by the fire.

Lara settled onto a low stool. Around the hearth, her companions were doing the same—arranging themselves in a loose circle, shoulders relaxing for the first time in days.

Two slaves moved among them, iron collars catching the firelight at their throats. They set down trenchers piled high: bread still steaming from the oven, cheese with a rind like old leather, and cured sausage glistening with fat. They filled wooden cups to the brim with ale, foam sliding down the sides.

Lara's mouth watered. She grabbed a piece of bread and tore into it. The taste exploded across her tongue—oats, yeast, and salt. She almost groaned. When had food ever tasted this good?

Around her, the others had bathed and changed. With clean clothes and skin, the transformation was startling.

Mor wore plain charcoal—a tunic that should have looked austere but instead clung to her lithe frame like a second skin. She'd let her black hair down, and it fell past her shoulders, still damp at the ends.

Lara's gaze drifted across the fire and stopped.

Alar's hair hung dark and wet across his shoulders. He'd traded his black leather for a fawn-colored tunic and breeches. She'd never seen him wear anything but black. The lighter color suited him; it made his pale skin glow warm in the firelight and contrasted with his dark hair.

She realized she was staring. Heat crawled up her neck. She jerked her gaze away, focusing hard on her trencher.

A woman had joined them. She was of middling years, with curly black hair, and she wore scarlet robes that seemed to drink the firelight. Mairead. A sacrificer. She'd declined to join them on their mission when they met her earlier, yet she agreed to travel south with them on their return from Darkmere. By then, Cailean would need the blood-letting. He'd have to wait until the full moon, but Mairead would be ready.

Cailean helped himself to some sausage, his gaze flicking to the sacrificer. "How did you escape Cannich?"

The question landed softly, but the air shifted. A subtle tightening.

"I was visiting family here when the Shee took the fort." Mairead's voice stayed steady, but her eyes slid toward Mor and her Ravens. A veiled glance. "I couldn't go back."

"There were many druids living there." Annis set down her bread, half-raised to her mouth. "What happened to them? Did any others escape?"

Mairead's face twitched. "I—"

"We executed them," Mor replied, cutting the woman off.

The warmth died.

Just like that. As if someone had thrown a bucket of water over the fire. Everyone went rigid. Breaths caught and held. The convivial ease of earlier shattered.

Lara's spine went rigid. Of course, they had. She'd known that. But Gods, did Mor have to put it so bluntly? Right now, when they'd finally started to relax in each other's company?

Vyr cleared his throat, the sound too loud in the sudden quiet. He shot Mor a look—pained, almost pleading. "Earth magic is dangerous to us. We couldn't let them live."

Around the hearth, jaws clenched. Brows drew down. Lara watched her companions' faces harden.

Heat pulsed in her own belly, anger rising. They'd killed druids. Her people. Executed them. And now they sat here eating bread and cheese like it meant nothing.

She forced herself to breathe. Forced herself to remember. The Marav weren't innocent either.

"We've killed innocents too." The words came out roughly. She didn't want to think about Cannich, and all those who'd fallen there. But she couldn't let their relationship fracture—not when they'd come so far. "My father hunted the Shee for years. Mercilessly." Cailean's shoulders went taut beside her, but she pushed on. "And when we took back Doure, we spared almost no one."

"It's war." Mor's voice stayed flat. On her shoulder, Eagal ruffled his black feathers. "Blood has to be spilled."

Lara's chin lifted. Her spine straightened. "Then let's end it."

Silence crashed down on them once more.

Everyone stared at their trenchers. No one moved. No one spoke. Not a single voice—Shee or Marav—rose to agree with her.

The lack of response made heat ignite under Lara's ribs. This was why the world was drowning. Because even now, even after everything, they couldn't let go.

The slaves had slipped away. So had Mairead, her scarlet robes vanishing through the doorway. Duana and Eithne lingered though. The sisters would stay here at Crask—it was too dangerous to take them farther. The rest would leave at dawn.

"Will you take us south with you?" Duana eventually broke the silence. "To Duncrag … when you return?"

Lara turned to her, grateful for something—anything—to pull them back from the edge. Bronze no longer glinted upon Duana's neck. Shortly after their arrival at Crask, the sisters had paid a visit to the crannog's smith to have their bed-slave collars removed.

Lara smiled, though it felt brittle. "Is that what you want?"

"Aye." Duana's voice went husky. Beside her, Eithne's blue eyes gleamed in the firelight. "It's not Dulross. But it's closer to home."

A few yards away, Alar shifted on his stool. The movement was small—just a tensing of shoulders, fingers tightening around his cup. Lara's smile faded. She watched him, wondering if he was sorry—if leading wulvers and Circines into Dulross kept him awake at night. If butchering the chieftain and his defenders had cost him anything at all.

Probably not.

And yet. He'd saved these lasses.

The man was a walking contradiction.

"You'll have a place in my broch." Lara turned back to the sisters, watched their faces soften, watched relief smooth the tension from their brows. "You have my word."

The fire crackled. Someone coughed. Slowly, the group began eating again. But the warmth didn't return. The ease was gone.

"Lara." Alar approached her as she was heading toward her alcove. "I need to speak to you … alone."

Halting, she cast him a wary look. The evening was settling in. Everyone's bellies were full, and their bodies cried out for soft furs. Cailean and Bree had retired before everyone else, and Mor shortly after. Lara couldn't wait to crawl into her sleeping nook. "*Now?*"

He nodded before gesturing to the door. "There's a storehouse next door."

Lara folded her arms across her chest. "Whatever it is, can't you just tell me here?"

Indeed, meeting him privately wasn't a good idea. Things had a way of spiraling when they were alone together. She had done her best to avoid him since they'd ridden double on Bracken, yet her cheeks still burned when she remembered his arousal. And her own.

"No." Stubbornness flared in his eyes. "This won't take long." He paused before softening his tone and adding, "*Please.*"

Moments passed. Then, huffing a curse under her breath, Lara pushed past him and grabbed a lantern from the wall. She just wanted to hide in her alcove until morning, but he wasn't going to let her. "Very well."

Outdoors, a thick mist wreathed through the crannog. The air was dank and so cold that their breathing clouded. Something feral howled in the night, the sound echoing across the water, and Lara's skin prickled. Fortunately, the storehouse was just a few strides away. Pushing open the wattle door, she stepped inside. The store was empty, save for a pile of sacks stuffed with oats in one corner. The lantern illuminated the drifting dust motes and stacked-stone walls.

Placing the lantern on a narrow ledge, she turned to Alar. "Out with it."

He stared back at her, his lean face all sharp angles in the shadowy storehouse. "I'm sorry," he said finally.

She stilled. "Sorry?"

"For everything. For lying to you. Betraying you. Hurting you." The words were halting, as if each one burned his gullet.

Lara's pulse started to thud against her breastbone. "You want forgiveness?"

A nerve flickered under one eye. "No … but *you* deserve an apology."

"So, you'll feel better, right?" Anger sparked then. "So, you can move on?"

He shook his head. "I'll never move on … but this isn't about me." He took a step forward, but she moved back, raising her hands, making it clear she didn't want him any closer. "I never deserved you."

"No, you didn't," she shot back. Dizziness swept over her. *Gods.* She was an idiot. She shouldn't have agreed to talk to him alone.

His throat worked. "From the moment we met in that dark wood, you enchanted me, Lara. You are beautiful and kind, yet resilient. Honest. Your decency in this depraved world is a brave flame that stands against the darkness." He halted there, breathing hard. "You gave me your trust … something fragile and precious … and I shattered it." His eyes glittered now. "I will always be sorry that I can never rebuild what I broke."

Tension throbbed between them, in time with the *Ord-ree seal* that now pulsed like an ember on her, casting the storehouse in golden light. Fury swept over Lara. Oh, he was good with words. But how dare he say such things to her? How *dare* he? "No, you can't," she snarled. She stepped forward, shoving him hard in the chest. To her surprise, he didn't budge. It was like hitting a tree.

His gaze guttered. "To be fair ... I did warn you that I wasn't good enough for you."

Lara barely heard him above the rush of blood in her head. Dizziness slammed into her. A crushing ache rose under her breastbone. "Get out," she rasped.

He didn't move.

"Leave, now!"

"Lara ... I—"

The crack of her palm connecting with his cheek filled the storehouse. She followed that up with a punch to the stomach. He grunted an oath. "Ashes. You don't—"

She stepped in then, her knee jerking upward, aiming for his cods.

Alar moved sharply back, avoiding the blow to his groin. She came after him, her fists pummeling into him.

And then, suddenly, she wasn't hitting him any longer. She was kissing him.

26: INSANITY

SHE WASN'T SURE how it happened.

One instant, she'd wanted to blacken his eye and shove his teeth down his throat. The next, she was climbing her husband like a tree.

The kiss was fierce. Instinctive. And he returned it, his mouth bruising hers.

Their hands clawed at each other. A wild hunger flared between them, while the *Ord-ree seal* continued to pulse. They both ignored it.

Alar drew her lower lip into his mouth and sucked it before capturing her tongue and doing the same. Dizziness swept over

Lara. She scrabbled at his vest, desperate to touch the skin beneath. Their bodies writhed together, limbs tangling, and she felt him, hot and hard, pressed up against her belly.

Growling, Lara bit down on his lower lip.

Alar snarled a curse against her mouth.

She then ground her hips against his. Goading him.

Their hands tore at each other's clothing now, even as their mouths remained locked.

Lara was vaguely aware of her tunic and under shift fluttering to the dusty floor, of the harness containing his daggers thudding against wood.

Her fumbling fingers burned to touch him. All of him.

Finally, they were both naked. Alar hauled her against him, his hands everywhere now, stroking, clutching, and squeezing. Frantic. Her fingers tangled in his still-damp hair. She then yanked his head back so she could bite his neck.

His gasp made excitement clutch at her lower belly. Reaching down, her fingers wrapped around his shaft, stroking its proud quivering length. Her breathing caught. Gods, he was beautiful.

He groaned into her mouth, and she thrilled at the sensual sound.

This was madness, but she craved insanity.

She didn't want to think right now—only to feel.

Their mouths attacked each other once more. Her hunger for him pounded through her, so fiercely now that her core started to ache.

Alar walked her backward so that she leaned up against the pile of stuffed sacks. The musty smell of oats embraced them. The rough sacking scratched her back, but she barely noticed. She was too busy sliding her hand up and down his prick, working him. Her stomach clenched once more as it grew harder still and swelled in her grip.

"Fuck!" He tore his mouth from hers. His teeth grazed the column of her throat, nipping the skin.

A desperate sound—halfway between a gasp and a sob—escaped her.

She released his shaft then, allowing him to move down her body. He cupped her breasts, pushing them together as he lathed each swollen nipple in turn with his tongue. He then started to suck.

Lara shuddered, her head falling back against the sacks. Pleasure pulsed straight down from her nipple to her aching quim. She writhed against him. "More!"

Alar growled another curse and sank to his knees before her, spreading her wide. Panting, he sat back on his heels, his hungry gaze raking over her exposed sex.

She started to tremble, even as she took him in. The strong lithe lines of his body. The glowing red eyes of his wolf's head tattoo. His parted lips, swollen from the violence of their kisses. The feral hunger in his eyes.

An instant later, he moved, throwing her legs over his shoulders. Then, his searing mouth dipped between her thighs.

Pleasure jolted through her womb at the first touch.

Lara canted her hips up to meet him, her hands tangling his hair once more as he devoured her. Shuddering, she thrust up to meet his swirling tongue. In response, he plunged it into her.

She bit down on her lower lip. Hard. *Gods*. She wanted to scream, but she couldn't. Others would hear. Heat smoldered in the cradle of her hips, the tension almost unbearable now. His tongue returned to the sensitive pearl of flesh above her entrance, teasing.

She shivered and groaned. And then, he was sucking her there, relentlessly.

It was too much. She shattered, bucking against him. Alar held her tight, continuing to pleasure her until she lay limp and trembling against the sacks. Sweat coated her skin, and her naked breasts heaved.

Her husband pulled back then, his gaze flicking up to meet hers. "Do you want me to fuck you, Lara?" he asked, his voice rough. "I'll stop, if you want."

Desperation clutched deep in her chest. "Don't you dare stop," she choked out.

His gaze smoldered as he moved her legs from his shoulders and rose smoothly to his feet. He then pinned her trembling thighs wide against the sacks. And then, staring deep into her eyes, he slid into her.

Lara gasped at the invasion. Despite how aroused she was, he was big, and she was tight. It almost hurt. Recklessness ignited then. She didn't fear pain. She welcomed it. Arching her back, she rolled her hips to bring him deeper still.

A whimper escaped her. And when their bodies were flush, she heaved a deep, trembling sigh. "This changes nothing," she ground out, meeting his gaze again. "I still hate you."

His eyes darkened, and he gave a slow sensual smile that made heat roll over her. "No," he said softly. "You don't."

And then, before she could reply, he gripped her hips tightly, withdrew to the tip, and drove into her.

Lara started to tremble.

Oh Gods, he was fucking her now—as she'd demanded.

This position, this angle, was intense. She could feel every inch of him, and when their bodies met, and he was buried to the hilt inside her, she clutched at his shoulders, her fingernails biting deep. Her tongue traced her lips, and her eyelids fluttered. She ground herself against him and was rewarded by a choked groan.

An instant later, he plunged into her again, harder still, and it was her turn to moan. Heat started to pulse in her lower belly. His prick rubbed up against a place that made her shudder and gasp. She could feel herself starting to unravel, and there was nothing she could do to stop it. Wet heat flooded through her loins.

"You'll be the end of me," he growled, fucking her hard now. "You know that?"

Lara swallowed a sob. No, he'd be *her* downfall. He already was.

Her pulse went wild then. His thrusts were deeper, more punishing. Something feral quickened inside her. He was relentless. Pushing her. Testing her.

"Oh, *Gods!*" Pleasure twisted and pulsed through her womb. She writhed against him, her head falling back as ecstasy pounded through her.

Alar slammed savagely into her. The heat of his release flooded through her loins. Letting go of her hips, he gripped the sacks on either side of her, bracing himself. His head had snapped back, his face twisting. A hoarse cry ripped from his throat.

Breathing hard, Alar bowed his head and squeezed his eyes shut. His body trembled in the aftermath of his climax. His eyelids stung, his throat thickened.

Ashes. He had to regain control.

Lara didn't speak. Didn't move. Their labored breathing filled the storehouse.

They stayed like that for a while, him still buried deep inside her.

Eventually, Alar raised his head, eyes opening. Steeling himself, he looked at his wife.

She stared back. Her cheeks glistened in the light of the glowing lantern. Earlier, when she'd come, it had flared bright. He'd barely noticed though. He'd been too far gone. And now, his chest constricted. She was weeping.

Swallowing, he raised a hand, brushing away the tears with his knuckles.

Before meeting this woman, words had come easily to Alar. But now they deserted him. He couldn't apologize—not after his disastrous attempt earlier. He couldn't make light of this though, or pretend everything was fine.

It wasn't.

They'd both needed this, but sex couldn't fix what was broken between them. It couldn't rewrite the past. He didn't know what to say.

"This never happened," Lara whispered finally.

He nodded, even as his gut clenched. "Is that what you want?"

"Aye."

Their gazes fused. "Then I will respect your wishes," he said, hating how wooden he sounded. "I will also keep my distance from now on."

Her pine-green eyes glittered. *Fuck.* He couldn't leave things like this.

"I swear it on my mother's memory ... but know this." Catching her hand in his, he lifted it to his lips, kissing the back of it gently. "You're the only beautiful thing in this Gods-forsaken world."

Lara entered the roundhouse first. Alar would wait outside for a while. The hearth glowed at the heart of the space. Slumbering bodies, wrapped in cloaks, lay around it. Skaal had stretched out before Cailean and Bree's alcove, her snores rumbling through the shadowed interior.

Lara darted for her own alcove, pushing the curtain aside and letting it fall behind her.

And only then did she let herself go. Hands lifting to her face, she lowered herself to the sheepskin rug. The dyke gave way, and hot tears coursed down her cheeks. A sob clawed up her throat, but she choked it down.

No. She couldn't crumble.

The Shattered Crown awaited her, and so did an important task. The shadows that were slowly smothering Albia had to be driven back. The rift her ancestors had made had to be mended. She couldn't focus on anything else.

She wouldn't let him break her.

But tears still flowed, and the ache in her chest was almost unbearable. It was just as well she was strong, for life seemed intent on testing her mettle. Tonight, she walked upon a knife-edge edge though. Her defenses were brittle, and her frenzied coupling with Alar had left her fragile.

Hiccoughing, she climbed to her feet and did her best to scrub away her tears. "Pull yourself together, woman," she whispered. "You've cried enough over him."

She moved then over to the shelf where her rosewood figurines sat. Their polished surfaces gleamed in the light of the flickering cresset on the wall above.

Lara picked up the figurine of The Mother. Then, whispering a heartfelt prayer, she brought the idol to her lips, kissing it lightly. That was a mistake, for the gesture reminded her of Alar's in that dusty storehouse. The pain in his eyes had been raw. The huskiness of his voice had betrayed him.

Heat washed over her as she recalled how she'd lost control. Her rage had felt good initially. Righteous. But then it had slid into desperation. Need.

I will always be sorry that I can never rebuild what I broke.

Gods. The anguish in his voice.

Tears rolled down her cheeks once more. She squeezed her eyes shut, her fingers tightening around the figurine.

"Hold fast," she whispered.

27: KEEPING HIS WORD

REEDAV SHIFTED BENEATH Alar, snorting and tossing his head. Alar leaned forward and stroked the stag's muscular neck with firm, steady pressure. "Easy," he murmured. "We'll move when I say."

The stag settled. Barely. His muscles still coiled like springs ready to release.

Alar understood the feeling. They couldn't linger here, not with the full moon so close. Nonetheless, for him, something else made him restless this morning.

Foreboding had woken him well before dawn—a cold certainty lodged behind his ribs like a blade. He'd lain there by the dying hearth, watching the embers pulse and fade, knowing something was about to go catastrophically wrong.

Then he'd remembered.

Something already had.

His jaw clenched hard enough to ache. Apologizing to Lara had been a mistake—what had he been thinking? The need had been building for days, a constant pressure under his breastbone, gnawing at him until he couldn't think straight. But giving in had led to an encounter that would haunt him until his last breath.

He was to blame. She'd initiated it—pulled him close, kissed him first. She'd made it clear what she wanted. But a better man would have stopped it, would have told her she'd regret it afterward. She would have been angry then, aye. But grateful later, once the madness of lust burned itself out.

He reached up and pinched the bridge of his nose hard. But he wasn't a better man. That was the core of it. And he'd never stop wanting her.

Behind him, the others were mounting up—horses, elks, and stags stamping, leather creaking, low voices murmuring farewells. Duana and Eithne stood at the edge of the walkway, wrapped in borrowed cloaks against the morning chill.

Alar stayed where he was. It wasn't him they'd come to see.

Roth moved forward and bent his head close to Duana's. Whatever he whispered made color rise in her cheeks. She nodded, shy and pleased at once.

Beyond them, a cluster of crannog-dwellers had gathered at the walkway's end. Connor stood among them, worry carved into the grooves around his mouth. The whole settlement had that look now—shadows under eyes, mouths pressed thin, the hunted wariness of people waiting for the next blow to fall. Life had grown brutal at Crask. But Lara had given them something: hope that the darkness closing in might finally end.

Reedav snorted again, tossing his head.

"Very well, lad." Alar let the stag move forward. Someone had to lead. It might as well be him. He'd deliberately left the roundhouse before Lara emerged from her alcove this morning—he couldn't face her, couldn't trust himself not to—

He cut the thought off. He'd keep his word. He wouldn't approach her again.

He urged Reedav to the front of the group, past Ravens on their elks and stags, past Vyr adjusting the weapons belt slung across his chest, past where Cailean and Bree whispered together. They all fell in behind him.

To the east, the last of the Goatfells reared up, their jagged tips catching the pale morning sun. To the north—their destination—the mountains of Darkmere rose like a wall against the sky. Alar's gaze lingered on those high-domed summits. Bleak country. Few Marav ventured that far into the northwest Uplands. It had brutal weather year-round: floods in summer, avalanches in winter. Nothing grew up there but tough grasses and lichen clinging to bare rock.

Only the Shee traveled there regularly, slipping in and out of Darkmere barrow like ghosts.

They left Loch Glass behind, riding into a steep-sided glen that carved north through the hills. A burn wound along the bottom, clear water bubbling over pale stones. The mist pulled back as they rode, but the clouds pressed lower, a grey ceiling bearing down.

After an hour, a wind kicked up—sharp, high-pitched, cutting through cloaks and tunics as if they were paper. The Whistle.

Alar pulled his borrowed cloak tighter. The wool helped against the cold biting at his face and hands. But it couldn't touch the ice lodged in his gut.

Nothing would.

He glanced back once—just once—to check everyone was following. His gaze skipped over Roth, just behind him. Over Bree and Cailean, and Annis, Ren, and Ruari hunched against the wind, and the Ravens riding in tight formation around Mor.

It found Lara.

She sat straight on Bracken's bare back despite the cold, chin lifted, eyes fixed ahead. Not looking at him. Deliberately not looking at him.

Good. And it *was* good. It was what they both needed.

Alar turned back to the path ahead, shoulders squared, and led them deeper into the North.

"There are cries on the air."

Lara's hands froze mid-motion, a stick halfway to the flames. She looked up.

Bree stood motionless, head tilted back, eyes scanning the darkening sky. Her body had gone still—the hunter's stillness that meant danger.

"The Slew?" Lara's voice came out hoarse. She dropped the stick, her fingers flexing.

Bree shook her head slowly. "No shrieking. Not yet."

"It's The Gaulas again." Mor approached the fire, her boots crunching on the sparse grass. She'd just finished tethering Dorka—Lara could hear the clag-doo's low growl behind them as she tore into a hare carcass. "Look north. The sky's turned pink."

She was right. The raw cold that had been flaying their skin all day had pulled back. The air felt wrong now. Too mild.

Lara twisted around to see for herself.

The northern sky had gone dusky rose, bruised at the edges. Beautiful, but beneath that beauty, voices tumbled over each other, worming their way into her ears.

You're pining for him, aren't you?

Her stomach turned to stone.

You're playing straight into his hands.

Her spine went rigid. She forced herself to turn back to the fire, to the circle of faces watching the sky with varying degrees of dread. "Aye," she said. Her voice came out flat. "It's The Gaulas."

Bree muttered something—a prayer or a curse, Lara couldn't tell. Beside her, Cailean's face had hardened. "We've got a rough night ahead then."

"I'll take my turn warding the camp." Vyr dumped an armload of dusty whin next to the firepit.

"As will I," Ren assured them, her sharp-featured face tight with determination.

Lara nodded, relief washing through her chest. She felt brittle tonight—stretched too thin, ready to snap. The fever had come back at dawn. She'd spent the morning caught between shivering and sweating, her body unable to decide whether to freeze or burn. By noon, it had receded, leaving her wrung out like a wet cloth. Then she'd lost time again. Most of the afternoon on this occasion—just gone, swallowed by a blank space in her memory.

Dread sat like a boulder in her belly. The last thing she needed was poison being poured into her ears all night.

You're falling apart! The voices crowed, gleeful. *You will fail. You will burn. You will—*

No. The word formed sharp and hard under her ribs. *No, I won't.*

She lowered herself to the ground, legs crossing beneath her. The earth was cold through her tunics, but the fire's heat washed over her face. Ruari and Annis were unwrapping food—oaten bread packaged in cloth, hard cheese, and apples that had gone slightly soft.

They'd made camp on a windswept hillside. Nothing grew here but heather, tough tussock grass, and clumps of thorny whin.

The food made its way around the circle. Bread torn into chunks. Cheese cut with daggers. Ale skins passed from hand to hand. Voices rose and fell—quiet conversations and forced laughter, the sounds people made when they were trying to pretend everything was fine.

Lara ate slowly. Or tried to. The bread turned to glue in her mouth and stuck in her throat. She chewed doggedly, her mind drifting, snagging on the flames that danced and flickered before her.

Gold. Orange. A core of white so bright it hurt to look at it directly.

She leaned forward. Just slightly. The bread in her hand forgotten.

The fire called to her. Whispered. Not with words—not like The Gaulas—but with something deeper. A pull in her chest. A hunger that had nothing to do with food.

Come closer. Give in. Let go.

Her fingers tingled. Heat bloomed under her skin, spreading up her arms, settling in her chest like coals banked for the night.

The urge to reach out—to touch the flames, to let them consume her, to stop fighting and just surrender—crashed over her like a wave.

She couldn't look away.

Around the fire, conversation continued. Someone laughed—Roth, maybe. Someone else asked for more ale.

Lara barely heard them.

And then her attention drifted to Alar. She didn't mean to look at him—she'd been so careful not to—but her gaze found him anyway.

He sat between Mor and Vyr, his profile sharp in the firelight. He hadn't approached her all day. She'd avoided him too. A careful dance of distance and deflection. He turned his head slightly, as if feeling the weight of her gaze, yet didn't look her way.

Her attention moved back to the flames. So warm. So bright.

"Lara."

A hand clamped around her arm, fingers digging in hard enough to bruise.

She blinked. The world swam back into focus—faces ringing the fire, all of them staring at her. When had the conversation stopped?

She stiffened, turning to Bree. Her warder's hand was still locked around her arm. "What?"

"I called your name." Bree's voice was quiet, controlled in that way that meant she was barely holding back alarm. "Five times, at least. You didn't hear me."

Lara's pulse kicked hard. "It's getting worse." The words scraped out. "Thank the Gods we're close."

"The fevers?" Mor leaned forward, firelight carving shadows under her cheekbones. "You're still losing time?"

Lara nodded. She looked down at her right hand, at the *Ord-ree seal* catching the firelight. "I'll be glad to be rid of this." Once, she'd worn it with pride. Now, she wanted to claw it off, tear it from her finger, and throw it into the fire.

The ring pulsed. Once. As if it had heard her.

"Soon," Mor said.

"We need to talk about what happens *after* The Shattered Crown." Alar's voice cut in.

He'd been quiet all evening, but now the authority in his voice made everyone turn.

"Assuming this works … that we close the rift and survive … what then?" He leaned forward, elbows on his knees, eyes locked on Mor. The firelight turned his face to planes and angles, all sharp edges. Never had he looked so much like his father. "Does our alliance end the moment the ritual is complete?"

Mor's jaw tightened. "Not necessarily."

"What kind of answer is that?"

Her dark eyes narrowed. The air between them shivered. "My first responsibility is to my own people."

"Of course it is," he said, his attention never wavering. "Just as Lara's is to hers. But that's not what I asked." He paused, letting silence swell between them. "Do we all go back to being enemies?"

Eagal shifted on Mor's shoulder, feathers ruffling, his beady gaze fixed on Alar. Vyr's face had gone carefully blank, while Sablebane watched his son intently.

"That depends." Mor's tone held a steely edge. "On whether the Marav … and wulvers … are willing to compromise."

Lara's gaze flicked between them, tension coiling in her gut. Alar was right to bring this subject up—she too wanted assurances from Mor—but his timing was poor.

"Alar." She didn't raise her voice; she didn't need to. He inclined his head slightly, acknowledging her, even as he continued to stare the Raven Queen down. "One thing at a time. Let's close the rift first. Then we'll figure out the rest."

He frowned. For a moment, she thought he'd push harder—demand commitments that Mor clearly wasn't willing to give.

He then sat back. "Very well," he said softly. "This conversation can wait … for now."

A nerve jumped in Mor's cheek, yet she said nothing.

Alar turned his gaze away from her then—from all of them—and stared into the fire. Lara watched him, noting the way he held himself apart now. The careful distance he'd been maintaining all day suddenly seemed deliberate. Calculated.

He'd do as promised. Stay away. No more watching her when he thought she wasn't looking. No more excuses to talk.

The realization landed strangely in her chest. Heavy and hollow at once.

She should be grateful. This was what she wanted.

Wasn't it?

You will never recover from him. The Gaulas slithered into her ear, gleeful and cruel. *He's an affliction you'll never cure.*

Her breath hitched. She shoved the vile voices back.

Aye, she would. Even if it killed her.

28: FROST AND FIRE

LARA PRESSED HER burning cheek to Bracken's neck and squeezed her eyes tight. For days now, dread had thundered through her every time the symptoms of fire-madness plagued her. They'd curdled her stomach and turned her mouth dry. But today, something had changed. Now, a dull fatalism filled her.

She was doomed. It didn't matter though. Not any longer. What did, was that she got to The Shattered Crown, that she sealed the tear in the veil. She kept remembering the hollowed gazes and strained faces of the crannog-dwellers. That silent newborn in Orla's arms.

She was going to fix this.

Around her, The Sharp Billed Wind tore across the bare hills, snagging at her clothing and blowing dust in her eyes. Its cold slap might have chilled everyone else to the marrow, but for her, it was a blessed relief. The first two days out from Crask, The Gaulas had pursued them, hectoring them like boggarts. But then, The Sharp Billed Wind had chased the spirit wind away. And with each furlong, the landscape grew bleaker and colder.

Lara glanced up at the sky then, searching for a glimpse of the sun. It was still hidden behind a dense curtain of low cloud, one even the wind couldn't budge. Mountains surrounded them now, gloomy jagged peaks that looked as if giants had hacked at the land with axes. Shards of black rock bit into the low cloud.

"I have something for the fever, My Queen." She turned from Bracken to find Ruari standing in front of her. He held up a cup of murky liquid. "The chieftain's wife provided me with some more healing herbs. This is a brew of willow bark." The seer's brow furrowed then. "I know your fever isn't the usual kind … but I thought this might help."

Lara forced a smile, touched by his concern. She took the cup and lifted it to her lips, sipping. It was woody with a bitter edge—she'd tasted worse. Tipping back her head, she drank it quickly before handing Ruari back his cup. "Thank you."

His gaze roamed her face. "We only have one more full day after this … will you manage it?"

Lara nodded, shivering as chills bathed her skin. "I will." The strength and determination in her voice made his eyes widen. But still Ruari lingered, as if he had more to say.

Lara didn't have the energy to question him.

Around them, the others had also dismounted and were passing around bread and cheese. Alar approached then, handing Ruari his ration. However, when he offered Lara hers, she shook her head.

"I'm not hungry."

He hesitated. "Shall I keep it for you for later?"

"Aye … thank you."

Nodding, he moved on.

When he'd gone, Annis moved close. The wind had reddened her cheeks and made her eyes water, yet she wore a resolute expression that Lara had come to know well. These druids had been through much with her over the past years.

"Have you told her about the bones?" Annis murmured to Ruari.

His brow furrowed. "I'm about to."

"Hurry up then … while we have some privacy."

Lara beckoned them both closer. "What have you seen?"

"I cast the bones this morning, My Queen," Ruari replied, his gaze flicking around him. He didn't seem to want anyone else to listen in. "Three bones fell together in an unusual formation. The burning crown, the frayed rope … and the triple spiral."

Lara frowned. "And?"

"They—" Ruari began.

"They contradict each other," Annis cut in. "The burning crown represents victory, but the frayed rope suggests failure. It would suggest that a choice is involved."

"And the triple spiral is usually a sign of an unpaid debt that must be settled," Ruari added, casting the counselor an irritated look.

Lara's mind churned. Her head was woolly as it was, but these two spoke in riddles. She didn't want to focus on them, but on what lay ahead.

"I also spied an omen this morning that concerns me," Annis whispered then. "We passed a lone pine at the mouth of this corrie ... I noted it had been struck by lightning ... its branches were charred, and its great trunk cloven in two."

"The Warrior's balls," Lara muttered, her patience fraying. "Just tell me what all this *means*."

"A choice lies ahead," Ruari answered. Hurt shadowed his eyes. "As well as a reckoning of some kind."

"My omen suggests destruction and rebirth," Annis added.

"But this could all be related to what we must do at The Shattered Crown," Lara replied. Her head ached now. Their voices droned in her ears like annoying gnats. "I don't think we should read too much into any of it."

Both the druids frowned, and Lara scowled back. "Why have you only approached *me*? Surely, Mor and Alar should hear this too?"

Annis's face pinched. "We serve you, My Queen. Not the Half-blood or the Raven Queen."

"Not everything needs to be shared," Ruari replied stiffly. "You might not wish to heed them ... but it might be wise to keep these warnings to yourself."

Lara watched Mor stroke Dorka's back.

The clag-doo was *purring*. And the contentment on Mor's face was also something to behold. Around them, the others huddled close to the flames, but the Raven Queen sat apart from them all, preferring to keep Dorka's company instead. She knelt next to the feline upon the stony ground, murmuring endearments. Eagal hunched on her shoulder. The Raven's gaze was narrowed, almost as if it was jealous of his queen's new pet.

But Mor didn't care, and as Lara looked on, she reached up and stroked between Dorka's ears. The clag-doo closed her eyes and lifted her chin, pushing up into the caress.

"Aye, well … now I've seen everything." Bree's murmured comment made Lara glance her way.

The wind howled tonight. They'd camped under a rocky overhang that provided some shelter from the elements. Nonetheless, Bree's shoulders were rounded against the chill, and she clutched her fur-lined cloak close.

For once, Lara was glad of her fever—even if it was a constant reminder of the illness that was slowly taking over.

"Why does Dorka matter to her so much?" she whispered back.

Bree's lips quirked. "I suppose a clag-doo is safe."

"Safe?"

Bree's smile turned rueful. "It won't try to steal your throne."

Her body was on fire.

Lara curled tight under her cloak. Eyes clamped shut, teeth grinding. Heat rolled off her in waves that made her skin feel too tight, too thin.

Around her, the wind howled through the rocky overhang. Their shelter was barely that—just stone jutting out enough to keep the worst of the weather off. Not enough to keep out the cold that would come after the fever broke.

Supper had been silent. No one spoke. They'd sat around the fire, gazes turned inward. Even the Shee looked miserable— shoulders hunched, mouths pressed thin. Lara had been grateful for the quiet. Following conversation had become impossible, words slipping through her mind like water through cupped hands. Roth and Cailean had taken first watch. Everyone else had rolled into their cloaks without a word.

Sleep dragged her under—and then, the dreams began.

Her father's voice, thick with contempt. Her brother facing him down. She stepped between them—crack—his palm struck her cheek, her head snapping sideways, blood flooding her mouth.

Then Dulross. On her knees in the dirt. Stones raining down from the walls. Circines and wulvers jeering. One stone caught her temple. Everything went black.

She awoke in furs. Naked. Alar's body against hers, their skin slick with sweat. His mouth on her throat. *Bite me.* The words tore from her lips as pleasure ripped through her, as his teeth sank into her shoulder—

She jolted into consciousness, shaking so hard her teeth clattered together.

The fever had broken. Now she was ice. Her feet and hands were dead weight, numb and tingling. The wind had died. Silence pressed down.

"My Queen." Roth's voice cut through the stillness. "We have a problem."

She rolled to her feet, yanking her cloak tight. Cold bit into her cheeks, her nose, and the tips of her ears. "Gods, it's freezing."

"Aye." His face had gone red and raw. He held a torch, the flame guttering and weak. A few yards away, Vyr threw the last scraps of firewood onto the coals—gnarled hawthorn branches, barely enough to keep the flames alive. His movements were frantic, jerky.

"What's wrong?" Her teeth wouldn't stop chattering.

"Knavoar." Mor stepped into the firelight, shadows carving her face into hard angles. "They've killed two of my Ravens."

Lara's heart kicked against her ribs.

She grabbed the torch from Roth's hand.

"My Queen, you shouldn't—"

She was already moving.

Out from under the ledge. Past Dorka crouched low to the ground, golden eyes fixed on something in the dark. A growl vibrated in her throat, constant and low.

Footsteps behind her—Bree, silent as always. Then Roth.

Her breath steamed as she moved.

She walked toward the ring of torches they'd placed at the camp's edge. Half were dead, smoke still rising from blackened wicks. The rest flickered weakly, struggling.

Alar stood at the edge with Cailean beside him. Sablebane and Fern had joined them. Skaal pressed against Cailean's leg, hackles raised, teeth bared.

They were all staring down into the corrie below.

Lara stopped beside them.

Moonlight turned the world silver. Frost crept across the ground in patterns that were too delicate, too deliberate. Two bodies lay sprawled on the sparkling carpet, just beyond the torchlight. No one moved toward them.

The air turned colder. Each breath scraped her lungs raw.

"Look." Alar's voice hardened. "They're coming."

Lara followed his gaze.

Silence swallowed them. It was a weight that crushed everything, even the whisper of breath in Lara's lungs.

Figures rose. Stick-thin limbs. Blue-white skin stretched over bone. They moved in stiff, jolting strides.

No faces, just hollows where eyes should have been. Their mouths hung open, exhaling vapor.

The cold hit Lara first. It sank through her clothes, into her skin, wrapped around her bones.

They were walking toward her.

Crunch. Crunch. Crunch.

Frozen grass broke under bony feet.

She couldn't move. Her legs had locked. Her heart slammed against her ribs—too loud, too fast. They would hear it. They would know where she was.

One of them turned its head. Its blank face angled at her.

It knew she was there.

Her throat closed. She tried to swallow but couldn't.

They kept coming.

Knavoar were rare. She'd never seen one, nor had she met anyone who had. Not even Cailean, who'd traveled The Uplands extensively, had mentioned encountering any. But now at least a dozen of them lurched toward them. They were surrounded.

"You need me," she rasped. She should be panicking right now, yet she was suddenly watching events unfold from above. Maybe it was the fire-madness. It was dulling her reactions. "Fire will deal with them."

"No," Alar said, his tone sharp. Final. "It'll take too much from you."

"He's right." A nerve jumped in Bree's cheek as she met Lara's eye. "You can't take the risk."

"Salt works against knavoar," Cailean said then. "If we had enough of it."

They didn't. Just a pouch each on their belts, and most of that was gone as they sprinkled salt around their campsite each night.

"Failing that … iron and steel," Alar added, unsheathing his blades. Cailean then drew his own weapons. Roth did the same, moving forward to join them, while Sablebane and Fern edged back from the ring of guttering torches, nostrils flaring.

Ren approached then, her boots sliding on the frost that crept over the ground where they stood. The bard's jaw was set.

"I'm ready," she said, raising her hands before her.

Cailean nodded to her. A moment later, the tattoos visible on their necks and forearms glowed silver.

Lara moved back, giving them all space. Nonetheless, her pulse now raced. Bree stepped up to her side then, iron blade drawn, ready to defend her High Queen. Skaal joined them too—this was a fight the fae hound couldn't take part in, for if her teeth or claws came in contact with a frost spirit, she'd die.

"Let them come to us," Cailean growled then. "They'll be weaker near firelight."

No sooner had he spoken when the spidery knavoar lunged into a shambling run.

"Don't let them get their hands on you," Alar warned his companions. "Just one touch will freeze your blood."

A wild song burst from Ren's throat, shattering the stillness.

Iron sliced through the air, biting into ice.

Lara's fingers clenched around her torch. Ruari and Annis drew closer to her, Bree, and Skaal, their gazes riveted upon the fight unfolding just yards away. Meanwhile, the Shee had all unsheathed their weapons, waiting.

Roth slipped on the icy ground then, rolling away just in time as long white fingers clutched for him. Snarling a curse, he bounced to his feet and sliced the frost spirit in half. Ice splintered.

Meanwhile, Cailean was a blur.

His earth magic made him devastatingly fast. Lanky bodies shattered under his heavy broadsword.

Lara's gaze seized upon Alar. Just like the first time she'd seen him, fighting off those powries, he moved like a dancer, his twin blades cleaving and stabbing. Knavoar surrounded him, but he dodged their snaking arms.

Mor muttered something under her breath then, pointing. Lara peered down the hill, her heart stuttering when she spied more lines of thin white figures staggering up the slope. Coming for them.

Drawing her own weapon, Mor strode forward, shouting to her Ravens.

Moments later, they'd joined the others. Steel rang amongst iron through the night. Ren edged back from the fighting, her voice faltering now. The cold was damaging her throat. She wouldn't be able to go on for much longer.

Lara, Annis, and Ruari remained there, watching the fight unfold, while Bree moved forward in a protective stance. All three knew how to wield the daggers they carried, but none of them were warriors. It would be foolish to rush into that fight. Nonetheless, dread now sat like a stone on Lara's breastbone.

Her limbs tingled from the deep cold that surrounded them. Each breath felt like inhaling shards of bone. The chill drilled deep into her torso.

"They are too many," Annis rasped finally. "They can't hold them back."

"I know," Lara whispered back. More frost spirits were filing up the hill now, closing the net.

Bree swiveled on her heel then, her expression fierce. "We must fall back."

Lara shook her head. "No … I must wield fire."

"No, Lara, you—"

"There's no other way," Lara cut her off. She understood the risk she was about to take. Fire-madness breathed down her neck, but she had to help. Heart pounding, she then turned to her counselor and seer. Annis's lips were blue. Ice glittered off her eyelashes.

Ruari had pulled his fur cloak close around his spare frame, yet now shivered uncontrollably. "B … but it's not s … safe for you," he replied through chattering teeth.

"No." Lara started fumbling for her cairn stone. Curse it, her numb fingers wouldn't cooperate. "But if I don't act, we're all done for." Her fingers curled around the icy lump of stone, and her chin kicked up. Curses rang across the hillside then. The press of knavoar was close to overwhelming their companions. "Grab those two torches over there. I'll need them."

Both Annis and Ruari nodded, stumbling as they hurried to do Lara's bidding.

Meanwhile, Lara flexed her numb fingers around the cairn stone and reached deep. *Gods.* She hoped her body and mind wouldn't fail her. Not now.

"Be careful," Bree's voice was low, urgent. "Don't push too hard."

Not like you did with the Slew. Not like last time when you lost control and nearly killed us all.

She didn't say it. She didn't need to.

Lara brushed past her, flexing her left hand. The fingers trembled. *Stop it. Stop shaking.* She clenched them into a fist.

Below, the fight was chaos. Blades striking ice. Bodies moving in a blur. Alar and Sablebane fought back-to-back—father and son—their movements mirroring each other. That was new. She'd never seen them—

Focus.

Her mind kept slipping, sliding away like feet on ice. The fever had only just broken. Her body felt hollowed out, scraped clean.

"Bring the torches." Her voice came out steady. That was better. "Drive them into the ground. There … a little farther right. Then get clear."

Annis and Ruari obeyed, their faces taut, hands shaking from cold and terror.

Lara stared at the torches. The flames guttered, dying. The frost spirits were choking them out. Soon there would be nothing left but smoke and darkness.

She reached out with her mind and touched the fire.

29: TOO FAR TO FAIL

ALAR SHOULD HAVE let someone else go to Lara as she crumpled to the ground, but he didn't.

He crossed the distance between him and his wife in long strides and scooped her up into his arms. He then turned and climbed the slope, back to where their fire pit still burned—brightly now, in response to the fire magic that had just roared through the hollow.

Lara had been magnificent.

He'd watched her flames whip around the frost spirits. Spindly bodies melted. Boiling water bubbled across the ground. Steam rose in thick clouds. And then, it was over.

However, her actions had come at a cost. She'd acted bravely, had driven back the knavoar and saved her friends' lives.

But she was burning up in his arms.

Fuck.

He lowered her by the fire and then reached for a waterskin.

"Here." Annis was at his side then, handing him a scrap of linen. "You'll need this."

He took it, wetting it thoroughly before wiping the sweat from Lara's flushed face and brow. Her breathing was quick and shallow, and when he felt her pulse, it fluttered like a caged moth against his fingers.

"It's worse than last time," he muttered.

"Let me help." Ren knelt opposite, her slender fingers moving in the air above Lara. Her voice, soft and tremulous, filtered over their camp. It was a haunting melody.

Bone to marrow, blood to vein, Let the fever break like rain.
What was scattered, gather in, Stitch the soul beneath the skin.
Root to earth and earth to stone, Call the wanderer back home.

Lara's breathing slowly deepened as Ren continued her sain.

Breath that falters, breathe again, Earth will mend what flame has rent.
Fire that burns too bright will fade, Cool the embers that you made.
Sleep now, daughter of the flame, Wake restored and whole again.

Alar bathed her face once more. Her skin was burning to touch. They had to cool her off.

Ren's melancholy song ended, and as it did, the fever receded just a little.

He continued to wipe the sweat from her brow, aware that the others now sat silently around the fire pit, watching. Alar paid none of them any notice though. He couldn't look away from his wife.

A groan escaped Lara then, and his breathing hitched.

She was returning to them.

Sitting back on his heels, he raised his chin. Bree sat opposite him. She'd been there since Ren had begun her vigil, her face taut with worry.

His gaze met hers and held.

It was the first time Lara's warder had met his eye without dislike glinting in her gaze.

Her expression wasn't friendly either though.

"I'll let you take over from here," he said softly. "She'd prefer to see your face rather than mine when she wakes up."

Bree snorted. "Aye … you're learning, Alar."

He stilled. *Alar.* Not 'Half-blood'. Could Lara's fierce protector be lowering her guard around him? "I am."

Rising to his feet, Alar shifted away. He realized then that some members of their group were missing. The Shee. Leaving the fire's warm glow, he emerged from under the overhang, and there, under the silvery glow of the moon, he found them.

The remaining Ravens were building cairns over their fallen warriors—tombs of stone.

Mor looked on, Eagal upon her shoulder, as they worked. She looked otherworldly, standing there, frosted by moonlight.

Vyr began to sing then. A slow, soft lament for the dead that drifted over the hollow. Among the Marav, it was women rather than men who sang such songs, but Vyr's voice was right for it.

Alar couldn't understand the words, for they were in the Shee tongue. But they settled into his bones, all the same. Longing rose in his breast. For a realm he'd never seen, and people he'd never known. The Shee were the other half of him. He'd spent his life hating his father, but underneath it all, he'd always been curious. This journey had taught him that the Shee were his people too.

He shared their strangeness, the difference that set him apart from Marav.

His gaze shifted from Mor then, to the tall lean figure who heaped stones onto one of the cairns that were quickly taking shape.

Wynn Sablebane's profile was stern, yet Alar studied it, searching for answers. Earlier, when they'd been battling the knavoar, he'd been surprised to find his father fighting at his back.

For a short while there, they'd been a team.

"Can you sit up?"

Lara's jaw tightened. "I'm not dying, Bree."

Not yet anyway.

Her friend's mouth pressed into a thin line.

Fine. She'd prove it.

Lara braced her palms against the ground and pushed. Her arms shook—a fine tremor that ran from wrist to shoulder. Her pulse hammered so hard she could feel it in her teeth, in her throat, and behind her eyes.

She made it upright. Barely.

Her vision swam. The nearby firepit tilted and then righted itself. Sweat slicked her spine despite the biting cold in the air. A shiver rippled through her, chills crawling across her skin.

The fever. Already clawing its way back.

"You did well." Cailean had hunkered down next to her, his concerned gaze roaming Lara's face. "There were too many of the bastards … we'd never have bested them on our own."

"They were relentless," Roth agreed, his voice gravelly with fatigue.

"Thank the Gods, we'll reach The Shattered Crown by tomorrow eve," Annis murmured. "None of us can take much more."

Silence followed these words. Meanwhile, Lara accepted the cup of hot broth Ren had just passed her. She took a sip, grateful for the heat that pooled in her belly. The chills were bad.

"Will you be able to ride tomorrow?" Ruari asked, concern shadowing his eyes.

"Of course," Lara replied with more conviction than she felt. "I'll be right by dawn."

"Will you?" Bree asked softly.

Lara sighed, lowering her cup and casting her gaze around the fire. The Shee were still building cairns for their fallen. Alar had disappeared for the moment. There were just the seven of them here. Her protectors. "All you need to focus on tomorrow is getting me safely to The Shattered Crown," she told them firmly. "And all *I* must do is take my place inside that stone circle and then throw this" —she held up her right hand, letting her ring glint in the firelight— "into the rift to seal it."

That was true. The binding didn't require her to wield fire. Mor would be the one doing all the work. The hardest part was getting to their destination. This grueling journey had proved that. It had tried to beat them but hadn't.

"We've come too far to fail," she continued, emotion constricting her throat. "Aye, fire-madness has its talons in me … but it won't have me … not until I'm ready, at least." She paused then, noting the tears that now sparkled in Bree's eyes. "And if I have to crawl into that stone circle to get this job done, I will."

30: THE MOST DANGEROUS OF ALL

DORKA PROWLED TOWARD Lara, Mor upon her back.

The clag-doo's tail swished with each stride. The steel collar on her neck still glinted, even in the murky early dawn light. Despite the bond that had formed between Mor and Dorka, the queen hadn't removed it, and she always carried the steel chain looped in one hand when she climbed onto the beast's back.

Mor didn't trust her pet entirely yet. Their relationship was still new. Untested.

Even so, the Raven Queen was a sight to behold this morning. Eagal perched upon her shoulder, claws digging into her fur cloak.

"Ready to go?" Mor surveyed Lara, brow furrowing; she was clearly unsure if she was up to traveling.

Lara managed a smile. She didn't imagine she looked great. Her body ached, sweat poured off her, and it was difficult to keep her spine straight. "Aye."

And she was. With the rising sun had come the certainty that fire-madness would soon consume her. But, strangely, acceptance of her fate was easier to deal with than dread.

She was oddly calm this morning. Resigned but ready.

Shifting her gaze from Mor's, she glanced up at where the eastern sky above the jagged peak that loomed over them was starting to lighten. The heavens had been clear overnight, but clouds drifted in with the dawn, obscuring the rising sun. It was eerily still this morning. The silence was unnerving.

Around them, the others were already moving out, their mounts picking their way down the slope, into a narrow defile that would take them north toward the Darkmere. The last leg of their journey. Tonight was the eve of Gateway. They'd make it, just, by the skin of their teeth.

Alar passed Mor and Lara, nodding to them both. Reedav loped forward in long strides. The gait must have been difficult to get used to, yet Alar sat easily astride his stag. There were no reins to hold onto, or a mane. Riding such an animal required excellent balance.

Lara nodded back, her gaze tracking him as he followed Vyr.

She then urged Bracken forward.

To her surprise, Mor fell in next to her, while Bree followed close behind.

Dorka didn't enjoy slowing her pace. She made a spitting noise in protest, but Mor leaned forward and placed a hand on her neck, murmuring to her until she settled.

"Your gaze often seeks him out," Mor said then. Her voice was quiet. No one else would have heard—but Lara did. "And he often watches you … when you're not looking."

Lara stiffened, not sure how to respond.

"It seems his betrayal didn't break everything, after all."

Lara swallowed. "I'm not sure about that."

Their eyes met and held for a heartbeat before Mor's mouth curved into a half-smile. "You don't love him then?"

Her pulse quickened. "It doesn't matter if I do. It's over."

A dull ache rose under her breastbone then: the weight of a love that had been doomed from the start. Aye, she loved the bastard. There wasn't any point in denying it. But love wasn't enough.

Mor didn't reply to that, and Lara found herself studying her.

They'd been traveling together for a moon's turn, yet didn't really know each other at all. They'd been guarded with each other. This was the first intimate talk they'd ever had, although Lara didn't wish to discuss Alar. It hurt too much.

"Why have you never taken a husband?" she asked finally.

"Shee don't have handfastings," Mor answered. "We take mates for as long as it suits us … and end the arrangement once things grow stale."

"Stale?"

Mor gave a soft laugh. "I've seen the turn of two thousand years. Even the most exciting of lovers grows boring in the end."

Lara supposed they likely would. "So, you'd never share power?"

Something moved in the depths of Mor's onyx eyes. "Never."

Silence settled between them. They'd left the corrie behind now, riding over wind-blasted hills studded with towering tors of stacked stone.

"Males … whether Shee or Marav … always want to be the ones in charge," Mor said finally. "When a woman rules, she can never show vulnerability … or others will exploit it." She paused then, eyeing Lara. "You've learned this too."

She nodded, even as she thought about Bree, Cailean, and the others who'd followed her north. She'd also learned that relationships were more complex than that. Ruari was right. Trust had to be given if you wished to receive it. There was vulnerability involved, and that could be terrifying.

"You can love and hate someone at the same time, you know?" Mor said then. "I loved my brother … and yet I had Bree hunt him down and chop off his head." A brittle smile tugged at the Raven Queen's lips. "The people you love are the most dangerous of all."

Alar had only ever traveled this far north once. When he was around thirty, and determined to see every corner of Albia with his own eyes. Even so, he'd found this place unsettling. Even with the low cloud, the sky was endless up here, the screech of eagles hunting echoing for furlongs across the hills and off rock. On that trip, he'd camped on the southern edge of the Darkmere but hadn't been able to sleep. He'd lain by the fire he'd lit, imagining something whispering to him in the darkness. Despite the fire's heat, cold had prickled his skin. It had been a relief to get up early, kick dirt over the embers, and ride south.

But here he was, decades later, approaching the same place.

Dusk was settling now, a bright, cold, windy day darkening into a murky gloaming. And as the shadows lengthened, the world grew quiet, as if it were holding its breath. The stillness had followed them all day; a watchful silence that had put everyone on edge. Even the Shee.

Reedav snorted then, tossing his head. Leaning forward, Alar stroked the stag's neck. "Aye, lad … I feel it too," he murmured.

The waters of the loch were dark and still, the color of beaten iron. The Darkmere sat in a cradle of mountains, sharp grey peaks that seemed to lean inward, shadowing the loch and glen below.

Urging his stag forward, Alar drew up alongside his sister.

Fern rode just behind Mor and Vyr. She cast him a wary glance.

"Have you ever visited The Shattered Crown?" he asked.

Something flickered in his sister's grey eyes before she gave a tight nod. "I was one of the party sent to report on the goings on at the stone circle."

"Did the spirits bother you?"

Her proud features tensed. "Aye … a little. Although we were careful to visit on a new moon. It's the safest night to walk amongst wraiths."

"And you saw the rip in the veil?"

Fern nodded. Their gazes met, holding for a few moments before she looked away.

Alar studied her profile, curiosity wreathing up. "Do you have any other siblings?" he asked after a pause.

Her gaze cut back to him, eyes narrowing. For a moment, he thought she might snap at him, but instead, her lips thinned. "No," she replied stiffly. "Shee families aren't large."

"And are our father and your mother still together?" Alar's gut tightened as he asked this.

Did it matter? Did he care? Aye, he did. He wanted to know more about the warrior who'd sired him, of the life he'd returned to in Sheehallion. He wanted to find the piece of himself that had always been missing.

"No," Fern replied. "Their relationship ended a century ago."

Alar stilled at that. Half-bloods lived longer than Marav, yet he'd never get used to the way Shee viewed time. As if a century meant nothing. They weren't immortal, but since their lifespans often stretched into thousands of years, a century was a mere blink of the eye.

"Does he have another mate then? Another family?"

"No." Fern looked away. "He's had little opportunity." Her voice lowered. "For he's only recently gained his freedom … he spent nearly seven decades in a labor camp."

Alar's heart kicked. *Nearly seven decades.* He was seventy-three, which meant his father had been imprisoned for most of Alar's life. The news unbalanced him.

"Aye, he was punished for his transgression." Fern now stared resolutely ahead. "Mor was … displeased."

Mind reeling, Alar took this in. All these years, he'd imagined Wynn Sablebane had gotten away with planting a bastard in a Marav woman's womb. But he hadn't. He glanced ahead at where his father rode alongside Vyr. Mor led the way now, stalking ahead on Dorka.

Suddenly, his head was full of questions, one tumbling over the other.

"And you don't resent him for what he did?" he asked finally. "He disgraced you, didn't he?"

Fern snorted, casting him a sidelong glance. "He disgraced *himself*, not me … and he's paid for it." She paused then, her features tightening. "My mother and I are estranged … he's all I have."

Alar inclined his head. Their gazes met and held.

His sister fascinated him—especially since he recognized some of himself in her. A loneliness she hid well from the world. For the first time, she'd lowered her shields and let him glimpse beyond.

Alar's chest tightened. He wanted to tell her that she had him too but wisely swallowed the words. Fern wouldn't want to hear them, and he wouldn't be stupid enough to make himself so vulnerable around her.

A mournful long cry echoed across the hills then, shattering the fragile connection between brother and sister. Grief distilled into one keening scream that made the fine hairs on the back of Alar's arms stand up.

The Weeper.

It warned them not to go any farther. But they would.

Behind him, someone shouted a curse. Glancing over his shoulder, Alar looked to where Roth was pointing east—to dark shapes boiling over the hill.

His heart bucked against his ribs. Next to him, his sister was silent.

Alar leaned forward, his sharp eyesight slicing through the murky gloaming. In amongst the approaching swarm, he made out heavyset bodies gripping pikestaffs, red caps bouncing as they ran. Alongside them were smaller wiry imps with hooked noses and sagging faces, gripping daggers. Powries and trows.

He swiftly drew his twin blades, his pulse thundering now as fury washed over him in a blistering tide. These creatures were the Shee's allies. Five years of service and they'd be able to return to Sheehallion.

A fucking ambush. Mor had turned on them.

31: AWAKENING THE WOLF

"LOWER YOUR BLADES!" the Raven Queen shouted. She'd drawn up Dorka and turned her around to face them. "The faerie creatures are here to help."

Alar's heart started to pound. Of course, they were—here to help *her*.

Lara urged her horse forward, flanked by Bree and Cailean. Her face was flushed, her skin gleaming with sweat, yet anger burned in her gaze. "What trick is this?"

"None," Mor replied, meeting her gaze calmly. "Our band is small … so I sent for reinforcements. These imps will ensure we actually reach The Shattered Crown."

No sooner had she spoken than the approaching swarm slowed. Panting, the powries and trows drew to a halt. Their eyes, some amber, others disturbingly red, glowed as they swept their gazes over the weary group of travelers.

"Why didn't you warn us?" Alar demanded.

Mor's gaze cut to him. "Because I knew you'd refuse."

"With good reason," he shot back. "These creatures are *your* allies … not ours."

"Not this evening." Mor stared him down, tension shivering through the air. "Tonight, we're all on the same side. Admit it, we need them."

Growling an oath, Alar shifted his attention from Mor then and looked at Lara. Her features were strained. Their gazes met. Wariness glinted in her pine-green eyes.

His fingers flexed around the handles of his fighting daggers. She was right to be wary. Mor's secretive behavior had just driven a spike through their band. Roth and Cailean drew their weapons as the Ravens urged their elks and stags forward, forming a semi-circle behind their queen.

"Perhaps I should have warned you." Mor's voice sharpened. "But don't look for betrayal where there isn't any. You can trust us."

"Can we?" Lara dragged her attention back to the Raven Queen.

Mor held her gaze. "Aye."

The Weeper's wail reverberated through the gathering dusk then—a sharp reminder that they had to keep moving. There wasn't time to debate this further. Mor had forced their hand, but the boulder was rolling down the mountainside now. They couldn't stop it.

All they could do was press forward.

"Let the powries and trows take the lead," Vyr said then, his tone brisk.

Mor nodded, relief flickering over her face. Her cousin was focusing on practical matters, reminding them all why they were here. Not that Alar needed reminding. "Lara is vulnerable," she added. "We must close ranks around her to ensure she reaches the crown safely."

Lara shifted uncomfortably on her horse's back. Her brow furrowed, and then she drew her iron dagger. "I can fight."

Mor pulled a face. "I've no doubt … but you're struggling. Let the rest of us look out for you."

Thunder rolled across the Darkmere.

Not from the sky, but from the earth. Hoofbeats and boot-strikes hammered out a rhythm. The war cries started next: powrie shrieks and trow bellows.

Alar crouched low over Reedav's neck, daggers already slippery in his palms. The stag's muscles bunched and released beneath him with each long stride.

His gaze snapped right, to where Lara leaned forward over her mare's neck, her jaw set. Wind tore at her braided hair, whipping loose strands across her face. Her mount's hooves drummed the packed earth, matching Reedav stride for stride. Bree rode at her flank, longsword raised and ready.

Keep her safe. Heat pulsed in Alar's gut. *Whatever it costs. Whatever you must do.*

Screams knifed through the air. His head jerked up. The western sky had turned black, not with clouds, but with bodies. Writhing limbs and tattered wings, smoke-hair streaming as the Slew descended in a swarm.

Then singing that was both beautiful and terrible joined the cries of The Unforgiven.

Pale figures glided across the loch's obsidian surface, arms outstretched like loving wives welcoming their husbands home. Their mouths moved as they sang an eldritch melody that made Alar's breathing grow shallow. Loch-Bhàns. One touch and they'd steal everything from you—your memories, your identity, your *self*—leaving nothing but an empty husk. You'd breathe and walk, but you'd remember nothing.

Movement *in* the water caught Alar's eye then. Slippery skin glistened in the dying light. Fish-eyes gleamed. Fuath dragged themselves onto shore, bog wights with webbed fingers and eel-like teeth.

Alar's pulse exploded. *They're all here.*

"Boggarts!" Sablebane's shout cut through the chaos.

Sallow-skinned figures with bloodshot eyes erupted from the shadows. They carried no weapons. They didn't need them, for boggarts had long fingers that could snap bone like dry twigs.

The trows and powries hit the first wave. The impact punched through Alar's chest. A heartbeat later, earth magic detonated around him like lightning striking a tree. It woke the wolf in his blood, set every nerve singing with borrowed power.

Reedav surged forward. Alar gripped with his knees, leaning into the charge as darkness rushed up to swallow them. The imps took the brunt—powrie curses mixing with trow war-cries. Blades bit into shadow.

Then the sky fell.

Slew poured down like black rain. Ice-breath blasted Alar's face, stealing the air from his lungs. Wings were everywhere—blotting out the sky. Spectral hands reached, grasping, desperate for warm flesh.

Mor struck first. The Raven Queen's blade carved through wraith-flesh. Vyr flanked her left, Sablebane her right. Steel sang through the air.

One Slew dove straight for them. It had long snarled hair and tattered robes that might have been burial shrouds.

Alar pushed himself up onto Reedav's back, knees locked, and leaped. His daggers slashed in crossing arcs. Iron swept through shadow-flesh. The Slew shrieked and wheeled away, trailing smoke.

Alar landed hard, nearly losing his seat, and caught himself.

But there was no time to recover, for the Fuath crashed into their circle.

A brackish stench hit him first—rot and stagnant water and things that lived in dark places. Teeth snapped. Webbed hands clawed. Mor's longsword cleaved through the first bog wight. Around her, Ravens hacked at slippery bodies that wouldn't stay down. Fern's blade was a silver blur.

Alar's pulse leaped. *Keep the circle tight.*

But they were slowing. Spirits pressed from all sides. Even the trows and powries up ahead were struggling, their war-cries turning ragged.

He fought on instinct. His body knew what to do even as his mind tracked something else.

Lara. Always to his right. Always within reach. She gripped her iron dagger fiercely, flanked by Bree and Cailean with Ren, Annis, and Ruari thundering at her heel. Brave. All of them.

A Slew dove. Alar's blade caught it mid-flight, driving it back. Another came. He sliced through shadow, felt resistance, and twisted the blade. The wraith dissolved into smoke.

His arms were starting to burn. How long had they been fighting? He'd lost track. Time had fractured into heartbeats and blade-strikes.

The light died. Indigo bled across the sky, deepening to black. The moon rose, riding high and cold above them.

They inched forward, every foot gained with effort. Spirits howled around them, screams layering over screams.

Alar's world narrowed to the space around Lara. *Protect her. Keep her moving. Don't let anything through.*

Silver light broke through the clouds and frosted the jagged stones ahead.

The Shattered Crown. Right there. Close enough to see the individual standing stones.

Lara's thighs burned from gripping Bracken's sides. The mare lunged forward, hooves pounding stone and earth in a rhythm that matched her own hammering pulse.

Around her, the world had turned to chaos.

The din threatened to split her skull apart. Slew screeches. Powrie war-cries that set her teeth on edge. The wet sounds of blades finding slippery bog wight flesh.

She clutched her iron dagger so hard her fingers ached. It felt too small and light in her hand. What good would one blade do against this tide of darkness?

Movement to her left caught her eye. Ren rode close now, right behind Bree, her face pale but focused, lips moving in constant song. The bard's voice wove through the chaos, a lifeline Lara clung to. Twisting, Lara caught sight of Annis hunched low over her pony's neck. Next to the counselor, Ruari's eyes were too wide, too white.

A Slew dove.

Lara's breath stopped. Tattered wings spread wide. Hungry eyes fixed on her. Reaching—

Twin iron blades flashed. The wraith screamed and wheeled away.

Alar.

He crouched low over Reedav's back, daggers moving in brutal arcs. His face was set in hard lines, eyes scanning constantly.

He was always there. Every time something came too close, every time the circle threatened to break, he appeared.

The Fuath hit their flank. Webbed hands tried to rake and claw their way through.

Bracken faltered and reared, a terrified whinny tearing from her throat. Lara grabbed the mare's mane with her free hand, thighs clamping down. With her other hand, she slashed and stabbed at shadows.

Bree's sword cut through a bog wight. Foul-smelling water broke over them. Her warder moved fast, her blade never still, her body always between Lara and danger.

"Stay close!" Bree's voice cut through the roar. "Don't let them in!"

Still, the wraiths came, crashing upon them. Wave after wave.

But they were moving forward. Step by brutal step, they pushed through the sea that boiled around the base of The Shattered Crown.

Lara's gaze swept right. Just a few yards away, Mor fought viciously—her blade singing—while her Ravens remained in formation around her.

Cailean's tattoos blazed silver as he slashed and stabbed. Skaal tore through bog wights with savage joy.

And Alar was there too—to her left—carving space, creating gaps, and driving back anything that came too close to her.

Her protector.

The realization pressed down on her chest, uncomfortable and undeniable.

A boggart lunged from nowhere. Long fingers reached for Annis. The counselor screamed—

Vyr's blade took the sprite's head. It crumpled. He wheeled his elk around, putting himself between the Marav and the next wave.

The circle stretched. Lara could feel it—the distance growing between Shee and Marav. Earth magic and iron drove them apart even as they fought to stay together.

The sky had gone fully dark now, but the moon was rising, and its light frosted the stones ahead.

The Shattered Crown.

So close.

But the spirits sensed it too. They sensed their prey escaping. The press intensified. The Slew dove in waves now, one after another after another. Fuath poured from the loch. Boggarts erupted from every shadow.

Panic hammered into her breast. There were too many.

Alar fought to her right now. His movements were starting to slow, just enough that she noticed. Blood ran down his arm. His chest heaved with each breath.

He was tiring. They all were.

A Slew broke through.

Not at her. At Ren.

The bard froze, eyes wide, her song rising to a scream. The wraith's hands reached for her face—

Lara moved without thinking.

She hauled Bracken to the right, put herself between Ren and the spirit. She drove her dagger up. Iron met shadow. Her arm went numb to the elbow. Cold shot through her bones, but it was worth it, for the Slew twisted away.

Yet more were coming. Faster and more aggressive than ever.

"Lara!" Bree shouted, alarm cracking her voice.

Alar appeared at her side, his daggers slashing as he drove the onslaught back.

Their eyes met for a heartbeat.

Heat pulsed between them, and then he turned and threw himself back into the fight.

The press of bodies—living and dead—became suffocating. Lara lost sight of him. One moment, he was there, the next, swallowed by shadow and writhing limbs.

Panic barreled into her.

Where was he?

A flash of blades to her left. *Alar.* He was—no. That was Vyr.

To her right then. Movement. Dark hair. It had to be—

Sablebane. Fighting alongside Mor.

Her pulse hammered so hard her chest ached. The chaos was total now. She couldn't track him. Couldn't see him.

A gap opened ahead. The Ravens surged through it, Mor at their head. The Marav followed, Cailean bellowing orders.

Sharp stones erupted before them. The base of the promontory, where powries and trows now formed a protective ring.

They'd reached it.

Lara's gaze swept back, desperate, searching through the chaos for Alar.

There. A flash of fawn-colored leather. Dark hair. Twin blades catching moonlight. Alar was still fighting. Still cutting his way through. Still alive.

Relief crashed over her.

Bree grabbed her arm. "We climb. Now!"

Lara slid from Bracken's back. Her legs nearly buckled. How long had they been fighting? Her muscles screamed. Her hands shook.

Around them, the others dismounted, weapons drawn, eyes wild. All of them were bruised and bleeding, their clothing torn.

And all the while, the spirits pressed closer, cornering them against the outcrop.

32: THE RITUAL

MOR LEAPED FROM Dorka's back. Slicing her steel blade at a bog wight, she severed its head. Water cascaded over her, but she barely seemed to notice. Taking a moment, she leashed Dorka to a gnarled hawthorn that grew at the foot of the promontory. The clag-doo yanked at the chain and howled in protest. Mor murmured something soothing, yet didn't linger.

Instead, she whipped around, her gaze slicing into Lara's. "After me!"

She then sheathed her sword and began the steep climb up to the broken stone circle.

Lara watched her go, still struggling to regain her breath.

Holding onto Bracken with one hand, she turned to Bree.

"We'll be right behind you," Bree grunted as she slashed at another Fuath, a slender female with a mane of wild, knotted hair. The trows and powries had formed a protective ring around the base of the crag, but wraiths had still managed to break through.

"Ruari!" Roth shouted then. "Watch yourself!"

Lara turned to see a Loch-Bhàn reach for the seer. Ruari had been slashing at a Slew, focused elsewhere. He hadn't seen the ethereal figure drifting toward him.

Roth had, but his warning came too late. Silver fingers enclosed around Ruari's wrist.

He staggered, his eyes snapping wide. The Loch-Bhàn released her grip then, drawing back.

A bewildered expression rippled over his face. His dagger slipped from limp fingers.

"Ruari!" Annis rushed toward him.

He blinked, turning to her. "Who?"

Two bog wights, seizing their chance, lunged then. Clawed, webbed hands grabbed the seer, and they dragged him backward.

Roth and Alar tried to get to him. The Slew dove, blocking them as they slashed and stabbed—even as the Fuath hauled Ruari toward the edge of the loch. Lara watched, heart pounding in her throat, helpless to stop them, as he disappeared under the cold dark water.

Just like that, he was gone. So fast. So final.

Lara flinched. *Gods. Ruari.*

"Climb!" Mor shouted. She'd already scaled the first few feet of the outcrop. The urgency in her voice tore through Lara's shock.

She staggered away from Bracken, following Mor. There was no time to tether her mare; it wasn't safe to do so anyway. Bracken needed to be able to flee, if necessary.

An instant later, Alar was at Lara's side. But so too, unfortunately, was a boggart.

"Half-breed fucker!" Spittle flew. "Freak! You're not fit to—"

Alar stabbed it in the throat, cutting off a tirade of jabbered insults. He then pushed her ahead of him. "Go."

Scrambling over rock, slippery with dew, her hands and feet fumbling, she followed Mor. The Shee queen was well ahead now, her black mink cloak billowing behind her. She climbed like a mountain goat, but Lara didn't find it so easy.

She was only a few yards up when her arms started to tremble and burn. *Fuck.*

"Faster," Alar grunted from below her.

"I'm trying," she panted, even as sharp rock dug into her palm. Gritting her teeth against the pain, she hauled herself upward. The Ancients hadn't made this stone circle easy to reach. "I … must … stop for a moment." She halted then, clinging to the side of the promontory, her pulse hammering in her ears. Farther below, the others were climbing the crag. Grunts and curses echoed through the icy air. "Just … need … a breather."

Alar pulled himself up next to her. "Can you manage this?"

Lara shook her head, too winded to answer. *Gods.* Her body was letting her down. Clenching her eyes shut, she made a silent prayer to The Warrior. *Just get me to the top of this rock. Please.*

"Climb onto my back," Alar ordered then. "I'll carry you."

Lara's eyes snapped open. Under other circumstances, she might have refused him.

But she didn't now. She needed help, or she wouldn't reach the top.

Edging closer, she slid onto his back. The next thing she knew, she clung to him. Her arms wrapped around his chest, while her knees gripped his narrow hips.

And then, he was climbing. Inch by inch. Foot by foot. The promontory suddenly seemed so much higher than it had from a distance.

Alar didn't speak as he scaled the crag. His entire focus was upon his task. He was sweating heavily, yet his body felt cool compared to hers.

Craning her neck, Lara gazed up at their destination, at the point where Mor had disappeared. "Just a few yards more."

Alar grunted. His arms were starting to tremble now.

"Not much farther," she whispered, tensing against his back.

Breathing hard, Alar finally reached the ledge above them. His body tensed as he prepared to heave himself over the edge—and then a slender hand snapped down, fingers clasping around his.

A heartbeat later, Mor heaved them both up. Lara swallowed a gasp of surprise. She hadn't realized the Shee queen was so strong.

Meanwhile, Alar rose to his feet, and Lara slid from his back, her boots hitting the dry grass that covered the rock. He braced his hands on his thighs as he recovered from the climb, before his gaze met Lara's. His lips then curved.

Her breathing hitched. *That smile.* She hadn't seen it since his betrayal. She'd almost forgotten how his cheek dimpled, how his eyes softened. How he looked at her as if she was something precious. Warmth spread across her chest before she caught herself. *Don't go there. Focus.*

All three of them then turned their attention to the massive stone slabs that rose before them.

The Shattered Crown formed a tight ring on the outcrop's summit. Time and weather had left their mark on the stones, blunting and smoothing their edges and covering them with patches of lichen and moss. The circle resembled the weathered crown of a giant. Some of the stones had fallen inward, while others leaned against each other.

Lara's gaze slid over the ring, her skin prickling. "Can you hear that?" she asked her companions. "They're humming."

"Aye," Mor replied. "It's coming from the rift in the veil." She met Lara's eye then, her head inclining. "Do you see why we needed the powries and trows? We'd never have made it this far without them."

Lara nodded, reluctantly giving her that.

Mor turned then and moved forward, heading toward the gap between the two nearest stones.

Lara and Alar shared a long look.

He stepped in close. "This is it … are you ready?"

Squaring her shoulders, she straightened her spine. "Aye."

"We need to be careful in here, Lara. Stay near me."

Lara's belly tightened. Slowly, she nodded.

Sweat slid down her back. Her limbs trembled. But none of that would stop her. She was here for an important task, and she'd see it done.

Walking ahead of Alar, she followed Mor into the circle.

Moonlight filtered through the stones, illuminating the crown in a soft silver light. This was an ancient place. Cailean had told her that The Shattered Crown was rumored to be the oldest of all of Albia's stone circles. Few mortals had ventured here over the centuries, and she couldn't help but feel that she was intruding.

However, a heartbeat later, she realized they weren't alone. Dark shapes flitted between the monoliths. Spirits.

Heart kicking, she moved close to Alar. He'd asked her to, yet it was an instinctive act, all the same.

Familiar voices drew her attention then. Glancing over her shoulder, she made out the shadows of their companions just outside the ring of standing stones. Bree and the others had also reached the top, and they were holding vigil as Mor had instructed. Howls and screeches rang through the night. The wraiths had followed them up here too.

Lara's gut clenched then. Had the powries and trows also climbed up to the stone circle? And if so, were they still allies?

"No one is to enter," Mor called. "No matter what you hear. The binding will only take if we three are alone."

Sweeping her gaze around the perimeter, Lara's gaze alighted on the space between two stones that leaned drunkenly on each other. Darkness swirled between them.

There it was. The rift.

Smoky shapes wreathed out of the gap, shapes that vaguely resembled men and women with glowing emberlike eyes.

Grimlochs.

Alar acted first, drawing his last handful of salt from the pouch strapped to his thigh and flinging it at the smoke wraiths. They fled, squealing, back through the rift.

But there was no time to draw breath, for a Slew burst forth. Its shrieks echoed off stone as both Alar and Mor unsheathed their weapons, slashing at it. Lara backed up, drawing her own dagger. *Gods.* How were they supposed to do the binding with spirits erupting like this? Wings beating, the Slew shot upward into the moonlight.

"Take your positions." Mor took charge now.

Lara obeyed, moving over to the southwestern edge of the circle.

Alar shifted to where a flat circular stone lay in the midst of the circle, worn and pitted with age. He cast his gaze over it before glancing Mor's way. "Here?"

"Aye," she replied, sheathing her sword. "On your knees. Face Lara."

Alar's gaze narrowed. However, he didn't obey.

"You need to kneel, Alar," Mor repeated.

"Why?"

"It's all part of the ritual."

Tension rippled over his lean frame.

"I've already explained this," Mor said, meeting his gaze squarely. "You are the bridge."

"Aye … but—"

"You need to be close to the earth when I begin the binding … and that means you must prostrate yourself upon the stone."

A nerve flickered in Alar's cheek. He didn't look any happier about this than earlier. Yet, he didn't argue with her now. Moments passed, and slowly he sank down upon the stone.

The sight made Lara's pulse stutter. Bathed in moonlight, he appeared a sacrificial victim from the old stories, back when sacrificers had been permitted to kill people to appease the Gods. The comparison disconcerted her.

Mor approached Alar. She then pushed back her cloak, revealing a row of blades strapped to her belt. The largest was a fighting dagger, the smallest the size of a boning knife. Mor selected one of the smaller ones, a thin-bladed dagger. "Hold out your hand."

Confusion flickered across his features. But this time, he didn't do as bid.

Making an impatient noise in the back of her throat, Mor grabbed hold of his wrist and slashed him across the palm.

Alar jolted, his hiss of pain following. His blood flowed thick, running through his fingers. "What the *fuck*?" he ground out.

"Let the blood drip onto the stone," Mor ordered. "It's all part of the grounding … connecting you to the earth through blood."

"But you said—"

"Quiet." Mor snapped.

Lips pressing into a thin line, he watched Mor warily as his blood dripped. Anger and suspicion blazed in his eyes.

Lara's own unease spiked. This wasn't right. Mor had said no blood was needed.

The Raven Queen moved back, taking her place at the southeastern edge of the circle, behind Alar. "Extend your right hand, Lara," she called. "Let the *Ord-ree seal* announce its presence."

Forcing herself to focus, Lara lifted her hand. Her gaze lowered to where the amber stone set against iron gleamed silver in the moonlight. "The ring feels warm."

"Good … it's seeking a connection to the Threshold. As anchor, you must hold fast. Don't take off the ring … no matter how hot it burns."

Lara nodded, sweat beading on her forehead. She stared into the swirling darkness between the two leaning stones. Moments passed, and her breathing deepened. Pushing her uneasiness aside, she concentrated on the task at hand. She'd made it. She was finally standing in The Shattered Crown. The wraiths hadn't taken her, and neither had fire-madness. Not yet. She'd survived, and now she had to end this.

Her fingers flexed. The void before her was mesmerizing.

And then her ring started to pulse. Red-gold light flooded through the stones. The *Ord-ree seal* was an ancient thing. Forged in another age, for a chilling purpose. There were many things about the ring she didn't understand, but she'd seen its legacy. It had brought darkness into their world. She couldn't wait to rid herself of it.

The ring grew warmer still against her skin, stinging now.

Mor began to sing then. Words in the Shee tongue. Lyrical. Beautiful. Poignant. Holding her hands aloft, the Shee queen dropped her head back, staring up at where the full moon hung above them. Her slender hands moved. Indeed, she did look as if she was lacing something together.

The anchor. The bridge. The weaver. They were all here.

The sounds of combat drifted into the stone circle then. Grunts. Muffled curses. The thud and scrape of booted feet. Lara's gaze cut right, alarm blooming under her ribs. *Gods.* Bree and the others were fighting for their lives out there. She couldn't let the wraiths best them.

The binding needed to take.

The buzzing noise from the rift grew louder then. And as Lara looked on, the gap in the veil seemed to pulse in response to Mor's voice. Still, her haunting song continued, more strident now.

And then a wind drove in—between the stones.

Dry and sharp, it held a vicious chill that stung her cheeks and caught in the back of her throat. Lara staggered forward before she braced herself against it.

Shapes started whipping past, hurtling toward the tear in the veil, ragged shadows with flailing limbs. They screamed. They fought. But they couldn't escape.

She watched the rift swallow them, and exhilaration tightened her chest. *It's working.* Mor's wind was pushing the wraiths into The Threshold.

More spirits poured through—a tide of them. Boggarts, their long fingers clawing at the air. Bog wights, hair billowing behind them like floating banks of kelp. Loch-Bhàn, mouths wide as they wailed. And the Slew too. Dark wings beating furiously. Elongated faces twisted with fear.

Still on his knees in the center of the circle, Alar crouched low, watching the spirits tumble past. Blood dripped from his clenched fist. It had formed a dark pool on the center stone now.

Lara winced then. The *Ord-ree seal* was scorching her skin. It hurt.

The wind continued to roar, a storm wielded from moonlight and Shee song. More wraiths streamed in, their wails rending the air. But there was no resisting this. The Raven Queen's binding was too strong.

Eventually, the spirit flow slowed, then stopped. When it did, Mor ceased her singing.

The wind died as abruptly as it had begun, and an eerie silence swallowed the stone circle.

33: THE BURNING CROWN

ALAR LIFTED HIS head, his gaze shifting to the writhing void. "Is it done?"

"Not yet," Mor replied, her voice tight. Eager.

Lara gritted her teeth. The *Ord-ree seal* had started to pulse harder now. It was like holding an ember against her skin. She could smell her flesh burning. *Shades.* She needed to rip it off. "How much longer?" she gasped, her voice catching.

"Just hold on," Mor barked.

And then Lara jolted, for an arm clamped around her torso, pinning her arms to her sides. Another hand covered her mouth.

"Apologies." Vyr's voice rumbled in her ear. "Change of plan."

Alar's chin kicked up, his gaze settling upon Lara and Vyr—just as Mor leaped on his back.

Taken by surprise, he grunted a curse, lurching forward.

Steel flashed. Mor drove a blade into his shoulder, just above the harness where his two fighting daggers were still sheathed. She pushed him onto his stomach, one knee pinning his spine. Alar writhed and bucked under her, but she dug the knife in deeper.

And then, with her free hand, she yanked his iron daggers free. She was careful to grab them by their bone hilts, avoiding iron. Nevertheless, she flinched, and her face screwed up as she hurled them away. "That's better," she panted. "Your blood will already be attracting the Fuath … and now you won't give them any trouble."

Alar snarled another curse, his voice cutting off when she ground the dagger deeper still.

"Behave, Half-blood," Mor warned. "Keep quiet, or Vyr will cut your beloved wife's throat."

A growl rumbled in his throat, yet he obeyed.

"Just to be clear … this isn't sacrifice." Mor's voice held a mocking edge now. "It's *murder*." Her gaze flicked toward Lara. "We both know the only reason you're here is for her. Love makes idiots of us all."

Panicking now, Lara fought against Vyr, but it was like trying to escape a steel cage. The Shee were fearsomely strong.

"What are you doing?" she tried to shout, but Vyr's hand muffled her words.

"Eliminating threats," Vyr answered quietly, as if he'd heard her.

Lara stared at Mor, mind whirling, heart thumping.

The Shee had just double-crossed them.

"It had to be done." Mor's voice was calm, even as she continued to pin Alar down, twisting the dagger every time he tried to free himself. She glanced at the swirling rift then. The shadows within boiled now. "It's time." Her gaze cut back to where Vyr held on to Lara, even as she fought him. "Don't let her go. Wait until the Half-blood is taken and then hurl her in after him."

And with that, Mor gave the blade a final twist. She then leaped off Alar, leaving the dagger embedded, and backed up swiftly, just as four bog wights exploded from the rift: large broad-shouldered males. They rushed at Alar, their webbed hands tipped in curving claws fastening around his arms.

He fought them. But they clung on—dragging him toward the rift.

Lara screamed against Vyr's hand, even as her ring flashed bright crimson. She needed to wield fire, but she didn't have a flame to connect with.

Mor looked her way once more. "This is the final stage. Two rivals eliminated in one stroke."

Lara jerked her gaze from where Alar struggled and twisted under the Fuath, to Mor. *You bitch!*

Meanwhile, Alar dug his heels into the ground. Mor had stabbed him to weaken him, to make him an easier victim. But, even injured, he was proving hard to wrestle into the gap. His eyes started to glow red then. His lips pulled back from his teeth as he snarled. Lara gasped. His wolf's head tattoo. The earth magic was fighting back.

And yet, only a few yards remained.

Panic surged through Lara.

They were going to take him, and she couldn't stop them.

A tall lean figure clad in black burst into the circle, dark hair flying behind him.

Mor snarled something in the Shee tongue.

Wynn Sablebane ignored his queen. Instead, his blade sliced into one of the bog wights, severing its head. He then stabbed another through the eye. Brackish water gushed over the ground.

Sablebane whirled, drawing his arm back to take down another of the Fuath.

Mor drew a dagger and hurled it at him. It hit him in the guts with a dull thud, embedding to the hilt. He reeled backward—even as two more Fuath crawled from the rift and hurled themselves at Alar.

Sablebane lay on his side, curled up. He'd yanked out the blade. It lay next to him, gleaming with blood. Face twisting in agony, he rolled toward Lara. However, his gaze didn't rest on her, but on the male holding her fast.

"You're expendable, Vyr," he gasped. "We all are."

"Idiot," Vyr growled. However, Lara felt his strong body tense against hers. "What have you done?"

"I've orders to kill you," Sablebane grunted out the words. "Once Alar and Lara are gone and the rift is sealed, I will slide a knife between your ribs." He grimaced as agony clutched at him. "She doesn't suffer rivals."

"Ignore him." Mor now stalked around the knot of Fuath who still struggled with Alar. She was heading toward Sablebane, her longsword drawn. "He's lost his mind."

A heartbeat pulsed.

"Close the rift," Vyr rasped in Lara's ear.

And then, to her shock, he let her go. Just like that.

Drawing his sword, he intercepted Mor. Alar was just two yards from the rift now. Agony twisted his lean features. Yet he fought on.

A savage cry tore from Mor's lips as she swung her sword at her cousin. He brought his blade up to block her. Clashing steel rang across the promontory, echoing off stone.

Another figure burst into the circle then—lithe and fast, her dark cloak billowing. Fern.

Alar's half-sister didn't hesitate. She rushed toward where her father lay bleeding, just as more Fuath began crawling from the rift, drawn by Sablebane's fresh blood. Her blade flashed as she positioned herself over him, slashing at the bog wights.

The ring finger of Lara's right hand was agony now. The char of burning flesh made her bile rise. The ring pulsed with power. Gold flames danced across its surface.

She tore it off. It was like handling a flaming coal. For an instant, it sat upon her palm, a ring of gold flames now. The burning crown. Ruari's warning.

Victory or defeat. She stood on the edge of a crumbling ledge. Which would it be?

Four strides. That's all it took.

The gap yawned before her—a tear in the world that pulled at her chest and made her vision swim. The Fuath swarmed over Alar, hissing and snarling, their webbed hands raking.

Lara's arm snapped back. The *Ord-ree seal* left her palm, a streak of gold spinning through air thick with smoke and screams, straight into the rift.

She didn't watch it fall.

Instead, her dagger scraped free of its sheath, and she lunged. The blade punched into slippery flesh at the base of a bog wight's skull. She felt resistance and then give.

Brackish water exploded across her face and chest.

The hum threading through the stone circle twisted into something sharp and high, a whine that drove needles into her eardrums.

White-hot pain lanced down her right arm. A Fuath had just clawed her from shoulder to elbow. Blood welled, hot and fast, but she ignored it, slashing her blade across a lean throat. More foul water erupted, drenching both her and Alar.

"Here!" She shoved her dagger into Alar's hand and felt his fingers close around the hilt. Two bog wights were left, but he'd finish them.

He did. Iron flashed beside her before water sprayed.

And then, something pulled at Lara from behind.

She swiveled, looking over her shoulder into a swirling vortex.

The rift had changed.

A whirlwind spiraled out from the tear, seemingly tethered to it.

Instinctively, she understood *she'd* caused it by throwing the *Ord-ree seal* into the rift. The veil was healing and creating a twister as it did so. This was nothing like the wind that Mor had summoned. It was stronger. Hungrier. It could take them all.

Lara's knees buckled. She dropped, palms hitting gravel, bracing herself against the column of air that tried to tear her away.

"No!" Mor's voice cut through—raw, desperate. "Not yet!"

The vortex caught the final Fuath attacking Fern. The bog wight reeled past where Lara crouched, its mouth gaped wide, needle-teeth gleaming. Webbed hands clawed at nothing but air. Then it tumbled backward into the gap, swallowed whole.

Lara couldn't breathe, couldn't think. She could only hold on.

A scream tore through the circle, furious and terrified at once.

Her head snapped up, and her breath seized.

Not all the wraiths surrounding The Shattered Crown tonight had ended up in the rift earlier. One had resisted Mor's binding. Until now. *The* Slew. The massive solid one with seaweed hair and a melted face. It had wrapped itself around Mor, arms locked, smoke curling between their bodies like a shroud.

Vyr staggered back, flattening himself against a standing stone as the twister lashed through the air. His face had gone taut, his eyes huge.

The cyclone roared louder.

Lara threw herself at Alar. Her shoulder hit his chest. They went down together, hard, his grunt of pain lost in the tempest shrieking around them. She pressed flat against him. His body was solid and real beneath hers while the world tried to tear them apart.

She lifted her head, just as Mor and the Slew, still locked together, spun past. Two figures embracing as they tumbled toward the gap. Lara caught a glimpse of the Raven Queen's face. There was no fear there, just fury.

Then they were gone. Swallowed by the rift.

Lara's forehead dropped against Alar's chest. Her eyes squeezed shut. The whirlwind still yanked at her. It wanted to drag her in with the rest.

They clung together, even as their bodies slowly slid across the ground, drawn toward the swirling maw.

And then the twister collapsed—abruptly—as if someone had just slammed the door, as if the world had remembered how to exhale.

Heart hammering, Lara sucked in a deep breath, tasting blood and salt.

Silence followed, hollow and profound.

All she could hear was her ragged breathing, and Alar's too, from beneath her.

She didn't move. Her body had locked in place, every muscle rigid with the certainty that the storm would come back, that it wasn't over.

But it was.

34: AN UNPAID DEBT

SLOWLY, LARA RAISED her head, twisting to look behind her. The rift was shrinking. No longer was it a gaping hole, but a thin silvery tear. And as she watched, it faded until nothing but the starry night sky was visible between the stones. Moonlight frosted The Shattered Crown.

Lara stared, heart pounding against her breastbone.

"You did it," Alar whispered hoarsely.

She swallowed.

"Lara!"

Bree rushed into the stone circle, still gripping her sword.

Reaching her side, she dropped to a crouch. Her gaze went to Lara's shoulder. "You're hurt."

"It's not deep." Lara waved her away. The scratch burned, but she'd put something on it soon enough. What mattered was that her body felt the strongest it had in days. Her mind was blessedly clear, and her skin was cool. The fever had gone.

More figures moved into the stone circle then: Roth, Cailean, Annis, and Ren. Skaal stalked after them.

"What happened here?" Cailean surveyed the interior of the stone circle, his narrowed gaze lingering on the knife hilt protruding from Alar's shoulder and where Sablebane lay, bleeding out. A deep groove then appeared between his dark brows. "Where's Mor?"

"In The Threshold," Vyr answered.

Lara shoved herself upright. Her arms shook. Her *entire* body trembled.

She turned her head. Vyr stood flanked by four Ravens, all of them pale and hollow-eyed. His leather armor hung in strips. Blood ran down his cheek in a slow trickle. He looked hunted.

Heat flared in her gut.

"Mor betrayed us." The words came out, harsh and flat. "And *you* helped her."

"Aye." Vyr didn't deny it. His gaze flicked to Alar, then away.

Cailean's fingers flexed around his sword hilt. Silver pulsed through his tattoos, painting his face in ghostly light. The air between him and Mor's cousin crackled.

Vyr's fingers flexed upon the grip of his drawn longsword. "Mor learned that she could draw wraiths back into the rift using her magic … but she needed a fire-wielder bearing the *Ord-ree seal* to close it." His mouth twisted. "Alar's presence served no magical purpose. She wanted balance restored … but she also wanted her enemies dead."

"Including *you*." Alar's voice was tight, threaded with pain.

Vyr's lips thinned, yet he didn't reply.

"The three of you were never meant to leave."

A weak voice made them all turn.

Sablebane lay on his back a few yards away, head in Fern's lap. Blood seeped between his fingers where they pressed against his stomach. Black in the moonlight. Fatal. Lara had seen enough injuries like this to know.

But he wasn't looking at his wound. He was looking at Vyr.

"Why do you think she contacted you after all these years?" Each word cost him. "The whispers that they were calling you the Elk King in the North. She needed your help. But she also feared you gaining too much power."

Vyr's expression hardened.

"You plotted against us." Cailean stalked forward, Roth and Bree at his sides. "You fucker."

Skaal moved with them, a growl vibrating in her chest.

Vyr and the Ravens flanking him raised their blades and dropped into fighting stances.

"Stop." Lara's voice cracked through the cold air. "All of you."

Cailean froze. A muscle jumped in his cheek. "But—"

"Listen to her." Alar was on his feet. Gods knew how—he had a dagger jutting from his shoulder, cuts covering his arms, and his hand still dripped blood—but he was standing. At her side.

Lara's heart kicked hard against her ribs.

The man was in a state, yet his first thought was for her.

She loved him. And he loved her. No declarations were needed, yet the truth of it hit like a fist to the chest. Mor had known, had used it.

Lara forced herself to breathe as she turned to Vyr.

"You went along with it. Betrayed us." Her voice stayed level. Barely. "I won't forget that. But you stood against her at the end."

Vyr stared back. He didn't try to justify himself. A wise move.

Lara took a step toward him. Alar shadowed her.

"Go." The word came out sharp. "But when you take her throne, when you tell them what happened here … tell the truth."

Vyr's throat worked. "You don't want blood?"

"I want cooperation." The words tasted strange. "Next time we meet, you negotiate with me. Do I have your word?"

His black eyes narrowed.

"We did this." Lara gestured at the sealed rift. "It nearly broke us all. Let it count for something."

Silence stretched. Then Vyr swallowed. Hard. "You have my word, Lara," he said, a hoarse edge to his voice. "Next time … we talk."

She nodded before glancing at Cailean. His tattoos still pulsed. His body still coiled tight, ready to spring. Only respect for her kept him leashed. How long would that last?

"Go," she said to Vyr again. "Before I change my mind."

Mor's cousin inclined his head. His gaze swept over them before he looked at Fern, still cradling her dying father. "Are you coming?"

"No." Her voice was barely above a whisper. "I'll see you in Cannich."

He nodded before gesturing to the Ravens. They backed away, melting into darkness beyond the stones.

Lara watched until they vanished. Her stomach churned. People broke promises all the time. Would Vyr?

Maybe. Maybe not.

But at least no one else would die tonight.

"Alar." Sablebane's voice drew her attention then. Weak. Raw. "My son."

Alar's breathing grew shallow.

My son.

Two words he'd never thought to hear.

He moved from Lara's side and crossed to his father. His palm pulsed with each stride, and a deep pain throbbed down his back. *Fuck.*

"Alar," Lara murmured. "We need to remove that knife … it's—"

"Later." He flashed her a weak smile before sinking down onto his knees next to Sablebane.

His gaze slid over the deep wound to his gut. Blood was everywhere. He looked up at his sister. Fern stared back at him. She knew he was done for too.

His father's hand lifted, trembling slightly. His fingers then closed around Alar's wrist. "I loved your mother … but I failed her."

Alar's pulse kicked into a sprint. He hadn't expected this.

Sablebane's face contorted then, as a spasm of pain seized him. His grip on Alar's wrist tightened. "After you were born, I returned to Dorne Forest … I watched you both from the trees. I planned to go through the stones and take Marav form … to disappear into Albia forever … but I hesitated too long. Mor had me followed. She discovered what I'd done."

Alar stared down at him, unsure of how to answer. For so long, he'd hated his father. And yet, as he stared into Wynn Sablebane's eyes, a lifetime of rage drained from him. "Fern told me you were sent to a labor camp," he admitted finally.

His father stiffened, a moan of pain tearing from his throat. "I overheard you that night," he panted. "When you told Lara about Struana's death."

Alar stilled. Telling Lara about that had cost him. The fact that Sablebane had been listening filled him with shame. However, there was no judgment in his father's eyes.

"You're not to blame for any of this, son … *I* am." Sablebane's breathing was labored now. Sweat coated his face. "For those scars on your face and neck too."

Placing his hand over his father's, he squeezed gently. "No," he said huskily, wishing his throat wasn't so damn tight. "You aren't."

And he meant it too.

He regretted his father's hesitation. If he hadn't waited, Alar's life would have been very different. His grandfather wouldn't have died trying to protect him, his grandmother wouldn't have withered from grief, and his mother wouldn't have been stoned to death.

He wouldn't have grown so bitter. So angry and desperate to prove himself.

But his path wouldn't have led him to Lara either.

Aye, it would have been a different life. A far happier one, perhaps. Yet it was the road not taken, and he wouldn't mourn it. Not any longer.

Silence settled, soft like falling ash.

Then Sablebane's fingers clamped tightly around Alar's wrist. His grip was hard enough to bruise, hard enough that Alar felt bone grinding.

"Kill me."

Fern jerked. "No."

"Hush." Sablebane's free hand found hers and squeezed. "A belly wound takes its victim slowly. Do you want to hear me scream?"

Tears cut tracks through the grime on her face.

Alar's gaze moved between them. His gut clenched.

All those nights, all those years, of imagining this. His blade driving into his father's chest. The light going out of his eyes while Alar watched.

But his father was asking for it now.

And he couldn't feel anything.

No—that wasn't true. He felt *everything*. Too much. It was choking him.

They'd both made choices. Bad ones. Selfish ones. Who was he to judge? After Dulross. After everything he'd done in the name of—what? Justice? Revenge? None of it mattered any longer.

"Son." Sablebane's gaze found his. "Will you make me beg?"

Something cracked in Alar's chest. "No," he whispered. "Don't."

"Then do it."

His heart started to slam against his ribs, hard and erratic.

He looked at Fern and marked the pain blazing in her eyes. She was shaking, barely holding on.

Reaching out, he drew one of the blades strapped to his father's thigh. His fingers closed around the bone grip. "Where?" he asked hoarsely.

Sablebane's gaze held his. Something flickered in his grey eyes—gratitude, maybe. Relief. "Drive it through the base of my throat."

Fern made a small and broken sound. Alar didn't look at her. He couldn't. If he did, he'd drop the blade and walk away.

Swallowing, he placed the tip in the hollow at the base of his father's throat. The steel dimpled his skin, and Alar's hand shook.

"Thank you."

The words barely made it out.

Then his father let go of Fern and wrapped his hand around Alar's forearm—above where he already gripped his wrist with his other hand—steadying him.

And yanked down.

Even dying, he was strong, stronger than Alar expected. The blade punched through—hit something, kept going, and then buried itself to the hilt.

Blinding pain exploded in Alar's shoulder. He bit down on a curse that wanted to turn into a scream.

Meanwhile, his father's eyes went wide, slitted pupils contracting into thin lines. His mouth opened, and blood dribbled down his chin, thick and dark.

Alar couldn't move. He couldn't look away.

The man who'd sired him. Abandoned him. Betrayed him. Saved him.

Dying.

The hands gripping his arm went slack and fell away.

Gone.

Fern started to weep. They weren't quiet tears, but deep sobs that tore from her chest. The rending sound echoed off stone, filling The Shattered Crown.

A hand touched his good shoulder.

Lara.

She settled beside him. He leaned into her without thinking. He needed the contact, needed something warm and real.

They sat while Fern wept. No one spoke.

Time passed. How long, he couldn't tell.

"Ruari predicted this." Lara's voice was soft and careful. "A couple of days ago. He cast the bones … and told me an unpaid debt had to be settled."

Alar looked at Fern. Her head was bowed, shoulders shaking. She hadn't heard, for she was too lost in grief.

An unpaid debt.

He remembered his father's words then. *You're not to blame for any of this, son … I am.*

Alar's throat started to ache. Sablebane had given his life to save his. Aye, the debt was well and truly paid, yet it didn't fill him with relief, or vindication.

Pain pulsed in his shoulder—bone-deep. Each heartbeat sent fire through the joint. His vision blurred at the edges. He closed his eyes.

Fuck being stoic. He needed—

The world tilted, and then he was falling.

Or maybe just, finally, letting go.

35: YOU KNOW THE WAY

"NEARLY DONE." LARA gently packed the last of the woundwort into the deep cut on Alar's shoulder. "I just need to secure this with a bandage."

"Take your time." His voice was husky with pain and exhaustion. "I'm not going anywhere."

"None of us are," Annis agreed.

Looking up, Lara cast a glance over at where the counselor sat, shoulders slumped, a few feet away. The rest of their companions—except for Fern, who knelt beside her father's corpse by the loch—surrounded them. They'd all descended from The Shattered Crown.

Roth and Cailean had helped Fern bring her father's body down as well. The moon was setting now. Not long until the sky lightened to the east. Lara worked by the light of a torch that Roth had lit. It gilded Alar's pale skin.

Now that the rift had sealed, what spirits still lingered in this place—those that had escaped being sucked back into Threshold—had fled. The powries and trows had disappeared too, following the Shee.

The silence was almost deafening.

In the aftermath of their success, Lara had expected jubilation to thrill through her. Aye, she was relieved the rift was mended and that balance had been restored, but Mor's betrayal had left a sour taste in her mouth. And viewing the expressions of those around her, she wasn't alone.

Stepping back, Lara busied herself with ripping off long strips from her undertunic. The material was tough, and she had to use her dagger. Then, she began to tie the strips diagonally across Alar's chest and shoulder, securing them under one arm.

"It's not the best of bandages," she admitted. "And your wound will need to be dressed properly ... but it'll do ... for now."

"Thank you," Alar replied.

"So, the satchel of healing herbs Ruari brought from Crask came in useful?" Roth asked then, his voice thick with fatigue and other emotions.

Lara nodded, even as her throat constricted.

Ruari.

A dull, dragging sensation settled in the pit of her belly as her gaze went to the glassy surface of the loch. *Gods.* She couldn't believe he was gone.

The young seer had been with her since just a couple of turns after she'd taken the throne. He'd always shown great talent, but over the years, he'd grown in confidence. In courage.

She'd watched, helpless, as the Fuath had dragged him into the deep. He'd had a terrifying end.

"You should never have listened to me," Bree's voice, low and rough, drew Lara's attention then. Her friend sat nearby, her hazel eyes dark in the torchlight. "I counseled you to trust Mor." She pulled a face. "Gregor was right."

Lara heaved a deep sigh. "She took us *all* in, Bree," she replied softly. "Don't blame yourself."

"And it doesn't change the fact Gregor is a worthless shitbag," Cailean added. "If our paths ever cross again, I'm killing him."

Silence fell at these blunt words. Lara had no doubt the chief-enforcer would make good on his threat.

Moments later, Roth cleared his throat. "What are we going to do about *that*?"

Lara glanced the warrior's way to see he'd gestured to where a dark shape crouched next to a boulder. Golden eyes glowed. Dorka was watching them. She was still chained to the hawthorn, waiting for Mor.

The Raven Queen would never return for her.

Lara studied Dorka's shadowed face, remembering how the Shee queen's eyes had softened every time she touched minds with the clag-doo, her joy when she'd finally managed to gentle the feline. It had meant so much to her and had revealed unexpected vulnerability.

A chink in Mor's armor. She'd hidden it well, but she'd been a lonely queen desperate for connection.

There was a price to pay for killing anyone who threatened your rule, a price for never letting anyone into your heart. Dorka had given Mor the intimacy she craved.

Not that Mor's connection with Dorka had altered her plans.

If she'd had her way, both Alar and Lara would be in The Threshold now.

Lara's belly tightened. No, she wouldn't feel sorry for Mor. She'd done this to herself.

"We need to set her free," Alar replied, heaving himself to his feet.

"I'll do it," Cailean grunted. "Sit down."

"Careful," Bree warned as he made his way toward the clag-doo.

A moment later, Dorka gave a warning hiss, and Cailean's pace slowed. Her tail started to lash, her ears flattening. She wanted Mor. No one else would do.

Ren stood up. Her sharp-featured face was haggard, yet she flexed her hands at her sides. "You'll need my help."

Cailean cast the bard a grateful glance. "Aye."

Stepping up to his side, Ren drew in a slow, deep breath. And then, the soft, beguiling melody that she'd sung to help gentle Dorka echoed through the still air. The hissing subsided, the tension easing from the feline's supple frame.

Eventually, Cailean moved closer once more, easing up alongside Dorka. She watched him warily, but Ren's charm had lowered her defenses. The chief-enforcer reached down, his hands sliding over Dorka's thick neck, to the steel collar. "Just bear with me," he murmured. "And I'll get this off … then you'll be free. Finally." His fingers worked swiftly, and with a 'click', the collar released, falling away.

It hit the ground, metal clanging against stone. The sound shattered the reverie.

Dorka sprang forward, knocking Cailean over as she went.

Racing past Ren in a black streak, the clag-doo disappeared into the shadows.

Dawn rose over Darkmere.

Mist evaporated off the loch's shadowy surface before rays of sunlight sparkled upon it. Streaks of rose, lavender, and gold painted the sky.

It was the most beautiful sunrise Alar had ever seen.

Walking across the dry trampled grass near the edge of the loch, the toes of his boots scattering small grey pebbles, he made his way to where a leather-clad Shee female finished building a cairn. The pile of stones sat back from the Darkmere, upon a rise, not far from the base of the outcrop where The Shattered Crown stood.

As he approached, Alar glanced up, taking in the grey monoliths. Sunlight now bathed them. They looked far less ominous with the dawn. Just an ancient ruined stone circle. Now that the rift had sealed, that was exactly what it was.

Farther down the pebbly loch-shore, Lara and her escort had gathered. Roth was making something out of reeds he'd collected. They were preparing to send Ruari's spirit to the Otherworld. Traditionally, the Marav burned their dead upon a pyre, but that wasn't possible for Ruari. Alar would join them shortly. But first, he needed to pay his respects to someone else.

The crunch of his boots alerted Fern to his arrival.

Turning, she glanced over her shoulder. Her gaze settled on him, noting the sling he now wore and his bandaged hand. "Lara took that blade successfully out of your shoulder then?"

Alar grimaced. Lara had worked as gently as she could, but it had still hurt. She'd given him a tincture for the pain, but his shoulder throbbed, nonetheless, in time with his heartbeat. "She did. Sorry … I wanted to help you build his cairn."

Fern snorted. "You aren't much good to me one-handed." She paused then, looking away. "Besides … I needed some time. Alone with him."

Alar nodded. He understood.

Moving up next to her, he surveyed the mound. Wynn Sablebane's final resting place.

The two of them stood silently then, listening to the cawing of a raven. Looking up, Alar's gaze rested on a large black bird. It perched upon an outcrop of rock jutting out from the promontory.

"Eagal," Fern murmured. "He wants to know where Mor is."

Alar glanced at his sister. "You're touching minds with the raven?"

She nodded.

"Have you told him?"

"Aye."

Eagal gave a raspy croak and took wing, disappearing over the edge of The Shattered Crown.

Alar watched the bird go, his gut hardening. "So, you knew what Mor was planning?"

"I did."

"And you had no problem with it?" He looked Fern's way then to find his sister watching him, her grey eyes shadowed.

"Not initially."

Silence fell between them. Fern lay the last rock on the top of the cairn.

"I've spent my whole life hiding," Alar said eventually. "Ashamed of who I am ... but I'm done with that now."

"Good," she said softly, surprising him. "You shouldn't suffer because of other people's prejudices. I'm sorry, Alar ... you deserved better."

His throat tightened, and he swallowed. Fern's words disarmed him; he wasn't used to being apologized to.

Their gazes met then before a wry smile tugged at her lips. "I've been jealous of you, you know?"

He raised an eyebrow. "Why?"

"Our father crossed lines for your mother ... and intended to leave Sheehallion forever to be with you both. He'd never have made such a sacrifice for me."

Alar huffed. "You don't know that."

Fern sighed, her gaze returning to the cairn she'd just built. "I used to visit him at the mine sometimes. We both thought he'd never leave it." She broke off then, tension rippling across her face. "But then Mor discovered a better punishment for him."

Cold washed over Alar. "His presence on this journey was *punishment?*"

"It was. As was mine. I was tainted by association. Mor never forgot a slight."

Alar's pulse quickened. "She used us all."

"She did." Fern's voice caught then. "But no one disobeys the Raven Queen ... to do so is unthinkable."

"And yet our father did."

Fern's throat worked. "And paid with his life."

They fell silent once more, listening to the gently rippling water stirred by a crisp breeze.

"Where will you go now?" Fern asked eventually.

Alar sighed. "I don't know." Something tightened in his chest then. "But I'll stay by Lara's side … unless she sends me away."

Fern observed him for a few moments, and then, to his surprise, she smiled. "You have the Sablebane loyalty, I see."

He huffed a laugh. "It would seem so … and you, Fern? Will you return to Cannich as you promised Vyr?"

She nodded, even as her expression clouded. "I shall … although whether or not I stay to serve the new king remains to be seen."

"He can't be any worse than Mor, surely?"

"No … but I'm not sure I want to serve anyone now."

Alar's lips quirked. "We have that in common too then."

Fern smiled back, even as a muscle feathered in her jaw. Turning from him, she placed a hand upon the cairn. She then bowed her head. "Go to your long sleep, father. Rest easy … until we meet again."

And with that, she nodded to Alar and swiveled on her heel.

"Wait," he said softly.

Fern glanced over her shoulder.

"You aren't alone." His pulse fluttered as he spoke. He wasn't used to making himself this vulnerable. It made him feel as if he were standing there naked. "I'm always here … if you need me."

Her proud face softened, her eyes glistening now. "Thank you … brother."

She walked away then in determined long strides.

Fern's stag trotted toward her, halting so that she could spring up on its back. An instant later, they were racing away, east.

Alar watched his sister go, wondering if he'd ever see her again.

When Fern was little more than a speck in the distance, he turned, his gaze traveling along the shore to where the others stood. He approached them cautiously. They'd gone through much together, but none of these people were his friends.

And as he walked down the shore, he caught sight of a magnificent red stag grazing a few yards away. A tired smile tugged at his lips. Reedav. He'd been sure the stag would have departed with the Shee. But he'd stayed.

Lifting his proud head, Reedav watched him. Dark liquid eyes.

Alar's smile widened. They couldn't touch minds, but his gut told him that the stag had stayed for him.

Hearing the crunch of his boots on gravel, Bree glanced over her shoulder. And then, to his surprise, she nodded to him. "You're just in time … Roth has nearly finished."

Drawing up to Bree's side, Alar watched as the warrior twisted the last reeds together.

A large swan, its neck curving majestically, sat upon his lap.

"You've hidden talents," Cailean observed as Roth climbed to his feet and handed the swan to Lara.

Roth's lips curved. "My mother is a basket weaver … I learned a few tricks from her."

"It's beautiful," Lara murmured as she moved toward the water's edge. "You've done Ruari proud." Leaning down, she set the swan on the water.

It floated away, bobbing on the rippling surface. The wind was getting up now. The Whistle had started to sing around them. Above, the sky was clear, the sun a golden halo to the east. It was the first time in nearly a moon's turn they'd seen its friendly face.

Alar exhaled slowly, the tension in his gut unraveling. The world felt right again.

Lara cleared her throat then. A moment later, she began to sing—a soft, sad lament.

> *"Bone-reader, dream-walker,*
> *May the current carry you gently*
> *To the shores we cannot see.*
> *This loch will remember,*
> *And we will not let you fade.*
> *Go softly on the dark water, Ruari.*
> *The veil is thin. You know the way."*

Lara had a soft voice. Not as clear as Ren's. Nor as powerful as Mor's. Yet the emotion in it made his breathing grow shallow. He hadn't been close to Ruari, not like Annis and Ren were, but he'd respected the seer.

The counselor and bard were both weeping now. However, although Lara's eyes glistened, she continued to sing, her voice never wavering. Next to her, Bree, Cailean, and Roth stood, heads bowed.

Watching them, a hollow sensation filled Alar. He was intruding upon their grief. He didn't move though, for he didn't want to shatter the moment or draw attention to himself. Skaal, who'd been sitting next to Cailean, padded over to Alar then. She pushed up against him. Grateful for her show of affection, he put an arm around her shoulders. The fae hound's warmth and musky scent reminded him of the wulvers—of a life he'd turned his back on.

How were his brothers and sisters faring at Dulross?

Eventually, the High Queen's lament ended.

The swan bobbed away, sunlight catching the reeds.

Blinking, Lara stepped back from the water's edge. "It doesn't feel like enough," she whispered. "He deserves more."

"He died with honor," Cailean said softly, glancing over at where Skaal now nuzzled Alar. His brow furrowed. "It's the best any of us can ask for."

"What now?" Bree asked. Her gaze still lingered upon the gently bobbing swan.

Lara sighed, drawing her cloak around her as a gust of wind whipped into them. "Now, we retrace our steps."

She turned then, searching for someone.

Alar stilled as her gaze settled upon him.

"Fern has gone then?"

He nodded.

"And yet *you're* still here," Cailean said gruffly.

Alar gave a soft snort. "Aye."

Bree nudged her husband in the ribs with her elbow, cutting him a sharp look.

"It was a jest," the chief-enforcer rumbled.

Of course, everyone here knew the reason he lingered.

Lara.

And he wasn't leaving, unless she told him to.

His gut tightened then as her gaze burned into him. Perhaps that moment had arrived. He wasn't going to ask though. He had his pride. If Lara was done with him, he'd let her spell it out.

"We're heading south now," she said finally. Her tone was veiled, her expression hard to read. "Are you coming with us?"

Alar cleared his throat. "Am I welcome?"

She nodded.

Warmth flooded across his chest, but before he could say anything else, she'd turned. He watched her walk away, back up the slope to where Bracken grazed. Fortunately, their horses and ponies hadn't bolted into the darkness the night before; none of them would be walking back to Crask. She then vaulted onto the mare's back and gathered the reins. "Let's go."

36: NO GOING BACK

WHAT ARE YOU doing?

Urging Bracken down the rocky hill toward where a burn sparkled in the silvery autumn light, Lara berated herself. Had she lost her wits? She'd had her chance to send Alar away. Their alliance had ended. The deed was done. But instead, she'd asked him to accompany them south.

Of course, she knew why.

She loved him.

Her pulse quickened, memories of that betrayal haunting her once more. The shock that had punched into her stomach, the slowly dawning realization that she'd been played. His face as he'd stood in the rain before her. Unrepentant. Scornful. Those memories were etched upon her forever.

Queasiness rolled over her then. Could she ever forgive that?

Don't think about him, she told herself firmly. *You're alive. The rift is closed. Focus on what you've achieved.*

An exhausted yet companionable silence had settled between the small group as they left the Darkmere behind them. They were all drained, all happy to travel without making conversation. Lara rode alone, deliberately so; she needed time to sort her thoughts out. Half a furlong ahead, Alar led their band, Reedav's long stride easily outpacing everyone else, while the others traveled in twos and threes behind him.

Despite that they were in the far north and winter now breathed down their necks, the sun held a surprising amount of warmth this morning. It soaked into her back and warmed her limbs. After days of fever, weakness, and a muddled brain, it was a relief to feel like herself again. The clouds had literally parted.

And despite that Alar kept intruding on her thoughts, relief glowed deep in her chest.

We did it.

After so many disappointments and defeats, something had finally gone right. Spirits still dwelled in Albia—as they always had—but its people would no longer dread the night. Nor would malevolent wraiths hunt them. Lara could now focus on other things. On dealing with her overkings properly. On uniting the south of Albia, at least.

And what about the borderlands? The wulvers and the Circines could prove a thorn in her side.

She pursed her lips, irritated that she couldn't just let herself enjoy this moment. *One problem at a time.*

Her gaze traveled forward once more, settling again on Alar's back.

She could spend the day ruminating, or she could face him. What was it to be?

Making her choice, she urged Bracken forward then, into a rapid canter. The mare leaped the burn at the bottom of the hill and raced up the other side, drawing alongside Alar and his stag.

He glanced her way. "Lara."

"Alar."

He looked rough, as if he'd been trampled by a clutch of trows. A bruise marked one cheekbone, and his eyes were hollowed. Crusting scratches marred his shoulders and arms. His long black hair spilled in a tangled mane down his back. His right arm was in a sling, and his left hand thickly bound with a bandage.

"How's the shoulder?" It was an inane thing to ask, but she was suddenly nervous.

He grimaced, giving Lara her answer. His gaze then roamed over her face. "And how are *you?*"

"Better," she admitted.

His brow furrowed. "So, the fire-madness … has it gone?"

Uneasiness shifted in her belly. She'd tried not to think about that. "I don't know," she answered honestly. "Maybe … we know so little about the effects of fire magic on the wielder."

"Don't use it then," he said, alarm flaring in his eyes. "There's no need."

"I don't intend to," she replied huskily. "Although my reign so far hasn't been easy … fire was a useful weapon in a tight spot."

"Then let me stay by your side … to help protect you."

Lara's heart started to pound. "Why would you—"

"We can't go back to how things were." His voice lowered, urgency in it now. "I can't be your husband any longer … but I could be your *warder*, like Bree."

They'd slowed to a trot now, the wind whipping against their faces. "I spoke impulsively by the lakeside," she said after a few moments, still reeling from his offer. It nearly made her lose her train of thought, or the reason she'd approached him. "Maybe you should go."

He gave her a long look. "Is that what you want?"

Misery twisted hard in Lara's chest—and a longing so sharp that she gasped. "I'm in love with you, Alar mac Struana." She choked the words out. "Gods, I wish I wasn't. I should hate you. Why don't I?"

Reedav slowed to a walk, and Bracken followed suit. The Whistle whined around them. Neither noticed. Instead, their gazes locked in a silent duel.

He gave her a tight smile. "I don't know."

Lara's fingers clenched around the reins. *Gods*. She was suffering, yet he just gave her a glib three-word answer.

"I've done terrible things … have given you little reason to love me," he continued, his gaze fusing with hers. "Although it's something I'll cherish until I take my last breath." A pause followed. A heartbeat. "So, no … I don't understand what you see in me … but I know exactly why I love *you*." Dizziness swept over her, yet he wasn't done. "You give me hope. Before I met you, I was a bitter bastard … searching for justice in a world where there is none. But just a few days in your company showed me there's light in the darkness. Beauty. You made me see it … and once you did, there was no going back. For that, I'll be eternally in your debt."

Lara cut her gaze away then.

Her throat ached, and her vision blurred. She didn't want to break down in front of him. That would be the last straw. And so, she dug her heels into Bracken's flanks.

The mare lurched forward into a canter.

Moments later, she was racing ahead of him. To her relief, Alar let her go. And as she rode, tears started to roll down her cheeks.

They rode into Crask in the late afternoon.

Even from a distance, Lara saw things had changed. The sod roofs no longer sagged. The wattle and daub walls glowed gold in the lowering sun instead of a dull dirty-brown. The loch sparkled, no longer lying flat and black like something waiting to swallow you whole.

The air felt different. Lighter.

Then the bairns came running.

They poured out from between the roundhouses, shrieking and laughing, their bare feet slapping on the wooden walkways. Then they ran alongside the horses as Lara and her escort approached, calling out questions that tumbled over each other.

"Did you fight monsters?"

"Did you make the ghosts go away?"

Lara's throat went tight as she looked down at their faces—flushed with excitement, eyes bright, questions spilling from their lips—and something knotted deep in her chest unraveled.

These children weren't hollow-eyed anymore. They weren't clinging to their mothers' skirts, too frightened to play.

They were alive again.

Connor appeared at the end of the walkway, Orla at his side. And when Lara saw what the chieftain's wife held against her chest, her breathing caught.

The infant she carried was moving and wriggling.

A happy gurgle reached her ears, and Lara's face split into a wide grin.

The silent baby who had haunted her all the way north—that tiny, still thing wrapped against her mother's chest—was laughing.

"My Queen!" Connor's voice carried over the excited chatter. "The sun has shone since Gateway. The nights are quiet … the wraiths have disappeared."

"The danger has passed." Lara slid off Bracken's back, her legs nearly buckling. Gods, she was tired. After three days riding, sleeping rough, her body screamed for a proper bed.

But she was smiling—she couldn't help it.

More people emerged from the roundhouses now, crannog-dwellers she recognized from days earlier. They'd once looked at her with a blend of hope and fear, wondering if she'd succeed or if they'd all die slowly as the world rotted around them, but they were all smiling now.

"You did it!" A woman called out, clutching her husband's arm.

Others took up the cry, and suddenly, excited chatter surrounded her. Relief and joy spilled over.

"The Loch-Bhàn are gone—"

"Haven't seen a boggart in days—"

"My nets are full again … the fish came back—"

Lara's vision blurred. She blinked hard. *Not now. Don't start weeping.*

A flash of crimson robes caught her eye.

Mairead. The sacrificer grinned, waving to her.

And then she saw two familiar figures pushing through the crowd. Duana and Eithne. The sisters looked different. There was color in their cheeks and light in their eyes now; they weren't just surviving anymore.

"My Queen!" Duana reached her first, nearly tripping in her eagerness. Her gaze went to the scabbed scratch on Lara's upper arm. "Are you hurt? Is everyone—"

"We're all fine." Lara caught the lass's hands and squeezed. "It's a relief to be back though."

Eithne smiled shyly then. "We haven't been idle since you left. We've been helping in the kitchens. I've been learning how to smoke eels."

"Come, My Queen!" Orla called out, beckoning to Lara. "We thought you'd return today … and have been preparing a feast in your honor. We've got ducks spit-roasting inside, bread straight from the ovens … and fresh goat's cheese."

"And ale," Connor added with a grin, winking at Roth. "Lots of ale."

The crowd began to move, drawing Lara along with them. Hands touched her arms, her back—not grabbing, just making contact. It was as if they wanted to reassure themselves that the High Queen was real, that she'd returned to them.

"Look at the chief-enforcer's tattoos," one of the bairns whispered.

"Is that really a fae hound?" another gasped. "I've never seen one."

"The man riding the red stag … how does he control it?"

As the chatter continued, Lara glanced back over her shoulder.

Her companions were dismounting, surrounded by crannog-dwellers eager to help with the horses. Bree was laughing at something someone said. Cailean looked bemused but pleased. Roth was already being handed a cup of something.

And Alar.

He still sat astride Reedav, watching. His face was tired, lined with pain he'd done his best to hide during the journey south. He watched the crannog-dwellers surround their High Queen—watched the people reach for her with joy and relief—and his lips curved into a half-smile.

Their eyes met across the crowd and held for a heartbeat.

Warmth suffused Lara's chest. Aye, she'd done this. *They'd* done this. Together.

Then someone tugged her arm, and she turned away and let herself be pulled along by the tide.

They led her to the largest of the roundhouses, the chieftain's residence. Inside, torches blazed in every bracket. Logs of pine roared in the hearth. As promised, ducks spit-roasted over glowing embers. Fat dripped, creating a fug of smoke, but no one seemed to care.

The rich aroma of roasting duck hit Lara as she made her way toward the hearth. Her stomach growled so loud that Eithne heard it and giggled.

"The ducks will be ready soon," someone assured her.

"Sit, My Queen, please." Orla motioned to a stool.

"Try a honey cake," a lass thrust a wooden trencher toward her. "They're still warm."

Women surrounded her, eager to share, to give, to make their High Queen proud.

Lara let them fuss, let them pour ale into a cup. And as they did, she couldn't stop smiling.

This was why she'd gone north—why she'd faced the Slew, the frost spirits, and the rift itself.

For moments like this.

She took a bite of cake that oozed with honey. "Gods," she mumbled. "This is incredible."

"My Queen." Connor appeared next to his wife. "We've prepared the east roundhouse for you and your companions. There's clean clothing for you all … as well as water for washing."

"Thank you." She swallowed her mouthful of cake and licked her fingers, suddenly aware of how she must look. Filthy. Exhausted. Probably smelling like horse and sweat.

She glanced around the hall at the happy faces, at the feast the people of Crask were preparing for her and her companions.

"Actually," she said, turning back to Connor, "Could I ask one small thing?"

"Anything, My Queen."

"A *bath*?" The word came out hopeful, almost pleading. "An iron tub if you have one. Hot water. And soap."

Connor flashed her an easy grin. "I've already got lads heating the water. Orla insisted."

Orla appeared beside him, the babe's tiny fingers grasping at her long braids. "I thought you'd want to wash before the feasting," she said, her lips curving. "The tub is in your alcove … it should be ready now."

Lara could have kissed her.

Leaning her head back against the rolled edge of the iron tub, Lara heaved a deep sigh. The water was perfect. Heat seeped into her limbs, soaking away days of grueling travel. The scent of rosemary soap enveloped her. Orla had made it herself. The sharp, woody scent tickled Lara's nostrils. Fresh. Like crushed pine needles.

The smell reminded her of Alar.

Lara's eyes snapped open, her contentment puncturing.

You can't ignore him forever.

Her pulse fluttered. No, she'd have to acknowledge what lay between them. She'd have to make a decision about the future. Like a coward, she'd told herself it could wait until Crask—but now, they'd arrived. Her time was running out.

And there was no running from this.

Her gaze went to the heavy curtain that shielded her small alcove from the rest of the space. Unlike their last stay at Crask, tonight, each of them had an alcove. Only Skaal would sleep by the hearth.

Alar's alcove was directly opposite hers. He, like the others, didn't have a bathtub to soak in. However, Orla had provided everyone with hot water, soap, drying sheets, and the clothes—now freshly laundered—they'd arrived in days earlier.

Picking up the soap, Lara started to wash. The bitter yet clean scent wrapped around her, coating the back of her throat.

Soft feminine laughter intruded then, making her tense.

Cailean and Bree had taken the alcove next to hers. The couple had spent little time alone over the past turn of the moon. Moments of intimacy had been rare. No doubt, they wished to enjoy their privacy; even so, Lara's brow furrowed.

She understood their eagerness. But when Cailean's throaty groan filtered through the wall, she stilled. Fingers tightening around the slippery bar of soap.

Irritation bubbled up. Surely, they weren't going to—

A muffled cry followed, and then another deep male moan.

Thick stacked stone divided the alcoves, yet that didn't stop noise from traveling.

Lara muttered an oath. She wasn't a prude, but she didn't need to hear her friends fucking.

"Aye … harder!" Bree whimpered.

Gods.

Squeezing her eyes shut, she slid under the hot water.

37: I WILL NOT YIELD

LARA REACHED FOR another slice of roast duck and avoided looking at Cailean and Bree.

The couple was oblivious to her anyway. They'd taken a seat farther down the chieftain's table. Cheeks flushed, eyes bright, they kept sharing lingering looks and secret smiles.

Lara pretended not to notice. Their *loud* lovemaking had ruined her bath.

Music filled the roundhouse. Two men playing bone whistles had struck up a tune next to the huge square stone-lined hearth at the heart of the roundhouse. The din of voices and the squeal of the bone whistles were deafening.

"What a feast."

She looked up to see Alar slide onto the bench opposite her. Clad in his usual black leathers, he looked dangerous. There wasn't much space, and Roth had to shuffle along to accommodate him. The red-haired warrior, who sat next to Duana, cast Alar a veiled look.

"Enjoy it," Lara replied, pouring gravy onto her duck. "It's in our honor."

"In *your* honor," Alar replied. "Connor mac Garth wishes to thank his High Queen … and rightly so."

Lara gave a soft snort. The crannog-dwellers had outdone themselves. It was a feast worthy of the ones her cooks prepared for special occasions at Duncrag.

Men, women, and bairns lined the long tables that formed a square around the hearth inside the chieftain's roundhouse, as they tucked into roast duck and smoked eel. They passed around baskets of crusty oaten bread, helped themselves to spoonfuls of soft goat's cheese, and drank mead and ale from wooden cups.

Next to Lara, Annis was spreading cheese onto a huge slice of crusty bread. The counselor then took a large bite, her eyelids flickering in pleasure.

A smile tugged at Lara's lips. Her attention flicked back to Alar, her belly fluttering when she found him watching her. It was a look she recognized; one he reserved just for her. A steady, smoldering gaze. Soft and knowing.

Aye, this man understood her. She'd never been able to hide from him.

Her cheeks warmed then. This was awkward; she wished he'd squeezed in elsewhere. But he hadn't. Dropping her gaze, she took a bite of duck. Rich flavor exploded on her tongue as she chewed.

"How long will we remain at Crask?" Alar asked then.

"Forever," Roth replied, pouring Duana and himself some more ale. "With hospitality like this, I may never leave."

Duana laughed, and Lara smiled. "We shall stay a few days at least. I think we've all earned it."

"A toast!" The chieftain shouted then, his voice cutting through the roar. "To our brave High Queen!" Connor had risen to his feet and now held a horn of mead aloft. His high cheekbones were slightly flushed. "She faced down the shadows and vanquished them. Songs will be sung about her bravery!"

Embarrassment prickled Lara's skin, especially when Roth murmured, "He's laying it on thick, isn't he?"

"A speech from our High Queen!" The chieftain thrust his horn high into the air, mead sloshing over the brim.

"Speech!" A roar went up, shivering through the smoky air and shaking the rafters.

Swallowing her mouthful, Lara exchanged a look with Alar—who was now smiling—and rose to her feet. A pause followed as she marshaled her thoughts.

"This isn't just my victory," she said once the cheering had died down, her voice carrying across the now silent roundhouse. "But that of those who have protected me on this journey. Cailean. Bree. Roth. Annis. Ren" —her gaze flicked to the man seated opposite— "and Alar."

Smiles followed these words, but Lara wasn't done. Over the years, she'd become comfortable with speech-making. She'd grown up watching her father hold an audience in the palm of his hand and had always marveled at his confidence. But it wasn't that difficult, once you learned how to connect with those listening.

"We lost our brave seer, Ruari, at The Shattered Crown. His soul has now traveled to the Otherworld … but I'd like us all to raise our cups now, to remember him."

"To Ruari!" Around her, a sea of cups thrust high into the air.

"Have you made peace with the Shee now?" Someone, a warrior with a florid face, shouted. There was a note of belligerence in his voice.

"Not as such," she answered. "Ruari wasn't the only one to fall at The Shattered Crown." She halted then, letting the tension build. "The Raven Queen is also dead." Shock rippled through the roundhouse. Once it had settled, she continued, "Mor's cousin, Vyrnek, now leads the Shee. He has promised to treat with us. We shall see if he holds true to his word."

A rumble followed this news. The crannog-dwellers exchanged wary looks. Clearly, few of them believed he would. However, none of them knew what had taken place inside that broken stone circle. Or that Mor had intended to betray her cousin.

"I can't give you all reassurances about the future," she went on, her chin lifting. "But you are proud crannog-dwellers. Uplanders. You've weathered many storms … and are strong enough to outlast more."

Connor, who still stood at the end of the table, nodded, raising his drinking horn high once more. "Aye!"

"Aye!" Cups thumped against wood.

"But there will be changes … both here in the North, and in The Wolds too," she went on, once the noise had died down. "Going forward, we shall learn to share our world with others.

It won't be easy. There will be obstacles, yet on this, I will not yield. My father persecuted the Shee, wulvers, and half-bloods. I won't."

A hush settled then.

Lara had spoken those last two words with deliberate emphasis, and fire pulsed in her belly as she stared the crowd down, daring any of them to contradict her.

No one did. Nonetheless, she marked the uneasy glances some of them shared. Change was coming, but that didn't mean it would be easy, or that they'd like it.

She lowered her gaze then, meeting Alar's eye across the table. Their gazes fused, and as their stare drew out, her pulse went wild. Suddenly, it didn't matter what anyone else in this roundhouse thought.

Only *his* opinion mattered.

The wulvers had turned on her, yet could she blame them entirely? Even at Duncrag, her people had treated them like vermin. Things had to change.

She wanted Alar to believe her, to know that she was committed to this. Over the last years, she'd teetered on the edge, torn between taking her father's path or her own. However, revenge only ever left a bitter taste in her mouth. Aye, she'd deal with her overkings. But that wasn't about justice or about restoring her birthright. It was about stopping greedy, ambitious men from destroying The Wolds.

Slowly, Alar smiled—and she knew he understood.

Lara rolled onto her back, staring up at the shadowed ceiling of her sleeping nook.

Curse it. The night drew out, and everyone else slumbered. But she couldn't.

The furs were deliciously soft, embracing her like a warm hug. After everything she'd endured of late, and with a belly full of rich food and drink, she should be sleeping deeply.

But she was wide awake.

And no, it wasn't Cailean and Bree's nocturnal activities that disturbed her. The alcove next to hers was mercifully silent.

Her mind wouldn't let her rest. Not with so much unsaid.

She'd said plenty earlier. Her speech had shocked many of the crannog-dwellers. The mood afterward hadn't been quite so merry as beforehand, yet Lara had lowered herself back onto the bench seat with renewed determination.

She voiced something that had burned inside her for a long time.

But not everything.

There were things she needed to say to Alar, and until she did, she'd find no peace.

Growling an oath, she threw back the furs and clambered out of bed. Her bare feet sank into the sheepskins as she threw her cloak around her shoulders.

She then ducked out of the alcove, stepping out onto the rush-strewn floor.

The hearth burned low. Above, the rafters creaked as wind buffeted the roundhouse. The drifting smoke swirled. A low rumble filtered through the air. Skaal lay curled up on a sheepskin by the fire, snoring.

Careful not to disturb the fae hound, Lara tiptoed across to Alar's alcove.

Halting before it, she hesitated, her courage faltering for a few instants.

Irritation surged up. *You're not backing away from this … or from him.*

And so, reaching out, she pushed aside the curtain and slipped inside.

Alar was asleep, propped up against a nest of rolled furs. Those furs covering his body had slipped down, revealing his naked torso. Fresh bandages wrapped around his chest and hand; he'd visited the crannog's healer shortly after their arrival. The light of a dying cresset played across his bare skin and the wolf's head tattoo.

The wolf's eyes glowed red then, as if it had just seen her.

Alar stirred awake, his own eyes opening. When he saw Lara, he stilled.

Embarrassed, Lara cleared her throat. "Sorry for waking you up," she said softly.

He stretched before wincing as his shoulder announced itself. Gingerly, he rolled it, testing it. "It's late … is something wrong?"

Her pulse started to thunder in her ears. Suddenly, she felt foolish. Tongue-tied. Maybe it would be easier if she just blurted everything out.

"I need to tell you *why* I love you."

He eyed her, his brow furrowing. "I thought you didn't know."

"Well, I do now." Gods, she wished she didn't sound so breathless.

His gaze softened, tenderness sparking in its depths. "You don't need to do this."

She shook her head. Aye, she did.

"You've always believed in me, even when I doubted myself," she began softly. "You listen. When you're at my side, I can take on the world." She paused, feeling lightheaded now. "Like tonight."

"That was a strong speech," he replied. "I didn't have anything to do with it."

She took a step closer. "You're wrong. You've opened my eyes to many things … even when I didn't want to see them." She paused then, her pulse fluttering. "You told me that Albia was changing … and that I couldn't put things back to how they once were, do you remember that?"

He nodded, his gaze veiling.

"Well, you were right. The old order died with my father. Why would I want to continue it?"

"I was harsh."

"You spoke the truth. I like that about you … the way you say things others don't. You have an ancient wisdom … one I want to learn."

He made a noise in the back of his throat.

She took another step forward. "You are a part of me now. Together, we've weathered betrayal, darkness, fire, and blood. We've emerged on the other side. Scorched but still alive. I love you, Alar. *All* of you. The darkness as well as the light. There's shadow in all of us."

"Not in you," he said huskily.

"Aye, *especially* in me." Her gaze fused with his, even as her pulse thumped in her ears. "Whether I use fire or not, I'm still a fire-wielder. Madness sleeps in my blood. I must always guard myself against it … and with your help, I will."

His eyes widened. "What are you saying?"

"When I ride back into Duncrag, I want to do so with you at my side. My husband."

Alar stared back at her. His chest rose and fell sharply. "You want me back?" His voice was hoarse, his eyes bright.

"Aye."

He swallowed. "Are you sure?"

Lara shrugged off her cloak, letting it fall to the sheepskins. She then reached down and grabbed the hem of her thin tunic, pulling it over her head so that she stood naked before him. "I've never been more certain about anything in my life."

38: SECOND CHANCES

STANDING UPON THE furs, cool air feathering against her bare skin, Lara let him observe her. And he did, his gaze tracking a hungry path down her body. "I could look at you all night," he whispered.

She snorted. "Please don't … it's not that warm in this alcove." Indeed, the heat of the smoldering hearth didn't reach this far. Cold drafts from the gusting wind outdoors pushed in through cracks in the stone and around the curtain that shielded them from the rest of the roundhouse.

"You'd better come here then," he replied huskily.

Lara's lips quirked. "I want to see you first."

His gaze hooded. "Very well." With that, he pushed aside the furs, revealing his own nakedness.

Warmth flushed over Lara as she took him in, admiring the lean hard-muscled lines of his chest. A thick solid erection thrust against his flat belly.

Her breathing hitched.

She moved then, climbing onto the furs and shuffling up so that she knelt between his thighs.

Her head lowered, her lips sweeping across his.

With a groan, he lifted his hands and cupped the back of her head. His mouth opened under hers, and they kissed—a slow, deep, sensual embrace that neither of them hurried. And into it, Lara poured all the emotion that still churned in her chest. She wasn't sure if he'd understood or accepted her love. But she'd show him now. Her teeth grazed his lips. Her tongue slid against his. Teasing. Demanding.

A low groan rumbled in his throat in response.

Reaching between them, she traced her fingers along the proud length of his prick. It responded to her touch, swelling larger still, straining toward her. She slid the palm of her hand over the swollen crown, thrilling as another groan escaped him.

He reached for her then with his good hand, but she brushed him aside. She continued to stroke him, marveling at how his shaft grew harder still. Moisture beaded on its tip.

His hand reached out once more, his fingers fastening gently around her wrist. "Wait," he said throatily. "I haven't touched you yet."

"And you will," she promised, heat pulsing in her womb now. "But, first, I need this."

He stared up at her, his pupils flaring dark. After a moment, his lips curved into a slow smile that sent her pulse wild. "In that case." He let go of her wrist and sank back against the nest of furs, spreading his thighs wider for her. "I'm all yours."

The challenge in his voice made Lara's breathing grow shallow.

She sat back on her heels and gazed down at his rigid prick.

Every time they'd lain together before now, she'd let him take the lead. But she was a different person now. Maybe he didn't think she'd take what she wanted, but she would.

Shuffling backward, the furs soft under her bare knees, she cupped his balls with one hand and wrapped the fingers of her other around the base of his shaft. He was rock-hard, his skin soft yet scalding to the touch. His shaft jerked, and he breathed an oath.

She leaned down then, her mouth greedily taking him in. When they'd coupled before, he'd pleasured her with his tongue, and she did the same to him now, flicking her tongue across the crown of him, tasting salt. And when she traced the underside of the tip, he gasped.

A thrill of power went through her, and she raked her fingertips over the tight skin of his balls.

He moaned, the sound sliding into a strangled noise when she took the length of his straining erection into her mouth. She took him as deep as she could, until it hit the back of her throat. Her eyes watered, yet she focused on stroking him, on sliding her mouth up and down his solid prick.

A shudder went through him.

A moment later, his fingers tangled in her hair, gathering it into a coil upon her crown so that it no longer hung in her face, so that he could watch her work him.

Excitement quickened like a flame on dry tinder in the cradle of her hips.

His raw sensuality awoke something inside her, a wildness that answered his call. Eagerly, she continued to slide her mouth up and down. Her jaws ached now, but she didn't care. She wanted to make him lose control, for him to spill down her throat.

"Touch yourself, Lara," he rasped then.

The command in his voice made her shiver, hunger quickening. And so, she obeyed, lowering her free hand between her thighs.

Her wetness shocked her, as did her sensitivity. She ran a finger gently over the swollen bud nestled there, and pleasure started to pulse deep within her core.

"That's it," he growled. "Good lass."

A groan rose in her throat, even as she sucked him, feverishly now. However, as her finger circled her wet, aching sex, her climax barreled into her. She cried out, the sound muffled against his throbbing prick.

He moved then, lifting her up from his groin. His shaft slid from her mouth, and she cried out in protest, reaching for him again. She wasn't finished.

"Not yet, mo rùin," he replied, his voice gravelly now. "When I come, I want to be buried deep inside you." With that, he pulled her astride him.

Excitement swooped through Lara. Still breathless from her peak, she slid her hand down his torso, wrapping her fingers once more around his shaft. She then lifted herself up, positioning herself over him. And then, inch by inch, she lowered herself down upon his heft.

A soft cry escaped her.

This position brought him deep, stretching her fully until she ached. And as she slid down his length, she shuddered. Her core was so sensitive now that even the slightest movement made her clench against him.

Alar's mouth fastened on her breasts then, sucking each one until mewing sounds tore from her throat.

"Grind on me," he growled as he nipped gently at a nipple. "Use me."

Heat flooded her loins, her pulse skittering. *Gods. This man.*

He leaned back once more, his chest rising and falling fast as his gaze captured hers.

Staring down at him, Lara rolled her hips, circling slowly. Pleasure rippled through her loins, and she cried out, the sound shockingly raw. She was making a noise, yet she didn't care. Repeatedly, she rolled her hips against him, bringing him deeper still each time. And with each movement, he touched a place that made her shudder and whimper.

Sweat trickled between her shoulder blades, and her eyes fluttered shut.

Alar grasped her hip with one hand, dragging her up and down his shaft in slow, deep strokes. He gasped her name then, the sound almost a sob.

And then he moved—so fast that she gasped.

An instant later, Lara found herself on her hands and knees on the furs. She barely had time to draw breath before he drove into her from behind. One hand tangled in her hair, he pulled her head back so that her spine arched, bringing her harder against him.

Lara's breathing came in ragged gasps as pleasure climbed and climbed. He felt so good. Every hard inch of him.

His breath fanned against her cheek then; he'd let go of her hair and now braced himself with his left fist, so that his uninjured shoulder took his weight. The wet slide of him inside her, and the friction of his lean sweat-slicked chest against her back, made her pant and whimper.

His tongue traced the shell of her ear. His lips and teeth grazed her neck.

"Mine," he whispered.

Lara shivered, anticipation twisting in her gut. This position was dominant. Possessive. His mouth was so hot. He was all around her now, overwhelming every sense. But it still wasn't enough.

"Please," she whimpered. "Mark me."

He growled, the sound low and feral. And then, thrusting hard, he sank his teeth into her shoulder.

The world spun. Suddenly, she was untethered.

Lost.

Blood pounded in her ears.

Pleasure pulsed in her womb.

A cry tore from her throat as she writhed, grinding herself against him.

The ragged sound of their breathing filled the alcove.

Alar withdrew from Lara in a long slow drag. The movement made her moan, and his gut clenched in response. *Ashes.* The sounds she made. They awoke something primal in him.

Gingerly, he lowered himself onto his back. Despite that he'd tried to be careful, his right shoulder now throbbed. He didn't care though. Not after this.

Panting, Lara collapsed against his chest, her thick auburn hair fanning out, tickling his skin.

They didn't speak for a while. Instead, he gently traced the indentation of her spine with a fingertip, enjoying the feel of her against him. His throat thickened then.

Nothing had ever felt so right.

He still couldn't believe she'd come to him tonight. The things she'd said. The emotion that blazed in her eyes. He didn't deserve any of it, but he didn't doubt her. They were well matched; he'd known that from the first days of their marriage. It was he who had set fire to it all. He'd thought he'd ruined everything. He'd believed it was over between them, despite that they loved each other.

But tonight, Lara had given him hope.

She raised her head then, tossing her curtain of hair over her shoulder. Her gaze sought his—but all Alar could see was the angry red crescent where he'd bitten her. It marred her milky skin.

His breathing quickened as he raised his hand, his fingers brushing the mark.

Peering down at her shoulder, Lara's brow furrowed. "Why do I enjoy that so much?"

He raised an eyebrow. "You've never heard of the wulver's mating bond then?"

She stilled, her lips parting. "No."

"They don't have handfasting ceremonies. Instead, when a wulver takes a mate, they mark them. They are together for life, after that. Only death separates them." His lips curved then. "Lyall and Dolph have such a bond."

Lara's pupils flared wide, her lips parting. Then, she reached out, her fingertips tracing the lines of his tattoo. Her touch made him shiver. Did this woman have any idea of the effect she had on him? He was utterly in her thrall.

She swallowed then, her gaze lifting to his once more. "So, I was yours then … even a year ago?"

Alar's eyes fluttered shut, recalling that heated night, the evening before Dulross. He'd lost control, had given himself to the hunger that had been growing for days. Aye, he'd marked her, and he'd hated himself for it ever since. He'd been a selfish bastard, doing that the night before betraying her.

"I always wanted to feel closer to the wulvers," he replied after a pause. "And ever since I had this tattoo inked upon my skin, something lupine now lives within me."

"I've seen it." Her fingers continued to trace the wolf's head. "When you fight … and when the bog wights had you at The Shattered Crown. Your eyes glowed red. You snarled like a wolf."

"It's a part of me now," he admitted softly. "Does it bother you?"

Her gaze lifted to his once more. "No."

They stared at each other then. "Your people aren't going to be happy about this," he said finally. He didn't want to shatter the moment, but he had to be practical. The sight of the Half-blood riding at the High Queen's side through the gates of Duncrag would likely cause an uproar. They all knew what he'd done.

Lara lifted a hand, stroking his jaw. However, her gaze never left his. "No. But I've weathered their anger before … and this time, we bring good news home with us. I will tell them of your valor. I will ensure everyone learns about the part you played at The Shattered Crown."

He snorted softly. "Other than being Mor's sacrificial goat?" His skin prickled then as he recalled kneeling on that stone. He'd known something was off. He should have trusted his instincts.

Lara's chin rose. "She thought she'd outwitted us all." Her eyes narrowed then. "She believed your father would stand by and watch you die. That was her mistake. She didn't understand love … or what people will do for it."

When Lara emerged from the alcove, cloak wrapped around her shoulders, with Alar at her side, she found the rest of their party already awake and seated by the hearth. Duana and Eithne had joined them. The sisters were frying oatcakes on a hot iron griddle. The sweet, nutty aroma drifted through the roundhouse.

Their hands wrapped around hot cups of broth, the others lifted their heads, their gazes tracking Lara and Alar.

None of them looked surprised, and warmth rolled over Lara.

It was too late to be embarrassed though. After overhearing Cailean and Bree, she knew how sound traveled. And they'd forgotten themselves. Alar had taken her twice more during the night, each time louder and lustier than the last.

She wouldn't be surprised if nobody in this roundhouse had gotten much sleep.

Lara didn't speak as she approached the hearth. Instead, she lowered herself onto a stool. Alar sat down next to her. Skaal rose from where she'd been gnawing on an ox bone a few yards away and padded over to him, nudging him with her nose.

Smiling, Alar ruffled her ears.

Cailean muttered something under his breath.

"You have reconciled then?" Bree's voice held a note of quiet resignation.

Lara took the cup of hot broth Eithne passed her. "We have."

"I knew this would happen," Roth sighed.

"We *all* saw this coming," Annis added, shaking her head. "The moment you insisted he travel south with us, it was clear."

Lara swept her gaze over their faces. "And you all disapprove?"

A brittle silence settled around the hearth.

"I don't," Eithne shattered the tension with a warm smile. "I think you're perfect together."

"As do I," Duana agreed as she flipped oatcakes.

No one else ventured a comment.

Taking a sip of broth, Lara sighed. "Alar will return to Duncrag and co-rule with me as prince regent."

Cailean gave a slow nod before his attention shifted to Alar. "I'll be watching you, Half-blood." His voice was low, yet with an edge she recognized.

Alar inclined his head, acknowledging the threat.

Tension rippled over the circle. Silence stretched out as the hearth crackled. Duana began dishing out oatcakes onto wooden trenchers.

Reaching out, Lara took Alar's hand, lacing her fingers through his. He squeezed gently.

"I'd expect nothing less of you, Cailean," she replied, her lips curving. Her gaze then traveled over their faces, meeting each of their eyes in turn. "From *any* of you."

She drew a breath then, inhaling woodsmoke and feeling Alar's steady presence beside her. "You've kept me alive through impossible odds. You've followed me into the darkness. Your loyalty has never wavered … even when mine did." Her throat tightened. "So, aye, hold him answerable. Hold us *both* accountable. That's what family does."

The word hung in the air between them—*family*.

Not advisors or even friends. She meant it too.

Slowly, Bree's shoulders lowered. Annis bowed her head, while Ren blinked, her eyes glistening. Even Cailean and Roth's expressions softened. And as the moments slid by, a small smile tugged at the chief-enforcer's lips.

Outside, a goat bleated, and somewhere in the distance, a bairn wailed. Life, with all its beauty, messiness, and uncertainty. They'd face whatever came next, the way they'd faced everything else—battle-weary yet stubborn.

Standing together.

Lara lifted her cup of broth toward them, smiling back at them. "To second chances," she said softly.

A pause followed, and then, one by one, they raised their cups in answer.

EPILOGUE: SHADOWS AND SUNLIGHT

Duncrag,
The Realm of Albia

Five turns of the moon later …

"ARE YOU READY?"

Staring down at the unraveled parchment before him, Alar nodded. Even so, nervousness fluttered to life in his gut. Ridiculous really. He could face down the Slew—but reading a poem made him falter.

Upon returning to Duncrag with Lara, one of the first things he did was learn how to read. He hadn't done so out of shame or even embarrassment that he didn't know his letters. Instead, curiosity had driven him to ask Gil for lessons.

A mountain of scrolls existed in the High Queen's archives, knowledge he'd never access—unless he asked someone to read them to him. He didn't want that. He wished to immerse himself in history and knowledge, to learn about the past.

"Go on then." Gil's tone, often laced with impatience, was gentle this morning. After many moons of painstaking lessons, of fumbled sentences and writing that looked as if a bairn had scrawled it, Alar had reached this point. It was an important day for them both. Usually, the two apprentices Gil had recently taken on worked alongside him in the archives, but this morning, he'd sent them away. His student needed privacy.

Clearing his throat, Alar began to read.

> *"Sometimes I stumble on the mountain path,*
> *Sometimes I find my footing sure and strong.*
> *Sometimes the battle ends in golden victory,*
> *Sometimes in ash and sorrow's bitter song."*

His voice was halting at first as he sounded out some of the words. But as he continued, the words flowed more easily.

> *"My choices carved this long road,*
> *But I'm more than their sum.*
> *My shadows do not own me—*
> *They show me how far I've come."*

He paused then, his chest tightening. The words on the page had come alive. Suddenly, another world opened to him. Swallowing, he completed the poem.

"Let ravens carry off my darkest deeds,
Let a cool burn wash my bloodied hands.
I am the spring that follows winter,
The seed of hope in barren lands."

His voice died away then, and he glanced up, meeting Gil's eye across the table. "How was that?"

Gil's lips quirked. "A good effort."

Alar harrumphed. Praise indeed from the sharp-tongued archivist. "I like that one."

"It's another by the High Queen's great-great-grandsire. He wrote many poems … some better than others."

"It speaks of hope," Alar murmured, running his fingertip down the edge of the parchment. "That we are more than our mistakes." His breathing grew shallow then. "Maybe that's true … for some people."

"You aren't still brooding about Dulross, are you?"

Alar's chin kicked up, his gaze narrowing. Gil sometimes pushed things. They rarely spoke about what had befallen The Brooch of Albia four moons earlier for a reason. Even thinking about it made Alar's gut clench.

It still haunted him.

They'd lingered longer at Crask than initially planned. And so, it was nearly a moon's turn later when Lara and her escort had stopped off at Dulross on the way home—only to discover that the wulvers and Circines had turned on each other.

A massacre had ensued, leaving the fort a smoking ruin.

Dolph had been among the survivors, and his despair had haunted Alar ever since.

His brother blamed him for the turn of events.

Alar had been the one to encourage them to want more than their former simple existence, and now Lyall was dead. Dolph had then departed Dulross with the few surviving wulvers—returning to the shadowy Upland forests and clear rivers full of fat trout.

In the moons following, Lara had sent a garrison to Dulross. The rebuilding was still going on. Roth now captained the Guard, and Duana stewarded the fort. She and Eithne hadn't continued to Duncrag, after all. Instead, they'd returned home.

But memories of the ruined fort remained with Alar.

He didn't appreciate Gil making light of it.

"Speaking of which." The archivist gestured then to a leather-bound volume that sat at his worktable a few yards away. "I'm writing about The Brooch of Albia at the moment."

Alar nodded. "How is your transcribing going?"

Gil pulled a face. "Slowly … there are a lot of blank pages to fill."

Alar's gaze lingered on the book. It would be the first to ever grace the archives of Duncrag. Gil had told him that such objects existed in Sheehallion, where they'd bind stacks of written parchment with glue and then make a cover out of leather. "You're writing everything we've told you down?"

Gil nodded. Of late, his role had widened to scribe as well as archivist. He'd spent much time with both Lara and Alar over the winter, taking notes as they recounted the events of the past years. Recording it all would take him a long while. Fortunately, Gil had the patience for such tasks.

"I'm up to the Circines and wulver clash," Gil admitted then. "But I need to check I've got things right." He paused, a groove appearing between tawny eyebrows. "Can I read it to you?"

Alar stiffened. He didn't want to relive it all, to be reminded of his mistakes. But Gil was only doing his job. After a moment, he gave a stiff nod.

"Iron, stop flagellating yourself over it," Gil muttered. "You aren't responsible."

"What if I am?" Alar snapped, pushing himself up from the table.

Few people knew how to get under his skin, but Gil did. Bree's brother was too sharp for his liking. He noticed things others missed. In truth, they were alike in many ways, and that galled Alar even more.

"Maybe you should pay greater attention to the poem you just read to me," Gil replied, his gaze steady. "You are more than the sum of your mistakes … we all are."

Alar's pulse thumped in his ears as he stared down at him.

Gil stood up too then. The two men were of a similar height, and their gazes locked in silent combat for a few moments before the archivist shrugged. "Aye, you encouraged the wulvers to want more for themselves … but you didn't put daggers in their hands. Nor did you put them at odds with the Circines." He paused then, his hazel eyes shadowing. "Your brother Dolph was grieving, and he lashed out. He didn't want to take responsibility for the part he played in things … but he wasn't blameless. Your shadows don't own you … but neither do his. Remember that."

Alar stared back at him. Anger still burned under his ribs, yet Gil's words calmed his pounding heart. Lara had told him similar things, yet in truth, he'd humored her.

He'd wrapped self-recrimination around himself in a tight cocoon.

But Gil had just pierced it.

Huffing out a sigh, he raked a hand through his hair. "Smug bastard. I hate that you're always right."

Alar emerged into bright sunlight, blinking.

Even with cressets, torches, braziers, and hearths blazing, the windowless interior of the broch was dark. But today, the contrast made his eyes water. It was a sparkling spring day. The sun was high in a deep blue sky. After another long and bitter winter, he welcomed the warmth upon his face. Noon drew near, and the aroma of baking bread drifted out from the nearby bakehouse.

Walking across the wide yard before the broch, Alar spied Cailean and Torran standing together near the gates. Skaal sat behind the chief-enforcer, scratching behind her ear.

He lifted a hand to acknowledge the enforcers, and they nodded back.

Both men smiled.

Seeing him, Skaal smoothly rose to her feet and padded over, pushing her nose into Alar's chest. He stroked her massive head before glancing back at Cailean and Torran. "Have you seen Lara?"

"The High Queen is out at the market," the chief-enforcer replied, gesturing to the open gates behind him. "Bree's with her."

"As is Mirren," Torran added, grimacing. "Which means they'll be a while."

Alar huffed a laugh. Of course. Duncrag held a weekly market, but the first of the new moon was the biggest.

Merchants came from all over The Wolds, although ever since Braewall and Baldeen claimed independence, the market hadn't been quite as busy. Nonetheless, Lara rarely missed it.

"The noon meal isn't far off … I'll see if they'll be joining us," Alar replied.

"Good luck," Torran quipped, "But if they've found a cloth merchant, you won't drag them back into the broch for a while."

Alar moved on. "We'll see."

Passing through the great stone arch, he walked out onto The Thoroughfare. As expected, a heaving crowd—mostly women with shopping baskets slung over their arms—greeted him. This high in the fort, the air wasn't too bad, and this morning, the aroma of freshly-baked mutton pies and grilled garlic sausages made his belly rumble.

He wove his way through the press, noting that the crowd parted easily for him. Of course, he was a distinctive sight: clad in black with his long dark hair, scars, and the grips of his fighting daggers protruding above his shoulders. A cloak rippled out behind him as he walked.

Many of the gazes were veiled, others curious.

Their return to Duncrag had brought an uproar, but these days, tempers were cooling.

Tales were still being told in ale-halls nightly about their 'adventures' in the North. About what the High Queen and the Half-blood had done. Even before their return to Duncrag, the people here had known something had changed. The Slew stopped hunting at night, and the host of malicious spirits that made them dread each dusk had disappeared.

One of the men nodded as he walked by. A lass then blushed and curtseyed.

Alar acknowledged them both, and as he did so, the lingering tension from his exchange with Gil unraveled.

He'd remained for a short while in the archive, listening as Gil read out his notes about the events that had unfolded at Dulross in early winter. He'd corrected a few things, and although his mood had improved by this time, he'd been relieved to take his leave. Gil was right. His shadows didn't own him. But that didn't mean he wanted to relive his mistakes either.

Weaving his way through the crowd, he scanned the sea of bobbing heads for a mane of auburn hair. Eventually, he spied his wife.

And as Torran had suggested, Lara, Bree, and Mirren were standing in a huddle at a fabric stall. A knot of the Fort Guard—leather-clad warriors wearing iron helms—waited a few feet back, hands on the pommels of their swords. Alar was pleased to note their vigilance. They could take nothing for granted these days, especially peace. Lara's overkings still had to be dealt with, and he wouldn't put it past either of the shitweasels to attempt an assassination. The guards at the gates into the fort questioned everyone coming and going now.

For the first time this year, Lara wore a light woolen cloak rather than her heavy fur-lined one. Dark-green like her eyes. Her hair, unbound but pulled back at the side with amber clips, tumbled down her back. However, she still carried a sheathed dagger at her hip, an incongruous sight against her fine tunic. His wife never went anywhere without it.

She laughed then at something Mirren had just said, the musical sound rising above the chatter of the surrounding crowd.

Alar's breathing quickened.

There were few sounds as lovely as Lara's laughter.

When they'd first met, he hadn't heard it often. But over the past moons, it had become increasingly more common. He welcomed it. His wife was sunlight, warming him on days when his mood grew bleak or regret twisted like a blade.

And after his session with Gil, he needed her.

"A productive morning?" he greeted the women, slipping in between Lara and Mirren.

"Aye … very," Lara replied with a smile. "Although there are always difficult choices to be made."

Bree rolled her eyes at this, flashing Alar a pained look. He swallowed a grin in response, remembering that she *hated* shopping.

"We can't decide whether we like the plum or teal fabric," Mirren added. "What do you think?" The Steward of Duncrag rested a hand upon the swell of her belly. Torran's wife was a few moons along in her pregnancy now.

Alar's gaze traveled over the two bolts of cloth the merchant had laid out. "Why not get both?"

Lara huffed before digging him playfully in the ribs with her elbow. "That's not helpful."

"The plum is nice."

"*Nice?*" The merchant flashed him an affronted look. "It is the finest weave you'll find anywhere in Albia."

"We'll get that one then," Lara replied, digging into her purse. "Package up ten yards, please."

The merchant nodded before deftly scooping up the bolt of cloth. "Right away, My Queen."

Alar turned to the waiting guards. "Bring the High Queen's purchase back to the broch."

The warriors nodded, allowing Lara and Alar to move off, with Bree and Mirren bringing up the rear. As he walked, Alar kept a protective arm around her waist.

"Missed me, husband?" she teased, glancing up at him.

"Aye," he replied honestly.

"How did your lesson with Gil go?"

"Well, enough." He paused then before admitting. "I read one of your great-great-grandfather's poems aloud."

Her gaze widened. "You did?"

He nodded. "There were two lines … at the end … I thought you might like."

"Aye?"

"I am the spring that follows winter … the seed of hope in barren lands."

She flashed him a smile that made his breathing quicken just a little. "That's beautiful."

"Aye … it reminds me of you."

Her eyes darkened. "It's not like you to flatter, Alar," she said, a husky note creeping into her voice.

"It's not flattery, mo rùin, but the truth. You're what Albia … and its people … need." He paused then, his grip tightening around her waist. "And you've certainly brought *this* cynical heart back to life."

The End

AUTHOR'S NOTE & GLOSSARY

As with *The Enforcer's Bride* duology, this one is steeped in Scottish folklore. I've been writing novels set in ancient and Medieval Scotland for years—and in 2024, I embarked on my first Celtic-inspired Romantasy.

Since then, there's been no looking back. I'm obsessed!

I hope you enjoyed the Pictish vibe of the story world, as well as the dangerous mythological creatures brought to life. I wanted Albia to be mysterious with an air of brooding menace, just like ancient Scotland.

Many of the names within this duology come from Scottish Gaelic. It's a beautiful language, yet written quite differently from how it's pronounced. As such, I have changed some of the spelling in the novel to make it more phonetic, and therefore more accessible to readers.

Below is a glossary of people and places from the novel and a bit of background on meaning and the original spelling.

Albia: a variation of 'Alba', the Scottish Gaelic name for Scotland

Ben Neeya: the Bean Nighe (see note below about 'the Washerwoman')

Caisteal Gealaich: the Shee queen's stronghold. It means Moon Castle. (pronounced *castel galeech*)

Dorka: Mor's clag-doo (Original spelling is Dorcha, which means 'dark one')

Reedav: Alar's stag (Original spelling is Rìgh-Damh, which means 'King Stag')

Sheehallion: Original spelling is 'Schiehallion'. Located in Perthshire, it's one of Scotland's most prominent mountains and is rich in legend. Its name derives from the Gaelic Sith Chaillean, meaning 'The Fairy Hill of the Caledonians'

Skaal: Cailean's Fae Hound ('sgàil' means 'shadow)

Slighe Fraoch: The Heather Path'. (pronounced *SLEE-eh FROHKH*)

The Marav: the name for the mortal race that inhabits Albia. Comes from 'Marbh' or 'mairbh', which means a dead person/people

The Shee: the name for the fae race that inhabits Sheehallion. This name is based on the Daoine sìth (pronounced: *doonyuh-shee),* the Scottish name for the fairy race.

In this novel, I use 'mac' with Malav names. Of course, this is from Scottish Gaelic, which meant 'son of'. In Pictish times, 'mac' was used as a separate word in a name with the father's name following. This was the origin of many Scottish surnames we see today.

During the novel, I refer to the *Ord-ree seal* (the ring Lara wears). This comes from 'Ard-ri' (High King in Irish Gaelic) and is pronounced *Ord-ree*.

The societal structure of Albia is based on the ancient kingdoms of Ireland and the Pictish kingdoms of Scotland, where a High King ruled several lesser kingdoms governed by 'Overkings'.

The creatures that are mentioned or feature in THE UNFORGIVEN duology, and their Scottish mythological origin:

Aughisky: The each-uisge (Scottish Gaelic, meaning "water horse") is a water spirit found in the Scottish Highlands (anglicized as aughisky or ech-ushkya). It usually takes the form of a horse—similar to the kelpie but far more vicious. Unlike the Kelpie (which inhabits streams and rivers), the each-uisge lives in the sea, sea lochs, and freshwater lochs. The each-uisge is a shape-shifter, disguising itself as a fine horse, pony, or handsome man. If you mount this creature while it's disguised as a horse, you are only safe out of sight or smell of water. Otherwise, your skin will stick to the creature, and it will pull you down to the deepest part of the loch and tear you apart. Find out more: **https://about-mythical-creatures.weebly.com/each-uisge.html**

Bavaan: The Baobhan Sith (pronounced Bavaan-shee) is a vampiric creature of Scottish origin. Beautiful, tall women with pale skin and icy breath, they dress in flowing green robes and are said to dance in the moonlight, seducing men, in order to kill them and drain their blood. Find out more: **https://folklorescotland.com/the-baobhan-sith/**

Ben Neeya: The Bean Nighe (pronounced *ben-nee'-yeh*), also known as 'the Washerwoman', is an old woman seen wandering near streams and pools, where she washes the bloodstained clothes of those who are about to die. The bean-nighe is sometimes said to sing a mournful dirge. She is often so absorbed in her washing and singing that she can sometimes be caught unawares. If a person sees her before she spies them, she will reveal who is about to die and will also grant three wishes. In my tale, I've altered things slightly so that she grants you one wish.

Boggart: A boggart is a mischievous, often wicked, supernatural being—a brownie that has turned nasty, often due to mistreatment. They cause trouble, hide things, make noise, and lead travelers astray. It's also said that boggarts crawl into people's beds at night and put a clammy hand on their face.

Corpse candles: also known as will-o'-the-wisps or fairy lights. In Scottish folklore, will-o'-the-wisps are variously depicted either as mischievous spirits (typically fairies), or even the ghosts of the dead, eager to lead travelers off their path and to their death. The lights typically appear close to a bog, marsh, or swamp, places where straying off the beaten path can become dangerous – or even deadly.
Find out more: **https://folklorescotland.com/will-o-the-wisp/**

Fae Hounds are a variation of the Cù-Sìth (pronounced *ku-shee*), a ghostly hound from Scottish folklore that roamed the Highlands. The name means 'Fairy Dog'. The Cù-Sìth were said to be the size of a bull with dark-green shaggy fur and a coiled or braided tail. People believed the Cù-Sìth was a harbinger of death—much like the Grim Reaper. Although mostly a silent hunter, this giant dog would sometimes let out three blood-curdling howls. If you didn't get away before the third howl, you'd be overcome with fear and die from sheer terror.

Powries: also known as a Red Cap, or a Dunter, a powrie is a type of malevolent, murderous goblin found in Border folklore. He is said to inhabit ruined castles along the Anglo-Scottish border, especially those that were the scenes of tyranny or wicked deeds, and is known for soaking his cap in the blood of his victims.
Find out more: **https://folklorescotland.com/the-fearsome-redcaps-of-the-scottish-borders/**

Trows: these creatures feature in Shetland folklore. They are similar to humans but smaller and uglier, and they live in the hills, particularly the heathery peatlands inland from the sea. They would only come out at night, to work mischief in the human world.
Find out more: **https://shetlandwithlaurie.com/the-blog/shetland-folklore-series-trows**

The Botach: The Gaelic word bodach (pronounced bot-ach) can mean 'old man' and also 'specter, ghost'. In ancient Scotland, it was the name of a mythological 'bogeyman' who comes down chimneys to steal children. He was also seen as an omen of death. He would prod, poke, pinch, pull, and in general disturb the child until he had them reeling with nightmares. According to the stories of most parents, the bodach would only bother naughty children. A good defense would be to put salt in the hearth before bedtime. The bodach will not cross salt.

Find out more:

https://www.tumblr.com/bestiarium/65069709351159398 4/the-bodach-scottish-mythology-gaelic-mythology

The Unforgiven/The Slew: The Sluagh Sidhe, or 'Fairy Host': spirits of the unforgiven or restless dead who soar the skies at night searching for humans to pick off. They always approach from the west and often prey on those close to death.

Find out more:

https://folklorethursday.com/folktales/the-sluagh-spirits-of-the-unforgiven-dead/

Wulvers: a Scottish mythological creature that is part human, part wolf. The wulver kept to itself and was not aggressive if left in peace. They would often guide lost travelers to nearby towns and villages. There are also tales of wulvers leaving fish on the windowsills of poor families. Unlike their werewolf counterparts, the wulver is not a shape-shifter.

Find out more:

https://www.scotsman.com/news/people/scottish-myths-wulver-the-kindhearted-shetland-werewolf-2463904

Fuath: (pronounced 'foo-ah') Malevolent water spirits from Irish and Scottish folklore that emerge from lochs, rivers, the sea, or during heavy rainfall.

The Weeper (Caoineag): This is a female spirit in Scottish folklore, a type of Highland banshee, with similarities to the Bean Nighe. She is believed to foretell death in her clan by lamenting in the night at a waterfall, stream, or loch, or in a glen or on a mountainside.

Some of the creatures and spirits mentioned in the book are entirely a figment of my imagination, although my inspiration for them comes from Celtic mythology:

Clag-doos: (*clag dubh* in Scottish Gaelic/the 'Black Claw'), a territorial, cat-like predator. It has long claws that grow constantly; as such, it must blunt them by scratching tree trunks, leaving scars that never heal.

Cnoc-banes: (CROCK-bain) Literally 'hill destroyers'. Ancient earth spirits that dwell within hills, mounds, and elevated ground. Highly territorial, they cause landslides and structural collapses upon those who invade their domain.

Grimlochs: these are shadow spirits that infest chimneys and hearths, snuffing out fires and filling homes with choking smoke.

Knavoar: these are frost spirits—of those who died of exposure in the mountains, their bones never properly buried. They seek to share their eternal cold with the living, drawing warmth from others to ease their own suffering. They appear as skeletal figures wreathed in frost, with ice crystals forming along their bone-white limbs. A hoar frost spreads before them.

Loch-bhàn (Lake woman): The wraiths drift on the water's surface and only appear upon a full moon. They are beautiful women with long hair that flows like water, sometimes silver like the moonlight, sometimes dark like the water. Their song is haunting, and if anyone touches a Loch-Bhàn, they'll lose their memory.

The Gaulas: (The Wind of Malice). A spirit wind that springs from The Threshold and carries the voices of those banished there. The wind gives voice to the damned souls of the Slew, calling out accusations and twisted truths.

The Grey Ghost: this spirit was inspired by the *Am Fear Liath Mòr* (Scottish Gaelic for 'Big Grey Man'), the name for a presence or creature which is said to haunt the summit and passes of Ben Macdui, (the highest peak of the Cairngorms). People have reported the crunching of gravel as it walks behind them and a general feeling of unease around the mountain. The spirit is described as very thin and over ten feet tall, with dark skin and hair, long arms, and broad shoulders.

Gods and Goddesses of Albia

The Five

The Mother: Goddess of enlightenment and feminine energy—the bringer of change

The Warrior: God of battle, life, and growth, of summer

The Maiden: Young goddess of nature and fertility

The Hag: Goddess of the dark—sleep, dreams, death, winter, and the earth

The Reaper: God of death

Gods and Goddesses of Sheehallion

The Ancestors

The Great Raven

Festivities of Albia

Earth Fire: Salute to new life and the first signs of spring

Day of the Hag: Spring Equinox

Bealtunn: Passage from spring to summer

Mid-Summer Fire: Summer Solstice

Harvest Fire: Festival to salute the harvest

Gateway: Passage from summer to winter

Mid-Winter Fire: Winter Solstice

Five 'paths' of druids

Enforcers: wear black and are the warrior druids who serve the king

Sacrificers: wear red and carry out ritualistic sacrifices to keep the Gods happy

Counselors: wear white and are the sages, you go to them for wise advice

Seers: wear green and are masters at divination

Bards: wear blue and sing and entertain, and tell lore through song and music

The Arch-druid: wears gold and is the one deemed to be the most wise

Initiates: wear brown and must choose their path

The four winds of Albia

The Whistle: high and shrill

The Sharp Billed Wind: pierces the land like a sharp-beaked bird

The Sweeper: whirling gusts that strip branches from trees

The Gales of Complaint: scatters food and crops

Source: **https://weewhitehoose.co.uk/study/the-cailleach/**

DIVE INTO MY BACKLIST!

Check out my printable reading order list on my website:
https://www.jaynecastel.com/printable-reading-list

ABOUT THE AUTHOR

Multi-award-winning author Jayne Castel writes epic Historical and Fantasy Romance. Her vibrant characters, richly researched historical settings, and action-packed adventure romance transport readers to forgotten times and imaginary worlds.

Jayne is the author of a number of best-selling series. A hopeless romantic in love with all things Scottish, she writes romances set in both Dark Ages and Medieval Scotland, and Romantasy with a Celtic vibe.

When she's not writing, Jayne is reading (and re-reading) her favorite authors, cooking Italian feasts, and going on long walks with her husband. She's from New Zealand but now lives in Edinburgh, Scotland.

Connect with Jayne online:
www.jaynecastel.com
www.facebook.com/JayneCastelRomance
www.instagram.com/jaynecastelauthor/
www.tiktok.com/@jaynecastelauthor

Email: **contact@jaynecastel.com**

www.ingramcontent.com/pod-product-compliance
Lightning Source LLC
Chambersburg PA
CBHW030102310726
48970CB00004B/1115